·THE·CURIOUS·AFFAIR·OF·

THE
WITCH AT
WAYSIDE CROSS

· THE · CURIOUS · AFFAIR · OF ·

THE WITCH AT WAYSIDE CROSS

JESPERSON AND LANE BOOK II

LISA TUTTLE

Jo Fletcher
BOOKS

First published in Great Britain in 2017 by

Jo Fletcher Books
an imprint of Quercus Editions Ltd
Carmelite House
50 Victoria Embankment
London EC4Y 0DZ

An Hachette UK Company

A CIP catalogue record for this book is available
from the British Library.

TPB ISBN 978 1 78429 959 0
EBOOK ISBN 978 0 85705 454 8

10 9 8 7 6 5 4 3 2

Typeset by CC Book Production
Printed and bound in Great Britain by Clays Ltd, St Ives plc

To the Murrays of Norfolk – Roy, Jean, Paul, Samantha, Megan and James – with love from the author.

CHAPTER ONE

A Corpse in the Hall

The man was dead, and although he had not cut a particularly large or imposing figure when he was alive, his lifeless body seemed to take up more space in our entranceway than a whole crowd of living, breathing visitors.

He lay as he had fallen, on his back, head towards the front door, the soles of his boots pointing up towards me where I stood upon the stairs. His face was frozen in an expression of terror, mouth gaping and dark eyes wide, their gaze forever fixed upon the last sight he had seen – me.

'Witch!' This stranger had shrieked, and cowered in abject terror. Yet I am a small, unthreatening woman, with nothing grotesque or fantastical about my appearance – nothing to alarm even the most nervous infant. It was hard to imagine that anything in my appearance could have given rise to such a powerful emotion in the breast of a total stranger – a fear so overwhelming that he had died of it.

Jasper Jesperson, my partner in detection, instantly crouched beside the stranger and checked for signs of life. No pulse, no heartbeat – the man who had pounded on our door only a few moments before had not lived long enough to tell us why he had come. Determined to be thorough, Jesperson went and fetched a small looking-glass, which he held before the figure's open mouth.

From the other room, the clock on the mantel chimed the hours: two o'clock in the morning. When the sound had died away, Mr Jesperson checked the glass for any trace of clouding, then looked up at me and solemnly shook his head.

My hand flew to my mouth, just as involuntarily I exclaimed, 'Do not say I have killed him!'

For a moment, amusement flickered across his mobile features, and I thought he would laugh, but the gravity of the situation checked the impulse. 'Why should anyone say that? The man is dead, but not by *your* hand, Miss Lane!'

'Not by my *hand*, perhaps, but – oh! Look at him! He has clearly died of fright.'

Up went the eyebrows. 'Is *fright* ever the cause of death, except in the penny dreadfuls?' His expression softened. 'Miss Lane, you are tired, and have suffered the most trying experiences over the past few days. To see someone die in front of you was a shock. But you have always prided yourself upon your ability to think rationally.'

The memory of what had just transpired was horribly vivid. I recalled how the stranger had flinched at the sight of me, eyes wide with terror. 'He thought I was a witch,' I reminded him. 'His fear was so great that he staggered back and dropped dead.'

My friend's reply was swift and calming. 'The man arrived here in a dreadful state, on the brink of death and probably hallucinating. He thought himself pursued by witches, and imagined he saw one standing before him. He did not see *you* – and if I had not answered his knock at the door, he would have dropped dead on the doorstep, or in the street.'

What strange power resides in a word like 'witch' and a man's terrified, accusing gaze! Fortunately, Mr Jesperson's argument was enough to restore my common sense, and I realised it was absurd to blame myself for another's nightmare fears.

'Forgive me; I was foolish.'

He waved it away. 'You have been under a great deal of strain; you need rest – goodness knows, we both do.' But the look on his face, so lively and interested, contradicted his words. 'But first, let us work out the mystery that sent him here to die.'

With that, he turned and knelt again, and began to search the dead man's pockets for clues. As he extracted each item, he commented upon it.

'Silver cigarette case – shiny and new – contents, two cigarettes – engraved: "Dearest C from your Loving A, 15-6-93".

'Leather notecase, embossed, gilded initials CM. Within: Two pounds, ten shillings. A train ticket – dated today – or rather *yesterday* – Great Eastern Railway, Norwich to London Liverpool Street. A card – aha!' He flourished the two-by-three-inch card, and even from where I sat I recognised it as one of our own business cards:

Jesperson & Lane

PRIVATE INVESTIGATIONS

203A Gower Street London

'Nothing to say where he acquired it,' he said, flipping it back and forth between his fingers.

'And as we have distributed only fifty or sixty at most, it should not take us long to trace its provenance,' I said, my spirits reviving.

He grinned without looking at me. 'Indeed. He may well be a friend of a friend of a friend. That is it for the notecase. No cards of his own, alas. Next – ah, this is better.

'Address book, with his own name and address inscribed inside the cover:

'Charles Manning. Twenty-four Gordon Square, London – crossed through – then, in the same hand, care of The Vicarage, Aylmerton, Norfolk.' He shook his head and looked up at me. 'I have never been to Norfolk. Do you know it at all?'

'I have been to Norwich, Great Yarmouth and a few seaside places, but I have never heard of Aylmerton.'

He began leafing through the little book. 'Hmm. Several addresses in Norfolk, all in Cromer; others in London. This should be useful.'

My head was beginning to spin with tiredness, and I sat down rather heavily upon the stair.

Mr Jesperson looked up. So far from flagging, his energy was magically restored in the interest of pursuing a new investigation. He stared at me briefly. 'You look done in. Why don't you go to bed?'

I gaped at him. 'And leave – this?'

'Yes, a fascinating puzzle, I agree. But if you are too tired to think clearly . . .'

'I meant – we have a dead body in our hallway. We must inform the authorities.' I stopped, realising I did not know the correct course of action, or who to inform, about a complete stranger who had entered our house and promptly dropped dead. Perhaps the information could be found in the copy of *Enquire Within* that sat upon the kitchen mantelpiece beside *Mrs Beeton's Book of Household Management*.

He grimaced. 'Yes, the police must be informed.' He rose and handed me the address book. 'They will want this, so would you mind copying it out? As quickly as you can?'

Despite his words, he was clearly in no great hurry to turn over this mystery to the police, and returned to his examination of the dead man's clothing. 'Pocket handkerchief, embroidered with a red "C". Leather coin purse, contents – five pennies, one ha'penny, two farthings.'

'Do you think he was murdered?' I asked, gripping the address book tightly. Unless I took it upstairs to my bedroom, I should have to step over the corpse to reach our office where the large desk was well-stocked with paper, pens and ink.

'I suspect he was poisoned, although he did not show the convulsive effects of strychnine, or the gastric distress of arsenic, and I cannot recall if hallucinations are a common feature of – hello, what's this?'

He held up a small object – round, silver, capped with a gleaming orange stone. 'A pillbox. Perhaps he was taking something for his heart?' But the little container proved empty. Jesperson held it close to his face, his nostrils flaring, before stepping around the body and offering the empty silver shell to me. 'What do you smell?'

I gave a cautious sniff. Something powdery, dusty, with a faintly acrid tang . . . 'I do not know.'

'Did you notice his eyes, Miss Lane? Emotion may dilate the pupils, but so do certain drugs. Whether or not it was the direct cause of his death, it seems likely that Mr Manning ingested something that made him see and hear things not of this Earth, and thus he fancied himself pursued by witches.'

He carefully replaced the pillbox in the pocket from which he had removed it, then bent close to the dead man's open mouth, and inhaled.

He got up, shaking his head in disappointment. 'No clue there, except that he has been drinking . . . and eaten oysters. Well, I had better not delay any longer, or I may become the chief suspect, if this *was* murder.' He stepped carefully around the corpse to the coat-tree and donned the coat and hat he had removed a few hours earlier. Then he looked at me, still sitting on the stair, and frowned a little.

'I hope you are not too tired to copy out his address book?'

I forced myself to rise. 'Of course not. Do you . . . should I . . . afterwards . . .' I tried to speak calmly, and managed not to shudder at the idea of tucking the little book away in the dead man's pocket, but could not help casting nervous, darting glances at the body. He understood.

'Hand the original to the police when they arrive. Nothing could be more natural than to check his pockets for a clue to his identity, and I shall tell them I have done so. We shan't mention finding anything else – they won't like it if they think we've been poaching on their territory, looking for clues,' he concluded, and, giving me a cheerful wave, went out the door into the night.

For a moment, as the heavy front door closed, leaving me alone in the hall with the dead man, I was tempted to rush upstairs and wake Mr Jesperson's mother. Edith Jesperson was both brave and practical, and, as I had found, a good person to have at one's side. She had left England after the death of her husband, undaunted by the task of raising her son alone in foreign climes where, I was certain, she had encountered many more frightening situations than this. But just thinking of Edith sleeping peacefully upstairs, knowing that I *could* call upon her, made it unnecessary to disturb her.

Gritting my teeth, I stepped over the legs of the corpse and went into the large front room which was both the household parlour and the office of Jesperson and Lane.

Although it was neither elegant nor beautiful, and the furnishings were old, the space was generous, the decorations homely and reflective of personal choices, so that overall the shabbiness was comforting rather than depressing. Although it had been picked up cheaply second-hand, the furniture had been chosen with good taste, and the walls, mantelpiece and bookshelves were adorned with a variety of objects that mother and son had acquired on their travels abroad. Although I had been part of the Jesperson ménage for less than half a year, I felt more at home in that room than anywhere else I had lived in my adult life. I particularly liked the corner where Mr Jesperson had placed his large desk (we often worked there facing each other, one on either side) in front of a wall filled from floor to ceiling with books.

Before settling down to my assigned task I added more coal and stirred the fire back to life. Then I took my accustomed seat at the desk, picked up a pen and a clean sheet of paper, and set about copying the contents of Mr Manning's address book. There were little more than a dozen entries, so it was quickly done. I had blotted the ink and hidden the page in a pile of others by the time I heard the noises from the street alerting me to the arrival of the police.

I did not recognise either of the uniformed men who entered a few moments later; they were, of course, from the local station, and therefore not members of the force who had helped us and made arrests at the Alhambra earlier in the evening, but it was clear from the deference they showed my partner that they knew all about our latest case.

Clearly, as heroes of the evening, we were on the side of the law, not to be considered as suspects. As Mr Jesperson had already given his statement in regard to what had happened, nothing more was required of me. In truth, I thought it remiss of them not to question me as well, but it was a relief. I handed over the little address book without comment.

With the police were two young men tasked with removal of the corpse, and they managed this swiftly with the aid of a large sheet and a canvas stretcher.

'You will keep me informed,' said Mr Jesperson to the senior officer as they made to leave. The man looked surprised.

'There is no need for you to trouble yourself any longer, sir.'

'It is no trouble. I wish to know the results of the autopsy – if not to attend it myself. Have you any idea when that is likely to be?'

The two policemen exchanged a look, and the first one answered, less politely, 'It may be no trouble to you, but it's not your business.'

Mr Jesperson relaxed his shoulders and seemed to gain an inch or two in height. He spoke softly, but with force. 'You are wrong. Mr Manning's death *is* my business – not merely because he died on my premises, but because he came here in fear for his life, and begged for our help. Unfortunately, the death he anticipated came before he could name his enemies or tell us anything more about them. But I had already promised to help – and I mean to keep that promise. Now, would you be so kind as to tell me the name of the police surgeon, and when and where the autopsy will be conducted?'

His cool conviction won the battle, bolstered by our recent success in solving not just one but an entire series of crimes.

'That would be Mr Blakely, sir, in the morgue. I don't know what time; that's up to himself, and depends on what else he has to do – if any more bodies have been fished out of the Thames tonight, say. If you go along there sometime in the afternoon he should be able to tell you what you want to know.'

CHAPTER TWO

Failure of the Heart

It was after three o'clock in the morning when we retired, so it is not surprising that I did not arise until almost eleven, or that it was closer to noon when Mr Jesperson at last came downstairs, in his dressing gown and blinking sleepily, his red-gold curls untamed, his face still unshaven, drawn to the kitchen by the irresistible scent of frying bacon.

His mother fussed over him fondly before adding more rashers to the pan. We all ate heartily and appreciated our good fortune in being able to do so. Not wishing to spoil such a fine breakfast, we said nothing about the late Mr Manning, although his terrified visage had haunted my dreams.

When he set out for the morgue, about an hour and a half later, Mr Jesperson went alone. It was not squeamishness that made me stay behind, but rather my awareness of how a female presence could upset the balance in such an environment. Even if the police surgeon did not resent my unexpected appearance, he might be overly concerned with my supposedly more delicate sensibilities. In any case, he was likely to speak more openly and honestly to Mr Jesperson alone.

I settled myself before the fire with a volume dedicated to the interesting subject of poisons and devoted myself to the search for any substance Mr Manning might have consumed, either knowingly or inadvertently, that would cause hallucinations and death of the sort we had witnessed. I was still reading when Mr Jesperson arrived home. He came in looking cold and rather cross, and immediately went to stand before the fire.

'Well?' I asked when several seconds had passed without a word from him. 'What's the verdict?'

'Heart failure.' He gave a short, unamused bark of laughter. 'What sort of diagnosis is that? We hardly needed a doctor to tell us his heart had stopped.'

'There are poisons that stop the heart,' I said, with a glance at my book.

'Mr Blakely has declared it a death by natural causes. He said there was no sign of any poison – although I doubt he looked for something he did not expect to find. He admitted he saw none of the usual signs of heart disease, but to him that suggested that this young and seemingly healthy man had suffered all his life from an invisible, inherent weakness which was only waiting for undue physical exertion or an emotional shock to become fatal. The expression on his face suggested that he'd had a great fright. '"Do you mean to say," I asked him, "that Mr Manning died of fright?"

'"It is entirely likely," he replied.

'When I described the setting in which he expired, pointing out there was nothing here to cause alarm, he proposed that Manning had suffered the shock somewhere else, and that it was the exertion of fleeing from this terrifying creature or event that over-taxed his heart.' Shaking his head in disgust, Mr Jesperson stepped away from the fire and dropped into the chair nearest mine.

'There was no point in arguing. But it is clearly absurd. Are we to think Manning met and was frightened to death by a *witch* on the streets of London? Unless the witch herself handed him our card and helpfully pointed him towards Gower Street, he must already have been on his way to see us before his fatal heart attack. Did he come to London to seek the help of a private detective, or was it only after he got here and something happened to him that decided him to come to us? And why us? Where did he get our card? If we only knew that, I think we would know much more.'

I put the book about poisons away from me, on a table, and said, 'Well, it doesn't matter now, anyway. He is dead, and his mystery, whatever it was, will be buried with him.'

Jesperson stared at me with a stunned expression. 'You cannot mean that, Miss Lane.'

'Certainly I do. You are disappointed, and I too, but as the police have decided there is no case—'

'We are not working for the police. Come, come, Miss Lane.' He leaned forward, engaging me with his intense blue eyes. 'The police surgeon's verdict is unsatisfactory and incomplete.

I cannot believe you do not feel, as I do, an obligation to our client.'

'Our *late* client,' I reminded him, and yet even as my heart was sinking at the prospect of another case that no one would thank us or pay us for solving, I felt some of his excitement about solving a mystery beginning to take hold of me.

'Our late client had a brother, his nearest living relation,' said Mr Jesperson. 'Mr Alexander Manning lives in Gordon Square – only a short distance from here. Given the circumstances, it is not merely acceptable, but positively required of us to call upon him – and sooner rather than later.'

'He has been informed of his brother's death?'

'Yes. He had to identify the body. I only missed meeting him at the morgue by an hour or so.'

'When shall we go?' Thinking of his 'sooner rather than later' remark I added, 'I can be ready in ten minutes.'

His nostrils flared. 'Mother is roasting a chicken. I think we may leave our visit until after dinner.'

Twenty-four Gordon Square was one of the tall, elegant houses that lined the quiet, green square, and seemed to me excessively large for the home of one unmarried man, even if he had until recently shared it with his brother. The curtains were drawn against the early dark, but they were not so thick as to hide the fact that lights were on in the downstairs front room.

Mr Jesperson rang the bell. After waiting awhile, he rang it again. Another wait, and I began to think that, in spite of the lights behind drawn curtains, perhaps no one was home, but then at last the door was opened by a man I knew must be Alexander Manning.

In my sole encounter with Charles Manning, his features had been distorted by strong emotion, but apart from that I saw how much the calm, grave man in the doorway resembled his brother. Brown-haired, brown-eyed, with a neatly-trimmed moustache beneath a short, straight nose above a full mouth, he appeared pleasant and quietly handsome.

'I do hope we are not intruding at this difficult time,' said Mr Jesperson. 'My name is Jasper Jesperson and this is my partner, Miss Lane. We should like to offer you our condolences, and deepest sympathy on your loss.'

Mr Manning's eyes widened slightly. 'You have heard already? How? I was just writing the notice to send to the papers.'

'We were with your brother when he died.'

This brief statement struck Mr Manning like a blow; he reeled back. 'With him? Where?' Then he held up his hand to forestall any reply. 'No, wait, please, won't you come in? I am glad he was not alone when he died; I want to hear all about it. Please, come in and let us speak in comfort.'

The drawing room into which he showed us was well pro-portioned, but stuffed with huge, dark furniture, every couch and chair layered with cushions and rugs, every surface crowded with useless ornaments, vases filled with artificial flowers, bowls with stone fruits, and every other kind of tasteless, old-fashioned clutter. It seemed entirely out of keeping as the home of this dapper bachelor.

He offered refreshments, which we declined, and we settled on to a pair of facing sofas to explain our business. Mr Manning spoke first, leaning forward tensely.

'The police told me my brother had collapsed in Gower Street in the early hours of this morning, dead of a heart attack. I had imagined him alone, and on his way to me here. But you say you were with him?'

'It was about half-past one in the morning; we were about to retire when there came a frantic pounding at the door. I opened it, and a stranger – whom I later learned to be your brother – all but fell into the house. He was clearly in distress, breathing heavily, covered in perspiration, his eyes dilated. He begged for our help, he enquired if he were safe – I assured him he was quite safe – but before we had a chance to learn what he feared, and how we could help him, he died.' Concluding his succinct description, Mr Jesperson leaned back, as if at his ease, but beside him, I could feel his nervous tension, and he never took his eyes from our host, who appeared at a loss.

'You say he was a stranger to you. Yet he came to your house, at such an unsociable hour. Have you any idea why?'

Extracting one of our business cards from his pocket, Mr Jesperson handed it across. 'He carried one of these. I can only assume, if he did not come across it entirely by chance, that someone recommended our services to him.'

Mr Manning stared at the card in a way that told me he had

16

not encountered its like before, so presumably he had not yet inspected his brother's personal possessions. 'Private investigations? What sort of investigations?' He looked up from the card and frowned at us in puzzlement that slowly changed to a look of dawning horror. 'You do not mean to say he came to hire you? To protect him? To uncover and foil some sort of fiendish plot?'

'It is possible,' Mr Jesperson agreed carefully. 'Alas, he did not live long enough to explain. All I can tell you is that he arrived in a state of palpable fear – he begged for our help – and made a few exclamations expressing his fear of witches.'

'Witches,' repeated Mr Manning. His mouth twisted bitterly. 'I might have known.'

His reaction was so unexpected that I had to ask: 'What do you mean? Did you know he had a fear of witches?'

'It was not a fear, Miss Lane. That would have been bad enough, a grown man who never outgrew nursery frights. No, it was worse. He had a sort of obsession with what he called "the old religion". Witchcraft, pagan mumbo-jumbo, the supposed ancient mysteries of Britain. He was a poet, my brother; a dreamer whose soul yearned for mystery and adventure he could never find in the workaday world, and he was always drawn to mysticism and had a childish love of fairy tales. As long as it was a hobby, it was well enough – I twitted him about it, but if he turned up to his job at the bank he could write poetry in his own time.'

'Then he threw up his job,' murmured Mr Jesperson.

'You have guessed it. He went to Norfolk one weekend – to walk on the beach and inhale poetic inspiration from the sea air – and when he came back, he was a changed man. He had made up his mind all of a sudden to quit the bank and devote himself to study and writing. And worse – he wanted me to sell the house and hand over half the proceeds to him.'

Mr Manning bowed his head. 'This house was our only inheritance.' He looked up again. 'In actual fact, it was left to me, as the elder son, but of course I always told Charles it belonged to him as well. By that I meant it would always be his home. He had no right to ask me to sell, and legally he could not compel me to do so. I told him he could continue to live here rent-free, as always, but I would not be answerable for his bills if he chose to leave his position. But to my great astonishment, he was giving up London along with the bank. Madness! If he truly wished to make a name for himself as a poet, or a scholar, London was where he ought to be – not the wilds of Norfolk.'

'When did he move to Norfolk?'

'June – near the end of June. I am sorry to say we parted on very chilly terms. I saw him only once after that, and when the police told me where he had died, naturally I thought he must have been on his way here, and I hoped it might have been for purposes of reconciliation, although from what you say,' he sighed, 'it seems unlikely.'

I sensed the aching sadness in him, the remorse for words that could never be unsaid or atoned for, and with some vague urge to comfort I said, 'If he had lived long enough to be married, his wife might have effected a reconciliation.'

He gave me an odd look. 'You did not know my brother.'

'True. I only meant that if love took him away from you, marriage might have brought him back – in a manner of speaking.' I almost squirmed under his astonished stare, and wished I had said nothing.

'*Love?*'

Mr Jesperson jumped in. 'Miss Lane and I had rather assumed it was an affair of the heart that drew your brother to Aylmerton. And that the most likely explanation for the silver cigarette case engraved with the date 15-6-93 and the words "To dearest C from your loving A" was that it was a present from his lover, possibly an engagement present. However, I see this is news to you.'

'He cannot possibly have been thinking of marriage.' Mr Manning rose to his feet and stalked to a table where he picked up a plain cotton sack that had been resting between a stuffed ferret and a ceramic shepherdess, and plunged his hand into it, pulling out the silver cigarette case Jesperson had described.

'The police gave me his personal effects, but I confess I scarcely gave them a glance.' He opened the case and read the inscription. 'And I am none the wiser for it now. I have no idea who this person A might be . . . or the significance of the date. Perhaps we should leave my brother his secrets.' With a hand that shook slightly, he dropped the silver case back into the bag and replaced it on the table.

As he turned back to face us, I had the feeling that he was

steeling himself to send us away; that he was on the brink of choosing to remain in ignorance about whatever story lay behind his brother's untimely death, but Mr Jesperson spoke first.

'If it was not meeting and falling head-over-heels with A, what *did* cause the sudden change in your brother? Do you know?'

'I do know.' He spoke decisively. 'One man is entirely to blame. His name is Felix Ott.'

I recognised the name as one I had copied, with an address in Cromer.

'Felix Ott,' repeated Mr Jesperson thoughtfully. 'Did he not give a talk – yes, I remember now; he was invited to speak by the Theosophical Society on the subject of Ancient Wisdom, but his particular stance was found objectionable by most Theoso-phists, for Mr Ott called upon the British people to look to our own historical traditions, rather than accepting the teachings of foreign masters in Asia.'

'Oh, he is worse than that,' said Mr Manning. 'As I understood from listening to Charles, the "ancient wisdom" Ott promotes is a mishmash of superstition and sorcery; everything a civilised person should find abhorrent – black magic, devil worship, human sacrifice.' He shuddered. 'How my brother could have been attracted to such vile rubbish, I do not understand; but he fell under Ott's spell upon their first meeting, and after that, he was a convert so absolute that, had I agreed to sell the house, his half of the money received would have gone to fill Ott's coffers, to support his so-called School of British Wisdom.'

'How peculiar,' Mr Jesperson mused, putting his head back to stare at the ceiling. 'Although it explains his preoccupation with witches, one must ask why, if he was such a staunch supporter of the School, he should have been so afraid of them at the end. For according to the tenets of Ott's School, witches were wise women unfairly demonised by the Church as part of the Christian practice of stamping out all the old native religions and pagan rituals. Of course, witches were thought to possess powers they could use against their foes.' He sat up straight and fixed his bright-blue gaze upon the other man. 'Did your brother fall out with Ott?'

'If so, he did not confide in me. I have told you we were estranged.' He gave a heavy sigh. 'It must be a source of eternal regret to me. So far as I know, Charles was still caught fast in Ott's occult toils. But he was an intelligent man. All that "ancient religion" was no more than his latest hobby-horse – he would have outgrown it, and learned to see through his teacher if only he had lived long enough.' The bleakness of loss came over him again.

'Were you aware that his heart was weak?'

Mr Manning shook his head, bewildered. 'No, not at all. He was always active as a boy – and into manhood. We both are – were – fine, healthy specimens rarely suffering even any minor illness.'

'So you were surprised when the police surgeon said he had died of heart failure brought on by shock and over-exertion?'

'He might have been speaking of another man,' he burst out. 'Indeed, until I saw my brother lying there on the slab I was all but certain there had been some mistake, a confusion of identity . . . I can still hardly believe he is dead.'

Mr Jesperson said nothing when the other man lapsed into silence. Painfully aware of Mr Manning's grief, I shifted uncomfortably and tried to catch my partner's eye, wishing to signal to him that we should leave. But he gave me no opportunity, his attention fixed on the grieving man with such intensity, I wondered if he were trying to transmit a thought to him.

At last, as the silence was becoming almost unbearable, Mr Manning spoke. 'Charles went to you because something had frightened him. And whatever that was, whether or not it caused his death, it must have been behind it. I would like to know why he died. And I think, by hiring you to investigate, I will be carrying out his last wishes.

'Will you do it? Can you? Find out what he wanted you for – and the circumstances that led up to his death? I will pay your usual fee, and all reasonable expenses – naturally you will want to go to Norfolk. You may send your bills to me. And any questions you have. I will assist you in every way that I can.'

He shook hands on it with Mr Jesperson; then I stood up, and he shook hands with me, clasping my hand warmly as he murmured, 'Please find out what happened to my brother.'

CHAPTER THREE

The Shrieking Pits of Aylmerton

Before we left Mr Manning, Mr Jesperson gave him instructions: he was to ask his brother's former associates if he had been in touch with them, and likewise ask at his old haunts in the city to discover if he had been seen there on the last day of his life.

'For we know he travelled down from Norwich on the one fifteen, arriving at Liverpool Street Station at approximately four forty-five; more than eight hours elapsed before he knocked on our door, which makes it most unlikely that his purpose of travelling to London was to bring a problem to Jesperson and Lane. No, he came to London for some other reason, but during the evening something happened which worried him and inspired him to seek out the services of a detective agency. Where did he get our card? Who recommended us to him? If his problem were connected with some concerns relating to Felix Ott it is unlikely he would have turned to any of *his* associates for help, and since he did not come to you, he may have looked up some old friend. You probably have ideas as to whom.

'We also know, from the contents of his stomach, that your brother dined on steak and oysters; also potatoes and cake. He consumed a great deal of alcohol, in the form of beer, wine, brandy and champagne – probably not all at the same time, so he may have visited several different licensed premises. Well, you will have your work cut out for you, tracing your late brother's movements.' Jesperson clapped Mr Manning on the shoulder in a display of manly support.

'Write to me at Cromer, poste restante. We will keep in touch, and if you learn anything important, or wish to speak to one of us urgently, send a wire. Good evening, and good hunting to you, Mr Manning.'

Our own immediate task, once we had returned to Gower Street, was to learn what we could in regard to the last known address of Charles Manning.

Aylmerton was not on a railway line, but it was only three miles south of Cromer, which was. After consulting a map and the latest issue of *Bradshaw's*, Mr Jesperson worked out our itinerary, and we set off bright and early the following morning with our bags and a picnic lunch prepared by Edith Jesperson.

We arrived at Liverpool Street Station with plenty of time to spare, and I was able to purchase a copy of a pocket-sized volume entitled *Tourists' Guide to Norfolk*. Once aboard the train, with a carriage to ourselves, we took it in turns to read aloud from it. The author, Mr Walter Rye, took a particular interest in the 'superstitions and peculiarities' of the inhabitants of Norfolk, which was very much to Mr Jesperson's taste.

Of Aylmerton the author had nothing to say except that a visitor might find it 'interesting from the open pits or earth dwellings, something like those at Weybourne, which are locally called "shrieking pits", from the local belief that the wraith of a woman is always wandering about looking into them at night-time, wringing her hands and shrieking. There are the ruins of a beacon on the high ground. The church is small and poor.'

Intrigued by the curious-sounding pits, I turned to the entry on Weybourne and read the following: 'Behind the village, on the heath, are the curious hollows somewhat resembling the Aylmerton *shrieking pits*, supposed by some to be the remains of British hut dwellings.'

The journey passed pleasantly through miles of interesting scenery, and with plenty of time for conversation as well as reading. Edith had prepared a substantial repast, which I thought would have served a multitude, but her son, whose slender frame gave no hint of the size of his appetite, polished off every scrap. 'No sense letting it go to waste,' he said, more than once. 'If you are quite certain you have had enough?'

We had only a short wait in Thorpe Station at Norwich before catching the train to Cromer. That journey took barely an hour, and thus it was still daylight when our cab deposited us in front of the Vicarage in Aylmerton.

I say 'cab', but the vehicle we hired outside Cromer Station was really more a cart. It was a big open carriage, the sort of thing hired by groups of holidaymakers wishing to see the local sights

25

on a summer's day, and although it was comfortable enough, it was hardly suitable to the weather, which had turned very cold. I could be pleased that it was neither raining nor snowing, but the buffeting wind had an icy edge to it which made me shiver and pull my woollen scarf up over my face.

Mr Jesperson, as usual, appeared indifferent to the cold, and obviously enjoyed the unimpeded views of the countryside and did not mind the slow pace of the old cart-horse. He was always keen to explore and learn about new places, and the elderly driver (he and his horse were a well-matched pair) indulged his interest with a story about everything we passed, no matter how ordinary or uninspiring in appearance. To me, his accent was a challenge, especially with the wind whistling about my ears, but I could see that Mr Jesperson understood him well enough, and I was happy to leave them to their half-comprehensible conversation.

Norfolk is traditionally known for its flatness, but it is not uniformly so, especially in the north-east parts of the county. This area would undoubtedly provide many charming excursions in warm, dry weather, I thought, knocking my feet together in a vain attempt to warm them. I was glad when the road descended into an area of woodland, where we were sheltered from the wind.

My ears pricked up when I heard the phrase 'shrieking pits' and I looked to where the driver was indicating, but could make out nothing in the shadowy depths of the forest.

'Are they only in the woods?' Mr Jesperson enquired.

'Nay, nay, master. Hardly. They used to be everywhere, especially on the heath. There are still some to be seen over Beeston way, and one right in Aylmerton – that one is in a field close by the Vicarage. If that's what you came to see, you won't miss it.'

He gave a gusty sigh. 'Can't see what the interest is, but the visitors do always ask about the pits. Back in me grandfather's day there must have been hundreds, but not now.'

'Why? What has become of them?'

'Oh, the farmers filled 'em in, mostly. So they could plough their land more handily, you see. And some got dug out. Or planted over.' He waved a vague hand. 'Anyways, most were disappeared before I was born. I suppose nobody cares about the one in the woods, no call to fill it in, even though it is said to be the deepest of all.'

Mr Jesperson quizzed him further about the pits, asking his opinion of their origins and purpose, and it was clear by his ready replies that our driver had dealt with the same questions many times before. It was generally said, although you might not think it to look at them, that they were the remains of ancient dwellings, where our prehistoric ancestors had dwelt. Furthermore, he added, quite a few of the local people believed these subterranean homes were still inhabited – by some sort of elves or boggarts, although he did not hold with such nonsense himself.

Mr Jesperson looked interested. 'You surprise me. I had thought such tales of an underground race were confined to the Celtic fringe, and connected with chambered cairns and hollow hills, rather than hut circles.'

Our guide frowned, thrown off his stride. 'Eh? Well, I cannot explain it except to say that folks round here know what they know, and that's all there is to it. Anyways, it may be you've heard of our famous ghost?'

'The shrieking woman?'

' No one can say when or how it happened, but long ago this poor creature was deprived of her baby, and ever since, her ghost haunts the pits, weeping and wailing and searching in vain for her lost child. If the wind is in the right direction you may hear her yourself some dark night . . . only pray you never set eyes on her, for it is said that no one ever survives that experience.'

'So I suppose that people generally avoid going anywhere near the pits after dark?'

'Oh, yes indeed, master. They surely do.'

'Even you?' he pressed.

'Why ever should I want to go roaming around the woods and fields at night?' the man replied, sounding indignant.

'Do you believe in ghosts?'

The driver frowned. 'I don't say that I do, but I won't say that I don't. I have heard her shrieking – and the sound fair gives you the chills, whatever you may say you believe – I tell you that.'

By this time we had come out of the woods and were approaching a crossroads with an inn. Although not mentioned in the guide book, it looked a reasonably comfortable place, and I thought we could do worse than lodge there, if there was no room at the Vicarage, although I imagined that as soon as we had learned all we could about the late Mr Manning from his former hosts we would move on to Cromer and tackle the mysterious Mr Ott. A signpost pointed straight ahead to Holt, right to West Runton and left to Aylmerton.

As soon as we had turned down the Aylmerton road I saw, straight ahead and on top of a hill, a building with a ruined tower.

'Church of St John the Baptist – Aylmerton Parish Church,' our guide announced. 'But you want the Vicarage, you said, master?'

'Yes, I do, although I will confess to you we have not been invited, and must throw ourselves on the Christian mercy of the minister, who will, I hope, be kind enough to take in two wandering pilgrims.'

The driver cackled with laughter at Mr Jesperson's words. 'Pilgrims, are ye? For by ye've come to the wrong place and I should take ye to Wayside Cross instead.'

'What is that?'

'Nay, I was only fooling,' he said, abruptly sober.

'But what is Wayside Cross?'

He frowned and fidgeted, obviously wishing he had kept quiet, but as Mr Jesperson would not drop it, finally he said, ''Tis a house by the old stump cross, said to mark the old pilgrims' route to Walsingham – the house takes its name from that. I meant nothing by it. And here is the Vicarage.' His tone lifted. 'Mrs Reverend Ringer will be happy to have more visitors from London. She finds it dull here out of season. And you'll both be very comfortable I'm sure, so long as you don't object to a bit of preaching from the Reverend.'

29

We came to a halt by the front gate of a large and comfortable-looking house. Mr Jesperson jumped down nimbly, unloaded both our bags, and paid the driver as I was getting down myself. My feet were hardly on the ground before the driver clucked to his horse and they were away at what seemed to me a brisker pace than any the old nag had managed throughout our journey.

A maid answered Mr Jesperson's knock on the front door and, incurious as to our names or business, scarcely looked at us before ushering us inside and depositing us in a neat and pleasantly furnished yet chilly sitting room. The fire in the hearth had burnt down nearly to ash. I suppose it was rather late in the day for callers; at any rate, the maid did not stay to build up the fire but merely told us the vicar would be with us shortly, before she left us, almost banging the door shut in her haste.

While I took a seat, Mr Jesperson discovered some coals lurking in the copper scuttle and set to work reviving the fire. It was soon blazing cheerfully and warmth was stealing back into the chilly room when someone else entered the room.

The newcomer was a short, powerfully built man, round-faced, clean-shaven and bald, a surviving fringe of light-brown hair appearing like a monk's tonsure. His collar marked him as a man of the cloth, but his face did not wear the pacific, welcoming expression one might expect. He looked rather pugnacious, in a righteous way, as if we had come to pick a quarrel with him – and he had decided to strike the first blow.

Without a greeting, without giving us the chance to introduce ourselves, he sternly announced, 'You are not members of my congregation. Nor are you residents of this parish.' He swept us both with a penetrating gaze, lingering a bit longer on my face than on Mr Jesperson's. 'I venture to guess that you have no friends or relatives here, yet you have come from Norwich – no, you have come all the way from London.'

I was baffled by his approach; even, I confess, rather intimidated, but when I looked at Mr Jesperson, I saw by his alert, amused expression that he was enjoying it.

'Bravo!' exclaimed Mr Jesperson. 'I perceive you are a devotee of detective fiction, Doctor Ringer. And you are quite right – so far. Can you deduce our purpose in coming to see you?'

'Nothing could be more obvious,' snapped the vicar. 'Do you imagine I have not met your kind before? Although I admit I do not understand why you should have chosen Aylmerton, rather than some more scenic village with a more celebrated church – there are several within as easy reach of Cromer.'

'We did not come here for the church, Doctor Ringer.' My friend smiled mischievously. 'And I fear we are at cross-purposes. Pray tell us, will you, the *obvious* reason?'

'Why, that you want to be married!' he growled.

I gasped, Mr Jesperson laughed, and the vicar for the first time looked uncertain. He frowned. 'No? I . . . I beg your pardon, but the maid told me . . . '

'The maid did not even ask our business!' I cried indignantly.

'Had she not been in such a hurry, I should have given her our card,' said my partner, producing one with a flourish. 'Jesperson and Lane, at your service.'

31

The vicar glanced up from the card, to search our faces once more. 'Private investigators? You are *real* detectives, then? You were quite right, to say I am a devotee. But, what can interest you here? What is your business with me?'

Mr Jesperson took his seat again. 'Charles Manning gave this as his address.'

'Yes, he has boarded with us since midsummer. But I am afraid you've had a wasted journey, for he went down to London three days ago and has not returned.'

'Nor will he,' said Mr Jesperson sombrely. 'We bring unhappy news. Charles Manning is dead.'

'How? Why? What happened?' The vicar leaned forward, his eyes fixed upon Mr Jesperson's face.

'He arrived at our door in a state of fear and distress, and died before he could explain.'

'Was he poisoned?'

The two men stared at each other for a long, charged moment before Mr Jesperson replied, 'The police do not think so.'

'How was it explained?'

'Heart failure.'

The vicar made a sound of disbelief. 'But he is – was – a strong, healthy young man. I never saw any signs of physical weakness in him.'

'His brother agrees with you,' I said. 'Tell me, why did you suggest poisoning? Is that simply due to your interest in mystery stories?'

Dr Ringer regarded me gravely. 'I wish it were only that.

But there have been three mysterious deaths in the parish this past year.'

Mr Jesperson gave an exclamation. 'What! Three unsolved murders in this quiet, rural place?'

The vicar looked a bit abashed. 'Well . . . not precisely. The first death was that of William Goodall, a farmer. He was undoubtedly poisoned. His wife was suspected of his murder, although she was not charged, and when she died the same way, seemingly by her own hand, this was taken as her remorseful confession. The third victim was not a local man, although he had resided for a time in Cromer. His body was found in the woods near here, after he had been missing for several days, and no one could say for certain how he died. Possibly it was an accident . . . the police are not looking for anyone in connection with the case, but the village gossip has it that he was killed. He was an acquaintance of Charles Manning, so, I wondered . . .'

'But Manning died in London.'

'Yes, but – why did he go to London? Could he have been fleeing someone, an enemy, who caught up with him there?'

Mr Jesperson glanced at me and I raised my eyebrows. He returned his attention to the Reverend Dr Ringer.

'Did he seem to you to be afraid? Did he say why he was going to London?'

His shoulders slumped, and the vicar sighed. 'No . . . He seemed much as ever. He told my wife he was going to London, but as he took no luggage, we expected him to come straight back. When he did not . . . well, we saw no reason to worry. I never imagined anything like this.'

'No, of course, why should you? Did you know Mr Manning well? Did he speak to you about his work?'

'His work? You mean his studies.' The vicar's expression became more reserved. 'He did at first, but soon realised that I did not share his interest in local superstitions; that in fact I felt his interest to be misguided – and dangerous. I do not believe it can do any good, and indeed may do much harm, to poke and pry into those dark recesses of the human soul, the lingering beliefs in magic and witchcraft, ghosts and fairies and other unchristian things.

'I liked Mr Manning – do not misunderstand me. I thought he was a gifted and intelligent young man who would soon get tired of investigating ancient obscenities – I beg your pardon! – and take up more wholesome pursuits. Some of his poetry was quite good – I used to think he might have written some rousing new hymns, if he'd been that way inclined.'

'Did he attend your services?'

The vicar sadly shook his head. 'Never.'

'Do you know why he chose to live here?'

'He came to Aylmerton because of the shrieking pits – you have heard of them?'

We both indicated that we had.

'You probably know they are reckoned to be the remains of prehistoric dwellings. Some have been excavated, but nothing of interest ever found. However, Charles was interested in them

less from an historic or archaeological view than for their reputation in local folklore. The well-known legend attached to
them is of a shrieking woman who haunts the pits, searching
for the body of her murdered child, but Charles told me he had
learned of another tradition, believed but not widely reported,
that the pits are actually the habitations of the little people –
fairies, you might say, as long as you don't think of anything
like Shakespeare's Titania and Oberon. Here in Norfolk there
is a tradition of a pygmy, troglodytic race, small folk who may
be kind and helpful if it pleases them, but who are more likely
to do you harm – or steal your baby.'

I sighed. 'You say it is not widely reported, but we heard the
same story from the old man who drove us here from the station.'

'That would be Royston Kettle,' said the vicar. 'Why am I
not surprised? Although whether he was Charles' informant or
had the story from Charles, is anyone's guess.'

'Did Mr Manning often interview local people about such
things?'

'Yes, of course. He meant to write a paper – or perhaps
even a book. That was why he came here. He began with
the shrieking pits, but he was interested in all the local folklore.'

Mr Jesperson said, 'Do you know a man called Felix Ott?'

As if the name has been a handful of grit flung in his face,
the vicar jerked his head back, muscles tensing, and blinked
rapidly. 'Ott! What of him?'

'You know him?'

'Not to speak to. I am aware of his occupation and his repulsive ideas.'

'Repulsive?'

'His description of Christianity is unspeakable. If he could, he would bring down the established Church of England, and replace it with devil-worship. He has said as much.' He stared hard at Mr Jesperson. 'Why do you mention his name in this house?'

Seeing the power in his tensed arms, and the unforgiving glare in his eyes, I thought that Christian he might be, but not of the meek and mild, 'turn the other cheek' variety.

'It was my understanding that Charles Manning decided to move to Norfolk after a meeting with Felix Ott.'

The other man nodded slowly, and some of the tension vanished. 'I see. Well, it is no surprise, considering the area Charles had chosen to study. No surprise, either, that he should never have mentioned him to me.'

'Alexander Manning was inclined to blame Ott for his brother's death.'

I expected Dr Ringer to agree, but he was dismissive. 'No, no. The man is poisonous, but I doubt he bothers with strychnine or cyanide. And Ott would not destroy a useful tool.'

'What if Charles Manning were not as amenable as Ott desired. What if he turned against him, threatened to expose him or spoil his plans in some way? Might not that have made him angry enough to kill?'

'Perhaps. Ott strikes me as a thoroughly immoral, utterly

selfish creature. He would not baulk at murder. And a man so interested in witchcraft might decide to cast a killing spell on his enemy – this would serve the purpose of demonstrating his powers to his followers, whilst keeping clear of the law. I hardly think that in this modern day anyone would be tried for, let alone found guilty of, murder by witchcraft.'

'Do you really think Felix Ott – or anyone – could do that?' I asked him. 'That he – or anyone – could have cast a spell to stop Mr Manning's heart?'

The vicar turned his gaze on me and nodded soberly. 'I believe in the power of evil, just as I believe in the power of good. And if ye hath faith as a mustard seed, nothing shall be impossible – this is unfortunately true for those who are determined to do evil as for the pure of heart. We are spiritual as well as material creatures; if I did not believe that, how could I devote my life to preaching the word of God? If witchcraft *were not* dangerous, why would I want to warn Charles away from it? If it had been only a waste of his time, I might have shrugged it off . . . but it was worse than that. It was far more dangerous than he knew . . . and in a different way than I expected. I was concerned about the state of his soul, you see; it never occurred to me that witchcraft might kill him.'

CHAPTER FOUR

A Night at the Vicarage

Reverend Ringer invited us to stay, and to consider his home ours for however long our investigation should detain us.

'It seems the very least we can do for our former lodger. Mr Jesperson, you will have his room. His things are all as he left them. We must, I suppose, soon pack and return them to his brother in London, but in the meantime, feel free to examine his papers and anything else that might provide a clue to his sad end.

'My daughters – I am blessed with three – are quite accustomed to changing about and sharing when we have visitors, so we shall easily find another room for you, Miss Lane. No trouble at all, I assure you. The girls, and my wife especially, find it a pleasure having visitors to enliven their quiet days so far from town.'

In due course we met the rest of the family in a more comfortable parlour than the one into which we had first been shown. Mrs Ringer was a stout, capable-appearing woman whose hair of faded gold and shrewd blue eyes hinted at the beauty she had possessed in her youth. The eldest daughter, Hilda, aged thirteen, brown-haired and blue-eyed, always had a book in her hand, or tucked into a fold of her skirt to be perused in any idle moment. The other girls, Louisa and Beth, were golden-haired children who took small interest in the adult conversation, preferring the game they were playing with their brother, a boy of about six years old called Richard. There were also three other sons away at school; we were told their names, scholastic interests and sporting achievements and shown their photographs in a red velvet album.

The Reverend broke the news of their erstwhile lodger's death to his family, presenting the official verdict of heart failure without any hint of doubt. We were introduced as acquaintances of Mr Alexander Manning, sent to collect his brother's effects and learn what we could about the last days of his life.

Mr Jesperson had told Dr Ringer that for the purposes of our investigation, we thought it best to remain incognito, and although I had not expected he would conceal the truth from his own family, it made good sense. Children may talk, or servants overhear, and thus the secret might be revealed to the very person we should least like to know.

Although all expressed shock and sorrow for a young life cut so suddenly short, none seemed personally affected, and the news did not cast a lasting pall over the evening. We spoke at first of Mr Manning, as seemed only proper, but as the family shared their memories of him with us I realised how little they had known him. He always took his breakfast in his room, and rarely dined with the family. Although invited to treat the drawing room as his own, he did not. If he was not in his room, working or sleeping, he was out – and he went out most days, and stayed out late into the evening.

Dr Ringer had made some attempts to become better acquainted with the stranger living under his roof, but their conversations had been largely dedicated to intellectual matters. They were on first-name terms, but were little more than acquaintances. Who Charles' friends were, with whom he dined or where he went at night, the vicar and his wife could not say. He was under no obligation to inform them of his movements, of course, Mrs Ringer interjected, but in the past, when they had taken lodgers, even if only for a month in the summer, the visitors had quickly come to feel like part of the family. But Mr Manning had not wished for that.

The maid who had answered the door to us now stepped into the room to announce: 'Dinner is ready, Cook says, if you please.'

As we were about to make our way to the dining room I noticed Mrs Ringer catch hold of her daughter's hand. 'Not at table, Hilda.'

With a sigh, the girl put down her beloved book and walked on. Always curious, I slowed my steps enough to discover what this fascinating novel could be, and was very surprised to find it was a mathematical text – quite incomprehensible to me.

Mr Jesperson saw – of course, he had also noticed Miss Hilda's surreptitious study going on whilst we grown-ups conversed, and with his sharp eyes he had divined the nature of the book before I could. He winked at me; I bit my lip and hoped no one else had seen.

Dinner was a more formal meal than the vicar had led us to expect, presented in a series of courses to the seven of us at table. The younger children were excused, but in addition to Hilda and her parents there were two others. Mr Mavesin was a thin, pale young man in spectacles, introduced as Dr Ringer's secretary, and youthful-seeming but grey-haired Miss Flowerdew was the family governess.

During the first course – a creamy leek and potato soup – Mr Jesperson and I became the conversational focus, as Mrs Ringer wished to understand our connection with Mr Manning, and asked immediately what was *our* relationship?

I had not given any thought to an answer, the decision to conceal our true occupation having been made on the fly. Fortunately, her questions came just as I had taken a spoonful of soup, so Mr Jesperson answered for me.

'We are business partners,' he replied. 'We are in the process of establishing a new publishing imprint, as Jesperson and Lane. Mr Alexander Manning is our banker, and he brought the poetry of his brother to our attention. It was our intention to publish his first collection.'

'I hope you will not abandon that idea,' responded Mrs Ringer. 'It would be lovely to have such a memorial of his brief life.'

'We must discover whether he left a sufficient quantity of work behind . . . and if all the poems are of the same quality.' He gave a sideways glance at the vicar to encourage him to join in.

'I have told Mr Jesperson he should feel free to sort through and examine all of Mr Manning's papers. I'm sure his brother could have no objection.'

His wife nodded her agreement, and the conversation moved on to more general observations about poetry, publishing and the need for more suitable and well-paid occupations for unmarried women. The talk was sufficiently engaging that it was quite some time before our hostess noticed that we had all long finished our soup, and that the empty bowls still sat before us, with no sign of the next course.

'Maria,' she said, raising her voice to call that name again. She frowned. 'Where *is* that girl? Never there when you want her. She has become so unreliable lately.'

Pushing back her chair, she got up and went to the sideboard for a bell, which she gave a vigorous shake. The clapper swung and the summons of the hand-bell pealed. Then she sat down again, and we all waited in silence.

After a few moments the door opened and a stout, red-faced woman appeared, hands on her hips, frowning.

'I am sorry, Cook,' said Mrs Ringer with a pacifying air. 'I did not mean to disturb *you*. Only . . . we are ready for our next course, as you can see, and—'

'And I am ready for you to have it and all!' the cook exclaimed fiercely. 'The fish will be that dry and cold, a-waitin', and I made it so lovely.'

Distantly, there came the sound of a slammed door, then hasty footsteps approaching.

42

Cook turned. 'And where have you been, I'd like to know? Keeping the gentlefolk waiting.'

'I'm very sorry, I'm sure.' It was the same maid who had taken us for an eloping couple when she let us into the house. She spoke distractedly, short of breath, wisps of hair escaping from under her cap, her clothing disarranged, with dark spots down her front, as if she'd splashed water on herself. 'Please, I'm sorry, Ma'am, but I had to – I had to go—'

'That will be enough, Maria,' her mistress said loudly, cutting her off. 'We do not wish for an explanation. Clear the plates and bring in the next course, and try to be more aware of the time in future.'

The fish was colder than it should have been, but perfectly cooked, with a lovely sauce. All the food was delicious and plentiful – not even the addition of two unexpected guests had forced a reduction in portions. I wondered if the Ringers ate so well every night, and if Charles Manning had known what he was missing, and where, on what, and with whom he had dined instead.

I received a partial answer to my question later that night, from Hilda.

Despite the vicar's cheery assurance that there were plenty of rooms, and that the girls were accustomed to moving, his wife had a different plan. She might accept me as Mr Jesperson's business partner and express her support for the idea of gainful employment for women, but she did not trust my morals enough to put me alone in a room overnight. Hilda was to be my bed-partner, to protect me from my travelling companion, or my own worse nature, or any suspicion of wrongdoing. She probably meant well, so I did not reveal my annoyance at her presumption, and pretended to believe that this was the best she had to offer, and I should be 'most comfortable' sharing with Hilda.

It did not help that, although the bed was large enough for two, young Hilda was a thrasher, given to rolling over suddenly, and kicking out with her long, skinny legs.

The one benefit of sharing was that she told me things about Mr Manning that her parents did not know. For instance, that he had a sweetheart whom he had visited most evenings.

We were in bed when this conversation began, lying in the dark.

'Do you know who she is?' I asked.

'She is one of the Bulstrode sisters. They live alone since their parents died, at Wayside Cross. Miss Bulstrode, Alys and Ann.'

I bit my lip, thinking of the 'A' engraved on the silver cigarette case. 'Which one?'

'Most likely Ann. She is the youngest and prettiest. Alys is pretty, too, but she has a sharp tongue. I'm sure she has frightened off more than one suitor already.'

'Mr Manning's brother had no idea of his brother's engagement. He cannot have written to her . . . They will not have heard the news,' I said. 'I should pay a call and let them know. Is their house far?'

'You may see it if you look up the road. They are our nearest neighbours.'

'Oh – well, perhaps your mother or your father would be

kind enough to introduce me. The sad news might better come from their vicar.'

She giggled and drummed her feet, making the mattress bounce beneath us. 'Papa is not their vicar! And we never socialise with them.'

'Why not?'

I felt the movement of her shoulders as she shrugged. 'Mama will not explain. But they never come to church – not to *our* church. But I think I know why, and – oh!' She gave a little gasp, and drummed her feet again. 'Perhaps that is the reason why Mr Manning never would attend Papa's services.'

'What is?'

'Why, if he was a Roman. For I think *they* are. And she wouldn't agree to marry him if he were not, would she? Or unless he converted.'

'You mean they are Roman Catholic?'

My own pillow shook under the force of her heavily nodding head. 'I think they must be. And it is quite a distance to the nearest R.C. church – Norwich, perhaps – so even if they are quite devout, they could not often attend a service. But I think the Bulstrodes are Christians – just different from *our* kind of Christian – and it is nonsense what some people say.'

I almost did not ask, for I had no need to hear the usual ignorant, prejudicial slander directed by pious Anglicans against the equally pious neighbours who had never abandoned the original Mother Church, but I wanted to keep her talking. 'What do some people say?'

'That Miss Bulstrode is a witch. Because she has a raven for a pet – it is a very clever bird – silly, ignorant folk call that her familiar. They say it is an *implet*. And because people go to her for powders and poultices and potions – but that is not witchcraft, you know, but *medicine*. She knows all about plants, the wild ones she gathers in the woods, and the ones she grows in her garden. And that is called *botany*. So you see – what she does is *science*, not witchcraft.'

'Do you believe in witchcraft?'

She squirmed and paddled her feet. 'I don't know. Define witchcraft. If A gives a mixture to B and B dies, does that make A a witch?'

'First I'd like to know the purpose of the mixture, and the relationship between A and B.'

'Very good. Is A a registered chemist, a trained doctor, a medical student . . . or a spinster with a raven perched on her shoulder?'

I gave a startled laugh. 'This is the lady that Charles Manning wanted to marry?'

'Of course not. I told you – Miss Bulstrode is too old for Mr Manning. And she is too clever. Mama says men do not like very clever women. But sometimes men must wish to talk to women they do not wish to marry. I think Mr Manning first called upon Miss Bulstrode to ask her about her knowledge, and to look at her books.' Her voice turned wistful on that word. 'They have a very fine library at Wayside Cross. People come from far and wide to consult it. I wish Mama would let

me go . . . but she says we have more than enough books here.'
She flopped on to her side. 'Anyway, Mr Manning went there
for information – for the books, and maybe to ask Miss B where
she'd learned to cast spells, but then Miss Ann cast her spell on
him.' She giggled sleepily. 'Isn't it funny how people talk about
ladies casting spells to make men fall in love with them? If spells
were real and I could do them, I wouldn't waste any of them
on anything as silly as that.'

'What would you use your spells for?'

'To go into space, to travel to other planets, to go deep under
the sea and find out all the secrets of the universe.'

I smiled. I liked Hilda.

'But they're not real.' She yawned. 'When Miss Bulstrode
helps somebody who goes to her, she doesn't do it with magic,
but with medicine – because she's been studying plants and
learning about the effects of chemical compounds on the human
body. And it would be the same if she ever harmed anyone.
People who say she is a witch – or that all the sisters are witches
– are simply superstitious, ignorant fools. Even Miss Flowerdew.'
She yawned again, heaved herself up and turned on to her other
side, facing away from me.

I asked another question before she could fall asleep. 'What
is Miss Bulstrode's Christian name?'

'Arabella,' she murmured drowsily.

Arabella, Alys and Ann. Three candidates for Mr Manning's
'dearest A'. In the morning, I hoped to learn which one – and
much more besides.

CHAPTER FIVE

In a House of Women

The problem with living incognito in a family home was that it made any private exchange of information with Mr Jesperson next to impossible. I was eager next morning to share what I had learned from Hilda, and to discuss our plan of action, but there were always others about, and, as we were still a novelty in the household, we were the centre of attention.

Breakfast was a family affair, with all the children present as well as their governess. The dishevelled, harassed-looking maid rushed in and out with bowls of porridge, plates of eggs and bacon, more tea and toast for us all. I felt sorry for her, and hoped she'd had her own breakfast already, although I suspected the food would have gone cold before she had time to eat.

'What are your plans for today, Jasper?' enquired Dr Ringer. 'I hope you do not mind if I call you Jasper.'

'It is my name,' he said equably, tucking into his bacon and eggs. 'But I fear you may change your mind when I tell you whom I plan to visit.'

'Felix Ott.' Dr Ringer spoke the name in withering tones, but his disapproval did not extend to his new young friend. 'I understand. He should be able to tell you much more about Charles' investigations, his comings and goings, and much more besides – if he is of a mind to be helpful. But I should not be too ready to believe whatever he says. And I hope you will take care, for I am certain he will do his best to involve you in his own scheme. Can you ride a bicycle?'

Mr Jesperson looked up alertly. 'I can.'

'Then you may take mine. It will get you to Cromer in under half an hour if you take it steady.'

'Thank you. That is most kind. I enjoy a good spin.'

As the two men beamed at each other across the table, I fumed in silence, trying and failing to catch Mr Jesperson's eye as I wondered why he did not mention me – did he expect me to toil along in his dust? Or did he imagine I should be happy to balance on the handlebars as he struggled to propel the overburdened machine . . .

I was still at a loss for words when Mrs Ringer intervened. 'What a happy thought, Robert. And do not worry about your friend, Mr Jesperson; Miss Lane and I shall enjoy ourselves together, and have a good, long gossip – stay in Cromer as long as you like.'

As she made to pat my hand, I pulled away, just managing to put on a conciliatory smile before she could feel the snub. 'That is very kind of you, Mrs Ringer, but I am afraid I cannot stay. I must pay another call today. There are other friends of Mr Manning who must be told of his demise.'

Her eyes narrowed. 'What friends? When you questioned us yesterday you implied – more than implied; I am certain you were entirely ignorant of any *friends* Charles may have made in Norfolk.'

'Perhaps "friends" is the wrong word. Indeed, we know nothing of his relationships,' I answered calmly, taking care not to look in Hilda's direction. 'But we have his address book, you know. And Mr Manning – his brother, I mean – was most eager for us to speak with anyone who had known him. We are only trying to carry out his wishes. Although you did not mention it, one address in his book is very near – Wayside Cross. Do you know the family?'

Mrs Ringer looked as if she had met with a bad smell. 'I know *of* them. Three sisters live there. If Mr Manning visited Wayside Cross, it can only have been for the library. The ladies inherited a large collection of books from their grandfather. He was a seafaring man who brought back a great many exotic plants from his travels around the world, and after he retired he settled down to collecting books and tending his garden.'

'Certainly Charles visited Wayside Cross, and more than once,' said the vicar. I wondered why he had not mentioned it earlier, but instead professed ignorance about where the late Mr Manning had spent his time, and perhaps he realised that he owed us an explanation, for he continued, 'The library was the great attraction to him, undoubtedly, and not for the volumes that most people would prize – works of natural history, botany, chemistry, geography and medical studies – but for a small collection of books in several languages dealing with magic and witchcraft.'

'Part of the "obscenities" you wished he would abandon?' Mr Jesperson suggested as he buttered a piece of toast.

'You do understand.' Dr Ringer sighed. 'One never likes to speak ill of the dead; I was so fond of Charles, it hurts me to say anything that would make others think badly of him. And—' He hesitated, then plunged into further justification for his previous prevarications. 'After all, you did ask specifically about his *friends* – and regardless of how much time he spent in her house, he could never have counted Miss Bulstrode as his friend.'

'Why not?'

Although it was I who had asked the question, he continued to speak as if confiding in Mr Jesperson alone. 'Because she was an enemy to Felix Ott.'

I gave an exclamation of surprise, and Mr Jesperson stopped eating to stare at the vicar, who nodded gravely. 'Miss Bulstrode has a reputation as a witch. She works as a healer, mainly with women – our doctor has said she is as good as any midwife he has encountered – and although she uses traditional remedies, they tend to work, and are often more effective than anything he could prescribe.'

He cast a glance at his children, sitting at the other end of the table, heads down, seemingly with no thoughts for anything but the food on their plates, although I would have bet money that the girls at least were listening with all their ears, and he lowered his voice.

'On the other side, she sells potions and casts spells – or at least people think she does. Whether true or not, nearly all the locals believe she is a genuine witch, mostly working for the good, but with the ability to strike down anyone who offends her, to kill swiftly and secretly without recourse to anything we would recognise as a murder weapon. I would never tell you all this if it were only rumour and superstition, but *Ott* believes in her powers to such a degree that he has tried everything to get her to become a part of his secret school . . . but she flatly refuses. So now he hates her. From flattering and wheedling he has turned to vilification. And Charles was so devoted to Ott and his cause that he could never have been friends with someone he hated.'

With that, Dr Ringer picked up his spoon and attacked his porridge, taking it in rapid mouthfuls. He clearly meant to say no more, but I had to ask: 'What of her sisters?'

'They are all as bad as each other,' Mrs Ringer said briskly. 'And this is not a suitable discussion for my family breakfast table.'

Mr Jesperson and I left the house at the same time, although we were going in different directions and by different means. The vicar walked to the gate with us, and offered to walk me to Wayside Cross.

'You are kind, but no thank you. I think it better that I arrive alone, rather than accompanied by a second stranger.'

'They know me. But I take your point: a solitary woman will surely receive a warmer welcome than a guest of the vicar of a church they shun.'

Still he lingered, and I thought I should never have a chance to speak to my friend alone, when Mr Jesperson, who had been standing holding the bicycle and gazing across the road, said, 'Is there a shrieking pit in that field there?'

'So they call it. But as I told Charles when he asked the same thing, I have never in more than twelve years heard a noise out of it – I think there must be a misunderstanding about the derivation of the name'.

'I should like to see it. Shall we, Miss Lane?'

'Rather!' I exclaimed cheerfully as he leaned the bicycle against the gatepost.

'The field is overgrown and muddy – you will muddy your boots – and your dress, Miss Lane.'

We ignored the vicar's peevish warnings and hurried to cross the road, confident he would not follow. We had to scramble across a ditch – which was indeed very muddy – in order to gain access to the field, but the terrain there, although rough and uneven, was not bad. But I could see nothing that looked like a pit; had I been alone I should probably have wandered all over the place and finally returned to the road none the wiser, but Mr Jesperson having had, as he told me, the benefit of perusing Mr Manning's notes before he went to bed, had a better idea of what to look for.

'There.'

I frowned at the shallow declivity that stretched ahead. The ground dropped gently away in an area that might have been fifty feet in diameter but hardly more than three feet deep. He walked down into it and I followed.

'Not very impressive,' I said. The soil was thin; weeds sprouted through a layer of pebbles or stone chippings. 'Was it really someone's home in the Stone Age?'

'That's the general thought. Although some scholars have suggested they were mines, or iron-working pits from Roman times.' He had bent nearly double and was shuffling about, examining the ground. 'You would expect to find some evidence of home-life, if they were dwellings, in the ones that have been excavated – bits of pottery and what have you – but nothing has been found. Hello, what's this?'

His attention had fastened upon a slab of rock. It was bigger than the others and quite distinct, being smooth and yellowish-brown whereas the smaller stones were mostly grey. It was roughly square in shape and more than a foot from side to side, like the top of a box, or a cake tin. It must have been there a long time, for it appeared very much a part of the earth, so I was surprised when Mr Jesperson picked up a thin blade-like stone shard and began digging around the edges until, before very long, he could prise the brown slab out.

'What are you doing?'

'It looks as if . . . Ah-ha!' he exclaimed as the stone came away. It could have been a paving stone, no more than two or three inches thick, and the sides were much more regular than they had appeared when it had been partly covered with soil and overgrown with some thin weedy grass. I saw then that by removing the slab he had uncovered a hole big enough to have been made by some large, burrowing animal.

'Someone has put this there to cover up the entrance,' he said, and stared at the hole as if it were something strange and wonderful.

'The landowner – to stop foxes, or badgers?'

He leaned down and sniffed. 'It doesn't smell like foxes.'

'Maybe it was a rabbit warren.'

'Have you seen any droppings?'

I stamped my feet, which were turning slowly to blocks of ice. 'That hole was not covered up yesterday. The slab may have been in place for years, even decades.'

'True.' He continued to stare at the hole; I could not understand the fascination such an ordinary thing had for him. He crouched down and thrust his arm in all the way to his shoulder and I could not hold back a small squeak of alarm. He grinned up at me, arm still buried in the earth. 'What's the matter? Do you think something is waiting to bite my hand off?' His eyes moved as if he were trying to summon the image of the space around his buried limb. 'It opens up – it is much bigger than you would expect from the size of the hole. Is it a chamber, or a tunnel, I wonder? Where does it go?' At last he withdrew his arm, and brushed off the dirt on his sleeve, once more gazing dreamily at the hole. 'It should not take long to widen it—'

'Whatever for?'

He gave me a puzzled look. 'Aren't you curious? We could be on the verge of discovering the secret of the shrieking pits.'

'You cannot just dig up someone's land without permission,' I said firmly. 'And that's not why we're here. For myself, I am far more concerned to find out which of the three ladies was Mr Manning's sweetheart – whether or not they were engaged to be married.'

I had recaptured his interest. 'Why so certain she lives at Wayside Cross?'

'Their names are Arabella, Alys and Ann. And Hilda informs me that he was courting one of them.' I sighed, and chafed my gloved hands. 'I do not like to bring them the sad news, but it is not fair to keep them waiting any longer.'

'Or to keep you here, freezing.' He wiped his hands on his handkerchief and helped me up the slope. I turned to look back; the hole in the earth, now revealed, looked dark and sinister. I almost asked Mr Jesperson to replace the slab, but then decided that would be silly, as well as a waste of time.

'I wish I could go with you to Cromer,' I said without thinking when we reached the road.

'Of course you can,' he said. 'We can walk, or take it in turns upon the machine. Do you bicycle? It is excellent fun.'

His ready agreement made me feel better, understanding that, like me, he would have preferred us to work together. But it made more sense to divide the work – we must make good use of our time. 'Thank you, but I cannot be in two places at once – and I feel my first duty is to speak to the ladies of Wayside

Cross. You will be able to tell me your impression of Felix Ott
– and surely I shall have another chance to meet him.' What I
did not add, before he peddled away towards Cromer and I set
off at a brisk march in the other direction, was that I had never
been on a bicycle in my life.

Wayside Cross – the name was painted on the gate – was a
plain, substantial building of white-painted stone, square and
handsome, set well back from the road amid a well-tended
garden that was still full of interest and beauty even in this bleak
season. I thought it would be a veritable paradise in summer.

A neat and pretty young maid answered the door.

'Good morning,' I said. 'Is Miss Bulstrode at home?'

'Certainly, Miss . . . ?'

'Miss Lane. But she does not know me.'

'Oh, Miss, that is no matter. This is her time for receiving,
and you are the first today. Come in. Let me take your coat.'

Once this was done she gave three raps on an inner door,
opened it and gestured me to go in. The room I entered was
large and full of shadows; it was lit only by the cool winter
sunlight that managed to make its way in through one front
window, and from the golden, flickering flames of the hearth,
and at first I thought I might be alone in the room, the walls
of which were lined with bookcases, filled to the ceiling. There
was the unmistakable scent of old books, but mingled with
something I took to be incense, containing notes of sandalwood,
cinnamon and others I could not identify. Looking around I saw

a fiercely grimacing monkey inside a bell-jar, the skull of some small horned beast, and a raven on a stone statue of Hermes.

'Good morning,' said a low, husky voice, and a woman stepped out of a shadowy recess and approached.

She was dressed all in black, a tall, dark-haired woman whose handsome appearance was only marred by a blotchy complexion, a redness of the nose and puffiness of the eyes that suggested she had either been weeping or was suffering from a heavy cold.

'Miss Bulstrode? I am Miss Lane. I must apologise for disturbing you'.

She waved a pale hand and smiled with the appearance of some effort, clearly wishing to put me at my ease. 'There is no need to apologise. I receive all who come to me. I hope I will be able to help you. You are new to the village? A visitor? How did you hear about me?'

I replied quickly, 'I am not here on my own behalf, but at the behest of another – a gentleman in London – Mr Manning.'

She tensed and her smile vanished. 'What? How – what do you mean? Mr Manning? When did he—?'

I bit my lip. 'I beg your pardon. The gentleman who sent me to Aylmerton is Mr Alexander Manning.'

Her eyes narrowed. 'I am not acquainted with that gentleman, and I should be surprised if he had heard anything of me.' Her voice and her manner were cold, and she turned her face a little away from me.

'True – oh, I am making such a hash of this. Forgive me. It is difficult to know how to begin. I came to Aylmerton to discover

– they told me at the Vicarage where you lived. I thought you should be told. It is about Mr Manning's brother.'

'Charles.'

'Yes.' I took a deep breath. 'I am afraid I bring bad news – the worst.'

She groaned. 'Worst? How could it be worse?'

There was a screeching cry, and then there was a great disturbance of the air, and something large and black swooped so close that I cried out as well, and ducked my head, putting up my hand to guard my face.

'He will not hurt you. There, there, Gabriel. Good fellow.'

Cautiously I looked up and slowly relaxed when I saw the big black bird perched on Miss Bulstrode's shoulder. I turned my head and confirmed that what I had taken for a stuffed raven was no longer perched on the marble head of Hermes. And I had been wrong to think it a raven – Hilda, too, had been wrong. The bird that cocked its head and peered at me with an eye like a shining drop of ink was a crow.

'Gabriel, this is Miss Lane. Miss Lane, this is Gabriel. Were you a friend of Charles'?'

I took note of the tense, as I am sure she intended. 'Then you know that he is—' When I hesitated over a choice of final clause – 'passed on', 'no longer living' – she said it for me, unflinching.

'Dead? Yes. And I mourn for our departed friend. As you see.' She swept one hand down her front, indicating her mourning garb. 'Of course, never having met me before, you may have thought I always wore black, but I can tell you I have a preference for brighter colours, the primary colours red and blue in particular. I had hoped, after the death of my stepfather, that I would not be required to wear black again for a good many more years.'

'I am sorry. Please accept my condolences,' I said awkwardly, and tried to explain: 'I never thought the news could have travelled so fast.'

'Bad news often does.'

The bird rubbed his head against the side of her face, as if to comfort her.

Miss Bulstrode stared at me, and two small frown lines appeared between her finely arched brows. 'I do not believe Mr Manning sent you. He knows nothing of us – or I thought he did not. Who told you to come here? What was your relationship to Charles?'

'It is a strange story, and may take a little while to explain,' I said carefully. 'I never set eyes upon Charles Manning before Saturday night – rather, in the early hours of Sunday morning. He was a stranger to me still when I saw him die.'

She covered her mouth with her hand and stared at me with eyes that looked as black as those of the crow on her shoulder. The silence stretched until she whispered, 'You were with him when he died?'

'Yes. And afterwards found your address, with others, in his pocket book. His brother greatly regrets the estrangement, and wishes to understand something of his brother's life and the things that mattered to him before his untimely death. Thus I am here.'

'Oh, you must tell me – tell me everything.' To my surprise, she seized my hand. Her fingers were ice-cold, colder even than the ring she wore on her left hand, set with a large, polished orange stone. I knew I had seen something very like it before, but her urgency made it impossible for me to think. 'Tell me exactly what happened. What did he say? Why – how?' She blinked rapidly. 'Did he . . . ? but wait.' She interrupted herself. 'My sisters must hear this, too. Will you wait here for me to bring them?' She tugged at me, directing me to a large, comfortable chair. 'Please, sit. Will you take a cup of tea, or anything else? No? Please, forgive me for my . . . my suspicion, my unfriend-liness before. May I get you something to eat?'

'No, thank you – I had breakfast not long ago. I am quite comfortable, and certainly I will wait – I should like to meet your sisters.'

'I will not be long.' She gave me a distracted smile and hur-ried away, her full skirt rustling noisily, the crow still clinging silently to her shoulder.

While she was gone, I stared into the fire, mentally assembling my first impressions of this woman Hilda Ringer had told me was reputed to be a witch, and who had been a friend to Charles Manning. A flicker of orange flame recalled her ring to mind, and I remembered the silver pillbox from the dead man's pocket. That was where I had seen it before. The polished carnelian set into its lid was the twin of the stone Miss Bulstrode wore on her finger.

She returned a few minutes later, without the bird, but

with two young women dressed, like her, in full mourning, whom she introduced as her sisters Alys and Ann. All three were dark-haired and dark-eyed, with the same straight nose, but while the two younger ones had the fresh bloom of youth, I thought Miss Arabella Bulstrode was equally handsome, and could not agree with Hilda Ringer's view that Miss Ann was the prettiest. She was certainly the youngest – possibly not even eighteen – but I found her prettiness a touch insipid, and her expression oddly blank, lacking the obvious spark of intelligence that animated the faces of her sisters. I told myself it was unfair to judge a woman in deep mourning in this way, and perhaps she was in shock since the news of Mr Manning's death.

Once more I was offered refreshments, and once more I declined. The younger ladies sat on a couch that faced my chair, and Miss Bulstrode pulled up a chair for herself and began, 'Miss Lane has said she was with Charles when he died, although he was a stranger to her. Please, tell us how it happened. We have been so worried – and so puzzled – by this terrible event. How did it come about?'

I moistened my lips and prepared to prevaricate. 'It was very late at night, but I had not yet gone to bed. I had just started up the stairs to my room when there was a frantic knocking at the door, and Mr Jesperson went to—'

'Who is Mr Jesperson?'

'He is my business partner. We lodge at the same address – it is his mother's household.' I paused, expecting a query about the nature of our business, but it did not come. 'Mr Jesperson opened the door, and a strange man all but fell inside. He was in a dreadful state, perspiring, panting, his eyes wide and staring.'

'This was Charles Manning?'

'So it later proved. But at the time, he was a complete stranger to us, and he made no introduction. He was far too perturbed for social niceties. He gave the impression of one pursued by . . . witches.'

I paused deliberately, and Miss Bulstrode took me up on it.

'Pursued by witches? What an odd phrase. Most people would say pursued by demons.'

I indicated my agreement. 'I chose that word with care. Because when we asked him what he feared, he said – *witchcraft*.'

Silent and still, the two younger sisters held hands and stared at me with big, round eyes.

'That is very odd,' said Miss Bulstrode. The little frown lines had reappeared above her nose.

'Yes, we thought so. But there was no mistake about it, for after he answered the question put to him by Mr Jesperson with that one word, he happened to look up, and for the first time he noticed me, where I had been standing all along, saying nothing, halfway up the stairs.' Recalling the moment still made me shiver. 'He saw me, and became even more frightened, if that were possible; he declared that I was a witch.'

'No – really? What were his words – his *exact* words?'

For some reason her mild expression of disbelief nettled me. 'I am hardly likely to forget. He stared at me as if he had never seen anything so terrifying – me! – and almost shouted, 'She is a witch!"

Miss Ann gasped and began to turn a silver ring around and around on the third finger of her left hand. I noticed, too, how Miss Bulstrode caressed the smooth, rounded dome of her ring-stone. Only Miss Alys remained absolutely still and silent, eyes cast down as she listened to my tale.

'Mr Jesperson told him my name and assured the stranger that he had nothing to fear from me, or anyone in the house. He assured him he was safe with us, and offered him a drink, but I am not sure he even heard, he seemed so locked in his own fearful imaginings. He said something more about witches – that it was too late, that he was cursed – and then he collapsed – dead.'

A brooding silence descended. After a time, Miss Bulstrode drew a long, shaky breath. 'Why – why did he go to your door – to total strangers – in his distress?'

I had already given some thought to how I should answer this, and began to lay out an explanation I hope she would find plausible:

'Mr Alexander Manning was sure his brother must have been going to his house – formerly his own address, for where else was he likely to be bound, so late at night? That is in Gordon Square, and Gordon Street is the next one over from Gower Street – in the fog, it is easy enough to lose one's way.'

From her face, Miss Bulstrode did not believe it. 'But his house was in a square, yours in a street – and he had lived there all his life. Even in the pitch dark, he could not be so mistaken.'

'Perhaps. Well, there is another thing that may have drawn him to our door. Although we had yet to meet Mr Charles Manning, we knew of him from his brother, who happens to be our banker. I mentioned before that Mr Jesperson and I are business partners. We are in the process of establishing a publishing company. Charles Manning was a writer, and we are interested in commissioning work from new, young writers on topics of interest. There had been talk of meeting, when he was next in London. Two o'clock in the morning is hardly the time for paying a business call, but, as we saw at once, and I am sure you will understand, Charles Manning was not in his right mind. He saw witches wherever he looked. He believed himself pursued and in great danger. Perhaps it is best not to dwell too much on his final moments. He may have been anywhere in the depths of his own mind, living out some sort of nightmare . . . He was, of course, dying.'

'But of what?' asked Miss Bulstrode. 'From your description he was suffering a feverish delirium before his sudden death, for which there could be several causes, but when I saw him on Friday evening he appeared perfectly well. What sort of disease could strike and kill a strong young man so suddenly?'

I watched her gently, perhaps unconsciously, stroking her ring as she gazed into my eyes beseechingly, and I asked, 'Why did he go to London?'

Miss Bulstrode looked at her sisters, who looked at each other. 'Why?' said Ann.

'He gave *me* no explanation,' said Miss Bulstrode. 'But . . .

there was an unusual sort of determination about him that evening, and I thought . . .' She shook her head.

'What did you think?'

'I imagined he meant to try once more to talk his brother into giving him his inheritance.'

'You mean, talk him into selling the house in Gordon Square?'

'I believe there is more than just that house. His brother has control of their parents' estate, and he tried to use it to control his younger brother as well. When Charles broke away from the life his brother wanted for him, determined to pursue his own interests, Mr Alexander Manning cut off his allowance and refused him all support.'

She must have heard that from Charles. I thought of the older brother with his sad eyes and mourning band on his sleeve, standing in a room furnished in the taste of an earlier decade, and I wondered who had been deceived. 'It was my understanding that the house was their only legacy, and it was left entirely to Mr Alexander Manning.'

'No doubt that is what he wished you to understand. Well, money and property alike are all his now – may they bring him little joy – and Charles is beyond needing any material things.' Unshed tears shone in her eyes as she made this bitter pronouncement.

'But Mr Ott is not beyond needing material things,' said Alys. '*He* will be sorry for his loss.'

Miss Bulstrode gave her a wounded look. 'Alys, how can

you? You know perfectly well that Charles was not merely a supporter of the SBW – Felix was his dearest friend.'

Alys gave an unrepentant sniff. 'According to *Charles*.'

'SBW – is that the Society for British Wisdom?' I asked.

'School of British Wisdom,' Miss Bulstrode corrected. 'You have heard of it?'

'Yes, but not from an unbiased source. The Reverend Ringer—'

A smile twitched at the corners of her mouth. 'Naturally, he cannot like it. The position of the Established Church has always been one of opposition to all pre-Christian beliefs. I have my own bias – on the other side. Although I have not affiliated myself with Mr Ott's school, I have come to think it is a good idea. There is a great deal in our native folklore that is well worth preserving, and much of value that has been suppressed or forgotten.'

Alys said, 'Charles hoped to become Mr Ott's partner as a founding member of the School. But he had no money to put into it. Neither has Mr Ott. Not even enough to take a long lease on some suitable premises. If the School is to come to anything he must attract a wealthy patron – or several.'

A thought came to me, and without stopping to think I blurted it out: 'Did Charles Manning leave a will?'

They all looked at me in surprise and, I realised, disapproval. I had crossed a line.

'I think you had better take such questions to his brother, Miss Lane.'

'Yes, of course, I only thought, as you were, clearly, so close to him, he may have mentioned . . .'

'He did not. And even if he had shared such a confidence, I cannot see how it could possibly be any of your concern.' Her dark eyes flashed. In another moment, I feared, I should be told to leave in terms which should end our acquaintance before it had fairly begun.

There was a knock on the door.

'Yes?'

The door opened and the maid put her head in. 'It's Mrs Poultney. Shall I tell her to wait, or come again later?'

'Give me five minutes, Nancy.'

'Yes, Miss.' The door closed quietly.

Miss Bulstrode looked at me. Her gaze was searching. 'I cannot believe Alexander Manning sent you to interrogate his brother's friends. Tell me the truth. Why have you come to Aylmerton?'

I took a deep breath. 'Have you ever seen someone drop dead in front of you?'

'Yes. My stepfather died suddenly in this very room.'

'But — a stranger? Someone of whom you knew nothing, not even his name, until you discovered it after his death?' Her look encouraged me to go on. 'It is very strange and shocking. Impossible to mourn someone you never knew, and yet, to be present at a death is very intimate; such a personal thing that one feels — at least, I felt — that something more was required of me than simply to go about my usual life.'

'I understand,' she said softly, and reached out to touch my hand. Her fingers were not so cold as before. 'Thank you for coming to tell us what happened to our friend – inexplicable and disturbing as it was, I am glad to have heard an eyewitness account. I must ask you to leave now, for one of my patients is waiting, but I hope you will come back, and we may speak more – I will be happy to share with you my memories of Charles, and I think Ann and Alys feel the same.'

The other two had arisen from the couch, and although they said nothing to indicate their agreement, they did not appear unfriendly; they walked close beside me, back to the front door, and Alys went to find my coat, and then they both wished me good day.

CHAPTER SIX

An Uncomfortable Conversation

I felt, as I walked down the path away from the front door that I was being watched, but when I turned around there was no one to be seen at any of the windows. And the feeling did not dissipate when I was on the road: all the way back to the Vicarage I had that uncomfortable tickling sensation at the back of my neck as if I were being spied upon, but I saw no one, apart from one man on horseback, who tipped his hat to me as he trotted past. I told myself I was imagining things; my interview with the Bulstrode sisters had unsettled me in some way that would prey upon my mind until I managed to work it out.

As I approached the Vicarage, I saw the little boy, Richard, absorbed in some solitary game in front of the house. He looked up and saw me, but instead of smiling or calling a greeting, he simply stared with his mouth hanging open. I had the idea that he was looking at something behind me, but when I whirled around, as before, the road was empty.

Richard ran to meet me at the gate. 'Why does he follow you?'

I confess, the absurd idea that I was being pursued by some spectre, visible only to the innocent eyes of a child, seized me with icy claws, but I managed to keep my nerve and did not look back.

'There is no one following me, and I am sure your mother could not approve of you saying such things, even in fun.'

He blinked rapidly. 'But it's true, Miss! Look, now he is watching from that tree.'

I slowly turned to look where he pointed. The tree was across the road, one of a row of elms, and in the bare winter branches there perched a solitary black bird.

I recalled a remark from Mr Jesperson once made: 'No one in London ever looks up.' And here was I, out in the countryside, beneath the wide open sky, not lifting my eyes even when I felt myself being followed, as unobservant as any dull city dweller – and I fancied myself a detective.

I gave the little boy a stern look. 'Was that crow really following me?'

'Yes, Miss, honestly. He was right above you, flying low. It looked so strange! Perhaps there is something on your hat that he wants?'

But there were no artificial cherries, shining sequins, or even a feather in my unexceptional hat. Although it was too far away to tell, and one crow looks very like another, I felt certain the black bird watching us from its high perch was Miss Bulstrode's pet. And I could think of no reason why it should have followed

71

me, except at her instruction. How would he report back to her, I wondered. Could crows be taught to speak?

I shivered. 'Let us go into the house, Master Richard. The wind today is too cold to linger outside.'

As we walked together up the path to the front door I recalled that Miss Bulstrode had named her bird Gabriel. Was that after the angel who had brought the good news to Mary? I had not asked just how or when the news of Mr Manning's death had reached Wayside Cross.

I scolded myself for my absurd imaginings. The news was more likely to have arrived by telegraph than via a winged messenger. And if the Bulstrodes and Mr Manning had no mutual friends in London, there was what might be called the 'servant telegraph' much closer to home. The Ringers and the Bulstrodes were neighbours, after all, and even if they did not socialise, their servants were almost certainly acquainted.

This simple application of reason relaxed my taut nerves. By the time I entered the Vicarage I felt my feet were firmly back on the ground. A bird had flown slowly over the road while I had walked the same route. That was no reason to let my imagination run away with me.

I settled in the drawing room with paper and pen, intending to write a full account of my conversation with Miss Bulstrode and her sisters whilst it was fresh in my mind. There was a fire burning cheerfully in the hearth, Hilda was sitting in an armchair, absorbed in her mathematical studies, and Mrs Ringer was busy with a piece of embroidery. Alas, embroidery work does not require the same mental attention as maths or writing, and Mrs Ringer welcomed my appearance as an opportunity to exercise her tongue on one subject whilst her fingers worked at another.

'Oh, leave your letter-writing for later, Miss Lane,' she said, 'Let us take this opportunity to become better acquainted.'

She began at once to quiz me about my life in London, beginning with my occupation. Fortunately, Mr Jesperson had said that our publishing venture was still in the planning stages, so I was not forced to invent an imaginary list of books or claim expertise in an occupation about which I was no more informed than any average book reader.

'But why did you think of attempting such a profession?' she pressed. 'Please do not imagine for a moment that I object to a woman who works – indeed, I admire you very much. Naturally, I consider motherhood the highest calling of womankind, but not all are called to it. But if I may ask, have you no family? Are you quite alone in the world?'

'Nearly. I have a sister – but our parents are no longer with us. My father was a classics master at Harrow School, and until his death I had quite a happy, settled childhood, full of books and music and games and companionship. I was barely out of childhood when all that ended. We had to move – the house was tied to his job – and there was not enough money for the sort of life we had known before – but I will not bore you with tales of long-ago trials and tribulations. I grew up, as everyone does, and must make my own place in the world.'

'What of your sister? Is she married?'

'No. She has made quite a successful career on the stage. At present she is touring America.'

'How very interesting.' Instead of the disapproval I had more than half expected from the wife of a minister, the light of fascination shone in her eyes. 'What is her name, may I ask?'

'Athene Lane.'

She sighed and gave a regretful shake of her head. 'I do not recognise the name. Before my marriage I was quite mad for plays – and even more the opera. But I am lucky now if I can get to London for one week in a year. So I doubt I have ever seen your sister. And you, Miss Lane, did you ever think of such a career?'

'No, I have never cared to put myself on show. When we were children, I must play supporting roles to Athene, but I was rather a disappointment to her, I fear. I am not very good at pretending.' I felt my cheeks heat.

'Well, there is nothing to be ashamed of in that,' said the vicar's wife soothingly. 'It means you are an honest, straightforward young woman – which was exactly my first impression of you, and I am a good judge of character. So, tell me, as you did not go on stage with your sister, what did you do, before you met Mr Jesperson?'

'Oh, this and that. I worked as a companion to an old lady, who was kind enough to pay for me to take a course in shorthand and typewriting. I thought, when she died, that I might work in an office of some sort, but before I could find a position I chanced to meet—'

Mrs Ringer broke in: 'That strangely attractive, energetic, and engagingly eccentric young man who calls himself Jasper Jesperson?'

I was shocked, I confess, by her interruption, especially as her tone was decidedly waspish. I replied reprovingly, 'I think you will find *everyone* calls him that – including his mother. And you are getting ahead of my story by several years. The person I met was another lady, in a similar position to myself, and we—' But I found that I did not wish to share my life story with Mrs Ringer. She liked the theatre, but I could not count on her approval extending to the realm of spiritualists and psychic phenomena which had been my own for more than four years.

I paused and cleared my throat. 'But I think you are not really so interested in *me,* are you, Mrs Ringer? I do not blame you – Mr Jesperson is a far more interesting character – what did you call him? "Engagingly eccentric"? Yes, he is. It is not surprising you wish to know more about him. And I am sure he will be only too happy to regale you with stories of his experiences. My own life has been less exotic. I can only apologise for boring you.'

Across the room, Hilda quietly got up, sidled to the door and let herself out.

Mrs Ringer looked not only discomfited, but positively mortified. 'You have done nothing of the kind! Oh, dear. Miss Lane, please forgive me. I am so sorry to have offended you. Truly, I did not intend anything . . . I did not mean . . . Oh, dear.' Making a great fuss with her embroidery, she finally managed to prick her finger, and then had to put her work aside, worried about staining it with her blood, before our conversation could resume.

'I am sorry, Miss Lane—'

'Please, no more apologies,' I said, feeling weary. 'It is truly of no consequence. I did not *ask* you to take an interest in me. Now, perhaps I may go back to my writing?'

'You may not believe it, but I am interested in you – and it is that interest, that *concern,* that leads me to warn you to take care.'

'I have been taking care of myself for a good ten years,' I said coolly.

'I am a mother. If your mother were alive, I know—'

It was my turn to interrupt. 'You did not know my mother. Now, what is it that so concerns you?'

'I do not mean to say anything particular against Mr Jesperson. He may be the best of men, but he is still a *man*, and a young one, impulsive, ardent – you cannot ignore his red hair!'

I think my mouth may have fallen open at that point.

'Miss Lane, even if this man could be trusted absolutely – which my years of experience make me doubt – you must still bear in mind how it *looks.*'

'His hair?'

'What?' She stared at me blankly for a moment. 'No! I speak of society – of social expectations – of wicked, wagging tongues. What people will think, what they may say, seeing an unmarried woman travelling about with a strange man. Once her reputation has been blackened, the stain is never expunged.'

As soon as she paused for breath, I jumped in. Although her

foolishness angered me (in particular her bizarre prejudice against beautiful red-gold hair) I think I managed to remain calm, my voice low and well-modulated. 'Mrs Ringer, your concern is unwarranted. I am not a girl of sixteen, but a spinster of nearly thirty. If you will forgive me, I think my understanding of what society considers acceptable is considerably more up-to-date than that of a vicar's wife in rural Norfolk. You claim to be in favour of more occupations being opened to women, but how is that possible if we are to be kept in purdah – even self-imposed – because we are worried about "what people may think"? My response to that is the famous motto of the Knights of the Garter: *Honi soit qui mal y pense*. Now please excuse me; I have work to do.'

I swept out of the room without giving her a chance to reply, and found myself in the entrance hall, with nowhere to go. Hilda had undoubtedly retreated to her bedroom, and I only wished to be alone. Voices from the smaller sitting room warned that the Reverend was in conference with one of his parishioners, and I could think of no excuse for intruding upon the servants in the kitchen, which left me with only one way out.

Collecting my coat, hat and scarf from the stand by the door, I made a swift escape.

Outside, it was even colder than before, the sun lower in the sky. I set off in the direction of Cromer, with no plan in mind except to keep moving. I certainly did enough of that; the road was busy with traffic, so I was forever having to step aside, on to the muddy verge. Occasionally I was offered a lift, and must explain that I wanted the exercise.

Just as I was thinking about turning back, I saw something that made me change my mind: a figure approaching from Cromer on a bicycle. I felt certain it must be Mr Jesperson, and a short time later, my hunch was proved correct.

He looked very surprised to see me and jumped off the bicycle when he reached me to ask with obvious concern, 'Miss Lane – what is the matter? No trouble, I hope?'

'No trouble – but there might have been if I had stayed another minute longer in the company of that meddling, moralising, *silly* Mrs Reverend Ringer – I preferred a long walk in the cold.'

'Moronic?'

I flinched, and his eyes widened in alarm. 'I only meant to chime with your alliterative scheme – the meddling, moralising, moronic Mrs R.'

'Oh, of course.' Now I felt silly. 'You are terrible.'

'More terrible than you? Come along, we'll walk back together and you can tell me about your visit to Wayside Cross,' he said, and began to wheel the bicycle. It seemed a rather contrary beast, requiring firm guidance, so our pace was slow.

'I found them all in mourning – already aware of the death in London. I should have liked to know how. Miss Bulstrode—'

'The witch?'

'It is easy to see why she has that reputation. Her familiar is a big black crow called Gabriel; her consulting room is a gloomy place with specimens in bell-jars and books from floor to ceiling.'

'A witch with a consulting room! It must make life easier, if you don't have to go wandering about a blasted heath in search of a witch when you want one. Does she have many clients?'

'They come regularly in the mornings, although she calls them her patients. I was taken for one myself, at first.'

'Pity you did not play along. I wonder what she would have said if you had asked her for a spell to get rid of some inconvenient relative?'

'You may play that card yourself later,' I said. 'I did learn that she is a sort of unofficial supporter of Felix Ott's School of British Wisdom – despite what Doctor Ringer told us. She thinks it an excellent idea, although she also took pains to let me know she is not officially connected with it, so she has reasons for keeping her distance, I suppose.'

'Ott described Charles Manning as his right-hand man. He made no mention of Wayside Cross, or the women who live there, and I could contrive no natural-seeming way to bring them up, at least not in our first interview. As delicately as I could, I enquired if there were a young lady who might have won his heart, who should be informed of his demise, but he said my question showed that I was utterly unacquainted with the younger Mr Manning, who had been a serious scholar, with neither the time nor the interest for courtship.' He looked at me with eyebrows raised.

I looked back, mirroring his sceptical expression. 'Fooled by his right-hand man.'

'Did you learn which of the sisters might have been "dearest A"?'

'Not beyond the shadow of a doubt, but . . .' I hesitated and then took the plunge. 'I believe Miss Bulstrode was his lover. Arabella Bulstrode spoke of him most warmly, and appeared the most deeply affected by his loss. I thought, when I arrived, that she had been weeping, and she wore a ring that she often touched. It was obviously very dear to her, and my guess is that it was a gift from Charles Manning.'

'Woman's intuition?' He smiled; this was an old joke between us.

'If you like. Now, tell me about Mr Ott. And quickly, for we shall not find it easy to have any private conversations at the Vicarage – Mrs Reverend has very old-fashioned notions about friendships between unmarried men and women.'

We had stopped, to keep ourselves and the bicycle well clear of a coach pulled by four galloping horses, and after they were past he did not move. 'Felix Ott is a man in his forties, a shade under six feet tall, brown hair going grey at the temples, an impressive moustache, but no beard, small scar on his chin, grey eyes flecked with yellow. He has a military bearing, and walks with a slight limp – I suspect an old knee injury. He had already learnt of Manning's death – an early edition of a London paper was open on his desk, turned to the obituary columns.'

We began to walk again, slowly. I did not think that the residents of Wayside Cross had read about Charles Manning's death in today's newspaper; they lived too far from the railway station, and it seemed unlikely they would have made arrangements for an early delivery of any London journal.

'What was Mr Ott's response to the news?'

'He was in a state of agitation when I arrived, although he seemed determined to repress any outward show of grief. But it was clear that he took the death very personally. Not only was he naturally grief-stricken by the loss of one he described to me as a close personal friend, but he found it alarming because Manning is the second of his associates to die in less than a year. Both deaths sudden, unexpected, and not fully explained; both young men who were devoted to his cause. He takes their deaths as an attack on himself, perceiving the hands of an enemy bent on strangling the infant School of British Wisdom in its cradle.'

'Two deaths? Who was the other victim?'

He frowned at my slowness. 'Surely you recall the man Doctor Ringer mentioned last night, as an acquaintance of Manning's? Ott identified him as Mr Albert Cooke. Originally from Bristol, he moved to Cromer late last year to devote himself to research into esoteric subjects, under Ott's direction, and to help him establish the school.'

Now I remembered: there had been a third mysterious death in the parish. 'Doctor Ringer said the police were not treating it as a murder.'

'Ott does not have a high opinion of the police, here or in London. He is certain both men were killed; he even named his suspect.'

'Who?'

He repressed a smile. 'The Reverend Doctor Robert Ringer.'

'Surely not.' The idea was too far-fetched to be shocking; it was simply ridiculous.

My friend laughed gleefully. 'Oh, but they hate each other. Each man thinks the other subscribes to a false and dangerous doctrine, a system of evil. And you must admit, possession of a doctorate in divinity does not make a man a saint. And even a religion of peace, as Christianity has been described, is used as a justification for many deeds of violence. Might not a righteous man do evil for the greater good?'

I remembered how concerned the vicar had been for his lodger's soul, and felt a shiver run down my spine. It seemed madness, yet not so very long ago the church had sanctioned torture and murder, on the grounds that sometimes the mortal body must be destroyed to save the soul. Was Dr Ringer secretly fanatical enough to feel the same?

'We must keep an open mind,' said Jesperson. 'At any rate, we now have two suspects for investigation.'

'Surely not for Mr Manning's death,' I protested, glad that I had something more than 'intuition' to back up my feeling that Dr Ringer was no murderer. 'According to Mrs Ringer, her husband has not been to London for many months – and it should be easy enough to discover if he was away from the parish at that time.'

'Ott declares he, too, was in Norfolk on the day Manning died in London. He also claimed to have no notion why Manning went to London – or even that he had gone, until he learned of his death from the newspaper. But I think he was lying about that.'

My heart beat a little faster when he said those words in a calm, reflective way. At last, a clue! Although I wished I had been there to witness it for myself, I knew Mr Jesperson's perceptions were to be trusted.

'Two deaths; possibly two murders,' he mused. 'It seems unlikely they are completely unconnected – after all, both men were close associates of Felix Ott, and both died under mysterious circumstances, yet their deaths are not being investigated by the police. Maybe they both died of natural causes; maybe there is no villain to be uncovered, no one to blame. Yet there is a mystery in it; and the truth will never be known, unless we find it.'

'So we are now to investigate a second case?'

He stopped and looked at me. There was really no need for him to answer.

CHAPTER SEVEN

The Second Case

Mr Jesperson stepped off the paved road and walked a few steps into the forest, pushing the bicycle with difficulty over the thick carpet of moss, grass and dead leaves. I followed, with no idea of where he was leading.

'Albert Cooke died in August, so I doubt there are many clues still *in situ*, but we may as well begin with a look at where his body was found.'

'In this forest? Do you really think you can find it?' I had no great desire to hurry back to the Vicarage, but I had my doubts about the practicality of an expedition into the dark woods, especially so late in the day.

'I have had a detailed description of the spot.'

'From Felix Ott?'

'Why should he tell me anything of the kind? To him, I am merely a friend of Manning's surviving relative. I had no wish to rouse his suspicions by interrogating him about another man's death. No, I went to the police station and identified myself as a private investigator from London.'

He stopped and hid the bicycle beneath a bush – it would not be hard to find, but there was no chance that anyone passing by on the road would catch sight of it – and then took my arm to guide me. 'There is a path . . . we should come upon it shortly. Mind those briars.'

'And they were happy to share the details of the other case with you?'

'The man in charge, Sergeant Canright, struck me as highly intelligent. When I informed him of Manning's death, he immediately recognised the possibility that it was connected to the unsolved case of Albert Cooke.'

'But I thought they did not see it as a case, only a natural death.' I tugged my skirt away from trailing branches and hoped Mr Jesperson knew where he was going.

'Although under pressure to declare Cooke's death nothing more than an unfortunate accident, Canright remains suspicious, and what he learned from me has inspired him to reconsider the evidence. Ah, here is the path.'

'Where will it take us?'

'Ultimately, to a picturesque area known as the Lion's Mouth, and from there to Aylmerton. But our way takes us past a shrieking pit – well hidden in the woods, and considerably deeper than the one in the field opposite the Vicarage. A few yards from that pit is the place where Cooke's body was found – the Poison Ring.'

His voice was matter-of-fact, and he laid no particular emphasis on the final phrase, yet it made me shiver.

'Was he poisoned?'

'He had been dead for at least two days when he was found, and with no witnesses to his death, it was difficult – the doctor declared it impossible – to say for certain. Local gossip thought it a death by poisoning, and linked it with the deaths of Farmer Goodall and his wife, although no one could think how Cooke, a newcomer to the area, might have been involved with them.

'The surgeon found a contusion on the back of the head, and decided, in the absence of any better evidence, that it was the cause of death. It is true that even a seemingly minor blow to the head may cause death in some people, depending on the fragility of the skull, the angle of the blow, and so on. The victim had not been robbed, and a quiet woodland glade seems an unlikely spot for a violent quarrel – although stranger things have happened. But, on balance, the coroner's court ruled it a death by misadventure, deciding it had been an unfortunate accident in which no one but the dead man had been involved.'

I looked down at the path, which was damp and muddy even though it had not rained for several days. 'Well, that sounds reasonable. Mr Cooke might easily have slipped, taken a tumble, and bashed his head. It only seems suspicious in connection with the death of Mr Manning.'

'You will understand how unlikely a solitary death seems in the case of Cooke, when you see where and how his body was found.' He stopped and peered around in the shadowy gloom of the mixed woodland. 'Ah, there. We are to leave the path and enter that stand of pines.'

I followed his lead into a darker area of the woods. Here, the tall, thickly branched evergreens blocked even more of the daylight, but it was easier to walk on the thick carpet of dead needles where nothing else grew.

He stopped, and I followed his gaze.

'There it is,' he said. 'The fatal spot – the Poison Ring.'

Sprouting through the ground cover where nothing else could flourish was the biggest fairy ring I had ever seen. We all know those circles of mushrooms that sprout overnight on lawns and meadows, and in woodland, but this was another species entirely. Not only was it very much larger – I estimated it was more than twelve feet in diameter – but it was composed not of the little white or brown mushrooms I was used to, but of the toadstools with red-and-white-spotted caps that artists often include to add contrast to the greens and browns of a forest scene. The more fanciful may include a fairy or an elf using one for an umbrella or a stool.

'*Amanita muscaria*.'

I felt that prickling at the back of my neck and looked around quickly. But the woods were still and quiet – not even the rustle of a crow's wing to suggest we could have been followed.

'Where was the body found?'

'Right there,' he said. 'In the middle of the ring.'

'You mean, the mushrooms were growing there even in the summer?'

'This ring formation has been known for generations and features in local folklore – hence, the name. You may be surprised to learn that this is not uncommon. The way that mushrooms propagate—' At my sigh, he stopped before his lecture on mycology was fully launched. 'However, what matters to us, and to the police, is that the corpse was found lying face-up in the centre of that ring of sinister reputation. As you can see, the ground there is soft and mossy, and there was nothing on which he could have struck his head; nor was anything found that matched the wound when police searched the area for weapons. Another thing which adds to the peculiarity of the situation, and surely encouraged the belief that he'd been poisoned, was that he was found with half a cap of the *Amanita* in his mouth.'

I shuddered. 'But that is poison.'

'No. Well, yes, in a way – they are called 'fly agaric' because they have been used as a fly-killer, and thus, the local designation of this as the Poison Ring. But one, even half a dozen, would not prove fatal to a grown man. Half a cap – which I point out, he had not swallowed – is enough to cause violent nausea and vomiting.'

I wrapped my arms around myself and he looked concerned. 'You are cold.'

'Merely uncomfortable,' I said. 'It is not just the chill in the air, but the thought of his lonely death in this strange place that affects me. What did the police conclude?'

'They concluded he must have taken a blow to his head somewhere near – possibly struck his head on a low-hanging branch – and then staggered away, and decided to lie down to rest in a more comfortable spot.'

'And take a bite of a toadstool?'

He shrugged. 'Peculiar, to be sure, but the blow to his head unhinged him. He was not in his right mind. He mistook it for a sandwich, perhaps – and died before he could swallow the first bite.'

We looked at each other. If the subject had not been so serious – and horrible – I should have been tempted to laugh. It sounded so unlikely.

'Come along,' he said. 'It does our health no good to stand about in this damp, chilly place. Only, before we head back, I should like to check my own idea of where he banged his head.'

I let him take my arm. As he led me further into the dark pine woods he warned me to take care and watch my step. 'It would not be a good thing to fall into the shrieking pit.'

But it turned out to be quite visible even in the crepuscular light, and we stopped at the edge and stared down into the shadowed depths. Then, before I had any hint of his intention, Mr Jesperson took a step forward, and dropped out of sight.

I gave a small cry of alarm, and heard his laugh, echoing slightly. I hurried closer and looked down and saw his face turned up to mine, barely an arm's length away. 'Forgive me for giving you a fright. As you see, I am in no danger. But if Albert Cooke had slipped on the edge and fallen head first, the stony floor *could* have been the death of him.'

Reaching into one of his pockets, he withdrew a box of

matches, and struck one, bending low to inspect the bottom of the pit by its light. When it expired he lit another, and then a third.

I hugged myself. 'Surely any evidence will have been washed away before now? What are you looking for?'

'Just assuring myself that there are rocks on which someone might have done himself an injury. If I want to see anything more I will have to come back with a lantern.' He replaced the matchbox in his pocket, reached up to grab the edge of the pit, and half jumped, half pulled himself out.

We did not linger, but immediately started back for the path.

'So you think Mr Cooke could have lost his footing, tumbled down head-first, struck his head, and then, dazed, managed to pull himself out and stagger to the Poison Ring before he dropped dead?' It seemed far-fetched.

'I am finding it hard to imagine,' my friend agreed. 'If he fell, he would likely have tried to protect his head. And getting out again would have required more energetic scrambling from him – Cooke was said to be delicate, even physically weak, and he was barely five foot tall. If he struck his head hard enough to cause death, I think it would have happened almost immediately, and he would have been found in a crumpled heap, at the bottom of the pit, not laid out on his back on a grassy spot some distance away. No, the evidence suggests there was someone with him either at the time of his death, or soon after. This person may have caused his death, or have been an innocent bystander who nevertheless preferred to remain unknown to the police. Out of pity, or superstition, or for some other reason, this unknown person lifted Cooke's body out of the pit where it might have lain undiscovered for weeks or even longer, and laid it out in a position and place where it was at once more visible, and more comfortable in appearance. The body was arranged neatly, eyes closed, hands crossed upon the chest – and a piece of mushroom had been placed between his lips.'

It sounded ritualistic. I wondered if this could have been one of the ancient British rituals Felix Ott was interested in reviving. Could it have been his doing? It need not mean he was a murderer; many people might fear coming to the attention of the police if they were the sole witness to a sudden death.

We had reached the path; Mr Jesperson proposed taking the most direct route out of the woods, rather than retracing our steps, as it would soon be dark, and, eager to return to the road beneath open sky whilst there was still light enough to see our way back to the Vicarage, I was happy to agree.

We emerged from the woods on to a road just as the sun was going down. I did not know where we were, but Mr Jesperson assured me that we were now no more than a ten-minute walk from the Vicarage.

'That Poison Ring is in a very out-of-the-way place,' I said. 'Who discovered Cooke's body?'

'Felix Ott. Cooke roomed in the same house, and they normally saw one another every day, so he was quickly concerned. Knowing of Cooke's interest in the shrieking pits, he began to search the woods and fields, fearing he had met with some accident.'

'Did the police find that suspicious?'

He shook his head. 'Oh, Canright is suspicious only so far as he would be of any man so openly antagonistic to the Established Church and promoting occult knowledge. But Ott had no motive to kill Cooke – quite the opposite. Although not a rich man, Cooke was in receipt of an annuity which was enough, apparently, to support Ott as well as himself. With Cooke's death, that support ended.'

'Did the annuity pass to anyone else on his death?'

'To his sister, a gentle, frugal, Christian soul who tithes regularly, gives music lessons from her home in Bristol, and never understood or approved her brother's interest in esoteric matters.'

I said, 'Mr Manning told us that his brother had nothing, and the house had been left to him entirely, but Miss Bulstrode believed otherwise. She thought he had a legal right to half the family estate – whatever that was.'

'Well, we had better look into it – and also discover whether Charles Manning died intestate, or left a will.' He sighed thoughtfully. 'Even though Manning has hired us to find out why his brother died, it would not do to assume he has been entirely truthful with us about every detail of their relationship.'

By now we had reached the gate outside the Vicarage. I felt there was still much more to be said and chewed over, but the wind had picked up as darkness fell, and I was too cold to protest when he opened it and ushered me into the front garden.

'We had better go inside, or Mrs Ringer may send out a search party,' I said.

Indeed, that lady must have been hovering by a window, looking out, for it was she herself who opened the door to us, and her expression was not friendly.

'I met Mr Jesperson on the road,' I said at once. Although I felt she had no right to an explanation, I wished to keep the peace.

'And where is my husband's bicycle?' she demanded with a fierce look at Mr Jesperson. 'If you have broken or lost it, you must pay for a new one.'

'I beg your pardon – it had quite slipped my mind. Do not worry – it is quite safe,' he said, apparently indifferent to her hostile glare.

'I shall believe that when I see it,' she retorted. 'Go and get it.'

His conciliatory smile made no impression. 'Will it not wait until morning? Surely Doctor Ringer will not want it tonight, and it is in a safe place. If I might speak to him . . .'

She responded as if to an impertinent servant. 'Don't you try and get around me. I have told you to go and get it. If you do not, I must assume the machine has been stolen, and you must answer to the consequences.'

With a shrug of resignation Mr Jesperson gave up the argument, turned and loped off.

'Oh, really,' I muttered, frowning at the rigid, unforgiving woman who now stepped back to allow me entrance. 'Was that necessary? It is cold and dark – he could get lost – without so much as a lantern.'

'If he will be that careless of the property he borrows, I am not inclined to add a lantern to the list. Do not make excuses for that young man; it is all his own fault. Now, will you come inside, Miss Lane, or do you intend to spend the entire night out of doors?'

Although I was tempted to run after Mr Jesperson, I could not ignore the implied threat in Mrs Ringer's invitation.

'Thank you,' I said coldly, walking in and past her. 'You are too kind.'

CHAPTER EIGHT

A Chat with the Vicar

Mr Jesperson was back safely with the bicycle in half an hour. I went into the hall to meet him, and at that same moment the vicar popped out to invite us both into his study at the back of the house for a chat.

This was – as I learned later – a singular honour, for Dr Ringer protected his territory very fiercely. The children were never allowed through the door, and neither were the servants. Only his wife was allowed to come in occasionally to tidy up or to have a private word with him, and she did not abuse the privilege. If the door was closed, it meant he was thinking or reading or writing and not to be disturbed except in case of direst emergency. Visitors, whether parishioners or relatives, were received either in the front parlour or in the family drawing room, depending on the closeness of the connection.

I thought I understood why as soon as we were inside, for the room was very small indeed, and although it must have been comfortable enough for a solitary resident, snugly ensconced behind his desk, surrounded by books, there was no obvious place for even one visitor, let alone two.

However, Reverend Ringer moved a stack of books to reveal a straight-backed wooden chair, upon which he invited me to sit, before excavating a three-legged stool for his other guest.

'I am very keen to learn how you have been getting on with your investigation – and this is the best place for us to confer, as we will not be overheard or interrupted in here. So, tell me,' he urged, clasping his hands together. 'How did Ott respond to the news of Charles' death? Did you see guilt written upon his countenance?'

Mr Jesperson shook his head. 'He responded as one who has already read the London papers – and asked me if his friend had been poisoned.'

The vicar's hands dropped into his lap. 'I see. Do you find that suspicious?'

'No more so than when you put the same question. Indeed, like yourself, Mr Ott found it hard to accept that Manning's could have been a natural death precisely because of his connection to another young man, also a supporter of Ott's School, who met his death in mysterious circumstances only two months ago. You know of whom I speak.'

'Yes, certainly – I told you about Mr Cooke myself.'

'Not by name. And you called him an "acquaintance" of Charles Manning, rather than the close friend that he really was. The two men spent most of their days together – but not, and perhaps most unfortunately, the day of Cooke's sudden death.'

Dr Ringer's brows knit. 'Well, what of it? When you asked about Charles' friends, it was in order to interview them. What point, then, in bringing up the name of the deceased?'

Jesperson nodded agreeably, but his keen gaze never wavered. 'You may be interested to know who Felix Ott suspects of being behind both deaths.' He paused, but the vicar said nothing. 'Well, it surprised me, I must say. He pointed the finger at you, Doctor Ringer.'

'Me? How absurd,' he replied, his tone contemptuous. 'But what can you expect from someone like that? No slander or lie is beneath him.'

'His assertion was not unsupported. He put forward the argument that you had the opportunity to poison both men. The fact that Manning lodged here would have given you the opportunity to dose his tea every morning. If the poisoning were gradual – small doses of arsenic, for example – he might have died anywhere, at any time, so there would be no need to look for his killer in London.'

'This is outrageous – do you expect me to sit here and be accused of such an infamous crime without taking action?' He glared across the desk at Jesperson. 'If you were not a guest in my house—'

'I merely inform you of Ott's argument. I know, even if he does not, how fondly you regarded Charles Manning.'

Some of the tension in the room was dissipated by Mr Jesperson's calm, reasonable tone.

'But to return to the case of Albert Cooke – I would not presume to describe your feelings towards him . . .'

'Feelings? I had no feelings for him – I hardly knew the man.'

'Felix Ott claims you were seen dining with Mr Cooke in the inn at East Runton, just hours before he died.'

I turned to stare at my partner, wondering why he had said nothing of this to me. Was it an invention, designed to provoke a response? If so, it was a successful one, for the vicar's frown became a furious scowl, and he had to struggle to keep his voice low. 'Well, then, he is revealed as a liar, for I never dined with that man in my life. I knew him by sight, that is all.'

'Did you see Albert Cooke in the inn at East Runton on the day he went missing?'

After a moment, he gave a grudging nod.

'And did you speak to him?'

He cleared his throat. 'We may have exchanged a few words.'

Mr Jesperson sighed. 'Oh, Reverend. More prevarication? I thought we were on the same side. But it seems you wish us to tell you everything we have learned, without returning the favour.'

The vicar shifted uncomfortably in his chair. 'Now, see here. You are not being fair. What do the movements of Cooke – and whether or not I passed the time of day with him – have to do with Charles' death?'

'Miss Lane and I are trying to discover if and how the deaths of the two men are connected – you yourself assumed a connection when first we spoke.'

'But you cannot imagine that I know anything about – that I could have had anything to do with either death.' He drew himself up. 'Would you take the word of that evil charlatan Felix Ott over mine?'

Mr Jesperson tipped his stool back, balancing precariously as he gave the vicar a long, thoughtful stare. 'But you have not given me your word, Reverend.'

'Must I swear to you that I am not a murderer? Very well – I give you my word that I did not kill Albert Cooke. I solemnly affirm I did not kill Charles Manning. I have never murdered anyone!'

'Would a man who would not stop at murder hesitate to perjure himself? Oh, calm yourself, sir. I do not imagine you a murderer. But you have not been honest with us. You are keeping things back, and your silence may mean a murderer remains at large. Surely you would not wish to be responsible for other deaths?'

Reverend Ringer stared, his eyes very dark, beads of sweat standing out upon his brow. 'Is it possible? Believe me, I had no thought of misleading you. After all, the police do not think there is a killer to seek – they said—'

'Never mind what the police said. Tell us everything you know about Albert Cooke. How did you come to be acquainted with him? And what of your encounter with him on the day he went missing?'

'Very well.' The vicar took a deep breath. 'I will tell you everything. It may be of no use, but at least you cannot accuse me of holding back. Albert Cooke came to Norfolk with Felix Ott early last year, in February, I think. The two men took lodgings in Cromer, and travelled about the area in search of what Ott is pleased to call "the ancient wisdom" but which most intelligent men would refer to as superstition. Ott's views on Christianity are notorious, but not all his followers agree. Mr Cooke, for one, attended several services.'

'In your church?'

'Yes. He was most attentive during the sermons; one is not always so blessed, alas. And when he returned not merely once or twice, naturally, I noticed, and felt gratified.'

'But he lived in Cromer – it seems strange, does it not, that he should have come all the way to Aylmerton on a Sunday to attend the service here.'

There were signs of a struggle on Dr Ringer's countenance; I imagined he was tempted to claim that his sermons were so clearly superior that any churchgoer of discernment would have done the same, but honesty won out. 'It may be that he wished to keep his practice of worship a secret from Ott. And Aylmerton had other attractions for him – the library at Wayside Cross, and perhaps also the young ladies who lived there.'

Jesperson leaned forward. 'Was he courting one of them?'

'There were rumours, but whenever a gentleman has paid a return visit to Wayside Cross, the tongues of the local gossips begin to wag. The three young ladies are very tempting marriage prospects, being single, attractive and in possession of some property.'

'Were there similar rumours about Mr Manning?' I asked.

'Naturally.' With a pained expression he continued, 'However, Charles never spoke of it, and I try not to give credence to gossip. Even if he had feelings warmer than friendship for one of the young ladies, we all know that poor young Mr Manning was in no position to take on the responsibilities and expense of a wife.'

'That need not have been a problem if he married an heiress,' I pointed out. 'In fact, the only wife Mr Manning could have considered would be a woman of property.'

'Please, Miss Lane,' murmured the vicar, looking pained. 'This is idle gossip, about a man who is beyond all such matters. If you must, speak to the Misses Bulstrode – ask them if there was any talk of marriage. I cannot see how it will help you find out why Charles died, can you, Jasper?'

'You never know what bit of information may be the key to unlock a mystery,' Mr Jesperson answered coolly. 'I would not be too hasty to dismiss anything as idle gossip – never, if Miss Lane considers it significant.'

The vicar did not like being reprimanded. He checked the time on the gold watch resting in a stand on his desk and gave an impatient sigh. 'Well, all this has taken up more time than I expected, and I should not like to keep the others waiting for dinner.'

'One last thing: tell us what transpired between you and Mr Cooke at your last encounter.'

Dr Ringer settled back in his chair. 'I had gone, as a favour

101

to one of my parishioners, who was feeling poorly, to the inn at East Runton to deliver a message to the landlord. I was on the point of leaving when Mr Cooke accosted me.

'I was not displeased to see him, until I discovered what he wanted. Not a discussion of spiritual matters at all, but information about something . . . something he had better not have asked me about.

'He was looking for the so-called Poison Ring. That is the name given by locals to a recurring fairy ring in the woods,' he began, but cut himself off when he saw we knew of it. 'Well, when I did not prove malleable, he changed his story and claimed it was not the toadstools themselves that interested him, but the shrieking pit he knew was located nearby – he had only asked about the Poison Ring as a marker to the location of the pit – but I did not believe him.'

'Why not? He had an interest in the shrieking pits, did he not?'

'Then why not say so? Why ask instead about those mushrooms?'

Mr Jesperson looked as confused as I felt. What difference did it make?

'Why did he ask you at all?'

'He had meant to go there with Charles – Charles knew the location well – but Charles was away somewhere with Ott – Norwich, I think – and I had the impression Cooke was feeling a bit left out – jealous, even, that Ott should have transferred his affections to this newcomer, when Cooke had been his right-hand man for so many months. Or perhaps he was simply bored, driven by idleness to fill his time in some way. So he decided to find it for himself. He had a map, but of course such things are marked on few maps. He told me he had spent nearly two hours tramping through the woods that morning, going over the same ground and getting lost. Finally he had given up and gone into Runton for his dinner. Refreshed, he was ready to try again, but he wanted a better guide than his useless map. The innkeeper could not help him. I gather he asked some old fellows in the bar, and they told him it was best to steer well clear of any of the shrieking pits, even in daylight. Then I walked in.'

'What made him think you would know?'

Dr Ringer glanced at the watch again and grimaced. 'Charles had told him. In one of our early conversations we had touched on the subject of the shrieking pits, and although as you know I abhor all those old superstitions, I was foolish enough to share one of them with him. I wish now I had kept silent.'

He passed a hand across his brow. 'It was something that happened in my first year in Aylmerton. One of my parishioners believed – as did many of the simpler folk, having heard that the pits had once been the subterranean homes of our ancient ancestors – that they were occupied still, by a race of little people – hobgoblins, pixies or fairies; the sort of creatures who generally shun our race, but have been known to do favours for the locals, unless they feel offended by them. Then they might find their cattle diseased and fields barren, or afflicted by any number of disasters.

'Well, this poor woman believed she had been cursed, by

creatures she never dared name. She hoped to make amends, by apologising and bringing a gift, but she was afraid to go alone. She begged me, as a representative of the Church, to go with her and protect her soul.' He sighed heavily and shook his head.

'I was young. I wanted to help. Reason made no more impression upon her simple mind than a stern injunction to reject the ways of Satan – i.e. the old superstitions – and cling steadfastly to the true faith. It seemed the only thing I could do to provide the support I was required by my office to give was to go along with her into the woods.

'I was there for her, but I kept my distance. I could have nothing to do with negotiations with imaginary beings. She went to the edge of the pit and mumbled her apologies, then dropped her offering – whatever it was – inside. When I walked her back home, she was much easier in her spirits.'

'Did it work?' I asked.

'How do you mean?'

'Was her petition successful?'

I could see he did not like my question, but with a glance at Mr Jesperson, he decided to give an honest answer. 'She believed it was. They did not lose their farm. The harvest was better that year – not just for them, for everyone, of course – and they were able to pay their debts.'

'So you did not regret having pandered to her superstition?' asked Mr Jesperson. 'But when Mr Cooke asked—'

Dr Ringer interrupted. 'Cooke was not looking for spiritual succour. He wanted a local guide. I am not sorry I did not go with him. I only regret that he managed to find that foul place on his own. But had I been with him, I could hardly have stopped him from doing what I guessed he meant to do.'

'What did you think he meant to do?' I asked.

'Why, to eat some of the toadstools – or gather them for distribution and later consumption. *Amanita muscaria* – is this truly not known to you? – causes extreme inebriation. Even though it is usually accompanied by sickness, the Laplanders and some other primitive peoples use it regularly – as part of a pagan ritual. Felix Ott wrote an article claiming our British, pre-Christian ancestors achieved enlightenment by consuming this fungus, and other allegedly sacred plants.' He looked again at his watch. 'Is that all? I would rather not keep my family waiting any longer.'

Dinner began in a similar fashion to that of the previous night, with the same group gathered around the dining room table. The soup was an elegant consommé; this was followed without delay by fried whitebait. The main course was beef brisket cooked with onions and carrots, and there were light, soft bread rolls, still warm from the oven. The conversation was less interesting than the food, but I found it a relief no longer to be the centre of attention, and everything was going well enough until, as we waited for our plates to be cleared away before the sweet course, there was a shrill, distant cry from outside.

'What sort of bird was that?' enquired Mr Mavesin.

Then we heard it again, closer.

Mr Jesperson jumped to his feet. 'That was no bird,' he said. 'It was a woman's scream.'

Footsteps pounded through the house and the dining room door flew open. The maid, Maria, staggered into the room, in evident distress, her eyes wide and staring, face white as a sheet.

'Help me,' she gasped. 'My baby – my baby is gone!'

After delivering herself of those words, her eyes rolled up in her head and she collapsed, senseless, in a heap.

CHAPTER NINE

The Stolen Child

'Hilda, my smelling salts,' said Mrs Ringer, rising from her seat without haste, looking down with some distaste at the collapsed figure of the maid.

'Shall I fetch the doctor?' Mr Mavesin asked the question generally.

'The village constable, too,' said Mr Jesperson. 'Or must a message be sent to Cromer?'

Both the Reverend and his wife stared at Mr Jesperson. 'She has only fainted, she is not dead,' said our host. 'No need for—'

'But her baby is missing—'

'Baby! There is no baby – the girl is delirious,' said Mrs Ringer impatiently.

'Delirious . . . I had better get the doctor,' muttered Mr Mavesin, and hurried out of the room.

The girl on the floor stirred and moaned and tried to sit up.

'Now, now, take it gently,' said Mrs Ringer, bending over her.

'My baby!' she cried. 'She's gone! It was only for a few moments that I left her, and now she has vanished.'

Mrs Ringer said gently, 'You have been dreaming, Maria. Perhaps you are overtired. There is no baby in this house. Why, even our little boy left babyhood behind some years ago. And he has Miss Flowerdew to tend to him, so there is no baby for you to worry yourself about.'

Maria stared at her mistress, looked wildly about the room, then wailed, 'My baby! My baby!' Covering her face with her hands, she shook and sobbed with a terrible grief.

Seeing that Mr Jesperson was heading for the door, I made haste to follow.

There was no one in the kitchen; after setting out seven little bowls of pudding to be collected and served by the maid, the cook had gone home for the night. It would be the job of the live-in servant, the maid-of-all-work Maria, to serve and clear away and do the washing-up and any other work necessary before she was allowed to retire. Mr Jesperson stalked past the sink piled with unwashed dishes and opened another door, and there it was, Maria's tiny room. In it was a neatly made bed, and a wooden chest that probably served as both table and chair as well as for storage, for there was room for nothing else in that small space.

Mr Jesperson stepped inside, opened the chest to glance inside, then bent nearly double to peer beneath the bed before he straightened and backed out again. 'She went outside,' he murmured to himself.

He looked at me. 'The Ringers keep a horse and carriage, do they not? So there might be a carriage house, certainly a stable.'

I tried to follow his thoughts. 'So you think there really is a baby?'

His eyebrows lifted. 'She was surely not pretending. Could a dream have seemed so real that she would continue to cling to it under the circumstances?'

Recalling her screams and tears, such obvious signs of grief and terror, I could not believe her anguish anything but real. I protested: 'But how could she keep it secret? Mrs Ringer at least must certainly have known if there was a baby in the house – and noticed before then if her maid was . . .' I struggled with a polite way to refer to something to which no unmarried lady was supposed to speak of to a gentleman.

'Certainly poor little Maria would have been out on her ear the moment she roused the least suspicion in her mistress. But if the girl managed to keep her condition a secret, and continued working until the last minute . . . Do you remember what Mrs Ringer said yesterday, when Maria came rushing in late?'

I gasped as the maid's distracted air appeared in a different light. I remembered her disordered clothing and the dark patches on her breast when she had arrived in the dining room last night, and realised all was explained if she had been sneaking out to nurse her newborn baby between courses. 'Mrs Ringer commented on it – she said Maria used to be so reliable, and now she was forever disappearing.'

'Yes, but now it is the baby who has disappeared.' His mouth settled for a moment into a grim line as he headed for the door to the outside, snatching up the lantern that hung beside it. 'Let us hope we are not too late!'

I hurried after him, into the dark, cold night.

The side of the stables loomed ahead, only a short distance from the kitchen door. Upon entering that building we found a warm, well-kept space. The carriage occupied one large area, with three stalls behind it. Only one of the stalls had a tenant – a glossy chestnut mare who put her head over the bars to observe us with an expression of intelligent interest in her large, dark eyes. Of the other two stalls, one was bare and swept clean, but one contained a pile of hay. It was only when we entered the stall and approached it, my partner holding the lantern high, that we saw what was hidden behind the hay: two wooden boxes, one overturned to make a rough seat, the other holding a hempen sack stuffed with hay. There was a hollow in that sack that clearly showed where something else had rested upon it, and my mind quickly filled in the missing elements, interpreting the two boxes as a stool for mother and a cradle for baby.

'I wonder if there is a stable boy in residence.' As he spoke, Mr Jesperson was peering around, looking up at the low ceiling. 'If we're lucky, he sleeps in the hayloft.'

Raising his voice he called, 'Hello?'

'Who is there?' The reply, in a boy's treble, came from the doorway.

Turning, we saw a short, sturdy-looking boy, dark of hair

and dirty of face, dressed in ragged old clothes that had been cut down to his size. I guessed his age as around eleven years.

'I am Mr Jesperson and this is Miss Lane. We are house guests of the Ringers. And you are . . . ?'

'Billy. Stable boy.'

'Do you stay here, Billy, or do you have family in the village?'

'This is my home,' he said. 'The Reverend took me in, gave me a job and a home after me mam died last Christmas.'

I murmured a conventional expression of sympathy as Mr Jesperson continued, 'I suppose you know Maria.'

A look of wariness appeared on the dirty face, and he took a step back. ''Course I do.'

'Where were you just now, Billy?'

'In the privy.'

Beside me I felt my partner tense. 'Show me it.'

The boy stared in surprise. 'Oh, no, sir, you can go in the house – that is for the servants and – Reverend wouldn't like—'

'Just show me. I do not intend to use it.' His voice was crisp, brooking no argument, and Billy responded obediently, turning and leading us out of the barn, and away from the house.

A weight like cold lead settled in my stomach as I understood Mr Jesperson's suspicion. Although it had taken place before I was born, the case known as the Road Hill House Murder remained a familiar object of horror to a later generation. The victim was a three-year-old boy; the confessed killer, his half-sister, Constance Kent, and the little boy's body had been discovered stuffed down the hole in the servants' privy, with his throat savagely cut.

As we followed Billy out into the grounds, I prayed we were not about to make a similarly horrid discovery, and when he indicated the wooden shed, half hidden behind some shrubbery, I hung back, letting Mr Jesperson enter to inspect the interior.

It did not take him long. He stepped out again and gave me a look to say all was well. 'Nothing there.'

'And what should be there?' Billy asked me as we followed Mr Jesperson back to the stables, but I made no reply. This boy was the first possible suspect we had encountered, and I thought it best to leave it to Mr Jesperson to handle his questioning.

'Show us where you sleep, Billy,' he said when we were back inside the building. Puzzled by his interest, but not unwilling, the boy led us up a wooden ladder into the hayloft and revealed his snug, Spartan quarters. Again, there was nothing to indicate that a crime had been committed by its occupant.

'Now, Billy,' he said, fixing the boy's eyes with his most compelling gaze. 'You are Maria's friend.'

'Yes, sir.'

'You know her secret.'

The boy flinched but appeared unable to look away. 'I will never tell it. I gave her my oath.'

'It has been discovered. Maria has told it herself. Did you not hear her screams, even from the privy?'

His eyes widened. 'Screams? Yes, I thought I heard some-thing – I thought it might be— But – that was Maria? Why? Is she hurt?'

'Her baby is gone.'

'Gone?' He broke away and ran to the stall, into it and around the pile of hay. At the sight of the empty box he gave a shriek. 'No! No! Where is she?' He began to cast about wildly, then to dig into the hay as the only possible hiding place. As he hauled out handfuls of the dried grass he gabbled, 'I said I'd keep watch . . . I said she would be safe . . . But I needed the privy, and the babe was sleeping, so I thought it would be all right, because I'd heard Cook leave, and I knew that meant Maria would soon be able to slip outside again. I thought she'd be no more'n a minute, and I really had to go.'

'Billy. Billy.' Speaking gently and taking him by the arms, Mr Jesperson managed to pull him away from his desperate but useless excavations. 'It was not your fault if someone else took the baby. I hope you can help us find who that was. Who else knew Maria's secret?'

The boy shook his head. There were tears in his eyes. 'No one. She didn't tell no one. She didn't even tell me – only I was here, when the baby came. I saw it happen.' His expression changed to one of dreamy wonder as he recalled the night the serving girl had given birth on the bare floor, alone.

'Like the baby Jesus, born in a stable,' he said. 'She was scared. She didn't know what to do. I didn't know either, but I helped her, gave her a knife to cut the cord, and helped her clean it up, and it were all right.

'I *thought* it were all right,' he ended bleakly.

★

We left him still searching the stables. In the kitchen, the seven pudding bowls were still untouched, and the door to Maria's little room was shut, but from within were sounds suggesting the doctor was in attendance.

In the family drawing room we joined Dr and Mrs Ringer. The children, including Hilda, had been sent up to their rooms, under Miss Flowerdew's supervision, and Mr Mavesin had returned to his own lodgings. I sensed the Ringers wished that we, too, would withdraw, but we were invited guests, and could not be dismissed as servants or children, so they must suffer our involvement in this private scandal.

Mr Jesperson asked a few questions about Billy. The answers accorded with what he had told us about himself, and the information that he was only just eleven years old removed any thought that he might be the father of Maria's child.

A rumpled-looking, grey-bearded, balding gentleman with a large, reddish nose came in and was introduced as Dr Vokes.

'I have given her a sleeping-draught; she will not wake for nine or ten hours now,' he said, sinking into a chair near the fire.

'And will she then be restored to her senses?' asked Mrs Ringer.

'How do you mean?'

'Will she have forgotten all this nonsense about a baby?'

'You cannot call it nonsense. From my examination, I found she has given birth very recently – I should say three days, at most.' He frowned at Reverend Ringer. 'You had no suspicions?'

Dr Ringer shifted uncomfortably, casting a sidelong look at his wife. 'I really have very little to do with the servants; my work keeps me busy.'

'I cannot believe it,' said Mrs Ringer firmly. 'How is it possible? If she was with child—'

'There is no "if" about it, I assure you,' said Dr Vokes. He looked expectantly at the Reverend. 'I wonder, as it is such a cold night, and I feel rather . . .'

Alert to the physician's unspoken request, the vicar jumped up. 'Will you take a glass of brandy? Or would you prefer something else?'

With a sigh of pleasure, Dr Vokes said, 'Brandy would be most welcome, thank you.'

'Forgive me, I should have offered you something at once.' The Reverend Ringer went to a cabinet, which opened to reveal glinting glass and crystal. He took out a bottle and a stemmed, deep-bowled glass. 'We are most obliged to you for coming at once. We had no notion that the girl had become a mother. Sometimes, lately, her service was erratic, but she looked the same as ever, and never even complained of feeling ill.'

'I think it came as a surprise to her,' replied Dr Vokes, stretching out his hand for the brandy glass. 'When I asked about the father, she declared she never had a sweetheart.'

Mrs Ringer scoffed. 'She certainly fooled us.'

'She is a remarkably ignorant child,' said the doctor. 'When I pressed her on the matter, explaining the facts of life, she admitted that something happened in the early spring – a man forced himself upon her; it was over quickly, and she put it out of her mind.'

'The father must be informed,' said Mrs Ringer. 'He must be made to do his duty.'

Dr Vokes contemplated his glass of brandy before he replied. 'That might do more harm than good. He is already married, and the father of Maria's two little nephews.'

Mrs Ringer gasped. 'I gave her leave to go and help her sister in her confinement – last Easter.'

'Yes, that is undoubtedly when it happened. To inform her sister would be an act of needless cruelty. Particularly needless since there is no child now to be taken care of, and Maria can continue to support herself by working in your household.'

Mrs Ringer looked as if she might object, but her husband quickly intervened. 'Yes, of course, although she has sinned, I am sure she is repentant, and it would be unchristian to turn her out. We must set an example. But why did she not tell us before? She could not have expected to get away with keeping such a secret for very long, not even with Billy's complicity.'

'Undoubtedly she was desperate, terrified of losing her position and being turned out with nowhere to go. Her mind may have been affected by her travails – I have seen it before,' said Dr Vokes. He swirled the brandy in the glass, sniffed, and then took a healthy gulp.

I was beginning to feel a bit desperate myself at the leisurely pace set by the physician. 'What about the baby? I think we should send for the police at once.'

He shook his head and looked at Mr Jesperson. 'Where did you search?'

'The privy and the stables. Also, immediately outside those buildings. Billy was certain that the baby was not left unattended for more than two or three minutes. There were no signs of violence, and I saw no footprints.'

'It is dark,' replied the doctor. 'Who knows what you may have missed? In the morning, the body will be discovered under a bush, or thrust into the hedge, or in some other nearby hiding place.'

My skin crawled with horror. 'You think the baby is dead?'

'Of course it is, my dear,' he said kindly, really looking at me for the first time. 'You do not want to think it, because you are gentle and soft-hearted, like all good women. I have seen a great many terrible things in my time. You imagine an abduction, but who would wish to steal a servant girl's illegitimate baby?'

'Who would wish to kill that baby?' I snapped back at him.

'Who else but the poor, desperate mother?'

'Oh, how horrible!' cried Mrs Ringer. 'Marie could not be so wicked! What about her maternal instincts?'

'I consider it a matter not of wickedness, but self-preservation,' responded Dr Vokes, 'to give her child a mercifully quick death as an alternative to slow starvation.'

'Doctor, you must know we would never have let them starve to death – no one would, not in England,' cried Mrs Ringer.

'There are people starving to death all over England. A quick death can be a mercy. Such things happen more often in the lower classes than those of us who are comfortably situated like to think.'

'You may explain the reason for *some* infanticides, Doctor Vokes, but it does not answer the facts in *this* case,' I said, my voice as reasonable as his. 'If she had smothered it immediately, perhaps, but she kept the baby, and took care of her, and when she found her gone – oh, if you had seen her anguish you could never accuse her of murder.'

'You seem to forget that I did see her. I spoke with her and questioned her long enough to be certain she was not acting – she has no memory of what she did. Her grief and bewilderment are genuine.'

'Are you suggesting she may have a split personality?' Mr Jesperson's face lit with excitement.

Dr Ringer sprang up from his seat, put another log on the fire, then seized the poker and stirred vigorously. 'Surely you do not suggest our meek little maidservant is in actuality some sort of Miss Jekyll and Miss Hyde? Do you suppose our cook prepared the potion to cause the transformation?'

Dr Vokes gave a rumbling laugh. 'Excellent – I can see that as a cartoon in *Punch*. I am sorry you do not include so many jokes in your sermons, Doctor Ringer. No, no, R. L. Stevenson's yarn was an allegory, of course. There are no such potions. But the premise is not entirely fantastical. Indeed, I have it on good authority that the author was inspired by the first diagnosed case of multiple personalities in one man.'

'Louis Vivet, 1885,' said Mr Jesperson.

The doctor looked at him in surprise. 'You are a medical student?'

'No. But I take a close interest in mental disorders, and read all the literature that I can find on the subject. A deal of good work is being done in France. I suppose your reasoning is that the trauma of unexpected motherhood, the necessity of keeping it a secret, could have caused a mental split to occur, and therefore it would be wrong to blame Maria for any act committed by her second self. She has no memory of it, and would never have harmed her child.'

'Well, someone did,' Reverend Ringer retorted, throwing down the poker.

'And no one except the desperate mother could have any reason to kill a baby,' said Dr Vokes, and finished his brandy.

'But we do not know that the baby is dead,' I objected, a little desperately. 'Unless we find it—'

In an instant, Mr Jesperson was on his feet. 'We must go out and search.'

'In darkness? Pointless. Much more sensible to wait until morning,' said the doctor.

'And aid in murder? Only think, sir. How would such a death be effected, especially in a divided soul? By smothering, beating, strangulation – or without violence, the way Spartan mothers were said to leave their less-than-perfect infants, to die of exposure.'

'She may still be alive,' I cried, understanding, and joining Mr Jesperson on his way to the door. 'Oh, we must hurry, before it is too late.'

CHAPTER TEN

The Search

Soon, wrapped up and equipped with lanterns, Dr Ringer, Dr Vokes, Mr Jesperson, Billy, Mrs Ringer and myself were searching the grounds, gardens and roadside areas near the house. From the stable boy's testimony we knew that there were only a few minutes in which anyone could have done away with or hidden the baby, and although it felt very cold, especially after the warmth of the fireside, we were all hopeful that even naked on a bed of leaves or under a bush, the baby would yet have survived.

We hunted with a will, and Dr Vokes, who had been so reluctant at first, was possibly the most energetic and determined of us all; his reluctance vanished as soon as he realised that he might be proved right about what happened and yet save the child.

We must have spent more than an hour going over the gardens and the area around the barn and the privy, investigating every nook and cranny. The moon was almost full, in a sky with fitful clouds, and it gave so much light that our lanterns were scarcely necessary.

The men searched the roadside to a distance much farther than Maria herself could have gone in only a few minutes; they looked not only along the bare verges, but clambered into ditches and hedges. Mr Jesperson went across the road into the field, as far as the shallow depression we had explored only that morning: the connection between a mother wailing for her lost child and shrieking pits was too obvious to ignore. But he returned empty-handed.

At last we all – except Mrs Ringer, who had already given it up as a lost cause and returned to the house – stood indecisively by the front gate, unable to think of any possible hiding places we had overlooked and feeling despondent.

'You go off to bed now, Billy,' said Dr Ringer. 'Keep yourself warm. You'll do no one any good by catching a chill.'

'What can have become of the little 'un?' the boy asked. 'Who'd steal a baby?'

By then, even Dr Vokes had to acknowledge that Maria could not have done away with her child; there had not been enough time for her to have gone further than our searches had taken us, or to have dug even the shallowest of graves.

'Book of Kings, Chapter Three,' replied the vicar. '*And this woman's child died in the night; because she overlaid it. And she arose at midnight, and took my son from beside me, while thine hand-maiden slept, and laid it in her bosom, and laid her dead child in my bosom.*'

'Of course,' said Mr Jesperson. 'A bereaved parent might well be tempted to take another baby as a replacement.'

'A pretty theory,' said Dr Vokes in a tone that belied his words. 'However, I am certain the Reverend will confirm he has not officiated at an infant funeral in recent months.'

'The last was a child of three,' agreed Dr Ringer. 'But—'

'Nor have I attended any still-births this year.'

'Praise the Lord for that. But it may be that some woman in the neighbourhood has recently miscarried. Or even a barren woman, trying for years to conceive, finally driven to take what the Lord has not been pleased to grant her.'

'If so, she has not sought *my* confidence,' Dr Vokes said flatly. 'You would be better to question Miss Bulstrode, for I understand that many women apply to her for tonics and traditional cures, even spells, to overcome fertility problems.'

I said nothing, of course, but inwardly resolved to return to Wayside Cross in the morning and do just that.

'Perhaps we are looking at this question the wrong way round,' said Mr Jesperson. 'We might come up with a list of women desirous of a child, and one of them might have been desperate enough to take what she considered an unwanted baby – but how would she have known of its existence?'

'Maria told no one,' I said. 'Billy was a witness – the only witness, we presume, but if anyone else was in the stables over the past few days they might have discovered a baby hidden in the hay.'

'Billy, have you seen anyone hanging about the stables? Any visitors I don't know about?' Dr Ringer asked.

'No sir. Not until these two.' He indicated Mr Jesperson and myself by a nod of his head.

'We have had no other guests.'

'That leaves your employees,' said Mr Jesperson. 'Did Mr Mavesin have any cause to visit the stables?'

'That's absurd! No one could suspect my secretary of—'

'No one suspects him of any wrongdoing, Reverend. Remember, we are simply trying to ascertain if anyone beside Maria and Billy knew about the baby. Rumours may have spread, and allowed someone to plan the abduction. Otherwise, we are left with an opportunistic kidnapper, a passing stranger, or someone known to the family, who entered the stables for some other reason, and made a spontaneous decision to take the baby they saw there. Does that sound likely?'

'Nothing about this situation is likely,' grumbled Dr Vokes, adjusting his scarf and turning up his collar against the wind. 'I can do nothing more tonight. I will stop by to see Maria tomorrow. Goodnight.'

We bade him goodnight. Billy having vanished to his hayloft, we went to the front door, and discovered it locked.

'My wife must have gone to bed,' said the vicar. 'Undoubtedly, she was overcome by the emotional stress of this evening. She will not have locked the kitchen door.'

The proved to be the case, and it seemed likely that Mrs Ringer had not so much as looked into the back regions of the house before she made her retreat upstairs, for we found the kitchen in the same state as when we had left it, piles of dirty dishes stacked to await the attention of the unconscious maid. Dr Ringer scarcely paused – such was his concern for his wife's fragile nerves – as he hurried through.

I considered it an unexpected gift, to have more time to discuss matters with Mr Jesperson.

'Someone has been at the pudding,' he said.

Indeed, one of the seven little bowls was now empty. 'Perhaps whoever cleared the table took it as her right. Who do you think: Mrs Ringer or Miss Flowerdew?'

'Hilda,' he replied, picking up one of the bowls and attacking the pudding with a clean spoon. I opened my mouth to remonstrate, but he pushed another bowl across the counter towards me, saying, his mouth half full, 'It is too good to waste.'

He was right. The sweet, custardy dessert was as delicious as everything else prepared by the Ringers' excellent cook. When he had finished his first bowl, Mr Jesperson took a second, and I confess I did the same. If there were any fault at all to be found, it could only been the size of the portions.

'Could Miss Flowerdew have known about the child?' he asked between mouthfuls. 'Remember, she was almost late for dinner, and I thought she looked flustered. What if she had been out to the stables, and whisked the baby up to her room? I really should have insisted that the house should be searched, but with everyone else convinced it was murder rather than abduction . . .'

I stared in astonishment. 'But why on earth should *she* want to steal a baby?'

'I do not claim any expertise in female psychology, but she is a spinster of a certain age who has seen her chances of marriage and motherhood disappear. I sensed an air of deep sadness about her. Did you not remark it?' He waved his spoon vaguely. 'Of course, it may be something else that haunts her . . . but unfulfilled longings can become obsessions, and lead to rash actions.'

Miss Flowerdew was sad and clearly dissatisfied, which struck me as entirely natural to one in her position. Governess was a role in life to which many women were driven by financial need, and few were temperamentally suited to it.

'Miss Flowerdew already has three children – four, counting Hilda – to look after; why should she want more?'

He pushed aside his empty bowl and reached for another. 'It is hardly logical, and yet I believe it is a fact that mothers often miss their babies when they grow up into little boys and girls. Women of all ages and ranks, even those who might flinch in distaste from a grubby four-year-old, coo and sigh at the sight of a new baby.'

I had noticed it myself, but . . . 'But *Miss Flowerdew*?'

He grinned. 'I know. But someone stole the baby. And no one has been able to name a single likely suspect. Living together in the same house, perhaps Miss Flowerdew noticed signs and suspected Maria's condition. Or Cook!' He paused, spoon suspended before his lips. 'Talented, irreplaceable Cook . . . She strikes me as altogether more down-to-earth than Miss

Flowerdew. Maybe Cook knew and, although disinclined to inform her employers, gossiped with her cronies? If so, the news may have spread to the one woman in the village who might be desperate and driven enough to take a child she thought no one else wanted.' He licked his spoon. 'Must ask Cook tomorrow. If she *did* gossip, she might know who might have done something with the information. Must take it carefully, though; important she should feel we are on the same side and there is no blame attached to her. I am certain the Ringers would never forgive us if we hurt her feelings.'

'You are good at sweet-talking cooks,' I said. 'So I will leave that to you . . . For me, another visit to Wayside Cross is in order. Miss Bulstrode may know which poor, desperate woman may have been driven to steal a baby.'

'Will you have some more of this delicious pudding?'

'No thank you.'

'Sure?' He wiggled the bowl.

'Quite sure,' I said. 'Now, about Miss Flowerdew . . .'

His eyes lit up. 'Of course! Take this with you. If she lets you in, you can sound her out, and look around for any sign of the child; if she refuses, we will know she has something to hide.'

I did not think it would be that simple. If Miss Flowerdew had already cleaned her teeth she probably would not want anything more to eat. I was barely an acquaintance; there was no reason for her to welcome my visit. Still, there was no reason not to try.

I carried the bowl and a spoon upstairs and knocked at her

door – hoping that memory served, and this was her room rather than one of the children's.

'What do you want?' Miss Flowerdew's pinched, startled little face appeared in the space between the door and frame, her eyes red-rimmed and puffy. 'Oh! Miss Lane. I thought it must be one of the children. What is the matter?'

'May I come in?'

'Of course.' Without the slightest hesitation she opened the door wide. I took a swift look around as I entered, noticing many places in which a baby might have been hidden: the wardrobe, behind the curtains, under the bed, even a dresser drawer. Unless it cried, an 'accidental' discovery might be impossible. I could drop my handkerchief and steal a glance beneath the bed when I picked it up, but what excuse could I have to look inside her wardrobe?

I held out my offering. 'A bit late, I know, but I thought you might like it.'

To my amazement, tears welled up in her pale-blue eyes. 'How very kind you are,' she whispered. Then, rapidly blinking, she cleared her throat and said in a more normal tone, 'But what about you?'

I think I blushed, recalling the secret feast so recently shared with Mr Jesperson. 'Oh, I was too greedy to wait, I'm afraid. Please, do eat yours.'

'Thank you, I will. Later. Won't you sit down, and stay for a while? If you don't mind?'

'I should like that.' I settled into the rocking chair she

indicated, and she perched on the cushioned bench in front of the dressing table, on top of which she set the dish and spoon gently, almost reverently, down.

'So very upsetting,' she murmured.

'I suppose Mrs Ringer told you . . . ?'

'Oh, yes. If not for the children – we must keep it from them, of course – I would have joined you in the search. You found nothing?'

'Nothing. If not for the doctor's confirmation, we might have thought the whole thing no more than a mad fantasy. Did you never suspect that Maria was in the family way?'

Her eyes widened. 'Not in the least. She seemed such a good girl, quiet, docile – and there were no young men hanging around. Never any cause for concern. Yet somehow it happened. Not here, of course. The brother-in-law, I believe? Dreadful goings-on.'

'And you noticed no physical signs? No changes in her?'

Miss Flowerdew's headshake was emphatically negative. 'She did not get fat; she looked no different, and made no complaints; she continued to work as usual. I have never known such a thing. And when it came to her time – well, I have been in this family for two confinements, and – such a fuss, I simply cannot imagine how anyone could keep it a secret! Do you suppose the doctor could have been mistaken? Do you remember that great scandal at court – no, you are probably too young to have heard about it – but one of Queen Victoria's own physicians declared a certain lady – and she was a *widowed* lady – was to become a mother? And it was not until she died of it that he realised he had mistaken a tumour for a child.'

'No, there is no mistake – unless the stable boy is lying. And why would he? He saw it all. He believed that she told no one, and that no one else knew, but he was wrong.'

'Why do you think so?'

'Because someone took the baby.'

She did not perceive my logic. 'Well, someone might have felt they were doing it a kindness, rescuing a foundling. Babies do get left on doorsteps.'

'Yes, but passers-by don't walk off with them, do they? If someone happened across Maria's baby – and it is hard to imagine anyone unconnected to the household casually passing through the stables – surely the obvious response would have been to tell the vicar.'

'Oh, yes, I see what you mean.' She sniffed. 'Who would steal a baby? Really, the abduction is almost harder to believe than the baby itself.'

'We thought perhaps a bereaved mother, like the one in the judgement of Solomon. Or someone driven mad by her inability to produce a child. Do you know of anyone like that in Aylmerton? Or can you think of some other reason for stealing a baby?'

She appeared to give the question serious thought. 'None of the married women I have met seem to fit your descriptions, but as we are not on intimate terms, I can hardly be certain. But – stealing babies. That reminds me of something. Why would

someone steal a baby? Was it something I read, or heard – oh!'
Her eyes widened as the memory came back to her.

'Mr Felix Ott. He said it. Yes, of course. How could I have
forgotten? Well, I did not really forget, only the circumstances
are so . . . Well, it was in the talk he gave one evening in Cromer,
back in September. Mr Manning mentioned it, and invited
me—' Her sallow cheeks flushed. 'Or, more truthfully I should
say I invited myself . . . Of course I knew the Reverend would
not approve, but Mrs Ringer said I certainly should go to the
talk if I liked, she thought it a shame I have so little social life,
and as it happened, Miss Goodall was going, she has her own
carriage and was kind enough to drive me home afterwards;
really, they say she is so proud and haughty but I can only say
she was entirely kind and accommodating to me.'

When she paused for breath I broke in. 'But what of Mr Ott's
lecture? What did it have to do with stealing babies?'

'I beg your pardon. He gave a talk on witchcraft. Did you
know, they are not only creatures of legend, but truly exist –
and not merely in the past, but even today. They continue to
practise their ancient traditions in secret, and although some
of their lore is part of the wisdom he wishes to preserve and
transmit through his school – the School of British Wisdom,
you know – he warned that we must be very careful not to get
involved with *evil* witches.

'For while many wise women and wise men were called
witches and falsely accused of heinous acts and condemned to
horrible deaths by the old, misguided Church, there were also

some who were deservedly feared and hated because they *did* do evil – when they rejected Christianity (and I had better say he thinks that is a good thing to do – you understand why Doctor Ringer cannot abide the thought of him or his teachings!) – these bad witches, instead of devoting themselves to the purity of their ancient traditions, they adopted a sort of negative image of the Church, which became known as Satanism.'

In full flow, she paused to draw breath, but this time I did not dare interrupt.

'These Satanic witches turned the ceremony of communion, in which we consume the metaphorical body of Christ, into actual cannibalism. They practised human sacrifice. And they still do today – so Mr Ott declared.'

Nodding her head, she gave me a strained, excited smile. 'He told us a great many horrid details about the wrong sort of witches, the Satanic sort, but this is what your question reminded me of: he said witches steal babies.

'When a new witch is invited to join a coven, as a part of her initiation she is required to provide a baby as a sacrifice to Satan. If she cannot bring one of her own, then she must steal one. The baby will be murdered and then cooked, either to be eaten, or to mix with other ingredients to make a magical ointment.'

Her eyes widened as if she only just realised the implication of her words, and she leaned in closer to me and whispered, 'Do you think it is true? Could there be real, live, evil witches living here today? Have they taken Maria's baby?'

CHAPTER ELEVEN

Witchcraft?

I was some time in Miss Flowerdew's room, calming her down – I could hardly abandon her in the state she had worked herself into. I told her very firmly that baby-boiling witches were a mythical creation of a more superstitious and fearful age, and that Mr Ott very likely told such horror stories to attract more interest. He was trying to make money, just like newspapers that published salacious details of gory crimes.

I changed the subject to favourite novels and then to pets we had known and loved – and heard a great deal about a particular bunny rabbit, dead now thirty years – before she ate her pudding.

'Would you like a cup of cocoa? Or perhaps some hot milk, just to settle you?'

'Oh, you are kind, Miss Lane! No, there is no need. I feel quite settled now. I shall brush my teeth and get ready for bed. It has been so lovely to remember Marigold . . . I am sure I will dream of her tonight, frolicking in the summer fields.'

'I am sure I shall, too. Goodnight, Miss Flowerdew. Sleep well.'

When I got back to the kitchen I discovered Mr Jesperson had nearly finished washing the dishes.

This was one of the more surprising activities I had seen him perform – I am sure he would never have done so of his own accord back in Gower Street – but I said nothing, and took up a towel to start drying.

'You have been a long time. I suppose you investigated every nook and cranny in Miss Flowerdew's room?'

'Not exactly.' I sighed. 'It took her a long time to express her own theory of what has happened to Maria's baby, and then it took me nearly as long to talk her out of it.'

'Why, what was it?'

'Oh, that witches have stolen the baby in order to cook and eat it.'

He paused, holding a plate suspended and dripping soapsuds over the sink. 'You think that is impossible?'

I gaped at him. 'You think it is likely?'

'The case that brought us to Aylmerton began with a man terrified of witches. No, I do not think it is likely – but I would not dismiss it out of hand.'

Rinsing the dish, he handed it to me to dry. 'Ritual infanticide is one of the standard accusations made against witches down the ages. Sometimes the children are stolen, sometimes they are the offspring of the witches themselves, conceived at bestial orgies. They are sacrificed to the Devil, or eaten by the witches in an unholy feast. Dead babies are well known to be the chief ingredient in the ointment that enables witches to fly. Mind you, I do not say that any of this is true, but people have believed it for centuries. And when something is widely believed, someone will try to do it.'

'I hope not in this case.'

'So do I. How did Miss Flowerdew come by this idea?'

'She said Felix Ott spoke of witches stealing babies for sacrifice to Satan.'

He shook his head. 'She must have got the wrong end of the stick. Considering the Reverend's attitude to Ott, that is not surprising. But what Ott really believes – or promotes – is the idea that witchcraft is an old religion, firmly British and worth preserving, nothing at all like the demonic madness it has been painted as.'

I set my jaw stubbornly. 'Miss Flowerdew told me she went to a lecture where Mr Ott made a distinction between the wise women wrongly accused by the church of witchcraft, and evil Satan-worshippers who are also witches, still active in the world today, who must be avoided. According to her, he said they were cannibalistic baby-killers. And, really, I cannot think where else she would have got such ideas.'

He emptied the sink, staring down as the water swirled away, and frowned. 'How very strange. You do not think she fell asleep halfway through his lecture, and missed the part about how that was the myth, but in truth witches today are all of the highest moral calibre?'

'No. She got the part about the good witches – but the warnings against the evil sort were certainly more vivid and easier to recall.'

'Evil is often presented in lurid colours, good in pale pastels. But Ott is canny – I find it hard to think he would make such a mistake. After all, he wants to attract followers – intelligent, civilised, *monied* adherents, not bloodthirsty lunatics. So far as I understand it, he's selling a new and distinctly British religion – though he calls it a school – rooted in old traditions. He knows he must steer clear of demons and emphasise morality and personal improvement. His aim is ultimately to create a movement that could be at least as powerful as the Established Church. He positions the Church as the old enemy, for its persecution and demonisation of good Britons who refused to give up their own rites and rituals and adopt those of an invading, foreign-born religion.'

'Well, according to Miss Flowerdew he warned his audience not to be taken in by the *wrong sort* of witch. The Established Church had tried to wipe out all those wise folk they called witches – but, he said, there were some who really were worshippers of Satan, and they must avoid them and not be taken in.'

'I wonder who he had in mind? Does he have competition in the ancient British wisdom arena? It sounds like a message aimed at someone in particular . . . only it hit a few other sensitive souls in its path. It would be useful to know who else attended that particular lecture . . . Could you find out the date?'

'She said it was in September.'

He helped me finish drying and putting everything away, restoring the kitchen to a state of tidiness that we both paused for a moment to admire.

'Mrs Ringer will think the elves have been in to do the work,' he said.

I laughed. 'She will not give it a moment's thought – she expects everything to be tidy when she comes down in the morning. Only Maria may be amazed and grateful, and wonder whom to thank.'

He replied solemnly as we left the room, 'I hope Maria knows one must never thank the elves, or admit to having seen them at work, or they will go away, never to return.'

Miss Bulstrode shook her head slowly. 'The name means nothing to me.'

'Maria is the maid-of-all-work at the Vicarage,' I explained. 'Are you sure she never came to you for advice, or for any sort of complaint?'

'Ah, now I know the girl you mean. No, I have never seen her, except in passing. She has certainly never paid a visit to me, but my girls are friendly with her, I believe. But why do you ask?'

'Last evening, while we were at table, the maid rushed in, shrieking that her baby was gone, and fainted. Her employers thought she had gone mad. They were adamant that there was no baby in the house, and certainly Maria had none of her own – she has worked for them for four years, and hardly a day of sickness. But when Mr Jesperson and I went out to the stables, we found the stable boy was able to confirm that for the past three days and nights, Maria had kept her baby hidden there, sneaking out to care for it whenever she could. He believed no one else knew about it; he was a witness to the birth, which seems to have been as much a surprise to the mother as to everyone else. He said he had watched the baby whilst Maria was in the house, and that it had been left alone no more than three or four minutes when it disappeared.'

Her brows knit and, as I had noticed her do before, she stroked the smooth dome of her carnelian ring with the ball of her thumb. 'Could the two young people be in league? Inventing a story about a baby that never was?'

'Doctor Vokes attended Maria, and he said there was no doubt that she had given birth in the past few days.'

'Then probably the maid or the stable boy did away with it — or both of them together.'

Her cool suggestion chilled my blood, but I reminded myself that she knew neither of those involved. 'Billy is only a child himself. And if Maria killed her illegitimate baby, the existence of which she had managed to keep secret, why then draw attention to it? Besides, we searched the stables and outbuildings, the garden and grounds and along the roadside, much farther than Maria or Billy could have gone in the short time available, and found nothing. The baby has vanished. Which brings me to my other question: do you know of anyone in the parish who is desperate for a child?'

Although she did not move, I felt her pull back. 'I would not tell you if I did.'

'Please, this information—'

'Is private and personal to the women who confide their troubles in me. I do not betray confidences.'

'But someone has stolen a child.' I tried to penetrate her coldness, to make her feel the urgency of the matter.

'So you say. And therefore, is every woman who has ever longed for a baby, or lost one, or tried and failed to conceive one, to fall under suspicion? And what is it to *you*, Miss Lane?' Her gaze sharpened; I felt she was on the brink of piercing through my thin disguise and ejecting me from her house as a spy.

'I cannot help but feel sorry for poor little Maria, that is all,' I said. 'I was in the house where this happened last night, and although it is nothing to do with me, I want to help if I can. And – a lost child! Surely you feel the urgency of that. There is no time to be wasted; it may be a matter of life and death. Everyone from the household is trying to help.'

She sighed and I saw her shoulders relax. 'Of course. I understand. And I hope *you* understand that I feel every bit as protective of my women patients as you do of that maid. I will not hand over anyone's secrets to be torn apart and used and put on public display.'

'But a child has been stolen,' I said emphatically.

'*If* a child has been stolen, that is a matter for the police,' she said, an edge of steel in her voice. 'Have they been informed?'

'I do not know.' I thought a moment, weighing the situation. 'There was some talk of it . . . Doctor Vokes, believing that Maria had done away with her child in a moment of madness, was not inclined to bring in the law. There is certainly the danger that they would accuse her of murder and lock her up. But, after all, there is no evidence of murder – a baby is missing, and the police might have a better chance of finding it. My partner inclines that way, I think; he was intending to go to Cromer later today, and might inform the police if we are still as much in the dark. But surely it would be better – and safer – for all concerned if we could settle matters without bringing in the police. I do not suppose you would be any happier to give the police a list of names . . . ?'

'I would not,' she said coldly. 'The police have their own sources, and will not scruple to use any bit of unfounded gossip or malicious rumour to add to the pain of women who have already suffered quite enough. But they will not find the missing baby in any of their homes. I will tell you this, although I will not name them, there is no need for me to name them. I would swear upon my very life that no one who has come to me for help with conception, or to prevent another miscarriage, has stolen anyone else's child.'

I saw that it would be useless to argue with her. And how likely was it that someone desirous of a baby would have known there was one lying unattended in the stable at the vicarage? Even Thomas Hardy might have baulked at coincidence bringing a bereaved stranger passing by, deciding to take shelter from the cold in a stable at the very moment that the baby was left unattended. Someone must have known about the baby already.

'You said that your servants are friendly with Maria – might I speak with them?'

'Of course. Will you come now?'

I followed her out of the large and rather gloomy parlour to a spacious kitchen at the back of the house. It was warm and clean and well-lit. Two young women sat at a big, scrubbed wooden table, one polishing silverware, the other engaged in peeling potatoes. I recognised the silver-polisher as the pretty maid who had answered the door to me on two occasions; the other girl was plump and fair but rather cross-looking, with masses of blond hair escaping from an unevenly pinned bun at the back of her head. Our entry had silenced them, but the echo of their voices still hung in the air as they stared up at us.

'Nancy, Elsie – no, do not get up. This is Miss Lane. She is a visitor from the Vicarage and would like to speak to you, if you do not mind? Good. I should be happy for you to answer her questions, and help her in any way that you can. Meanwhile, I shall put the kettle on, and make a pot of tea for us all.'

The two young women gave up their previous occupations to fix their attention firmly on me as I asked my first question: 'I understand that you are friends with Maria Murry, the young woman who works at the Vicarage?'

Nancy nodded agreement, but blonde Elsie objected: 'I should not say *friends,* exactly.'

'But you know her.'

'Oh, aye. What has it been, three years now?'

'Did you know that Maria had a baby?'

'What, before she come to Aylmerton?' Elsie's eyes narrowed, sparkling with interest. 'What a dark horse! She must have been awfully young?'

'No, I mean just recently. Had you any idea that she might be in the family way?'

'What? No! She never did – she could not – impossible! And her without a sweetheart – she never walked out with anyone!' Their disbelief tumbled out in a jumble of protest and explanation. I learned that that Elsie thought Maria fancied herself too good for the local young men, whereas Nancy felt that the girl was shy, and young for her years – possibly a bit simple.

'I expect someone took advantage of her,' said Nancy. 'The poor soul.'

'Yes – her brother-in-law, most likely. At least, so the doctor inferred from what she told him, and the dates fit. Maria herself hardly understood what had happened.'

'You see?' said Nancy to Elsie. 'Oh, the poor child. But – we saw her only a fortnight ago.'

'Bonfire night, that was. Nearly a month.'

'Even so . . .' She frowned, remembering. 'She did not look . . . Well, no one could have guessed . . . How did she manage to hide her condition?'

'She hid it even from herself, I suspect,' said Miss Bulstrode. 'Sometimes, if the baby is small and carried high, it is not so obvious. And a naïve young woman might manage to ignore the changes in her own body. If that was the situation, how terrified she must have been when the baby came. Some instinct may have driven her to hide herself rather than seek help. And once she saw the baby . . . perhaps she decided to hide it, well aware of the consequences once it was known, but more likely, I think, that she did not plan, only adapted herself to this new demand, and struggled to carry on as best she could.'

'What will happen to her now?' asked Nancy. 'Will the Ringers throw her out? I suppose she'll have to go to the workhouse.'

'The baby is gone,' I said.

The maids stared in astonishment. 'What? How?'

'Last night, when Maria went out to check on her child, hidden as usual behind a pile of hay in the stable, it was not there.'

'But who would take a baby?' asked Nancy.

'No one,' said Elsie, looking at me with narrowed eyes. 'Did *you* see this baby, Miss?'

'No.'

'Did no one else but Maria see it?'

'Only the stable boy.'

'She is lying,' said Elsie flatly. 'And she's got Billy to believe a piece of wood wrapped in a blanket was her babby. Don't kick me, Nance. I do not blame her. Look at her life! I could never have stuck it at the Vicarage for half the time she's put up with being their overworked, under-appreciated slavey. I don't reckon she's as simple as you say, either. For once she is the centre of attention, and at the end of it, they'll all feel sorry for her, and she'll still have her job. There never was a baby.'

'But there *was* a baby,' I told them. 'According to Doctor Vokes, Maria had given birth within the past few days. And

Billy saw it. He is the reason we know almost to the minute when the baby went missing.'

This silenced them for a few moments. Miss Bulstrode was about to speak when Elsie got there first. 'But who is to know if the baby was born dead . . . or died soon after? Billy saw Maria tending to something wrapped in a blanket . . . and only slowly realised she was caring for something that required no care. Maybe he is the one who finally took the cold body away and buried it. That would explain her hysterics.'

I was impressed by Elsie's reasoning abilities, and found her theory more likely than any other I had heard or managed to come up with myself. It was more reassuring to think that the baby had died of natural causes – it may have been too small and sickly to survive. Maria was thereby cleared of infanticide, and her grief and horror at the loss of the baby (which she had gone on trying to nurse in her simple-minded way) was explained. The only problem with this story was Billy. Having seen the boy, I did not believe he had anything to hide. He was as surprised by the disappearance as Maria. I did not think the boy could be such a skilled actor, and even if he had been, *where* was the baby? Surely there had been no time for him to dig a hole and bury it.

I was still turning Elsie's suggestion over in my mind, preparing to argue it out point by point, when Miss Bulstrode took over again.

'Thank you very much, girls,' she said, rising from the table. 'We'll not detain you from your work any longer. The kettle is on the boil – Nancy, please make the tea and bring it to us in my office; Miss Lane will stay long enough to enjoy a cup, and we are not to be disturbed except for some emergency.'

As soon as we were inside her parlour, she shut the door and turned her back on it to regard me with a grave expression.

'Miss Lane, you are very good to take up Maria's case like this, but the best thing you can do for her now is to lay it down again. Above all, do not bring the police into it.'

I stared at her, bewildered. 'Why?'

'Maria never had a baby.'

'But Doctor Vokes said—'

She cut me off. 'Yes, and whatever I think of him, he is not such a fool as to make a mistake like that. But it may be she had a miscarriage, or the child was stillborn – either might explain why no one suspected she was *enceinte*. At present, no one but Maria and Billy can say they saw it. There is no body. If a body is found, the police will be involved, it will be treated as a crime – and Maria will bear all the blame. For bearing life, for dealing death.' I tried to speak, but she would not let me. 'No, listen to me; it does not matter what "really" happened. If it was born dead, or Maria smothered it by accident, or in a moment of panic or fear. Doctor Vokes will not go to the police. I will not. Maria will not. If you care about the girl, you will not. The best thing for her is that she should forget it ever happened.'

'But the baby!'

'The baby is dead.'

A fusillade of sharp raps, like a scattering of gravel against glass, startled us both. Turning towards the sound, I saw a crow perched on the ledge outside the window. It cocked its head.

'Oh! Gabriel,' Miss Bulstrode cried, and hastened to open the window. 'Come in my dear, come in!'

The black bird hopped inside, and she shut the window again. 'Too cold outside, I quite agree. Now, I have left a treat for you on the shelf – fly up and get it.'

With a single loud '*caw!*' the bird launched and flew to the top of the bookcase, where I saw it peck up something with its beak, then put its head back as it swallowed. It cawed again.

Miss Bulstrode turned back to me, smiling and relaxed now, the intensity of our confrontation in the past. Although I wanted to argue against her assertion that Maria's baby was dead, I had no compelling counter-argument to make. I did not think my hostess would respond favourably to Miss Flowerdew's idea of cannibalistic witches.

I went to stand before the fire and as I was warming myself, I looked around the room, noticing things I had not seen before. In particular, there was a glass-fronted case – a medicine cabinet, it must have been, for the shelves were filled with labelled jars and other containers, some of which were like those you see behind the counter at the chemist's shop. I could not quite read the labels, but thought they were in Latin.

'How do your clients respond to your pet crow?' I asked.

'Some are nervous, some are charmed by him. At least one lady considers Gabriel more in the role of my colleague, rather than a pet.'

'And some, I suppose, must think he is your familiar?' I turned around so I could see her expression. 'Have you ever been accused of being a witch?'

She did not seem at all put out by my question, but almost pleased. 'Oh, yes, indeed,' she said calmly. '*Accused* is an interesting word. Should I be *accused* of being a doctor or a midwife? I could accept the title of healer or wise woman with pride. But witch? That is still considered beyond the pale. I should be happy to reclaim the title. The Church did a good job of demonising us.'

'"Us"? You include your sisters?'

'My sisters in the tradition, not Alys and Ann. Our mother taught me, but neither of them have ever been interested – although Alys has a bit of a green thumb, so she likes to help me in the garden and the glasshouse.'

'So, you learned your skills from your mother – and she from hers?'

'No, she was instructed by a childless old woman in the village. The tradition is not only transmitted by right of birth; it requires devotion and dedicated practice. Bearing children, raising them and looking after a family do not really fit with having a true vocation. To have *one* child, perhaps, under the right circumstances . . . but not the obligations imposed on most wives and mothers. My mother was unmarried; I have no father. Fortunately, her own father was an unusually tolerant man who let her make her own choices, and he had money enough to pay servants, giving her leisure to work and study. I was a curious child, eager for instruction; I was her apprentice before I was four years old.'

It was a delicate subject – an unmarried woman with three children – but I had to ask. 'Your sisters?'

'When I was thirteen, my grandfather died. Less than a year later, my mother married a man by the name of Joseph Peacock. He arrived one day to look at her late father's library, with the plan of buying it. She had no wish to sell it, but nevertheless he ended up in possession of it – and the house – and her. Their first child was born about a month after their marriage. Ann came along two years later. Two years after that, our mother died in childbed. The baby she carried was badly deformed and did not survive.' Her hands clenched in her lap, and her mouth was a tight line as she spoke. 'She should have known better. She knew ways to prevent conception, but the Peacock wanted a son to carry on his name.'

'I am sorry,' I murmured.

'Ancient history,' she said. 'But it shaped me. It was a powerful lesson about the dangers of letting a man rule over you. I saw, too, how the demands of motherhood, even more than that of being a wife, wore her down and took her away from her vocation. Fortunately, by then I was old enough to assume her mantle in both her occupations – witch and mother.'

'And what of Mr Peacock?'

Her nose wrinkled. 'What of him? Well, he died, eventually. None too soon – but at least before he could sell the house from under us, or marry a wicked stepmother.'

'Your sisters do not bear his name.'

'Are you surprised? No, they look upon me almost as their mother, and naturally wished we should share the same surname.'

'But that will change with marriage.'

'Yes, when they marry – and I think they will – although it would not surprise me if Alys did not insist on her husband taking her name as part of the conditions of their betrothal.' She laughed and I could not tell how serious she was.

'And what about you?'

'I shall never marry,' she said firmly. 'I have been asked, and I have refused, so this is no idle promise. I told you about my mother's experience. It made me determined never to allow a man to have dominion over me, making my choices, absorbing all my energies and telling me what to do.'

'All men are not like Mr Peacock.'

'I know that. But why risk it? I have my vocation.'

'You speak as if you were a nun. Is witchcraft so like a religion?'

She looked thoughtful, turning the ring around on her finger. 'There are elements that have some similarities, I think – devotion, ritual observances – but in truth I know very little about religion. I was not raised in any Church. My grandfather was proudly atheistical. My mother . . . had her private spiritual beliefs. However, Mr Ott thinks that witchcraft should be considered one of the ancient religions of our land, along with Druidism. And unlike Druidism, the truth of which has been entirely lost to us, many of the rituals of witchcraft have been handed down over the generations and continue to be practised in secret.'

I was fascinated by the movement of the ring on her finger. 'Was that ring your mother's?'

'This? Oh, no. It was a gift, from a gentleman – given in

friendship. It is certainly no engagement ring.' My attention sharpened at this – surely unnecessary – denial. I noticed how her cheeks were flushed, and her eyes seemed brighter as she contemplated the large orange stone, turning her hand so it caught the light, and I felt more certain than ever that it had been a present from Charles Manning, echoing the pretty little *bibelot* she had given to him. Judging by her words, she could not have been engaged to him, but her looks spoke of a fonder emotion than friendship. Perhaps they had been lovers, and this had roused jealousy in another, and led to his death.

'It is certainly unusual – and attractive – why should it not be an engagement ring?' I said, speaking almost at random as I tried to think of how to question her about her relationship and who had known of it.

She turned her hand from side to side. 'It is not what most people would choose as a *friendship* ring, either,' she said. 'Let me show you.'

She touched the side of the stone, caught with her fingernail at a gap beneath the setting, and flipped it open, revealing a small, hidden compartment. It was empty – I thought again of Mr Manning's pillbox.

'That might hold a lock of the beloved friend's hair,' I suggested.

'A pretty idea,' she said, looking amused. 'Much prettier than the truth! In fact it is designed to hold a lethal dose, in pills or powder. Have you never seen a poison ring before?'

CHAPTER TWELVE

Still Seeking Answers

Miss Bulstrode checked the time on the gold watch pinned to her lapel. 'I hope you will not think me inhospitable, but other matters compel my attention. Please do not feel you must rush off.'

When she rose, I did too. 'Thank you . . . While I am here, I had hoped I might speak to your sisters.'

Like a shadow, an expression of wariness crossed her face. 'You are not still pursuing the phantom baby? I can assure you, my sisters know nothing.'

I spoke quickly. 'No, it is about Charles Manning.'

She did not look reassured – and I confess, she was right to suspect my intentions – so I pressed on. 'You know why I have come to Aylmerton. And you have been very kind. If Ann or Alys had memories of Charles Manning they could share, I know his brother would be grateful.'

'Do you? I do not think he would be glad to learn of a connection between his brother and my sister.'

I recalled the cigarette case with date and initial. 'Do you mean to suggest there was one? A special understanding, or—'

'That is not for me to say.' She gave a weary sigh. 'Oh, very well, I shall tell them. Let it be her decision.'

'Thank you, but this is your office – I do not wish to discommode you—'

'No, not at all, I have to go out. Please, make yourself comfortable. And while you wait, feel free to explore the library. Not all the works are scholarly tomes; you may find something here to divert you. Good day, Miss Lane.'

I was glad to have her permission, for I should have found it impossible to resist having a browse once I was left alone in that room full of temptations. The only difficulty was in knowing where to begin, since I did not even know by what plan they were organised. As I wandered, searching for a familiar title by which to orient myself, I found the volumes were in a variety of languages, including Latin, German and Arabic, ancient and modern, and although mostly grouped according to subject matter (medicine, astronomy, botany for example) some seemed to have been shelved at random.

Seeing the name of Sir Walter Scott on a dark blue spine was like glimpsing an old friend in a room full of strangers, but this was not one of his novels, but a copy of *Demonology and Witchcraft*. Beside it, three leatherbound volumes comprising the *Compendium maleficarum* of Fr Francesco Mario Guazzo. I pulled one out and opened it to a woodcut illustration. It showed a devilish beaked, horned, tailed man welcoming a group of men and women dressed in the style of the seventeenth century, with a fat naked baby lying at their feet. I did not need to be able to read the Latin text to understand. A few pages later I came upon another woodcut, this one far more horrible, showing one infant being turned on a spit over a blazing fire, and another about to be dropped into a boiling cauldron.

Had they ever been true, those accusations of infanticide and cannibalism, the confessions of sacrifice and devil-worship elicited under torture? Or were they nightmares and deliberate lies invented to demonise the followers of an older religion?

I closed the book and put it back in its place. I wondered if the woman and murdered child legend of the shrieking pits had anything to do with witches. Who, after all, had killed her child? From there, my mind jumped to Felix Ott, and whether he'd had anyone particular in mind when he warned his audience against the wrong sort of witches – Satan-worshipping, child-murdering women at large in the world today. Miss Bulstrode claimed to be happy with the maligned name of witch, but she was a healer, a wise woman who helped other women with their problems – wasn't she? I believed her. But what made me think I was such an expert at recognising goodness and seeing through lies? If people's sins were written on their faces for all to read, no criminal would ever escape the consequences of his evil deeds.

I moved away from the *Compendium maleficarum* and its companions, walked right to the end of the room, and looked up. On the shelf above my head I saw Bewick's *A History of British Birds* beside nine volumes of *American Ornithology* and felt this would be a more calming section in which to browse. I stretched up, meaning to take hold of *The Dodo and its Kindred,* but my fumbling fingers caught hold of something else.

It was a small, slim book bound in soft, pinkish skin. There was no lettering on the spine or the cover, and when I opened it, I discovered the heavy rag paper pages were handwritten, in a language I could not read nor even recognise.

Turning a few more pages, I discovered the text was frequently broken up by small, carefully drawn sketches of various plant parts – mostly detailed depictions of roots and seeds. There were also mushrooms, and one picture that took up half a page showed a ring of *Amanita muscaria,* the red caps lurid and bright as drops of fresh blood.

This coincidence – a depiction of what might be the very same Poison Ring I had seen yesterday, in a book picked up by chance in the room where its owner had showed me her own poison ring a few minutes earlier – made my skin crawl, and I quickly closed the book and went up on my tiptoes to replace it.

I had only just done so when the door opened behind me. I turned around, my heart pounding ridiculously fast, as if I had been caught spying.

'Hello again,' said the smiling girl. As before, she was dressed in black, but today the sombre impression was undercut by a coral necklace, even redder than her full lips. She looked both younger and more beautiful than I had recalled, and for a moment I was uncertain which of the sisters she was.

'Miss Alys?'

She pouted at the implied question. 'Who else? Surely you did not mistake me for that baby Ann? Two years younger and one whole inch shorter than me. And she has a crooked tooth – although you only see it when she laughs – and lacks my beauty mark.' She touched the little brown mole beneath her mouth.

'I do beg your pardon – why, I see now you are so distinctly different in appearance, one would never dream you were sisters,' I said dryly, and she giggled. 'But I had hoped to speak with Ann as well.'

'Ann is not well,' she replied. 'She is grieving, of course. I am sure you will forgive her reluctance to speak with a stranger about the man who was all in all to her.'

I could not get the measure of her; was she mocking me, or her sister, or was her arch manner a reflection of her own discomfort? I spoke cautiously, feeling my way: 'I understand. Naturally, his death was a shock. I am very grateful to you for agreeing to speak to me, as I know Mr Alexander Manning will be, when I am able to share your recollections with him.'

She gave a careless shrug and plopped down on the nearest sofa, then patted the seat. 'Come, let us be friends. Standing here reminds me too much of being called in for a scolding – or worse – from Mr Peacock.'

'Your father.'

'Please do not remind me.'

I sat beside her. 'Well, I had much rather hear about Charles Manning. Did you know him well? What was your impression of him?'

'He was all right, I suppose. If that sounds half-hearted, I am sorry, but after all, *I* was never in love with him.' She smiled provocatively. 'That should mean I saw him more clearly, although my sisters may disagree.'

Did she mean to imply that both her sisters had been in love with Charles Manning? I held my tongue, hoping she would reveal more if I let her rattle on.

She gave a thoughtful sigh. 'Portrait of a young man. Hmm. Well, you know what he looked like, so I shall not dwell on his outward appearance. Inwardly, he seemed gentle, intelligent, well-read, well-spoken, interested in all sorts of curious and occult matters – like his good friend Mr Ott – so naturally Bella found him agreeable. And he treated Ann like a proper grown-up young lady, always complimented her on something or other, asked her opinion on little things – since she had nothing to say on great matters – and when she spoke, he stared into her eyes as if she were the most fascinating creature on two legs – pardon my English!' She laughed at her own joke. 'And then he started bringing her little presents – flowers and sweets – and it began to seem that he was coming to Wayside Cross just to see *her*. Ann never had a suitor before, she took it very seriously; of course she was positively *bouleversée* by what happened; she really thought they would be married, and now, now she groans and cries and thinks there will never be anyone else who wants to marry her in her whole life. What rubbish! I can't see why she'd want to get married anyway. *I* don't.'

'You think he was only being kind, that he was not serious in his intentions?'

She frowned. 'Oh, no he wanted to marry her, all right. Went down on bended knee before her. She still wears his ring – only a frippery little thing, but the meaning could not be plainer: two hands clasping a heart.'

'So they were engaged to be married.'

'Not *really*. Bella wouldn't have it. She said Ann was too young and Charles could not afford a wife – and she was quite right. He had no job, no position except as an unpaid associate of Mr Ott, and any money he managed to make went to that silly School.'

'But was Charles counting on an inheritance? Perhaps, if his brother had known he wished to marry, he would have been more generous?'

'No. He told – he told *Ann* there was no money, nothing but the house in London, and if he took her there as his wife, as he meant to do, they would have to share with his brother.'

'How did Ann feel about that?'

She gave a gusty sigh. 'Oh, what does it matter how she felt? It was nothing but a dream. It was never to happen. It was all romancing, castles in the air. Ann is still a child. She gets her ideas about love from books and plays. She liked having a lover and talking about marriage, but we are her family and this is her home, and she is far from ready to leave it.'

'How old is your sister?'

'Ann turned sixteen in October.'

'When did she meet Charles Manning?'

'Why, the same day we all did – it was sometime towards the end of June. Mr Ott brought him here and introduced him.'

'Mr Ott is a good friend of Miss Bulstrode, I think?'

She smiled slyly. 'You had better ask *Miss Bulstrode* about that.'

'He comes here often?'

'Oh, yes.' Then she stopped and considered my question. 'That is, he used to. Now you mention it, I have not seen Mr Ott since the summer.'

'Since Mr Manning was introduced?'

'Oh, no, much later than that. They both visited us all through the summer. But, let me think.' She cocked her head thoughtfully. 'Why, Mr Ott has not called upon us since early September. And how strange it is that he has not made a condolence call.' She gasped. 'Is it possible he does not know that Charles—?'

'He knows,' I said. 'He read about Mr Manning's death in a London newspaper.' Seizing the opportunity, I asked, 'And how did you hear about it?'

Her eyes widened. 'Me? Well, I suppose . . . Why, from Bella.'

'You do not subscribe to a London paper?'

'No.'

'So how did she learn it?'

'I did not enquire. Someone told her. What does it matter?' She stared at me suspiciously.

'Forgive me. I did not mean to offend.'

'You are very inquisitive,' she said coldly.

'It is my nature to be so, I fear. Mr Jesperson and I brought

157

the news to the Vicarage. Until we arrived, the Ringers had no idea that their lodger would never return. So I had steeled myself to be the bearer of sad tidings here, too, only to find you all in mourning already.'

'I am sure we are all very sorry to have disappointed your expectations,' said Miss Alys icily, and stood up, indicating clearly that our interview was at an end.

'I do beg your pardon. I only meant to explain how the question rose in my mind.'

'It is of no importance.'

'No,' I agreed, as false as she. 'It is of no importance whatsoever.'

This time I walked back to the Vicarage from Wayside Cross with no sense that I was being followed or spied upon. Arriving, I encountered Mrs Ringer.

'Oh, Miss Lane,' she said. 'Mr Jesperson has left you a note.'

She handed me a paper, which had been folded over and edges glued shut.

'Come into the parlour – you may use my paper-knife, and read your letter in comfort by the fire,' she said kindly, and although I did not relish another cosy *tête-à-tête* with her, I followed her instructions. The paper-knife was a necessity.

The 'letter' did not take long to peruse, consisting as it did of only two lines:

What colour was the baby's blanket?
Meet me for dinner, Chapman's Inn, Cromer, 1 p.m.

'You will be happy to learn that Maria is much recovered,' said Mrs Ringer as she picked up her knitting. 'So much recovered, that, rather than rest in bed all day, she is now sitting up in the kitchen, helping Cook with a few small tasks. Her strength will not be overtaxed, and she will have someone to keep an eye on her, as doctor ordered.'

'That sounds reasonable,' I said cautiously. 'And what of her future?'

'Why, she will stay on here, working for us. You did not imagine we would turn her out?'

This was exactly what I had feared, but I did not like to say so.

'Maria is not a *bad* girl – only unfortunate. She cannot be blamed for what happened, except as her own innocent ignorance may have contributed. Naturally, it would have been better if she had confided in us, but there is no point in crying over spilt milk. We cannot change what is past.' Mrs Ringer spoke placidly as her fingers worked and the needles clicked. She was making something green – perhaps a scarf, perhaps part of something bigger. I thought of Mr Jesperson's question. No one would have made a blanket for Maria's baby, and yet she must have wrapped it in something.

'And what about the baby?'

'There is no baby.' The needles never faltered.

'There is,' I said stubbornly. 'There is a missing baby.'

'That is not your problem.'

'I beg your pardon, but it must be someone's. I do not think it fair to leave Maria alone to bear the burden. I would like to help her if I can.'

'If you would like to help Maria, you would do better to forget she ever had a baby. Surely you must see that she is better off without the burden of an illegitimate child. And it would in no way help her to find its tiny corpse in a ditch or hedgerow.'

'So you believe she killed her baby?'

She stopped knitting. 'I said no such thing.'

'You do not say it in so many words, but in every other way you imply it,' I replied. 'I do not believe that Maria has committed any crime – and yet a crime has been committed. Someone stole that baby away, and it may not be too late to save it. I am determined to find out the truth.'

'Well, now you are honest. You do not wish to help Maria, as I do, but only to satisfy your own curiosity. You are as foolish and as arrogant as that young man who is your travelling companion; you are self-centred and dangerously wilful in your determination to find what you call "the truth". Curiosity killed the cat, Miss Lane. *Some questions should not be asked.*'

On that final, warning note, she stood and swept out of the room, leaving me staring at her abandoned piece of knitting, still too small to make a blanket for anything bigger than a mouse.

'Curiosity killed the cat.' How often had I heard that? And 'Some questions should not be asked.' That might apply in polite society, but was not that why polite society was so stuffy and stultified? Human beings could not grow, nor society advance, without asking questions. Only, when choosing facts over belief, and asking questions, one must be prepared for uncomfortable answers. It was certainly possible that Maria would not like, nor be helped by, whatever we found, but I would not, could not, turn away from this problem out of fear or pity for her situation. If the baby was alive, we must find it. If the baby was dead – I still wanted to know that, and to learn how it had met its end, and while I would do whatever I could to see she was not unjustly punished, I thought Maria deserved to know the truth.

I got up and went to the kitchen where I found Maria all alone, sitting and peeling a pile of potatoes. I wondered what had become of Cook – I could only pray that Mr Jesperson had not offended her in some way with his questions and caused her to leave, for I guessed the Ringers would far more easily forgive him the loss of a bicycle than the loss of their cherished Cook.

'Hello, Maria,' I said. 'Do you remember me? I am Miss Lane. Do not get up – I only want to ask you a few questions.'

I pulled out a chair and sat down beside her.

'What sort o' questions?'

I looked into her worried grey eyes, and felt a pang of remorse. What if I was wrong and the doctor was right, and she had killed her baby in a moment of despairing madness? But I took a deep breath and forced myself to go on. 'I should like to help find your baby.'

'Oh, Miss, if you could! Doctor told me not to think about it anymore, and then Mrs Ringer, she said the same – she said we should forget all about it, and carry on as before, only . . . I can't forget, and I don't want to forget, my little Annie.'

'You called her Annie?'

''Twas my mother's name.' Worry constricted her small

161

features. 'But . . . she wasn't baptised. There wasn't time for that! I called her Annie to myself and to Billy, but there was nobody else I could tell. I should've told the Reverend, shouldn't I, and asked him to baptise her? I was so afraid they'd turn me out, if they knew, and I'd nowhere to go – except to my sister's, and I couldn't go back there.' A sob welled up and choked her off.

'Did your sister know – about Annie?'

'No, Miss, I told you – *I* didn't even know, before . . . didn't know until . . . I thought I was dying, the pain was so bad – but then it was all over, and it was like a miracle, my own little baby girl!' From tears to sunshine, her face wreathed in smiles, recalling that happy moment when she found herself no longer alone in the world, the mother of a baby girl. Looking at her, listening to her, I felt entirely certain that she could have done nothing to harm her child.

'Did you have a blanket for your baby?'

'I wrapped her in my shawl – the good, blue woollen shawl Mrs Ringer made for me last Christmas.'

'Light-blue or dark-blue?'

'Sky-blue – beautiful.' She sighed. 'Nicest thing I ever had.' She bit her lip. 'I didn't have no clothes for her. So I just wrapped her in the shawl.'

'Now, you say you did not know you were expecting a baby, and you did not speak to anyone about her, but – perhaps you wrote to your sister, after the baby was born? Or to someone else?'

'No, Miss, how could I? I cannot write.'

'And you're quite certain that you told no one else?'

'No one. I told no one. But someone saw.'

'Someone besides Billy?'

'Someone else must have seen. You know they say: They see you, but you don't see them. It was them took her. Oh, why didn't I tell the Reverend? They couldn't have took her if she was baptised, could they?'

As she spoke, I felt a crawling sensation on the back of my neck, as when the crow had followed me unseen, and I entertained an unwelcome recollection of the old German woodcut that illustrated the uses witches made of babies.

'Maria, what are you talking about? Who saw? Do you have any idea of who could have taken your baby?'

Her eyes darted nervously around the room. 'Mustn't say,' she muttered.

'But you think you know?'

She gave the tiniest of nods.

'Won't you tell me? Please – I want to help.'

Head down, she spoke to the table: 'Them.'

'Who?'

Her eyes flashed up to mine. '*You* know.' But she must have seen from my look that I did not, for finally she whispered a brief phrase, so low that I caught only the last word: 'neighbours.'

Before I could confirm it or ask anything more, the kitchen door banged open, and there stood Mrs Ringer, staring at me in forbidden conversation with her servant.

I stood up quickly, knowing from her grim expression that nothing I could say would made any difference.

'Miss Lane, you have been a guest in my house, but you have not had the decency to abide by my clearly stated wishes. I must ask you to leave.'

'Very well.' I walked past her, out of the kitchen, and she followed close behind. 'Please pack your things. When you have done, Billy will drive you to the station.'

I was startled and, I admit, a trifle flustered by the suddenness of my eviction. 'Could I not wait until—?'

'Not another hour. It is in your own best interests – at this time of day, you should have no problem getting a train – or, if you prefer, a hotel room in Cromer.'

'What about Mr Jesperson?'

'What of him?'

'Are you evicting him, too?'

'What business is that of yours?' She frowned even more darkly. 'I may make my own decisions about whom to admit to my house. That man is no relation of yours, and therefore—'

'We have a *business* relationship, as we told you the evening we arrived.'

'Oh, yes, your *publishing* business,' she said with a sneer that made it clear she did not believe in it. I wished for a moment that her husband might have shared the truth with her, but probably that would have made no difference; indeed, she might have been even more suspicious of a woman who admitted to making her career out of being curious, and asking questions that should not be asked.

164

CHAPTER THIRTEEN

A Fish Dinner in Cromer

The carriage was waiting in front of the house by the time I came back downstairs with my valise; Mrs Ringer had no intention of allowing me any more time for questions. This was fine with me, as I had no wish to linger, and appreciated the luxury of such easy transport to Cromer, where I would be able to meet Mr Jesperson for a meal, but it was rather annoying to be banished from Aylmerton just when I finally had what might be a clue to the fate of Maria's baby.

Maria thought the neighbours had taken her. She might well be mistaken, but presumably had some reason for her suspicion. The Vicarage was in a rather isolated spot; the only 'neighbours' worthy of the name were the inhabitants of the nearest house, Wayside Cross.

Three unmarried, childless women lived there, and were gossiped about as witches. Miss Bulstrode did not even deny that label – and although I could not connect her civilised, sensitive intelligence with the horrific imagery of babies boiled in cauldrons, such things had been a matter of folk-belief for centuries and, as Mr Jesperson had said, when something was believed to be true, someone was bound to attempt to do it. Maria's whispered words might have been nothing more than a reflection of those nightmare fears, roused by her loss, but it would be remiss of me not to investigate.

No smoke without fire, I thought before I could help myself, and then I winced, because it seemed like something Mrs Ringer would say.

Billy hopped down from the driver's seat to take my valise. 'Mrs Ringer says I am to take you to Cromer Station. You are leaving us?'

'I am leaving the Vicarage, but not Norfolk,' I said. 'Do you know Chambers' Inn?'

'Yes, Miss. Will I take you there?'

I hesitated barely a moment. 'Not straight away. First, I must speak with someone at Wayside Cross. I would very much appreciate it if you could take me to that house first, wait for me there, and then take me on to Cromer.'

'Right-o, Miss,' he said cheerfully, and leaped up to the driver's seat.

We were there in a twinkling. The maid who answered the door was surprised to see me. 'You are back quick, Miss Lane.'

'I know I am, Nancy, and I know your mistress is busy, but please could you tell her I promise not to detain her more than a minute or two, if she will see me now.'

She gave me a searching look. 'Best come along with me

now, and save time,' she said. 'This way – Miss Bulstrode is tending her plants.'

I followed Nancy through the house to the kitchen, and out the back door, then along a path lined with rhododendrons to the glasshouse, where she stopped and stepped back.

'Just you go in,' she said, making a gesture to encourage me to open the door, and so I did.

It was like walking into summer. In marked contrast to the chilly November air outside, within the glasshouse the atmosphere was moist and humid and heavily scented, redolent of tropical perfumes and rot. Everywhere there was green and brown, with occasional flashes of brighter colours, red or pink or yellow, where flowers and fruit bloomed out of season.

'Hello? Who is there?'

I walked towards Miss Bulstrode's voice, and there she was, a canvas apron covering her dress, and her hands deep in soil as she repotted a plant. 'Why, Miss Lane; I did not expect to see you again so soon.'

'Forgive me; I must apologise for disturbing you,' I said, already breathless in the clinging heat.

'Not at all. Perhaps you'd like to take off your coat? If you will give me a few moments to bed this little darling down, I shall be happy to give you a guided tour. My sisters will tell you, I love any chance to show off my beauties.'

'That is very kind, but I really cannot stop for long – I am on my way to Cromer – but I wanted to ask you – that is, I mean, I wanted to tell you that I am no longer resident at the

Vicarage. In case you wanted to get in touch with me. I seem to have managed to offend Mrs Ringer, and she has thrown me out.'

Her mouth dropped open a little. 'You do not mean it?'

'I am afraid so. She was kind enough to lend me her carriage as far as Cromer Station, so eager is she to be rid of me.'

'So you are going home to London?'

I took a deep breath – it was a struggle to fill my lungs – and wiped the moisture from my brow. 'Not yet. I thought I might find a room to rent in Cromer – perhaps you could suggest a suitable inn, respectable, but not too expensive?' I hoped she would attribute the blush in my cheeks to the heat.

'Suggest? Oh, Miss Lane, you must stay *here,* of course.'

'Oh, I could not possibly impose—'

'It is no imposition – believe me. Rather, it would be my great pleasure to have you stay as our guest. We have a very comfortable guest bedroom – it is yours for as long as you like.'

'Are you sure? That is most kind. I never expected . . . I would hate to be a bother. Believe me, it would only be for a few days . . . Perhaps you would let me pay you something towards my board?'

'Do not even think of it,' she said firmly. 'It is no hardship, and I am certain my sisters, especially, will enjoy hearing some news from London. I never care to travel, but they have not been anywhere in months and they find life in this small village rather dull sometimes.'

'Thank you,' I said again, feeling very mixed emotions. I was pleased to have achieved my aim so easily, mortified at the necessity of deceiving – and suspecting – such a friendly lady. 'If there is any way I can repay your kindness . . .'

'You will have to tell us what you did to offend the vicar's wife.' She smiled, and a malicious sparkle lit her eyes.

'Perhaps later,' I said uneasily.

'Oh, yes, at supper tonight, when we're all together. Or will you stay for dinner? I had better ask Elsie what she has planned, but there should be enough for one more—'

'No, no I have a meeting in Cromer at one o'clock,' I said, cutting her off in some desperation. 'The carriage is waiting for me outside.'

'Of course. Please, consider our house your home. You may come and go as you please – if you will be out late, let me know and I shall lend you my key. I hope you will be able to join us this evening; we usually have a light repast at sometime between seven and eight, but if that does not suit—'

'That will suit me very well; thank you.' I began edging towards the door.

'But what about your bags?' She looked at my empty hands.

'Only one – it is outside, in the carriage.'

'Well, bring it in – Nancy will show you to your room, and you can freshen up before you go, if you like. You are looking quite flushed. It is the heat, of course, that you are not used to.'

I fetched my bag from the carriage and asked Billy if he minded waiting another half an hour for me. I was glad when he said he did not, for there seemed to me no benefit in arriving to meet Mr Jesperson much before his stipulated one o'clock. It was agreeable to be able to take the opportunity Miss Bulstrode had suggested, to 'freshen up', before I left.

'Do you mind if I ride beside you?' I asked Billy when I returned.

He looked a bit taken aback. 'You will be warmer inside, Miss.'

'I do not mind the cold,' I lied, hoping I would not give myself away by shivering too obviously. I did not wish to pass up what might be my last opportunity to question the stable boy.

'What do you know about the ladies at Wayside Cross?' I asked as we started off.

'I know that Mr Manning meant to marry one of 'em.'

'And how do you know that?'

'Because he told me.' He grinned at the memory. 'It was when I dropped him off in Cromer. He said he expected to be married and living at Wayside Cross by Christmas, with any luck, and then he gave me a nice tip.' The smile dropped off his face. 'That was the last time I ever saw him. How sad, for such a kind young gentleman to die so sudden.'

'Do you remember his exact words?'

'Near enough what I just said.'

I looked at the woods, pushing my chin down into the warmth of my scarf. 'Where did you let him off? At the station, I suppose. Did he say where he was going?'

'No, Miss. At first, he said he wanted the station – but when we arrived, he remembered something else he needed to do, and told me to drive on. But then, we met a wagon unloading kegs of beer – the streets are so narrow, further in, that I had to stop; there was no way around it; and he got impatient, and hopped out, said he'd make his own way. He wasn't cross, though; he was always nice and friendly to me; he laughed and made a joke of it; said that when people said something was worth waiting for, he reckoned it was even more worth *not* waiting, if you could find a way of getting there quicker.'

I rubbed my cold nose. 'Apart from Mr Manning's engagement, do you know anything more about the ladies at Wayside Cross?'

'I don't know anything about them, Miss.'

'But have you heard people talk about them? Do people say they are witches?'

Looking uncomfortable, Billy avoided my eye, and fiddled unnecessarily with the reins. 'People say all sorts of foolish things.' He sighed. 'Their mother was a wise woman, and so is Miss Bulstrode, that is well known. But it is women's business, that, and not for me.'

There was something so final in that remark that I knew I should get nothing more from him on this subject. Out of idle curiosity, then, I asked, 'And what about men's business? If men can't ask a wise woman for help, what do they do?'

He perked up a little. 'Men have different sorts of problems; stands to reason we would need to see another man, don't it? There is a cunning man in Cromer, I have heard. He can take spells off of people, and tell you what's to come in the future. Once he even found some buried treasure, or so they say.'

By the time he had finished elaborating on the abilities of this unnamed wonder, we had reached Cromer, and all Billy's attention was required to navigate amidst the traffic.

'There, that's Chapman's Inn, just down there,' he said, pointing. 'Oh, and look – is that not Mr Jesperson? Why, there's luck for you!'

'Luck, indeed,' I said, and quickly scrambled down. 'Thank you, Billy. You'd best be off home now.'

I met Mr Jesperson in front of the inn. He looked past me at the departing carriage. 'Well, you have come in style! How did you manage to get the use of the Ringers' carriage, when I was not even offered a second chance at the Reverend's bicycle?'

I sniffed. 'Mrs Ringer told me to pack my things and get out; Billy was supposed to get me to Cromer Station in good time to make the last connection to London.'

He began to laugh. 'What have you done to offend that good lady?'

'I questioned Maria, against her express orders.'

He pressed a hand to his breast. 'On my instructions. So it was my fault.'

I protested. 'I should have wished to speak to her again in any case. No one tells me there are questions that should not be asked.'

Biting his lip to repress more laughter, he said, 'Come along inside. We may continue our conversation over dinner. And I suppose you will wish to take a room here . . .' He frowned. 'But where is your bag? Not held hostage by Mrs Ringer, I trust.'

I smiled sweetly. 'I left it in the guest room at Wayside Cross.'

'Oh, well done!' He clapped my shoulder briefly. 'The Vicarage is about exhausted as a source of information, I am sure you agree; and you will learn much more about Manning – and Cooke, too – from the Misses Bulstrode.'

We went inside. The waiter spotted us instantly, was effusive in his welcome and hurried to find us a table with a good seaside view, his delight easily explained by the sparsely populated dining room. November is not a very profitable month for businesses in English seaside resorts.

'What do you recommend?' Mr Jesperson asked the waiter when we were seated.

'The fish is always good, and today—'

'Then we shall have fish. I am sure we may leave the manner of its preparation to your chef. Bring us a good meal, and a decent bottle of white wine, and do not disturb our conversation any more than necessary, there's a good fellow.'

'Very good, sir.'

Mr Jesperson turned his alert, inquisitive gaze on me. 'You know the colour of the blanket?'

'Blue – sky blue. Not a blanket, but Maria's own shawl.'

'Of course,' he said softly. 'No blanket, no garments for her little stranger. She had to make do.'

'Why did you wish to know the colour?'

'I found something this morning – it may have been nothing, but I thought otherwise. What you report encourages me in that belief.' He reached into a pocket and brought out a folded handkerchief, inside which was a tiny scrap of sky-blue wool.

I gasped. 'Where did you find it?'

'In the field opposite the Vicarage – in the shrieking pit – caught on a briar.'

A young girl brought a basket of bread to our table and marched away.

'In the shrieking pit,' I repeated blankly. 'But last night you looked—'

'I missed it last night,' he said, sounding cross with himself.

'Such a small thing – it is not surprising. I am sure most people would not have noticed it even in daylight. But why did you go back?'

Before he could reply, the wine waiter appeared, and the bottle must be opened, wine poured, tasted and approved of by Mr Jesperson. When at last the waiter withdrew, my friend held up his glass and gazed at it, saying, 'I found that the stone had been replaced.'

'What stone?'

He set down his glass, frowning. 'Surely you recall the slab that I removed from the ground yesterday?'

I recalled it, and remembered turning back to see the uncovered hole gaping like a mouth, before we left the field. 'This was last night?'

'No. Last night I could still see the opening – I shone my light into it. But when I went to look this morning, it was covered again.'

'Then most likely it was replaced by the landowner. After all, it must have been covered for a reason.'

'Oh, undoubtedly there was a reason.'

Our first course arrived: bowls of beef consommé. Looking down at the circle of murky brown liquid, I thought of the hole in the field, imagining the threatening darkness of it under the moon. It was big enough to take the body of a baby. But if anyone had put it there last night, Mr Jesperson could not have failed to find it. I imagined a cloaked, hooded figure with a baby in its arms, scuttling down the sloped side of the shrieking pit to hide there for a few minutes, alerted by the sound of Maria's screams. Once the coast was clear, it could have scrambled out again and crossed the field, staying away from the road, and never noticing that a tiny scrap of wool had been snagged on a briar in passing.

'Aren't you hungry?' asked Mr Jesperson.

With a little start, I returned to the present, and picked up my spoon. Alas, the consommé tasted more of pepper, salt and flour than of beef. 'Not up to the standards of the Vicarage,' I said. 'Which reminds me – what of your interview with Cook?'

'Disappointing. She said she thought Maria had been putting on weight, but ascribed it to her "washing the plates with her tongue" every time she cleared the table. She was surprised to learn Maria ever had a baby, but her best suggestion regarding its disappearance was that it was carried off by a stray dog, or possibly a fox.'

The thought made me feel rather ill – or perhaps it was the

pepper in the soup. I put my spoon down. 'Would a fox – *could* a fox or a dog – do such a thing?'

'It seems unlikely. Especially since it was carried off *in* the shawl, leaving no trace behind. Unfortunately, I cannot think of any answer to this peculiar affair that could be described as a reasonable suggestion. Perhaps we should move on to discuss the case of Charles Manning, which is, after all, why we came to Norfolk.'

I pushed my soup bowl to one side. 'My reason for wanting to stay at Wayside Cross has more to do with Maria – she suspects someone in that house of taking her child.'

He frowned. 'Why?'

'There was no time for her to explain, and she was too frightened to say their names aloud, but it was clear who she meant. Of course, it may be nothing, but once you begin to ask *why* anyone would steal a baby—'

'Then the old calumnies are recalled,' he said briskly. 'Babies sacrificed to the devil, or boiled up to make magical ointments. That Felix Ott, of all people, should resurrect those lies – and yet it appears that Miss Flowerdew was correct in her assertions.

'I have spoken to two others, both followers of Mr Ott's, who confirmed that in his late September lecture in Cromer – but at no other time or place – he warned against "Satanic witches" – making a distinction with the "wise women" who were *good* witches – and darkly intimated that there were some people alive in England today who did the very things that the Church accused witches of in the past.'

'How did you find these witnesses?' I asked.

'Surely you remember the names in Manning's address book? Miss V. Goodall and Mr Simon Crisp, local residents.'

The girl arrived to take our soup bowls away, but hesitated over mine, which indeed I had scarcely touched. 'Shall I leave it, Miss?'

'No, take it away,' I said emphatically.

When she had gone, Mr Jesperson continued his tale.

'Miss Goodall is unquestioningly devoted to Mr Ott and could not entertain the thought that he could ever be mistaken in anything. Since his warning against the wrong sort of witches she has been on her guard. I had the impression that, with only a little more encouragement, she could have given me the names and addresses of suspicious, witch-like characters in the area.

'Mr Crisp, on the other hand, found those remarks quite out of character. He felt there was something vindictive in them, that they were not to be taken at face value, but were aimed at someone in particular – possibly Manning.'

I furrowed my brow. 'Manning? Why?'

'I only repeat his impression. He said that afterwards, when time was allowed for questions, Manning tried to argue that the Church had invented the notion of Satanic witches, and that they had not existed in the past, and certainly not now, but Ott cut him off. Later, Crisp says, he saw the two men in heated argument – the only time he had ever seen them disagree. But they must have made up their quarrel, for by the following week the two were again as thick as thieves, and witchcraft was never again represented in anything but an entirely benign and positive way, as part of the ancient British wisdom promoted by the School. Crisp wondered if Ott's slanders against witches were never meant to be taken seriously; if they had been a tease, or possibly some sort of test, aimed at Manning.'

The waiter arrived at that moment bearing two plates of beautifully golden, crisp, steaming hot fried fish and potatoes, and for the next few minutes everything else was forgotten. It tasted even more delicious than it looked. This was food on another level entirely from the so-called beef consommé; the fish was perfectly cooked, the batter light and crispy, a glorious mixture of soft and crunchy, smooth and salty. Mr Jesperson topped up our glasses with the mellow wine, and we sipped and munched away in contented silence.

At last, he enquired about my conversations at Wayside Cross.

'The two maids there are acquainted with Maria, but had no notion of her situation. Miss Bulstrode said she had never met her.'

He raised an eyebrow. 'Is that a note of suspicion I hear?'

I thought I had spoken neutrally, and said only, 'I reserve judgement.'

'So you do not think the sisters are in reality a coven of demonic, baby-stealing cannibals?'

It sounded quite absurd, and yet . . . 'Of course not. But Miss Bulstrode admits she is known as a witch, there is a baby missing, and of course there is a long tradition connecting witches to such vile activities.'

'There is a long tradition of ascribing the worst imaginable atrocities to one's enemies in order to justify one's own dreadful deeds. Thus, the Church justified torture and violence against women and men they claimed were guilty of performing even more hideous and depraved acts. Strange, is it not, that the accused witches were never able to call upon their supposed powers to save themselves.' He stabbed a piece of fried potato with his fork. 'Ott was playing with fire when he suggested there might be baby-murdering Satanists at large in the countryside. Rousing old fears is far easier than putting them to rest; it would not be difficult to resurrect the age of the witch-hunt.'

I said, 'I do not know which would be worse – if Ott truly believes in those evil creatures, or if he only said it out of mischief. And why should Manning have taken it so personally?'

'I wondered that myself. Could it be Ott was driven by jealousy? If both men were courting Miss Bulstrode – and if Manning had managed to become engaged to marry her—'

I hastened to correct this idea. 'It was not Miss Bulstrode he meant to marry.'

'No? You seemed certain of it before.'

'Perhaps his first interest was in Miss Bulstrode, but when she made it clear she had no intention of ever abandoning her single state, he became engaged to Miss Ann – the youngest of the three. At least, if it was not a formally acknowledged engagement, it was understood between the two of them. Miss Bulstrode said they must wait until Ann was older and Mr Manning could afford to support a family. It is possible, of course, that her objections to their marriage were tinged with jealousy, for she told me she had recently turned down a proposal. And I must say, I sensed she may regret it – certainly, she still has strong feelings for her suitor.'

'Charles Manning?'

'Who else? And to see him find solace, so swiftly, in her sister . . .'

'Such inconstancy is brutal,' he mused. 'It might make her wonder if he had ever truly loved her.'

'Billy told me that Mr Manning boasted to him that he would be married and living at Wayside Cross by Christmas.' Something about that boast still jarred, and now I knew why. 'Do you not think that a man in love would speak of his lover? Would say, "I shall be married to Ann Bulstrode", rather than name her house?'

He met my eyes, and once again I felt that little spark of connection, of shared intellectual excitement, that was a feature of our relationship. 'I do,' he said quietly. 'He gives himself away in his words, speaking only of what he considers important and wasting no breath on anything else.'

Leaning back in his seat, he said, 'In whose interest would it be to scotch his plans? Was the action inspired by jealousy, or something else? Was Cooke's death really an accident? I wonder . . . Perhaps the real target all along has been Felix Ott and his School of British Wisdom.'

CHAPTER FOURTEEN

The Cunning Man

The sweet course consisted of treacle tart with heavy cream. I found it excessively sweet, but it seemed to please Mr Jesperson, and he consumed every scrap, telling me, between mouthfuls, what he planned for the afternoon.

'A visit to Cunning Verrell is the next thing,' he said. 'Although he did not mention him to me, I have discovered from my other informants that Felix Ott considers him someone of great importance, and has been trying to engage him in the development of his School.'

I smiled. 'People do have the most original names in Norfolk, do they not?'

'Possibly so. However, in this case, Cunning is not his Christian name, but a title, like Doctor or Professor. The cunning man is the male equivalent of the wise woman – but never call him a witch, for one of his most vaunted powers is the ability to discover, trap and destroy evil witches.'

'Ah, I wonder if it was he that Billy meant when he spoke of the male counterpart of the wise woman. And if he is actively opposed to witches, I suppose he is no friend to Miss Bulstrode.'

'Correct. He claims to be unable to set foot in Wayside Cross, which is rather a hardship for him, because there is something in that house that he considers his rightful property. He must therefore use go-betweens, and this has become a bargaining chip with Ott, who thinks he might name his price, if only he can find the book.'

'What book?'

'It is supposed to be an ancient grimoire – something Ott naturally feels would be of great importance as an addition to his knowledge, although as it is apparently written in some unknown and so far undecipherable language, it may be of more symbolic than practical use. Verrell was unable to make any better use of it than to sell it; now, knowing how keen Ott is to have it, he declares that it is still rightfully his own – that he never meant to sell, but only to *lend* it to old Admiral Bulstrode in the expectation that that learned and much-travelled gentleman would be able to decipher it for him. But the Admiral was unable to oblige – the thing is either in code, or written in a language he has never encountered anywhere else in the world. The cunning man admits he was paid a goodly sum for the thing, but insists it was always understood between the two of them to be a loan – the Admiral, of course, is no longer here to confirm or deny.'

'Is this a handwritten book?' I asked.

'Yes.'

'Illustrated?' At his nod I continued: 'A small book bound in soft skin, without a title or anything else on the spine or the cover?'

Eyes wide, he put down his fork. 'Are you speaking of a book you have seen?'

'I found it quite by chance tucked between two books on ornithology. I was actually meaning to pull down one of the others, but suddenly found myself with this odd little volume in my hand. I could not read a word of it, but there were pictures – one looked just like the *Amanita muscaria* fairy ring in the woods near here, which made for a rather spooky coincidence.'

'Amazing,' he said. 'You found it, and in a way that fits the prophecy – well, the first half, anyway.'

'What prophecy?'

He ate the last bite of his dessert before replying. 'According to Simon Crisp, who had it directly from the mouth of Felix Ott, there is an ancient prophecy about this book – which Ott described in typically grandiose fashion as one of the lost sacred books of England (I do wonder about the others). The prophecy is only a bit of doggerel which Ott probably made up on the spot: it claims that this book would be found, when the time was right, by one who searched without knowing that they were searching, and the finder would be one who had need of it, again, unknowing, not for himself, but to redeem something else that had been stolen, referred to as The Book of Life.'

'Well done me,' I said sarcastically. 'Do you suppose I would be able to put my hand upon it again, if I went looking for it, this time *knowing* what I am looking for? Or will it have magically relocated to another shelf?'

The waiter came to ask if we wanted anything more. Mr Jefferson gave me an enquiring look. 'Coffee?'

'Yes, a cup of coffee would be very nice,' I agreed. When the waiter had gone away again, I reverted to the subject of the missing book. 'Is there *really* a prophecy? Because if Mr Ott made it up, he is a fool, to deny himself any prospect of finding the book he wants so badly. And if the prophecy existed, and he believes it, then he should have known from the start that his search would be hopeless. And by telling followers like Mr Crisp, does he not realise he has made it likewise impossible for them? They can never find the book so long as they know they are looking for it. He may as well give up.'

Mr Jesperson looked as if he were enjoying my little rant, and I was encouraged to go on.

'Does he believe the things he preaches?' I felt a burst of distaste for this man I had never met, this self-styled preacher who would promote witchcraft as a religion one day and denounce witches as demons the next. 'He must be a complete hypocrite – or very selective in his beliefs, changing as the wind blows.'

'You are a harsh judge, Miss Lane,' he said gently. 'I do not think he is a hypocrite. Deluded, certainly. But the desire to find wisdom and certainty is not to be sneered at. Perhaps he is more a tourist than a genuine explorer, one who picks up gaudy souvenirs and takes trash for treasure. He has no reliable guide. As to the prophecy, he says it came to him in a vision, and he is most interested in the second part, which he interprets as referring to the old religion of these islands – the precious thing that has been lost – The Book of Life which will allow us to understand the journey we are on. Thus, in his interpretation, the book that Cunning Verrell sold to Admiral Bulstrode, when it has been found and reclaimed, will offer a first step towards rescuing the great lost religion of the British Isles, returning it to the people whose birthright it should have been. It is they, us, the people, who do not know what we have lost, nor why we are all searching – and it is he, Felix Ott, who believes he can give us what we need.'

Cunning Verrell lived in one of the narrow houses that lined a mean, sloping street with a stink of drains about it. The buildings there were packed so closely together that the sea breeze that lightened the atmosphere everywhere else in the town was kept out, and the laundry displayed from upper windows hung limp and dispirited in the damp, chilly air.

Although his address was not recorded in Charles Manning's address book, Mr Jesperson told me that amongst the dead man's papers were directions to the cunning man's house.

'But there were no questions, and no notes about their conversation, which inclines me to believe that Manning went there for an entirely personal reason,' he explained, keeping his voice low as we picked our way carefully along the rough cobblestones.

'Perhaps he had been feeling unwell,' I suggested. 'He might have felt the first symptoms of the heart trouble that was to kill him.'

Mr Jesperson stopped abruptly to peer at one of the wooden doors, and although I saw no number or anything else to mark this particular hovel out from its neighbours, he rapped his knuckles against the boards.

The man who opened the door to us was old and dressed in clothes that were even older than he. He wore a linen smock of coarse weave, woollen knee-breeches, black stockings and flat felt slippers. His hair, thick and white, fell in heavy waves to his shoulders, but his face was clean-shaven, and apart from the nests of fine lines around his grey-green eyes, the skin was taut and unwrinkled.

'Good day to you, Cunning Verrell. My name is Jasper Jesperson, and this is Miss Lane. If it is not inconvenient, we would like to speak with you.'

'You've come a long way to speak to old Verrell,' said the man. 'London, is it? It must be serious. I won't ask you to spill your business on my doorstep.' He stepped back to allow us entry.

I almost held my breath, expecting the interior to be as noisome as the street, but in fact the room we entered was as neat as a pin and scented with smoke from the resinous logs crackling in the hearth and dried lavender hanging in bunches from the rafters.

Indicating two wooden chairs for us, the old man perched on a three-legged stool and fixed his sharp gaze on me.

'Women don't usually come to me with their troubles,' he said. 'I don't know as I could help you.'

'We are not here about any personal problems,' said Mr

Jesperson. 'I believe you met Charles Manning? We should like to know—'

The old man narrowed his eyes. 'His business with me is his business.'

'So it must die with him?'

The thin, arched brows arched higher. 'Ah! Dead? How?'

'It was very sudden. Heart failure, according to the surgeon.'

'No!' He thrust out his lower lip and shook his head vigorously. 'His heart was sound. And he was a young man, and well – quite well – when I saw him. The eye does not lie.'

'What do you mean by that?'

'I mean what I say. I looked him in the eye, and saw no ailments there. The eye is the key, young man. The eye is the key to the whole. Not all can read it – but I can. I need no book to tell me how to read the eye.'

He looked at me as he finished, and I felt he laid a heavy emphasis on *book,* as if he knew . . . But that was absurd.

'Did Manning come to you about the state of his health?' asked Mr Jesperson.

The old man snorted. 'No. He told me he was very well indeed, no cause for any alarm – but I looked very carefully into his eyes – as I always do, when—' He shut his mouth suddenly, his eyes shifting away.

'What did he come to see you about?'

'His private business.'

'Manning is dead. There can be no objection.'

'I object! Who are you, anyway, to come poking and prying

into another man's affairs?' He glared fiercely, but if he expected Mr Jesperson to flinch or apologise he was sadly mistaken.

'We were present at his death, which was sudden and unexpected. His brother asked us to come to Norfolk, to learn about the final days of his life, and if anything that happened might hold some clue to the reason for his demise.'

This cool explanation had its effect; the suspicion with which the cunning man had regarded us faded away. 'He died in London?'

'He did.'

'Then you should look in London for the cause.'

'Perhaps. But first, we think there is more to be learned from the people he associated with since he came to live in Norfolk.'

'I could tell you how he died if I could see his corpse,' the old man muttered. 'For certain, I could, if I had seen him die.' He frowned, then leaned forward, elbows on his knees, and peered closely at Mr Jesperson. 'You were there. Tell me how it happened – and when.'

'It was nearly two hours past midnight – Saturday night. I opened the door to a furious knocking and a stranger in great distress rushed in. He begged us for help. He believed he was pursued by witches.'

Cunning Verrell exhaled gustily. 'There be witches in London?'

'That is not generally believed to be the case,' my friend responded dryly.

'You think they followed him from Norfolk?'

'I think he was hallucinating, in the grip of some nightmare.

His pupils were dilated, he was perspiring heavily, clearly terrified – but, before he could explain more, he dropped dead. The police surgeon said he died from heart failure, but could not say what caused the heart of this healthy young man to fail.'

'A witch's spell. He said so himself.'

'Who was the witch?'

The cunning man leaned back again. 'Why ask me?'

'I understood that witch-finding was one of your talents. Is that not so?'

'Oh, aye, but hunting a witch takes time and a deal of preparation. If you want me to name the witch who sent death to strike down that young man . . .' Holding up his left hand, he made the familiar sign for money.

'We can pay,' Jesperson said coldly.

'But I do not want your money. There is something else I would have.' He turned his calculating eyes on me as he spoke, and I flinched. 'You have been to Wayside Cross, Miss.'

'How do you know that?'

He cackled. ''Tis my business to know.'

I felt annoyed with myself for letting him surprise me. 'Mr Manning probably told you how often he visited that house.'

'He never told me. No need. I have my ways.' He tapped the side of his nose with a long, knobbly forefinger. 'There is something that belongs to me in that house. I want it back. If you fetch it here to me, I will tell you everything you want to know about the death of that poor young man.'

Mr Jesperson tapped the side of his own nose and spoke in

an imitation of the cunning man's Norfolk drawl: 'It is a book you want, an old book hidden in the library Miss Bulstrode inherited from her grandfather. I have my ways of knowing.' Reverting to his normal voice he asked, 'Why do you say it belongs to you?'

The old man looked nonplussed. 'Why? Because it is mine. I came upon that book nigh on sixty years ago, and it showed me the way I must take in my life. Everything changed in that moment.'

'But you could not read it.'

'True, but I could understand the pictures. And the thing itself was a sign . . . It showed me the path I was destined to follow.'

'Where did you find it?'

'In the ground. Under a rock. I was only a lad, but a strong one, helping a farmer clear his field when I came upon it. I hid it inside my shirt, until I had a chance to look at it better. I thought to sell it, or trade it, but when I saw those drawings of roots and mushrooms and other such things, I knew it was meant for me, if I could puzzle out its meaning. And that was how I began to learn about plants, which ones aid and which things harm . . .' He trailed off and fixed me once again with his gimlet eye. 'I want it back.'

'Go and ask for it,' I said. 'If it really is yours . . .'

'Nay, I cannot go there,' he said. 'But you can.'

'You expect me to steal a book for you?'

'It is not stealing when you return property to its rightful owner.'

'It ceased to be your property when you sold it to Admiral Bulstrode,' Mr Jesperson said firmly, and I nodded my agreement.

'No, that is not so.'

'He bought it from you.'

'No,' the old man repeated stubbornly. 'He gave me money when I needed it, and I gave him the book, but we had an agreement – he was to tell me what the words meant. And he never did. He kept the book to the end of his life and never could tell me what it said. I let him keep it, thinking he might come good some day, but he never did, and so, by all that is fair and right, the book should have come back to me on his death.' He smacked his lips. 'You help me, and I will help you.'

'By giving us the name of someone you say is a witch?' Mr Jesperson shook his head dismissively. 'It was no spell that killed him. Quite possibly he did die of natural causes, as the police surgeon said. He must have been suffering from some complaint when he came to you. What did Manning come to see you about?'

The cunning man cackled. 'His heart, o' course! Yes, he had a complaint . . . An affair of the heart, so some might say, but in truth, it was a different organ that needed my help.' With a swift, sideways look at me, he sobered. 'Let it go. There was nothing wrong with his health – I made certain of that. The poor man's dead now. We won't gossip about his affairs.'

'A love affair? Did he tell you he was engaged to be married?'

'I do not pry,' he said rather prissily. 'I would not expect him to risk a young lady's reputation. All I knew was that he had arranged a *rondayvoo* with this young woman, and he was nervous in case the first time he should disappoint her. He worried that he might not rise to the occasion. He had no experience with the ladies, you see, and although I says to let nature take its course, put two healthy young folk together, all they needs is the opportunity, no special knowledge required, he insisted he could not take the risk. So – I gave him something.'

'What was it?'

'Just the usual. Nothing that would harm a healthy young man.'

'Did he tell you when his amorous meeting was to be – or where?'

'It was soon – I think that very night.'

'He saw you on Saturday morning?'

The cunning man made a gesture of assent.

'Then he must have walked here from the railway station, and gone directly back to catch the train to Norwich,' said Mr Jesperson, and I felt as often before that our thoughts were running along the same course, for I had been remembering my conversation with Billy.

'He did seem in a bit of a hurry,' Cunning Verrell agreed.

'He did not tell you he was going to meet a woman in London?'

'He did not say where he was going. I did not suppose he meant to spend the night at the Vicarage,' he said, with his dirty laugh. Then he slapped his knees and stood up. 'Enough. If you want any more help from me, you know my terms.'

We stepped out of the house and were back in the mean little street. Eager to get to a more salubrious part of town, I hurried away, for once outpacing my friend. We had almost reached the top of the road when he stopped.

'What is it?' I asked.

'Wait.' He turned and galloped back to Cunning Verrell's house and, as I watched in some perplexity, I saw him readmitted.

What could he have forgotten? I wondered and waited and shivered as the air grew chillier and the day darker as clouds gathered and thickened overhead. I could smell rain, or maybe even the prospect of snow, and I wondered how long I must wait. Yet I knew Mr Jesperson must have had his reasons for going back; there might be questions the cunning man would be more likely to answer if I was not present. I guessed he was not often in the company of women. Perhaps there was some taboo against it – why else should he find a visit to Wayside Cross impossible?

At last, I heard the distant click of a latch and a squeaking of hinges, and saw Mr Jesperson emerge. Jamming his hat on to his head, he broke into a run and, on reaching me, seized my arm and pulled me along.

'What was that about?'

'Oh, nothing. Never mind.' Looking up, I was surprised to see a red flush creeping over his normally pale face.

'Why did you go back?' I persisted. 'Why will you not tell me? I suppose you thought of some more questions, but even if it was totally useless—'

'It was not useless,' he said, so quickly that I realised the very suggestion had wounded his pride. 'I suddenly thought it could be useful to have a sample of the – of whatever pills or potion he supplied to Charles Manning.'

'A good idea,' I said encouragingly. 'And he agreed?'

His flush deepened, and he kept his gaze fixed ahead, as if there might be some danger in catching my eye. 'Well, I tried to purchase them . . . as if for myself, you see. He would have found it suspicious – would have thought, and quite rightly, that I suspected him of causing Manning's death. Why else should he emphasise his ability to detect ailments and weaknesses in his clients?'

'Must we go so fast?' I gasped.

'Forgive me! I was hoping we might reach the Post Office before it starts to rain.'

But I was not to be distracted. 'It took you some time to convince him.'

'Indeed it did. He inspected my eyes quite thoroughly and declared I was in the very pink of health – and such a vigorous young man as I could not possibly have need of, er, what I was determined to buy. He did his best to talk me out of it; in fact, I began to fear he would simply refuse to sell it to me – so, as a last ditch, I "confessed" that I had been sent by another, to purchase it on his behalf.'

He laughed. 'If Verrell was half as careful and concerned about his clients' health as he claims he should have sent me away with nothing. Especially as I would not say who it was for. How could he know my unnamed "friend" was fit and healthy, and would not have a bad reaction to the ingredients? But my ruse worked. He thought he had guessed who I was buying for. It made him laugh, made him feel he had something over him . . . Ah, there is the Post Office,' he cried, with something of the relief and joy of a sailor spotting land after many weary weeks at sea, and quickly steered me across the street.

CHAPTER FIFTEEN

Meeting Mr Ott

I stopped him outside the Post Office, before he could steer me inside. 'Wait a moment,' I said. '*Who* did he think you were buying it for?'

He looked at me very seriously, except for the twinkle in his eye, and said gravely, 'Mr Felix Ott.'

'Mr Jesperson.' The loud, disapproving voice addressed him from the street behind.

We both turned around, startled. A tall man in his mid-forties, dark-brown hair beginning to go grey, beardless but with a handsome moustache, wearing mustard-coloured tweeds and a somewhat military demeanour was approaching at a rapid, yet slightly stuttering, pace. I knew at once this must be the very man of whom my friend had just spoken, and he had such an unfriendly look that I wondered if he had been following us, and had overheard all.

Now he turned his glare on me. 'Miss Lane, I presume? I had not realised that the partner of the famous Mr Jesperson was of the fair sex, but I can imagine it makes your job easier. I never suspected the youth filled with bright-eyed enthusiasm was acting a part – was in fact a *spy* – and I can well imagine that such a very sober, serious-looking young lady has deceived many others.'

Jesperson frowned, moving protectively in front of me. 'I say, this is a bit much – explain yourself, Ott.'

Felix Ott snorted. 'The way you explained yourself to me? How dare you suspect me of the murder of my dearest, truest friend!'

'Who told you that?'

'No one had to tell me. I have *deduced* it from the evidence,' he responded. 'Do you deny that you are a detective? That the two of you are, in fact, the famous London partnership known as Jesperson and Lane?'

Even as I wondered where he had acquired the notion that our still-fledgling operation deserved to be called 'famous', Mr Ott reached into his breast pocket and withdrew a small card which he flourished in Mr Jesperson's face.

'This is your card, is it not?'

Jesperson peered down his nose. 'It does appear to be.'

'Well then! Detectives, as I said. No better than spies. And you cannot deny that you are here to investigate the circumstances that led to the death of Charles Manning.'

'I have never denied it. I told you within moments of our first meeting that I had been sent to Norfolk by Manning's brother with instructions to learn as much as I could about his time here and the people he had known.'

'But you implied you were acting as a friend – you never said that you were a hired detective – nor that you had a partner, also working on the case. That it should be considered a case at all strikes me as . . . as far-fetched. The police did not find that Manning's death was the result of foul play.'

'Do you mind if I ask where you got that card?'

'Eh? It was given to me by a chap at my club.'

'Because you wished to hire a detective?'

Felix Ott scowled. 'Certainly not! Why should I?'

'Well, despite your protestations of faith in the police, I do not think you were happy with their treatment of the death of Arthur Cooke.'

'They are fools to call it an accident. How could it have been? Do they think he laid himself out so neatly? Someone else was there; someone killed him, and they have no idea,' he muttered.

'Precisely. And perhaps the London police are just as foolish? It seemed to me – perhaps I misunderstood – that you were shocked by Manning's death.'

'Of course I was! He was in rude good health when I saw him last; there was no reason at all to think he had any problems with his heart.'

'And when did you last see him?'

The corner of his mouth twitched. 'Friday . . . Yes, Friday evening, in Cromer. I already told you that.'

'Yes, you did. And you said then that you had no idea he was going to London the next day.'

'Absolutely no idea.' The look of wounded outrage on his

face was utterly convincing: Mr Ott still felt the betrayal by his late friend.

'Perhaps you picked up that card advertising a detective agency because you were still hoping someone might find out for you . . .'

'Absurd!' He gave his head a shake as if to dislodge an annoying insect. 'It was handed to me – had not the least thought of ever needing a detective – we only took the cards to be obliging – one doesn't like to offend a fellow member, especially not ex-Army, a very gentlemanly old buffer – had no interest, but he was handing them out; I tucked it away in my pocket without even looking at it, and had forgotten all about it until I came across it today. Then – imagine my surprise to see *your* name. A London detective! That put a very different complexion on things.' He gave the card a hard flick with his thumbnail that should have sent it into collision with Mr Jesperson's nose, but my friend caught it neatly in his fingers.

'I apologise for the deception,' said Mr Jesperson. 'There was nothing personal in it, only we thought it best to keep a low profile, rather than risk alerting the wrong people that we were investigating a suspicious death.'

'The wrong people,' muttered Mr Ott, staring at the ground. Then he looked up, to frown at us. 'Go back to London. Any suspicious circumstances must surely be there, where Charles met his end.'

Mr Jesperson looked at the card in his hand, turning it over and over. 'Yes, we shall have to go back to London.' Then he looked into Mr Ott's face again. 'But first, I must fulfil my promise to you – and my obligation to the memory of Charles Manning – by giving the lecture tomorrow evening.'

I had to bite my tongue to keep from asking my friend what he meant. I saw Mr Ott look surprised, but then relieved.

'You mean it?' he cried. 'It was not all pretence, then?'

'None of it was pretence – except the necessary, slight evasion,' said Mr Jesperson. 'Everything I said to you was the truth – I only kept back the fact of my profession.'

'You have a genuine interest in the ancient ways and wisdom?'

Mr Jesperson inclined his head. 'Indeed I do. I cannot pretend to any expertise . . . and must admit that the existence of the shrieking pits was entirely unknown to me before this week. However, Mr Manning left behind some interesting notes. His point of view strikes me as original and compelling – what a pity he did not live to write the paper that he had planned. But I think I shall be able to cobble together a talk that he might have approved, and that students of folklore and ancient history will find interesting.'

'And I shall be very grateful to you for giving it,' said Mr Ott, whose manner and expression were now transformed. 'And not only because I had already announced it.' Smiling with more than cordiality, he thrust out his hand for a manly shake; in that moment, I noticed Mr Ott wore on his little finger a gold ring set with a familiar orange stone.

We proceeded into the Post Office after Mr Ott had left us.

'What was that about your talk?' I asked in a low voice as we joined the queue. 'You said nothing of it to me.'

'Did I not? I do beg your pardon; with so much else on my mind . . .' He was so casual in his apology that I felt even more aggrieved.

'With so much else to think about, you nevertheless have managed to arrange a lecture! When did you mean to tell me? Or was I to hear about it afterwards, from other members of the audience?'

He looked at me in surprise. 'Why of course you will be in the audience – and working harder than I in your observation of those attending. I hope you will not have too inflated a notion of this so-called lecture, which barely exists. I fear I misled Ott in regard to Manning's notes. He left very few. I shall be obliged to make up most of it out of whole cloth.'

Having reached the counter, Mr Jesperson asked if there were any letters for him. The clerk went away to look.

'Well, at any rate you seem to have assuaged Mr Ott's suspicions,' I said. 'I wonder where he got our card?'

Mr Jesperson laughed politely, as if I had made a joke, as the clerk was returning with two letters. We immediately withdrew to a more private corner to inspect them.

The first letter was from the firm of solicitors who had long handled the Mannings' affairs.

'I thought it best to go to them direct, in the unlikely event that Mr Manning was not being entirely honest,' my partner reminded me as he quickly scanned the letter. 'But it is as he said – Alexander, as the elder son, inherited all – and apart from a few stocks and shares, "all" is the house and its contents. Mr Charles was not honest if he allowed his lady friends to imagine he had any expectations.'

He tore open the other letter, which was from Mr Alexander Manning himself.

'Any news?' I asked. 'Has he discovered where his brother went or who he saw on his last day in London?'

'No, of course not,' he replied, refolding the letter and thrusting it into his pocket. 'He went to none of his old haunts, saw none of his former friends.'

'That is disappointing.'

Again he laughed, as if I spoke to amuse him. 'Hardly! Come along – no time to waste.'

With that, he rushed me outside and along the road in the direction of the railway station. The sky was now very dark, the wind whipping up in anticipation of the coming storm, so I had no doubt of our destination, and was relieved that we reached it before the heavens opened. Even more fortunately, we arrived as a trim two-wheeler cab drew up and let out two passengers, and the cabby met Mr Jesperson's interrogative stare with a nod that meant he would accept us as his next fare.

As the driver was helping his passengers with their luggage, Mr Jesperson looked at his pocket watch and made a satisfied noise. 'I shall catch the next Norwich train, and easily make the last connection to London,' he said.

I stared in surprise. 'Why should you go to London?'

He looked equally surprised by my question. 'Why do you suppose?'

'I have no idea.'

'Really? But now that we know where Manning was only hours before his death . . .'

I was amazed by his remark, considering that Alexander Manning's letter had contained no useful information. 'How do we know that?'

'Why, from this, of course.' He flourished one of our own business cards at me, and smiled encouragingly, as if something very obvious had simply slipped my mind.

'Is that the card you took from Mr Ott?'

'Of course. Look at it,' he urged, pushing it into my hand. I turned it over, but there was nothing written on either side, and no changes to the printed information we had designed and ordered some six weeks ago.

'What do you expect me to see? How many times must I look at our own address?'

'That is not *our* card, but a copy. Call it a reprint, although as it must have been ordered from a different printer, it is effectively a separate original.'

I scowled and shook my head in bewilderment. 'How can you say that?'

'Because it is so. Look at it. The difference is obvious. At least, it would be if you compared it side by side with one of ours. I noticed when I found the card in the dead man's pocket. At least, I *should* have done.' He screwed up his face in an expression of self-disgust. 'I was aware of a slight difference, but could make no sense of it. I did not appreciate the significance. It niggled at me . . . yet I did not pursue it, and almost managed to convince myself that I had been mistaken. But I was not mistaken.'

I stared at the card so hard my eyes should have burnt a hole in it, but I could not see what he claimed was obvious. 'Really, Mr Jesperson, I am not blind, but I do not see!'

He took pity on me and explained, 'Different paper stock. Although superficially the same, it has come from a different batch, and probably a different mill.'

I did not doubt his knowledge, but what did it mean? 'Well, then, perhaps our printer was forced to order more paper after he printed the first one hundred of our cards. For why should anyone want to make copies of our business card? Who would benefit?'

He smiled broadly. 'We would – and no one else. It was done for our benefit. I saw it all as soon as Ott revealed how he had obtained it – he did not pick it up, but had it thrust upon him by a "fellow member" – he must have meant a member of his London club. And he made the slip of saying "we" – to whom else could he have referred but his companion that evening, the friend he had invited to be his guest, a person he was determined not to name for fear of self-incrimination.'

'You think he was with Mr Manning?'

'I am sure of it. Manning acquired his card from the same source and now I know it must have been in Ott's club on Saturday evening. Initially, I was misled by finding our card in

Manning's pocket into thinking he must have come to London in order to appeal for help from a detective agency, but in fact he never had any intention of looking us up until, in fear for his life, he remembered the card in his pocket, and sought out our address – fortuitously not far away, and in a neighbourhood he knew very well from his prior residence.' He broke off to make arrangements with the cab driver.

'You should have asked Mr Ott for the name of his club,' I said. 'How will you find it?'

He smiled. 'There was no need to ask him. You wondered why anyone would copy our card, and I said that it was for our benefit. Who could have helped us in this way? Ott referred to his fellow member as 'ex-Army', a gentlemanly old buffer. Do we know anyone of that description who might have gone to the trouble and expense of printing copies of our card to distribute to his friends and acquaintances?' Mr Jesperson helped me climb into the carriage and then continued, 'Who else could it be but a certain elderly colonel for whom I did a trifling favour a few weeks ago – who was very eager to return that favour in any way that he could?'

He shut the door. 'Here's the rain! And my train will not be far behind. Farewell, Miss Lane, until tomorrow.'

I leaned back as the cab rolled away, and remembered our brief meeting with Colonel Robert Mallet in a London street where Mr Jesperson had performed his 'trifling favour' – climbing up the side of a house to rescue a stranded kitten. The kitten was the pet of the old gentleman's granddaughter, and he had been extremely grateful, promising to treat Mr Jesperson to dinner at his club, eager to repay the favour. Well, if my friend were right – and I did not doubt it – Colonel Mallet had repaid it more than handsomely now.

CHAPTER SIXTEEN

Poisonous Babies

Opening the door to me at Wayside Cross, this time Nancy looked not merely startled but dismayed. 'Oh, Miss, you needn't knock – you are a guest here, so you may come in as you please.' Hurrying me in out of the rain, she relieved me of my coat, which she patted and shook in an attempt to rid it of water before hanging it on the hall coat-tree.

'Do you need me to show you to your room?' she asked.

'No, thank you, Nancy, I think I remember where it is.'

My words, although joking, gave me an idea as I mounted the stairs. To learn if there was anything in Maria's suspicion of her neighbours I really ought to search the house, and sooner rather than later. If I was discovered poking into somewhere I should not have been, I might get away with the claim of being lost today but not tomorrow.

Thus, rather than going directly to my room when I reached the top of the stairs, I walked to the other end of the passage, and (the words 'I beg your pardon, I thought this was the bathroom' waiting to be uttered) took hold of a door handle and boldly opened it.

Within was dark and shadowy, only the late afternoon daylight streaming through a single window. I saw a canopied, four-poster bed, a wardrobe, a dressing table, and a few other items of furniture, one of which at first I took for an unusual coat-and-hat stand designed to resemble a bare, leafless tree. But as I absorbed more details – a purple shawl, a red scarf, the hint of a familiar perfume, and books, everywhere, piled on the bed and floor, ribbons and bits of paper protruding as place-markers – I felt certain this was Miss Bulstrode's bedroom.

Cautiously, I entered, pulling the door to behind me, and began to search, opening the wardrobe, looking underneath the bed – with every move I made, I felt more and more the guilty spy, prying into an innocent woman's private space, and I hurried, eager to get away as soon as I managed to convince myself that there was most certainly no living creature but myself anywhere in the room.

Back in the corridor, I opened the next door and found what was probably known as the lumber room. Here were trunks and boxes, a folding table, extra chairs, other bits and pieces that would only be taken out on special occasions, or were awaiting repair. I saw at once that it would be impossible for me to investigate further without moving things about and making noise – and I could think of no acceptable explanation for a guest to go digging through the things stored away here, so I satisfied myself with sniffing the air. Although my olfactory sense was not as keen as that of Mr Jesperson, I could smell dust and wood, old furniture wax, a trace of silver polish, but nothing that suggested a baby.

The next door I tried was the bathroom. Immediately beside it was a door labelled 'WC'.

That left three rooms. One was mine; the other two must belong to Miss Ann and Miss Alys. Were they in residence? I stood listening to the steady drumming of the rain on the roof, and decided that they certainly were.

Rather than risk embarrassment, I went into my own room. It was warm and welcoming. Whilst I had been out, someone had lit a fire in the grate. I added more coal, and sat down to write some notes. Soon, though, the warmth of the room, the comfort of the padded arm-chair and the after-effects of a good dinner and wine lulled me into setting aside my notebook and pen and I closed my eyes for just a moment . . .

The sound of knocking roused me. The room was quite dark, the fire nearly out. So much for my 'moment'! But who had knocked? I held my breath to listen. From the passage outside I heard a woman's voice, low but penetrating, call, 'Annie!'

I nearly jumped out of my skin. In fact, I did leap out of my chair and was on my feet, half-crouching and tensely alert, in one swift, unconscious motion.

Annie was the name of Maria's baby. This was my first, over-whelming thought. The voice came again: 'Oh, open up, Annie dear! *Do* come down and have some supper.'

I recognised the voice of Miss Alys, and realised she must be speaking to her sister Ann, whose room must be the one next to mine. When I heard the impatient rattle of the door-handle, I guessed she had locked herself in.

'Ann, please.'

Miss Ann's response was too muffled for me to make out, but Alys heard it well enough, and gave a derisory snort. 'Nonsense! Don't be such a child. You will make yourself sick. Come down now — if not for yourself, then for the sake of our guest.'

A key turned, and I heard Ann say in a tragic voice, 'How can you expect me to care about food or company? My life is over — ruined. I shall never love again.'

'Don't be such a big silly.'

'You would not talk like that to me if I had been his widow.'

'Thank goodness you are not. Listen to me: he did not love you, and you only played at loving him. Now you are playing at grief. I *know*. Be a good girl and come with me — or do I have to send Gabriel up to pull you down by your hair?'

Ann shocked me by giggling. 'Beastly thing!'

'Yes, he is a beast, but he is Bella's beast.'

'I meant *you*.'

'Ah, but I am *your* beast.'

Another giggle, then footsteps, and a rustling of dresses: I envisioned the sisters in an embrace as they made up their disagreement, and listened to them walking away together down the stairs.

I had not heard Ann lock her door after she came out. My

heart raced; I could not resist, I would not miss the chance to search her room. Grief could drive people to do extraordinary things. What if Ann, half-mad with grief over her dead lover, had gone for some reason to the Vicarage stables; might she not have imagined she was rescuing an abandoned baby? I must seize the moment and learn the truth.

Quickly, and as quietly as I could, I slipped out of my room and into the one next door. She had left a lamp burning, and I saw at a glance something that appeared to be a child's bedroom, rather than one of a woman of an age to be married. Everything was in soft pastel hues of pink, yellow and lavender. The walls were adorned with sentimental pictures of kittens and puppies being embraced or bathed or dressed by cherubic children. At least half a dozen dolls were on display, staring at me with shiny wide eyes and pursed painted lips. There was a baby doll and a stuffed dog on a pillow. The bookshelf contained mostly school stories and old-fashioned novels like *The Wide, Wide World* and *Dorothy's Vocation,* but there was also a complete Shakespeare and a number of poetry anthologies.

I looked beneath the bed. Stuffed away behind the dust-ruffle was a pair of knitted pink slippers, a cheap novel with a lurid cover, a crumpled handkerchief and a silver cake tin. I did not open it, deciding Ann's treasures might remain her secret, but rose and quickly went to peek behind the heavy curtains that enclosed a window seat, upon which rested more dolls, more novels, and a box of chocolates. I no longer expected to find anything incriminating, but for the sake of thoroughness, I opened the wardrobe, which was filled just as it should be with dresses, skirts, scarves and shoes. It had been absurd of me to imagine she might have stolen a baby, but at least I could put that idea to rest now. I departed as circumspectly as I had entered and returned to my own room to fix my hair and otherwise make myself tidy before going downstairs to join the others.

Although we ate from fine china in the dining room, supper was, as I had been told it would be, a simple meal: soup and bread, with cheese and fruit or cake to follow.

'Or both,' said Miss Bulstrode.

'Beware of cheese before bedtime,' warned Alys. 'It can give you nightmares. Cake is a safer choice, and always delicious when made by sister Ann.'

Ann flushed and dropped her eyes, the picture of modesty.

'Did Ann also make this lovely carrot soup?' I asked.

'Elsie made it, but all of us can cook,' said Alys. 'Of course we have our specialities; Ann does love her sweets. I like baking, and also making stews and roast meats. Bella is happiest when she can serve us the fruits and vegetables she has grown herself.'

'This is not the best time of year for me,' said Miss Bulstrode. 'Unless you include my pickles and preserves.'

I relaxed, enjoying the food and the company, relieved I need no longer suspect my hosts of any involvement in the disappearance of Maria's child. She must have been influenced by evil rumours about witchcraft and her neighbours, and for that I blamed Felix Ott.

However, I told myself I must not forget why I was here.

They might be able to give me some useful information about Charles Manning and his other acquaintances in the county. I was particularly interested in what they might have to say with regard to Felix Ott, for the revelation that he had lied to us about his last meeting with Mr Manning, and his whereabouts on the night he died, had, in my mind at least, moved Mr Ott to first place as a suspect. That two of his closest associates should have died so unexpectedly, in mysterious circumstances, could hardly be a matter of chance.

But as soon as I tried to raise the subjects of most interest to me, I was foiled by Alys. I understood and sympathised with her desire to protect her sister by avoiding sensitive topics, but, remembering how Alys had needed to coax Ann to join us this evening, I realised she would require careful handling, and I resolved to give it more time. It would not help my cause if I upset her with clumsy questions; I could too easily imagine how her sisters would close ranks against me. It was bad enough to have been evicted from the Vicarage; I should be most heartily ashamed if I made myself a pariah in a second household today.

'I cannot go on calling you "Miss Lane",' said Alys. 'You know *our* names – I call that unfair, until you tell us yours.'

This question was one I always dreaded, for the name my father bestowed upon me, although well-intended, had always felt wrong – I am no Aphrodite. I took a deep breath and replied, 'My friends call me Di.'

'Diana, the huntress, Goddess of the moon, the Roman

equivalent of the Greek Artemis,' said Alys, her eyes alight. 'May we call you Artemis? A is for Arabella, Alys, Ann and Artemis!'

I hardly knew how to respond, and was grateful when Miss Bulstrode leaned towards me, saying, 'I should like to call you Di, if you will call me Bella.'

'I should like that very much, Bella.'

'Well, *I* shall call you Artemis,' said Alys, a stubborn set to her jaw.

'I shall take it as a mark of your special favour,' I murmured.

Bella chuckled. 'Never underestimate the value of that.'

Taking this as good advice, I allowed Alys to set the direction of the table-talk, and, although I never liked being the centre of attention, I accepted this as the price I must pay. Since I was not admitting to my present occupation, I spoke of my previous one, as companion and assistant to Gabrielle Fox, aka 'Miss X', working for the Society for Psychical Research, and related some amusing anecdotes about fraudulent mediums and make-believe spirits.

'And are they all frauds and make-believe?' Bella asked.

'No. I should not like to give that impression. The real work of the SPR is not to uncover fraud but to expand our understanding of the world, to show how many things generally considered impossible according to the physical laws of science may actually take place – thought-transference, creating physical effects by force of will alone, the existence of other states of being, the survival of personality after death, even perhaps such things as witchcraft and magic spells.'

Bella did not look pleased at my attempt to connect her own field with spiritualism. 'Witchcraft is nothing like that – we do not make the claims that mediums do,' she said sternly. 'Naturally, superstitious people may believe what they like, but I assure you, everything a so-called witch, wise woman or a cunning man does – or ever did – can be explained in scientific terms. Some people are too inclined to give the label "magic" to anything they do not understand.'

'Is that Mr Ott's belief, too?'

'You mean, the principles behind his School? Well, I should not speak for him, but it is certainly my understanding that—'

Alys gave a dramatic groan. 'Please, may we not speak of something else for a change? I am sick to death of that silly School! Artemis, what of your personal life? Your parents are dead, but have you no family?'

'Only my sister. We saw much of each other when we both lived in London, but she is often travelling. Currently she is on tour in America.' Seeing her look of puzzlement, I explained: 'Athene is an actress.' I was quite unprepared for the excitement with which this information was greeted, as Ann and Alys burst out with a volley of comments and questions.

'On the stage. How wonderful! How proud of her you must be! Do you attend all her opening nights? Of course not! In London, I mean. Is she a leading lady, the ingénue, or does she take character parts? I wonder if we have ever seen her? Who has she acted with? What is her favourite role?'

The questions came thick and fast. Only Bella abstained,

sitting back in her chair, casting a fond, tolerant look at her siblings. Gradually they wound down and stopped, watching me expectantly.

'I hardly know where to begin,' I said, with a little laugh. 'Of course, I am very proud of my sister, and happy to speak of her, but we do lead our own lives; I have not seen her every performance . . .'

'Forgive us,' said Alys. 'But we do so adore the theatre . . . The great sadness of my life – really, the only fault I find with Wayside Cross – is that it is so far from theatre-land. Sometimes in the summer there may be a travelling troupe in Cromer, or we attend plays in Norwich, but – as you must know – nothing compares to London. And it is all but impossible to convince Bella to leave Aylmerton for a week or two in the city.'

'I can live quite well without the bright lights and spectacles of London,' said Bella. 'And you girls are quite old enough now to go there without me, whenever you feel you must have another dose of theatre. Of course, you are right to consider the expense, but there are ways to economise. It might be cheaper to stay in lodgings with half-board for a month – in that time, you could have such a surfeit of theatre and other cultural events that it would last you a whole year.'

'Or why not simply move to London?' I said helpfully. 'You could surely find some gainful employment there – maybe even something to do with the theatre.'

Alys gave me a dark look. 'You are very flattering, but I could never be an actress.'

'There are other jobs besides that – I did not mean—'

She did not wait for my apology. 'I love theatre, but it is not my life. My life is here.'

Remembering that not everyone shared my feelings about the importance of a meaningful occupation, I did not pursue the question of what she actually *did* with her life in her sister's household, but asked, 'When were you last in London?'

She gave a heavy sigh. 'So long ago, I can scarcely recall it. Just after Easter. We had hoped to go again before Christmas, but,' she cast a sidelong glance at Ann, 'that is probably out of the question now.'

Ann had been looking pensive, and now spoke almost to herself: 'Charles promised to take me to the theatre. He knew how I loved Shakespeare. But no one is playing *Romeo and Juliet*. Surely next year there will be a new production. If we lived in Gordon Square after our marriage we could see everything, and Alys could come to stay as long as she liked. Oh why, why?' She jerked her head back and looked about wildly. 'Why am I still here? Why did I not die with my beloved? Oh, Charles, Charles! Why did you leave me, Charles?'

Alys got up and rushed to embrace her sister as Ann burst out in noisy, wracking sobs. Bella rose, too, and calmly took charge. 'Take her to bed, Alys, and stay with her. I will bring up something to help her sleep.' Even amid the turmoil, she did not forget her duties as hostess, telling me to help myself to cheese and biscuits or a piece of cake from the stand on the sideboard while I waited for her return.

I had not long to wait; rather to my surprise, Bella swept back into the room a few minutes later, carrying a decanter.

'All is under control,' she said briskly. 'Alys will stay with her until Ann falls asleep. Poor girl . . . It is mostly self-dramatics, of course, but when she works herself into a state like that there is no point in trying to reason with her.'

This struck me as a rather insensitive response, and I could not help objecting: 'Surely there is never any point in applying reason to an emotion as powerful as grief. Especially when the wound is still so raw. The man she loved is dead.'

'She did not love him. You think me cruel and unfeeling – I am not. I know my little sisters. Ann is still a child, and more interested in her own fascinating emotions than with another real person. She was in love with being in love, and now that Charles is dead, it is not *he* she grieves over, but the loss of all the fantasies that she had built around him.' She held out the decanter towards me, asking, 'Will you try a glass of my plum brandy? It goes very nicely with Ann's poppy-seed cake.'

'Thank you, I will. From your own plums? You are multi-talented, indeed.'

She laughed as she poured out two small crystal glasses of the dark purple liquid. 'I suggest you taste it before you decide if liquor-making is one of my skills.'

'I am no expert on brandy, but I like this,' I said after taking a sip. 'And you are by all accounts a skilled gardener.'

'I love tending my plants and watching them thrive,' she

replied. 'I suppose some might say I find in them an outlet for my thwarted maternal emotions.'

'Hardly thwarted, when you have raised your two half-sisters.'

'True.' She drank off her glass in a gulp and then gazed at her hands, resting on the tablecloth. She touched the orange stone of her poison ring, and then covered it with her other hand. 'But not quite from infancy. Of course, I love them dearly, they could almost be my own, yet it must be different to hold one's own newborn baby, the fruit of one's own womb. I wonder . . . is it too late for me?'

The hairs on the back of my neck prickled. I held my breath, not daring to speak, fearing to break the spell of this unexpected intimacy. But then in an instant her mood changed again; she looked at me, smiling, and asked, 'Would you like to come and meet my green children now?'

In truth, I have next to no interest in plants and flowers, but I made a show of eagerness and allowed her to lead me to the back of the house where she made sure we were both equipped with lanterns, although we did not bother with coats or capes against the icy rain for the short distance we must run to the glasshouse.

By contrast, this time, the warm and humid air was a welcome blessing, and despite my lack of interest in exotic flora, I was happy to spend a little time in this man-made jungle, the litany of botanical names falling from Bella's lips in musical counterpoint to the drumming of rain against the glass.

She pointed out fruits and flowers and leaves and spoke of

edible qualities and medicinal uses. Some of her 'children' I was invited to admire for their vigorous growth or beauty. Many of the plants were descendants of samples her grandfather had brought back from India or a South Sea island; others she had grown from seeds ordered from a catalogue.

'Now take care,' she said, holding up her lantern as we came to the far end of the long, hot room. 'We've left behind the friendly plants with their pretty flowers and tasty fruits. Do you recognise this one?'

I saw a bush with soft green leaves and shiny black berries. The berries looked succulent, and I could easily imagine they might be good to eat, although her warning suggested otherwise. 'They look like bilberries,' I said. 'But you will have to tell me.'

'This is *Atropa belladonna,* or deadly nightshade. Eating the berries is a fairly certain route to death, although some get away with a fever, hallucinations and a rapid heartbeat, possibly a mild seizure.'

Although I had failed to recognise it, I was familiar with this deadly plant. 'Have you nothing good to say about it?' I asked her wryly.

She laughed. 'Well, it *is* rather pretty, don't you agree? And small amounts of the chemical – atropine – can be mixed with other ingredients for medicinal purposes. I believe that in the past, women used it for cosmetic purposes – that is supposed to be the origin of the "belladonna" name.'

Moving along, she pointed to a small, slender tree in a blue pot. '*Strychnos nux-vomica,* more commonly known as the strychnine tree. I am sure I do not have to explain further.'

I frowned. 'The only thing you might have to explain is why you should grow your own poison.'

She gave me an odd look. 'You mean, rather than buying it from the chemist, like other people?'

'Surely it has no beneficial uses?'

Her lips quirked. 'You do not consider the extermination of vermin beneficial? But, in fact, in minute doses, strychnine is a stimulant. It may also be used to treat intestinal worms. For those reasons – and because we are occasionally troubled by moles in the garden and rats in the pantry – I include strychnine in my pharmacopeia.'

'And you are not afraid it might be stolen? I heard that a farmer and his wife both died from strychnine poisoning earlier this year.'

'I keep all my jars in a locked cabinet, to which no one but myself has access.' She patted her waist, producing a slight, silvery jangle from the keys hanging from her belt. 'I am quite certain that it is more secure there than it would be behind the counter in a village pharmacy. Although I have met their daughter, neither Mr nor Mrs Goodall – the farmers you mentioned – have ever set foot in this house. Mrs Goodall's name is down in the poison register, since she purchased a quantity of strychnine in Cromer, for the declared purpose of exterminating the moles who had ruined her flower beds.'

'I do not mean to accuse you of anything,' I said, uncomfortable beneath her gaze. 'I only thought, the existence of such deadly plants might be a risk . . . and despite what you said about your medicine cabinet, the door to this glasshouse has no lock.'

She gestured at the strychnine tree. 'Can you explain to me how the would-be murderer would extract the poison from that, even if he recognised the tree?'

I stared at the tree. 'Er, boil the leaves perhaps?'

'No.'

I thought harder. 'I suppose there is a fruit, some sort of nut, perhaps.'

She nodded her approval of my guess. 'But not at the moment – as you can see. I have long since taken its paltry harvest – it never has produced many nuts; I keep it warm and watered, so perhaps it is the soil that is at fault – and ground the seeds to powder. So, even if someone were aware of its existence, and knew how to extract the poison, and came creeping in here some dark midnight – little good would it do him, or her. Even if someone wished to go to so much trouble to avoid putting his name in the poison register, I hope I shall not have to count too many potential murderers amongst those I have introduced to my poisonous offspring!'

She touched my arm. 'Come, shall we go back to the house? I am used to this atmosphere, but you are looking flushed.'

'No, I am fine. There is no need to cut our tour short.'

'I fear I have overstretched your interest.'

'No, certainly not.' Glancing around, my eyes fell upon a healthy-looking shrub in the corner. It had glossy, dark-green, blade-shaped leaves and some peculiar, knobbly green fruits. 'What is that? Not ripe yet, I suppose.' I reached out to touch it, and she stopped my hand.

'Poisonous?' I asked.

'Very.' She half-turned to walk away, but I made no move to follow. My curiosity was piqued by how less forthcoming she was regarding this, compared to her other 'children'.

'*Cerbera odollam*,' she said at last. 'Also known as the suicide tree. The meat of one of those nuts would be enough to stop your heart within the hour – although the meat is so bitter, no one could make the mistake of eating it, except with suicidal intent.'

'But it also has some medicinal use?'

'Its only use is death. Hardly known in this country at all, on the southwestern coast of India where it grows it has the reputation of providing an easy release for women who have come to feel the conditions of their lives as unbearable. Death is said to be swift and painless, and the bitter taste is easily disguised by mashing the white meat of the nut with the local palm sugar. It may then be added to whatever she has chosen to make her final meal.'

I found it interesting that she spoke of the imagined suicidal person as female. 'Is it only women who kill themselves in that way?'

She looked puzzled by my question. 'I doubt it . . . although in their society, women undoubtedly have the worst of it. And there is the element of food preparation involved . . . No, I give you the description of *Cerbera odollam* as my grandfather gave it to me. Nothing more sinister than that.'

Yet I did find something sinister in the way she spoke of it. 'Why do you keep it? If it has no other purpose, and the fruits are so deadly?'

'It is part of my grandfather's collection. It survived him, and it may survive me. I have told you how I feel about my plants. I exaggerate when I call them my children, but they are certainly my pets, and I would find it as hard to destroy any one of them as I would to kill Gabriel, or any other living creature.' She moved closer to me and took my arm, directing me firmly away from the suicide tree and back in the direction of the door. 'Few even know of its existence. It is safe here in my glasshouse. It does no harm.'

But it might be used for harm, I thought, and not only for self-harm. The woman who sweetens the pounded flesh of the nut to make her final meal less bitter could as easily serve it to someone else – perhaps the very person who made her unhappy enough to consider suicide. I could not help noticing that there were three nuts hanging from long, fleshy stems, and that a fourth stem in the cluster terminated abruptly. Had there only ever been three nuts, or had the fourth one been picked?

I did not dare to ask Bella that question, and I could not get it out of my mind.

CHAPTER SEVENTEEN

Thinking Things Over

The rain continued through the night, and was still falling when I went downstairs, rather later than usual, the next morning.

I found Alys breakfasting on toast and tea in the dining room, and joined her. When I asked after her sisters, she told me that Ann never ate anything in the morning and that Bella had already started upon her day's work, and was now conducting a private consultation in her office.

'Her office is your family parlour – do you not find that a bother, to be shut out of the best, most comfortable room in the house?'

She gave me a look that mingled suspicion, reproach and amusement. 'I think my own room is the most comfortable, actually. Perhaps you mean that *you* are feeling shut out?'

I tried not to be flustered by her astute remark. I was aware, too, that had she but known it, she might have posed the very same question to Edith Jesperson, who never complained that her son and I had commandeered her sitting room for our office.

'Do not look so disheartened,' she said more kindly. 'Bella rarely has more than one or two visitors of a morning – you will soon be at liberty to go in and browse amongst the books to your heart's content. I suppose that is what you wish to do?'

I sighed with relief. 'Yes. I do find time drags – especially on a rainy day like this – without a good book to read, and I brought nothing with me but a guidebook to Norfolk.'

'Oh, dear. How awkward. I should tell you, there are not many books in the Bulstrode library that I should consider a good read, but come up to my room after you have finished your breakfast, and I can give you something more entertaining than anything from the old Admiral's collection.'

'Thank you, Alys, that is very kind.' Her invitation would give me the chance I wanted to inspect her room. Even though I no longer expected to find a baby secreted in the house, I wanted to understand more about these three sisters who had featured so prominently in the final months of Charles Manning's life. I fancy that the rooms where someone lives may offer a glimpse into their soul.

And Alys, despite the teasing and play-acting I had sensed in her earlier, was now, it seemed, quite happy to show me hers. Having finished her own breakfast, she lingered at the table until I was ready, and we went upstairs together.

Her bedroom contrasted with those of her sisters. It was neat and tidy, with everything in its place, and there were few remnants of childhood on display, no toys or trinkets or dolls, but everywhere evidence of some craft or hobby: a basket of embroidery threads, needlepoint cushions on the chairs; a box of watercolours, framed landscapes on the walls. On the marquetry-topped table ('not very good, I fear, and it took me a very long time,' she said modestly) was a photographic portrait of the three sisters, and a much older picture of a young woman I took to be their mother.

She directed my attention to her bookcase and invited me to take my pick.

Apart from a few 'how-to' books (*Practical Marquetry, The Needlewoman's Handbook*) and some biographies, they were nearly all novels or plays, arranged alphabetically by author. Alys had her own one-volume *Complete Shakespeare*, and some anthologies, but her taste in fiction tended towards the sensational, with many works by Mrs Braddon and Mr Wilkie Collins. My own interest is more for travel narratives and personal histories – perhaps I encounter enough of the sensational in my profession – and I am afraid Alys found my choice (Mrs Gaskell's *Life of Charlotte Brontë*) somewhat disappointing.

I took my leave of Alys and went to my own room, not to settle down with Mrs Gaskell, but to write to Mr Jesperson. I did not mean to post the letter, but if we had no opportunity for private conversation when next we met, at least he could be brought up to date with my own investigation. Writing a proper letter, rather than simply jotting a few notes to myself, also helped me to think about the significance of my observations.

Ann had a childish liking for dolls, and Bella was haunted by unfulfilled maternal longings, but I had found nothing to suggest that they had so much as suspected the existence of Maria's baby; her suggestion that they had taken it could only be the result of superstitious fear, possibly stoked by Mr Ott's recent defamatory remarks connecting witches to infant sacrifice.

In regard to Mr C. Manning's death, however, I am not inclined to acquit them of all involvement. There are a few things that bother me. For one, Ann is deeply upset by the loss of her fiancé, which is surely natural, yet her sisters continue to make light of her feelings and insist she is self-dramatising and never truly loved him but only the idea of their love.

If Bella loved C.M. as I suspect, this may reflect feelings of jealousy on her part, and a natural desire to dismiss his relations to her sister as being less deep and meaningful than his true feelings for her. Or did his betrayal of her turn her love to hate, in which case – could she have been driven to murder him?

Certainly, if CM was poisoned, that poison very likely came from this house. Some of B's most dangerous medicines are kept locked away, but there are also deadly plants in her glasshouse, which is not locked, and could easily be accessed by anyone with the knowledge of what is there.

The berries of the deadly nightshade produce hallucinations and fever, an increased heart-rate with the end result of death. Would the police surgeon have recognised the cause if CM did not eat the berries themselves but consumed them in powdered form, disguised in something else (I am relying on your encyclopaedic knowledge).

Another death-dealing plant is <u>Cerbera odollam</u>, also known as

THE WITCH AT WAYSIDE CROSS

the 'suicide tree'. Miss B showed me this plant, which is practically unknown in our country (where it would surely not survive outside a glasshouse); it is known to the people of the part of India where it grows for nut-meats that will provide a swift death from heart failure. The nuts are very bitter to taste, but quite palatable when sweetened, and easily disguised in a sauce. No one would ever guess the death that resulted was not by natural causes.

Mr O surely knows of Miss B's poisonous plants, and would have had easy access to them. If he was with CM the evening of his death, drinking and dining with him at his club, he would have had the opportunity to administer the killing dose. Only – what is his motive?

I am eager to hear what you have learned in London. I can get no further on my own. How I long to discuss it all with you. I hope we may speak soon.

A.L.

I had been aware, whilst writing, of movements downstairs, voices in the entrance hall, the opening and shutting of the front door, but now all was quiet again. As I folded my letter and put it away in my pocket book, I dared to hope that Miss Bulstrode had entertained her last client of the day, and that the coast was now clear for further investigations.

Downstairs, I knocked on the parlour door. Then I knocked again. I waited a few moments, but answer came there none. Retreat, or go ahead? I had already made my choice, and turned the handle.

'Miss Bulstrode? Bella?' Even as I spoke I stepped inside and saw I was alone in the room. With a rapidly beating heart, I shut the door behind me and walked swiftly to the cabinet which had been so much on my mind since my discussion with its owner about poisons.

The doors on the front of the case were of tawny, varnished wood set with heavy, leaded glass; old, greenish, pocked with little bubbles, but through it the rows of pottery jars and smaller blue glass bottles were easily visible, lined up on the shelves within. The labels were in the usual abbreviated Latin and mostly incomprehensible to me, although some I recognised from chemists' shops, including the deadly *Strych. Nus-Vom.*

I moved closer to inspect the keyhole. It was small and looked similar to one in a cabinet from my childhood home. I remembered when the key had been lost, how easy my sister and I had found it to open using a hammered nail.

A shadow fell across me and there was a sudden, terrifying commotion in the air. Instinctively I cowered, my hands up to protect my face, as I felt the beating of wings, and glimpsed the brutal beak of the crow aimed at my eyes, the claws about to snatch at my hair.

I shrieked and crouched and scuttled backwards before I turned and rose, still cowering with my hands above my head for protection as I hobbled towards the door.

There I stopped. Realising I had not been pursued – and was in fact unharmed – I straightened, let my hands fall away from my face, turned round and looked back.

Gabriel was perched on top of the cabinet, looking nearly twice his size with feathers ruffled up and his neck extended as he glared a warning at me. This time, he had not drawn blood, but if I dared try to touch this cabinet again, it would be a different story – or so I interpreted his posture. Now I understood why Bella had no fear that her drugs might be stolen.

'So you are Bella's watchdog,' I said shakily. 'Pity the poor thief who tried to break in here – he would think himself attacked by devils!'

Pride made me stay – I would not be banished by a bird! Although I kept a nervous eye on him as I walked slowly to the bookcases, I guessed I would be safe enough if I avoided that corner, and so it proved: Gabriel's remit did not extend to protecting anything left on the open shelves.

Just to prove to myself that it had been no fluke, I found the fabled grimoire in the same place where I had come across it before and had another look through it. The writing was like nothing I had ever encountered elsewhere. Some elements appeared to be illustrative, like Egyptian hieroglyphs: I recognised a slug, a fish, a mushroom and a cup or bowl. Then there were some that more resembled primitive alphabets, constructed of straight line, dots and curved lines. Of course, I was no expert, and could not claim to be able to recognise every written language in existence – but the more I saw of this one, turning page after page, the more I suspected that it was too varied and odd for a real language. Could it be code? Or perhaps it was a private language, never meant to be read or understood by anyone but its creator. The whole book was a work of art. The pictures were lovely, and clearly representational, even the ones of things I could not name.

Returning it to its place, I browsed contentedly for the next half an hour, and was absorbed by a book about an expedition through outer Mongolia when Bella finally entered.

'Oh, here you are,' she said pleasantly. 'I am glad you have found something to read – but now here is something else, a letter for you.' When she gave it to me, I recognised Mr Jesperson's handwriting, and I was eager to read it in privacy.

My Dear Miss Lane

I write to you in transit, on the train, and will drop this by the house, or send someone to deliver it to you so you may be up-to-date with my latest findings even before I see you in Cromer this evening.

Upon my arrival in London I went directly to the club Col. Mallet had given as his address & by good fortune he was there. (He practically lives there, since the death of his wife.) He was pleased to see me – sends his best regards to you – and immediately confirmed my suspicions: Yes, he had taken liberty of ordering another printing of our business card, for wider distribution – he hoped we did not mind – I assured him we considered it a great kindness & indeed I learned when I got to Gower St that we have had three enquiries already, undoubtedly attributable to his missionary activity – but I digress.

Col. Mallet is acquainted with Felix Ott & remembered giving cards to him and his friend. Of Manning (whom he had never seen before) he had the impression that he was in business with Ott, and subordinate to him; also that there was a tension or rivalry between them.

Over the course of the evening, this erupted into a quarrel.

All our friend could tell me about it was that the argument was over a woman. Manning said something which caused Ott to erupt with fury: 'You cad! You do not mean to ruin her?'

Manning said he meant to marry her. His words: 'I mean to make sure of her – she will have to marry me.'

Unfortunately, the Colonel had no reason to know how grateful we should have been for more information, or he might have listened, hiding behind his newspaper. Instead, uncomfortable at being privy to revelations of unworthy behaviour, he rattled his paper and coughed to let them know he was there. They continued to argue, although they lowered their voices. Rather than risk being made into an eavesdropper again, he withdrew to the smoking room, and the two men were left alone together.

Tho' I pressed Col. Mallet for more details, he could recall nothing else that was said, but was able to give me his impression of the affair, which I consider trustworthy. He thought Manning was hurt and surprised by Ott's reaction – the suggestion being that M told O his plans expecting his full approval.

The Colonel naturally thought it quite shocking that one gentleman would expect another to approve of his plan to force an innocent woman into marriage. He hazarded a guess that the lady in question was in possession of a large fortune, but unless Ott and Manning had been brothers, and the marriage was intended to save *an old family estate or something like that he could not imagine why Manning should reveal his caddish designs to another man.*

But if we replace the idea of 'family' with that of 'School' we may easily imagine how much Ott might stand to benefit from any advantageous marriage made by Manning. And if Manning considered the School their joint venture, he might have been willing to sacrifice much for it, including his own marital happiness.

Col. Mallet did not hear the end of the argument, but he witnessed Manning leaving the club, alone and looking very grim; then, only a minute or two later, he saw Ott go hurrying outside, and he wondered if he was going after his friend, presumably, for he did not look friendly, intending to pursue their quarrel.

No wonder Ott lied about when he last saw Manning. This does not look good for him.

I let the letter fall to my lap and stared unseeing at rain outside my window, imagining Felix Ott in a fury, charging through the foggy London streets after the man he had decided to kill, rather than allow him to harm an innocent woman.

That scenario would have made more sense if Charles Manning had been bludgeoned to death with a walking-stick, had his throat cut, or been strangled. But the manner of his death had been one that left no mark for a police surgeon to find. His heart had been stopped – by nature, by poison, or perhaps by magic.

Charles Manning had seemed to think he was being killed by witchcraft. And even though he had been looking at *me* when he reeled back in horror from the witch he imagined I was, it would not to do forget that witches could be men as well as women.

Was Felix Ott himself a practitioner of the dark arts?

I was glad I did not have too many more hours to wait before I could speak with Mr Jesperson, but as I gazed at the rain, I could not help imagining how wet I would get, walking to Cromer, if the rain did not stop in the next few hours. The Bulstrodes kept a carriage, I remembered. Would they think me awfully forward if I begged the use of it tonight?

Then I had a better idea. I would invite them to come as my guests to the talk my friend was giving tonight in Cromer. I hurried downstairs and, my mind already leaping ahead to compose the invitation, went into the parlour without stopping to knock.

The three sisters stood in a huddle before the fireplace, turning startled faces on me as I entered. Was it because the flames lit their faces, otherwise shadowed by the dimness of the room, so strangely, or was it the way they stood, tensed almost aggressively at my appearance, that I found myself reminded of the three weird sisters in *Macbeth*?

'I do beg your pardon,' I cried. 'I should have knocked; I have interrupted.' I turned to go, but Bella called me back. When I turned again, they had moved apart and the strangeness was dispersed – perhaps it had never really been, except in my imagination.

'Come in, come and join us – you are not interrupting anything; we three can meet and talk anytime; it is lovely to have you here. Please, sit.' To encourage me, Bella sank on to a couch and patted the cushion beside her.

I took the place she offered as Alys and Ann found other seats for themselves.

'I do not wish to keep you from your work,' I said, still feeling I was an intruder.

'Work? No, I have finished with my work for today,' Bella replied. 'As for my sisters, they are like the lilies of the field, who toil not and neither do they spin.'

'That is so unfair!' cried Alys. 'It is true, I have not yet learned to spin, but—'

'And I have been helping Elsie in the kitchen this morning,' said Ann. 'I was going to bake a cake, but after such a remark, you do not deserve it. Perhaps I shall make a small one, just enough for me and Alys and Artemis, but not you, *Bella*,' she concluded, giving a popping emphasis to the B.

The barely repressed smiles made it clear they all enjoyed such routine teasing of one another, and I felt a sudden, sharp, entirely unexpected pang and missed my own sister. Can anything ever replace the loving relationship with someone who has known you forever?

'I have just come in to ask you,' I began, and then started again, 'I mean, to invite you to come as my guests to a lecture in Cromer this evening. I hope it might be something that interests you.'

'A lecture,' said Alys with a suspicious frown. 'In Cromer. Not in the Templars Hall, by any chance?'

'Yes.'

'And a Thursday evening, too.' She sighed. 'You mean well, I have no doubt, dear Artemis, but I must tell you that a lecture by Mr Felix Ott is not something I have *ever* enjoyed. Bella feels differently, of course. But when Mr Ott is at the podium, if he does not make me feel stupid, he simply puts me to sleep. I know Ann feels the same.'

'Oh, but Mr Ott will not be giving this evening's lecture,' I said quickly. 'He has invited a guest speaker – my friend, Mr Jasper Jesperson. He is to give a talk in memory of the late Charles Manning, based on notes he left concerning his investigations into the shrieking pits. I think it will be very interesting.'

'We must go, of course,' said Ann, sounding unusually determined. 'Charles would have wished it.'

'I should like it very much,' said Bella. 'Thank you, Di. Alys, you need not come, of course.'

Alys scowled. 'Do not think you can leave me out.'

'But you have said you are not interested.'

'I am not interested in the stupid old holes in the ground they call the shrieking pits, no indeed; but I am very interested in seeing your Mr Jesperson,' she said, with a bright, mocking look at me. 'Your friend, you call him. Your fellow lodger. Is he your lover?'

My cheeks felt very hot, although I tried to keep my expression neutral.

Bella chided her, 'Alys! You are impertinent.'

'I think my question is very pertinent,' she said smartly. 'And

I suppose Mrs Ringer thought he was . . . and that is why she threw you out – am I right, Artemis?'

'You had better ask Mrs Ringer her reasons,' I said coolly. 'I would not like to pretend to know her mind.'

'We will take the carriage,' said Bella, clearly determined to change the subject. 'It will not matter if the rain continues. What time is the lecture? We had better have something to eat before we go . . . I must have a word with Elsie.' She rose. 'Alys, will you go out to the stables? Ann, I need your help in the kitchen. Come along, girls!'

CHAPTER EIGHTEEN

Mr Jesperson Gives a Lecture

The rain had cleared before sunset, and when I arrived in company with the Misses Bulstrode there was a queue at the door of the Templars Hall, and more people approaching, eager to pay their shilling for enlightenment.

As we waited to get in I examined the countenances of nearby strangers, wondering how many were members of Mr Ott's School of British Wisdom, and how many others had been driven by idle curiosity or boredom to one of the few entertainments on offer in this seaside resort out of season.

A poster had been plastered repeatedly on the walls and doors of the hall, showing a lurid illustration of a woman in ragged dress, her hair wild, arms uplifted and mouth open wide in a scream of anguish. Below this picture, in large letters:

Discover the **TRUTH** about the 'Shrieking Pits'

As revealed through the research of the late Charles Manning (SBW), presented by Jasper Jesperson, Esq.

Introduced by Felix Ott, Founder and President, School of British Wisdom.

TONIGHT ONLY

Applications available on the door to join School of British Wisdom.

½ price entry to registered students.

On the door (I was surprised to discover) was Felix Ott himself, collecting the admission fee and dispensing brochures advertising his School.

'Bella,' he cried, his businesslike demeanour transformed at once into a look I could almost call worshipful. 'What a lovely surprise! But I will not take your money. Had I known you might come, I should have sent tickets with my compliments.' He made a gesture, pushing away her attempt to pay. 'There is no charge for you.'

'And my sisters?' Without taking her eyes from his face, she indicated the two young women standing behind me.

'Certainly – you must know I hold your entire family in the highest esteem. I am flattered by this attention! Miss Lane, of course, is friend to Mr Jesperson—'

Alys spoke up sharply. 'Please, may we come in? You are blocking the entrance, sister dear. There are people behind us, you know.'

'Yes, yes, quite so,' murmured Mr Ott, still in a rapt exchange of looks with Bella, and at the same moment, each reached out to the other; he seized her hand in his, then bent his head over it, brushing her knuckles with his lips.

Once again, I noticed Mr Ott wore a ring on his little finger, and now, seeing their hands joined, I realised the stone in his ring was, as in hers, a carnelian. Before I could make sense of this connection, their hands had parted, and I was forced ahead, propelled by a determined push from Alys.

'Look at this crowd,' said Alys peevishly. 'We shall never find seats together; I wish we had not come.'

'Stay with Ann – you will find two seats easily. Do not worry about us.' Not giving Alys a chance to object, Bella swept me away to the front of the hall, and secured two seats for us in the second row. 'Will this be all right for you?'

'Yes, of course.'

'I thought you might like to be closer to the speaker – since he is your friend. It does not matter where the girls sit, and certainly there is no necessity for us to sit like a line of ducks.' She gave me an appealing glance, as if she feared she had done wrong, so I hastened to thank her for her thoughtfulness in finding me a seat near the front.

'They are too possessive of me, I fear,' she went on. 'Perhaps it is not unusual, having been orphaned so young, that they

241

should cling . . . but they are grown up now. They must learn. They will soon be embarking on their own adventures.' From her words, it seemed she was still preoccupied by her sisters, but there was a brightness in her eyes and colour in her cheeks that had nothing to do with them.

A full-figured, fair-haired young woman had arrived to claim a seat in the front row, and it was clear by the muted flurry of excitement that greeted her that it had been saved for her, as a person of some consequence. It was, evidently, the best seat in the house, and she preened and smiled with satisfaction, nodding regally as she accepted the greetings of her admirers. She was dressed in half-mourning, and as she adjusted the fine black woollen shawl, I saw that it was pinned with a carnelian brooch.

It could hardly be coincidence, unless the stone were a particular Norfolk fad.

'Who is she?' I whispered to Bella.

'Miss Goodall.'

I remembered that was the name of the farmer who had been poisoned by his wife – and also a name from Mr Manning's address book – just as Bella leaned closer to murmur in my ear, 'The daughter of the late farmer, and now owner of the farm. She is a student in Mr Ott's School, and one of his chief benefactors. She has given him land on which his school might be built – if he can raise the funds.'

'Did Mr Ott give her that brooch?'

She nodded, and I saw her give a surreptitious stroke to her own ring. 'Carnelian, the stone of the Sun and Venus, is his personal talisman. He has the habit of giving some sort of token incorporating the stone to his friends and close associates. Mr Manning had a small silver pillbox that he always carried about his person, although he could not display it as obviously as I do this.'

Only then did I understand how wrong I had been about her feelings for Charles Manning. If she loved anyone, it was Felix Ott: that was obvious from her heightened colour, the look they had exchanged, and the way she treasured his ring. She had refused his offer of marriage, choosing to remain single, dedicated to her profession. And he had not taken that rejection well, judging by the vindictive remarks he had made in his September lecture. Yet he had probably repented of that, and hoped it might be forgotten. I felt certain from his adoring gaze and the kissing of her hand that Mr Ott was still deeply in love with the woman who sat beside me.

This went some way towards explaining his quarrel with Manning. Would that love have been enough to drive him to murder? When he discovered Manning's despicable plan – whichever one of the sisters it was aimed at – had a jealous, protective rage made him kill his former friend, either by poison or by mental force, as the only certain way to stop him? Such an emotion was a powerful driver, and Ott had certainly had the opportunity to kill Manning on the night he died.

The buzz of conversation in the hall died down as Felix Ott approached the podium at the front.

'Welcome all,' he said, his voice booming out and silencing the last few chatterers. 'What a pleasure it is to see so many of you have decided to venture out on such a cold night – it makes me feel that my message is getting through, and reaching the very people I wish to attract to our School. I hope those of you who have not yet done so will join the School of British Wisdom after tonight's lecture, whether as a novice scholar or as a supporting member. The information is all in the brochure, so I will not take up any more time on that now.' He cleared his throat.

'Tonight's lecture is given in memory of my late friend Charles Manning. His death was sudden and unexpected, and has taken away a fine young man who had given evidence of much promise, which he sadly was not able to live long enough to fulfil. Even in his short residence in Aylmerton he made many friends who mourn him. He was, as well as being a close personal friend of mine, one of the most diligent and devoted of all students in our fledgling School, which is much the poorer for his loss.

'How well I remember our first meeting with this ardent young scholar. Charles had come to Cromer for a short holiday, two or three days to walk along the beach, think about his writing, and let the sea air clear the soot and grime of London from his lungs. On one of his walks he encountered another young man, Albert Cooke, who told him about my School. Charles was immediately intrigued, his own studies having suggested to him that there must be a source of hidden knowledge closer than India or Tibet; ancient wisdom that could be found right here in his native land. Albert brought him along to meet me, and we three talked long into the night. By dawn, his course was set; Charles returned to London just long enough to resign his job and pack his things, then he came back here to begin an exciting new phase of his life, dedicated to the rediscovery and transmission of ancient British wisdom. Alas, that life was cut short.'

With a tragic expression, Ott paused to compose himself. He repeated, 'Alas, that life was cut short. However, before he left us, Charles Manning had time to research a subject little known outside these parts, but of potentially great interest: the mystery of the shrieking pits. Who made them, for what purpose, and when? What can folklore and legend tell us about this peculiar feature of the north Norfolk landscape?

'Although he did not live to publish his report, and his final conclusions will never be known, Charles did keep a notebook, and I know he would have wished his work, even unfinished, to reach a wider audience. Therefore, I have invited Mr Jasper Jesperson, who was one of the last people to see Charles Manning alive, to prepare a paper based upon the notes he left behind.

'Gentleman, ladies, please will you give a warm welcome to tonight's speaker, all the way from London, Mr Jasper Jesperson.'

As he spoke his last sentence, the audience broke out in polite applause as a door in the wall behind him opened, and Mr Jesperson emerged, wearing his black evening clothes, and an unusually solemn expression on his long, pale face. As he stepped up to the podium the light from the gas jets gave an uncanny glow to his red curls, so that for a brief moment he seemed to wear a nimbus of light, a radiant halo around his head.

245

Stirred by the rising inflection of Mr Ott's voice as much as by the guest speaker's appearance, the audience clapped more enthusiastically. When it eventually died down, Mr Jesperson began to speak in a relaxed, authoritative way, without notes.

Having often been the recipient of one of Mr Jesperson's *ex tempore* lectures, I knew what a powerfully retentive memory he possessed, and that his mind was well-stocked with facts and figures relating to any number of unlikely subjects.

'Most of you are local residents, and therefore need no lengthy introduction to the feature known collectively as shrieking pits,' he said. 'They are found in an area stretching along the coast from Cromer to Cley, with those at Aylmerton, Weybourne, and Beeston being the best known. In the last century there were many more than we see today.

'When were they made? And what for? There are two main theories, the most popular being that they are the remains of ancient dwellings where our prehistoric ancestors made their homes.

'None of the Aylmerton pits now extant had ever been the subject of specific study – prior to the arrival of Mr Albert Cooke, whose work was then carried on by our Mr Manning – but some forty years ago the Weybourne pits were extensively excavated by Mr Harrod, who found no evidence of human habitation in them and concluded that they were Roman in origin and had been used for metal-working. However, some twenty years after that, Mr Spurrell, the well-known antiquarian, argued that while *some* were undoubtedly associated with iron workings, *most* were far older than the Roman occupation, and they were better described as hut-circles or pit-dwellings.'

He paused and, leaning forward over the podium, smiled a mischievous smile. 'So much for the scientific evidence. What else is there? Memory. Of course, there is no one alive today who remembers a time so long ago, but what about folk memory? The memory of the race is reflected in our language; in stories, songs, even place names. Consider the name: *shrieking pits*.

'Why are they called that? Well, there is a story that explains . . . I see many of you smiling and nodding – yes, you all know the story. It is represented on the poster made to advertise my lecture. A woman – some say she is old, with long white hair; others that she is young and dressed in white; some that she is veiled; but all agree that she is the source of the shrieking as she runs about, peering down into the pits and wringing her hands. Why is she distressed?'

Mr Jesperson paused and looked out at the audience as if expecting an answer, and a young man obliged, shouting out, 'She lost her baby!'

'In the pits? That seems a *very* odd place to leave a baby.' His delivery of this line won him a burst of laughter.

The same young man obliged again: 'Somebody else done it. Her man. He threw it down the pit.'

'Is that the story known to you all?' Mr Jesperson cocked his head and listened to the babble of response from other members of the audience. A few agreed; the greater number did not.

'Tell me what other explanations you have heard for such

behaviour, please,' he said. 'If you would be so kind as to raise your hands . . . You, sir? Yes?'

A thin, middle-aged man rose to his feet and said, 'There is no explanation required. She is a spectre, and behaves in standard fashion of her kind, repeating a few simple actions over and over again in the same place, in her case, shrieking and wringing her hands. I have never seen her myself, but I have heard the shrieks.'

More hands were up, waving for Mr Jesperson's attention. He called upon a man who said he had heard that the woman had been driven mad by an unspecified crime and ever afterwards her spirit haunted the pits. Another man said she was looking for something she had lost, and could never rest unless she could recover it, but no one could say what she had lost. The next one said it was certainly a baby, but he had never heard why she should be searching for it in the pits.

'After all, it's only a ghost story; you can't expect it to make sense,' declared one gentleman with a long nose and bushy eyebrows.

'Ah, but I *do* expect them to make sense – their own kind of sense,' replied Mr Jesperson, leaning forward intently. 'Mr Manning was hardly the first investigator to believe that folklore and local legends, including ghost stories, may contain a core of truth. The difficulty is in sifting out the later accretions, the helpful "explanations" from the original matter. It is like panning for gold.

'There is no evidence that the legend of the shrieking woman reflects an actual, historic crime – infanticide, abduction, or a woman driven to madness – and there is no written reference to this shrieking woman prior to about 1830, but of course that tells us nothing about the antiquity of the oral tradition. Perhaps it reflects a prehistoric crime, the primal horror of which continues to haunt the human mind through the ages. Or perhaps the legend was a deliberate creation – the fear of meeting such a disturbing apparition could serve better than any physical barrier to inhibit exploration of the pits, at least amongst the credulous.'

'Let us return for a moment to that question of what the pits were *for*. Were they, as the majority opinion has it, truly the homes of our ancestors?

'I find the idea strange. We have heard of the cavemen, but to take up residence in an existing cave is surely different from deliberately excavating a hole in order to live underground when they might have felled trees or piled up stones to create a warm, dry, airier and altogether more comfortable residence. A perusal of Mr Manning's notes shows he thought the same. If these pits were homes, as the antiquarians insist, might they have been inhabited by another race? Not our lineal ancestors, but an earlier form of human being – which may have coexisted with our own earliest forebears. We have evidence of Neanderthal Man. And if there were two distinct forms of human being living at one time – why not more?

'Manning is not the first and will not be the last scholar to suggest that stories about elves, goblins and fairies are a distant folk memory of a time when early humans shared their world with other intelligent species. There are pygmies still in Africa, and so there may have been long ago in Britain. Whether they were naturally subterranean dwellers, or forced to go underground for some reason, this could explain the shrieking pits.

'Both Cooke and Manning were interested in the possibility that this pygmy race continued to survive into recent centuries, spending their entire lives in hiding, having become ever more fearful of the dominant human race. On the rare occasions when they were seen, they were taken for ghosts or fairies – and as such, in some places, they are even seen today.'

Beside me, Bella sniffed. I did not have to see her expression to sense her scornful disbelief. I wondered where Mr Jesperson was going with this – and why.

'In Ireland and Scotland and in all the Celtic fringes, mounds, earthworks, chambered tombs as well as hills and caves are said to be the entrance to the otherworld, where the fairy-folk live. Norfolk is peculiarly bereft of fairylore – we might also consider the lack of hills, and the fact that more than tumuli, Norfolk has . . . pits.'

There was a titter from somewhere in the hall in response to the dramatic pause before he emphasised the final word, and for a moment I was afraid Mr Jesperson had misjudged his audience. They might begin by laughing, and quickly turn to jeering.

Mr Jesperson smiled. His shoulders dropped and he tilted his head slightly, looking very much at his ease. 'Do you know, before I came to Norfolk I was led to believe it was very flat. And then I came here, and was agreeably surprised by how varied and interesting the landscape is, with so many good viewpoints, and actual hills – not as high as in Scotland, to be sure, but distinctive enough to be given names. And so, having learned that the general knowledge relating to Norfolk's flatness is not to be swallowed whole, I am cautious also about the supposed dearth of fairy lore. It may be that the stories are, like the hills, hiding in plain sight. There is evidence, if you know how to look, of their existence in plenty of stories, most of them seeming to have nothing at all to do with this subterranean, pygmy race. For there is another tradition about them, which is well known, and that concerns their secrecy. They do not wish to be spoken of. Even to acknowledge them when they have helped you can have a bad result – as in the stories of the farm-wife who knits warm garments and leaves them out for the brownies who had been cleaning her kitchen at night.

'So, they are spoken of indirectly, in a roundabout way, under different names. Not fairies or brownies or pixies or elves but – "them", "the others", and "the good neighbours".'

I almost jumped out of my seat at that. In my mind I heard that same phrase repeated, not in Mr Jesperson's clear, penetrating tones, but in Maria's hurried whisper. 'The good neighbours.' That was the whole phrase; and now, belatedly, it occurred to me that she did not blame her human neighbours, and had not been thinking of witches and human sacrifices, but of something else entirely.

'There are no stories I can find in Norfolk about babies who are stolen and a stock left in their place, although in Ireland

and Cornwall the fertility problems of this other race are well-known, providing an explanation for why they should wish to take our children.'

I became convinced that Mr Jesperson was trying to send me a message. Had he not found a scrap of Maria's missing shawl in the shrieking pit across the road from the Vicarage? But what he meant me to understand from all this nonsense about fairies, I could not imagine.

'Yet consider the shrieking woman, searching for her child,' he went on. 'Perhaps this story, with its mysterious lack of detail, reflects an actual event from a more distant day, something prehistoric and long lost to present knowledge, yet surviving, like a vestigial tailbone, a reminder of a species now extinct.'

He paused. 'Or, perhaps, the survival of the story serves a purpose, with the particulars stripped away – its purpose is to frighten; to make people avoid the pits. Many of them are gone now, filled in by farmers. But there is one shrieking pit at least that still survives. It is protected by its location, not marked on any map, and by surroundings that do not appeal to picnickers. Rumours of adders in the woods, the boggy ground and sinkholes, references to bad air, and those toadstools, spotted red and white, growing in a formation known locally as "the Poison Ring" – all these things, so insignificant in themselves, work by cumulative effect to provide safety from spying eyes and accidental discovery.'

An arm went up in the audience, and was vigorously waved

until Mr Jesperson could no longer pretend not to see. 'Yes, sir? You have a question?'

'I certainly do.' A wiry, white-haired man of pugnacious aspect sprang to his feet. 'You imply one moment that this pygmy race is extinct; the next that it continues to coexist with us, and relies on superstitious fears to keep from being discovered.'

Mr Jesperson inclined his head and with a slight smile asked, 'And your question?'

'Well, which is it?'

'Which . . . ?'

'Are these creatures still living or not?'

Mr Jesperson raised his eyebrows. 'I really could not say. However, I think it is fair to assume that Albert Cooke met his death trying to answer that very question.'

There were some gasps in the hall, and an undercurrent of muttering that grew louder, until a young man called out, 'You say the fairies killed him?' And there was a general outbreak of laughter.

Mr Jesperson waited for it to die down before he went on. 'No, I do not say that. I tend to agree with the police, that Cooke met his death by accident, striking his head. If he slipped on the grass, perhaps as the result of a sudden fright . . . The only problem with that theory is that the nearest and most likely place where he could have acquired a fatal injury is at the bottom of the pit. And if he met his death at the bottom of the pit, why was his body not found there, instead of lying in the middle of the Poison Ring?'

His first questioner, the white-haired gentleman, was still on his feet, and now spoke up again: 'But what do you think?'

'I am not here to give my opinion,' he replied gently. 'My opinion does not matter. Before this week I had never heard of the shrieking pits, nor given any thought to the idea of an aboriginal race of British pygmies. All of this was new territory when I first encountered Charles Manning's notes. My intention this evening is not to pass judgement on his ideas and discoveries, but only to give them a public airing, so that his work may outlive him, if it is found worthy.'

The old gentleman would not give up. 'Well then, what did Manning think? Did he think there was something still living in the pits?'

'That was a question still under investigation when he died.'

'So there's no answer?'

'This may be something for future investigation by Mr Ott's School,' said Mr Jesperson. 'Thank you for your kind attention.' He bowed.

Recognising that Mr Jesperson had concluded his presentation, Felix Ott came forward to invite questions from the floor. A sea of hands appeared, but as he called upon various individuals, it was soon apparent that although many people wished to be heard, very few had anything that could be described as a question. Some wished to express agreement, disagreement, or disapproval, but most had a story to tell: inexplicable experiences, strange encounters, disappearances, noises in the night – I found it all quite interesting and should have been glad to hear more, but Bella claimed my attention.

'I cannot believe it,' she murmured, frowning. 'Charles never said anything of this to us.'

'You mean about the . . .' I hesitated over what word to use. 'About the pygmy race?'

'Not anything. He never even expressed any particular interest in the shrieking pits.'

'I thought it was for the shrieking pits that he came to Aylmerton?'

'He never said so. I understood that the shrieking pits were an interest of his friend, Mr Cooke.

'Perhaps Charles took it up as a subject to investigate, to honour his friend,' she mused. 'But it never struck me that the question of the shrieking pits – how they came to be – was the sort of mystery that Felix's followers go in for. I cannot pronounce on Mr Cooke's interest, for he never shared any particulars of his researches with me; I only know that when he used my library, the books he consulted were on the subject of mushrooms.'

CHAPTER NINETEEN

After the Meeting

When the last opinion had been expressed and the meeting had been brought to a formal close by Mr Ott, I asked Bella if I might introduce her to Mr Jesperson.

'Thank you, I should like that very much. I hope you will not mind if I question him rather ferociously on this matter of a pygmy race dwelling beneath the ground in these parts. I had never heard such a thing, in all my years here, and I should like to know where Charles came across such an idea.'

Although the general movement in the hall was towards the exit, there were others who had the same aim as us, and Mr Ott and Mr Jesperson were encircled before we could reach them.

'This may take a little while,' I said apologetically, but Bella smilingly indicated that she did not mind waiting.

'*There* you are.' I looked around to see Alys bearing down on us, her sister in tow. 'Come along, what are you waiting for?'

'Di is going to introduce us. Would you not like to meet her friend, too?'

Ann looked compliant, if somewhat sleepy, but Alys frowned. 'No, thank you. I had quite enough of his fairy tales – what nonsense! I am sure Mr Manning never said anything of the kind. I think that Mr Jesperson simply made it all up. Perhaps he thinks we are such unsophisticated yokels in these parts as to swallow any whopper. I beg your pardon, Artemis; I know he is a friend of yours, but – troglodytic pygmies in Norfolk! Quite absurd. Now come along, my darling Arabella.'

Bella laughed. 'I quite agree, it sounds absurd, but we must let the man speak in his own defence before we convict him of being either a liar or a fantasist.'

'No, why should we? I do not care to hear another word from him. And look at poor little Ann, how pale and tired she is, nearly dropping. And, you know I hate to complain, darling, but I must confess I am feeling a bit unwell myself. This hall is not warm. If I have to stay in it much longer, I am sure I shall catch a cold – if I have not already.'

Bella sighed. 'Very well then, go home. Go, take Ann with you. We shall stay.'

But the firmness of Bella's tone seemed only to increase her sister's resistance. 'Leave you? And how will you get home?'

'I told you – do not worry. Miss Lane and I will manage perfectly well.'

Alys spoke flatly: 'You mean me to drive?'

'Yes, why ever not? You love to drive – you always—'

'Not at night – not when I'm feeling like this. Do you want me to die of cold?'

'Don't be silly.'

'I am not being silly. I have told you how unwell I feel. The best thing for me is to go straight to bed. It is always best to nip these things in the bud – prevention is better than cure; you say that yourself. If I am worse tomorrow, it will be your fault. And if you do not care about *me,* think of our little Annie!' She grabbed her younger sister's arm, to pull her forward, and I strongly suspect she gave her a hard pinch, as well, for Ann sucked in her breath and tears welled in her eyes.

'Please,' she whispered. 'I should like to go home now.'

It was, in my view, the most obvious, childish attempt at manipulation, and yet it worked. Bella proved as liable to feelings of guilt as the most tender-hearted mother there ever was. 'Oh – poor little Ann, you do look done-in. I am sorry, dear, I should not have made you come out.' Heaving a sigh, she turned to me, 'You must excuse us . . . Will you come, too?'

'No – I must have a word with my friend. He will see me safely back to Wayside Cross. Are you certain you cannot wait a few more minutes?'

She only shook her head, mouth turned down ruefully. 'Please, give him my apologies, and invite him to call tomorrow, or another day. I should very much enjoy meeting him some other time. And please tell Mr Ott I was sorry to rush off, but that my sister is unwell. I know he will understand. Tell him . . . tell him I was very pleased to see him again, and only wish there had been time for us to talk. Tell him—'

Through all this, Alys had been tugging at Bella's arm, and

at last dislodged her, pulling her away in midsentence. Mr Ott, although caught up in a discussion with Miss Goodall, did not fail to notice their departure, and from the yearning look that crossed his face I thought that, if not for the restraining presence of that other lady, so clearly one of his inner circle, he would have run and intercepted Bella at the door.

There was no need to hurry now, so I waited until everyone else had left, and I was alone in the hall with the two men before I approached them. Mr Ott looked relieved when I passed Bella's message on to him.

'Ah, of course. I understand. Poor little Ann. I had feared, if only for a moment, that there might have been a misunderstanding when I saw how Miss Bulstrode hurried away, but—'

Mr Jesperson interrupted: 'You mean you imagined she might still mistrust you since your attempt to blacken her name?'

Mr Ott gave a start. 'What do you mean?'

'I refer to your September meeting. Prior to then, you referred to "wise women" rather than witches, feeling that the name of witch had been debased, tarred with the brush of evil by the Christian Church.'

'Yes, and so I firmly believe.'

'Then why, in the talk you gave in September did you raise those old – and according to you *now*, false – spectres of infant sacrifice and devil worship, and declare there were women here in the county today who behaved so abominably?'

Mr Ott stared at Mr Jesperson with a wide, fixed gaze. After a moment, the tip of his tongue crept out to wet his lips. He cleared his throat. 'Well, that is not right. Someone must have misunderstood what I said.'

'No, they understood exactly what you wanted them to understand. You are very careful in how you express yourself on these subjects. You know how ill-feeling has been stirred up in the past by accusations of witchcraft. You knew, when you spoke of infant sacrifice and evil women just how that would be interpreted, and believed, and spread to others . . . It was a deliberate and malicious act on your part.' Mr Jesperson spoke without heat, as one who passes a final judgement, and remained unmoved by Ott's faltering attempts to object.

'I know what you said. I do not ask *if* you said these things but only *why*. What did you think you would achieve?'

'Nothing! I did not mean – I was misunderstood!'

'Why did you do it?'

Ott drew a hand across his brow. 'I . . . may have said a few things that were wrong. All right, I admit that I did. It was done in a moment of weakness. If you will allow me to explain . . .'

'Please do.'

Ott looked around, and so did I. A young man had come into the hall and was now noisily moving the chairs and stacking them against the walls. 'Perhaps we should go somewhere else. My rooms?'

'As you wish.' We followed Felix Ott out of the hall, into the chilly night. The clouds had cleared away, and although the streets were still wet, the air smelled of sea-spray rather than rain. A short walk took us to a fine stone house overlooking the seafront where Mr Ott occupied the whole of the first floor.

The reception room was large and comfortably furnished; it was a trifle chill, but the makings of a fire waited in the grate, and Mr Ott soon had it blazing. 'Would you like anything to eat?' he asked. 'Or tea? Brandy?'

'No, thank you,' said Mr Jesperson before I could say that I did fancy a cup of tea. He stood blocking the doorway, staring across the room at the man standing before the fire. His expression was stern. 'Let's not drag this out, Ott. This is not a social call. I asked you questions which you have evaded, and they are questions I think I may answer for myself.'

Toying with the poker, Ott smiled uneasily. 'Go ahead.'

'You called it a moment of weakness. Miss Bulstrode – Arabella Bulstrode – is your weakness. You asked her to marry you, she refused. You minded that refusal more than you could say. You were cut to the quick. You pretended to be her friend, but you were not. Perhaps it was, as you say, only a moment's weakness, and soon regretted, but during that evening's meeting you sought your revenge by painting her as a witch – not the sort of "wise woman" witch your School holds up for admiration, but the villain of legend, the devil-worshipping child-killer who never really existed, except as an excuse to torment and murder helpless old women. Did you really mean to stir up that atavistic fear in your listeners and create a witch-hunt?'

'No!' He scowled down at the fire, then bent and carefully replaced the poker in the stand before turning to face his inquisitor. 'I never *meant* anything. There was no plan. I lashed out in a moment of weakness – of vileness, I admit – that I regretted immediately. I let myself get carried away in that talk – I often am, when lecturing; some other spirit seems to take over. What was meant to be a sly dig, a hurtful jibe, somehow grew and changed into something worse. Afterwards, I was horrified by myself. I could only hope my ill-judged words would not linger long in anyone's memory. Fortunately, that meeting was not terribly well attended. *She* was not there to hear it, at least!'

He sighed, stepping away from the fire, gesturing at the plump sofa and padded chairs. 'Please, won't you be seated? We may as well continue this uncomfortable conversation in some comfort.'

I took one of the seats and after a moment Jesperson perched on another, but Felix Ott remained standing. 'Are you sure you would not care for some refreshment? Whisky or brandy, or a nice hot cup of tea?'

'No thank you,' Jesperson replied again. 'No more of your delaying tactics. I want your confession.'

Ott widened his eyes. 'But you have heard it!'

Jesperson smiled grimly. 'Not all of it. You have admitted your sin against the blameless Miss Bulstrode, but said not a word about what you did to Mr Manning.'

He paled. 'What do you mean?'

'You killed him.'

Ott staggered and all but fell into the nearest chair. 'How – how – how—?'

Jesperson leaned forward, his gazed fixed. 'As to that, you must enlighten us.'

Shaking his head helplessly he replied, 'I had nothing to do with it! And you know it was a natural death! No one's fault.'

'Then why pretend you did not see him again after he left Cromer? Why did you lie to me? The game is up, man! You were with him in London. Either you went there with him, or you encountered him by chance, but in either case you invited him to your club. And there you were witnessed quarrelling with him over a woman. When he left, you followed him, and when you caught him up—'

'No!' Ott straightened up as he protested, then sagged again. 'I did go after him, yes, to try to stop him, but by the time I reached the street, he was out of sight. It was a foggy night. I had left it too late, I realised, and gave up any idea of pursuit, then and there, and retired to my room for the night.'

'Because you had no need to catch up to him,' Jesperson said. 'You served him a drink laced with poison, and let him go, knowing he would be far away when he died, imagining there was nothing to connect you to him. But you were wrong.'

'*You* are wrong,' Ott declared, his face flushed. 'I did not kill Charles Manning. I had nothing to do with his death. The news came as a great shock – and sadness – to me. He was my friend. I had no reason to want him dead.'

'Oh no?' Jesperson gave him a cool, sceptical look. 'You were very angry with him, according to my witness. He meant to do something – you tried to argue him out of it, and failed. When words fail, men often turn to violence.'

'I did not kill him.'

'I should believe you now, despite your previous lies?'

Felix Ott frowned as he began to recover his self-possession. 'You are not the police. You have no right to question me.'

'I told you when we met that I was enquiring at the behest of Manning's family. This is still the case. You pretended you were willing to help me, but in fact you misled me. If you had nothing to hide, why not tell me the truth?'

'Excuse me, I must have a brandy,' he said, jumping up from his chair and crossing the room to a drinks cabinet. We watched and waited in silence as he took out a bottle and glass and poured himself a generous measure, from which he took a large swallow before he returned to his seat.

'I did not think it was your business. If I told you I had met Charles in London, if I had told you why he was there . . .' He shook his head. 'I would not have her name dragged through the mud.'

'You had better tell me everything,' Jesperson said grimly. 'Otherwise, I shall deliver you up to the police. There are poisons which leave little trace, which may stop a man's heart – you could have had access to them, and you certainly had the opportunity. As for motive – jealousy is a strong one.'

'Jealousy?' He sounded incredulous. 'How could I be jealous of Charles? He had nothing that I wanted – he was my acolyte – he did everything to please me.'

'You were overheard quarrelling about a woman. And you have just told me—'

'That was not jealousy.'

Jesperson shrugged. 'You wished to protect her from him.'

The hand not holding the brandy glass curled into a fist, and he struck the arm of his chair. 'He told me – he brought it to me like a cat bringing a mouse to its master – that he meant to marry one of the Bulstrode sisters. He thought it would please me – please, yet also sting, this proof that he had succeeded where I had failed. That is how he thought of it – that we were alike; that we had the same end in view.'

'He told you he meant to marry Miss Bulstrode?'

Ott snorted. 'He would have no chance with Miss Bulstrode, and he knew it! It was Ann – he found her the weakest link, young and foolish and susceptible to his flattery. But because she was so young, and because he had so little to offer, it would be a long engagement – and Miss Bulstrode, who is more like the girls' mother than their half-sister, decreed that a formal engagement should have to wait until Ann was older. Charles pretended to agree – but he was plotting a different outcome.'

'How long had you known?'

Ott took another gulp of brandy and shook his head. 'I learned of the attachment for the first time that very day. I met Charles by chance, in London, and invited him to my club when he admitted he had time to kill.

'He was in a strange mood; nervy, excited, yet also repulsed – by himself, or his own intentions, as I realised later. He hinted at an assignation, a secret rendezvous, but when he'd taken a few drinks he confessed that he had talked Ann into coming to London and meeting him that evening. They would have supper in a private room, where he intended to have his way with her. If she was willing, all to the good; if not, he would force her. After that, he believed, there could be no impediment to their marriage, and no delay.' With a look of disgust he paused to drink off the rest of his brandy.

'I was horrified, of course. How could he speak so casually of committing such an act against the girl he claimed to love? But he did *not* love her – that was his crime. He wanted her for what she represented to him – because he knew I had paid suit to Miss Bulstrode – he imagined it would be some sort of dynastic alliance, to have this old Norfolk family, with their ties to the ancient knowledge, connected to our School – oh, it was foolish.' He stood, and made as if to get another drink, but then sat down again abruptly, and put the empty glass on the floor.

'I tried to explain he had it wrong; told him in no uncertain terms he must not do such a dreadful thing – imagine, how she would feel about the husband who had forced her into marriage – but he would not be dissuaded. He had no money or prospects – *she* did – she must be his wife.' He sighed heavily, shoulders slumped. 'I could not stop him. I tried – tried going after him, but he was already lost in the fog. So I went back to my room and I prayed.'

I suppose I must have moved, or made a noise of disbelief – my response, whatever it was, captured Mr Ott's attention, and he looked at me directly for the first time since he had started his story.

'Oh, yes, I prayed. Not to your foreign, desert god, but to the gods of *this* land. I asked them to intercede, to stop Manning before he could harm anyone.'

He turned his eyes away and gazed blankly at the floor. 'I did not imagine such a fatal intercession, but, after all, one cannot dictate to the gods. My prayer was granted. Not as I should have liked it to be – the School has lost one of its sturdiest pillars – but the woman's innocence was protected.'

'You would have us believe Manning was struck down by the power of some ancient god?'

He shrugged. 'You may believe what you like. Charles died of natural causes, as the police surgeon found. But what caused his heart to stop?'

'Your prayer?'

Ott looked calmly at Jesperson. 'It is no wonder you Christians have so little luck with all your prayers – such bloodless affairs. Mine was not like that.' He held out his hand, palm up, and we saw how it was lined and scarred; amongst the old scars was one more recent cut, red and inflamed.

'Only a few drops of my blood, but enough to make it more than a symbol. The gods granted my prayer. Does that make me a murderer?'

CHAPTER TWENTY

An Appearance and a Disappearance

As we walked back to Aylmerton, I told Mr Jesperson what I had written in the letter he had not yet had time to read.

'*Cerbera odollum* contains a poison so powerful, yet so little known in this country that its results would undoubtedly be seen as death by natural causes,' I said, as we walked along the road under a large, bright moon. 'And Mr Ott knew where to get it. He was at one time a regular visitor to Wayside Cross, and even afterwards he might have crept into the glasshouse secretly to steal one of those deadly nuts.'

'That presumes premeditation,' my friend objected gently. 'Unless you think he always carried it with him, just in case a deadly poison might come in handy. From everything we have heard, the two men were on friendly terms, and Ott had no reason to wish any harm to Manning until he revealed his dastardly plan.'

I was not ready to give up my idea of Ott as a murderer. 'But what if Ott had learned of it earlier — what if he had gone to

London precisely with the intent of stopping Mr Manning, and what Colonel Mallet witnessed was not their first argument, but the last of several?'

'How did Ott manage to administer the poison – the men did not dine together.'

'He could have put it in his drink.'

I thought this a reasonable suggestion until I saw Mr Jesperson's grin. 'Even ground to powder, a nut that size would turn a glass of brandy into bitter, undrinkable sludge.'

'Well, maybe they did eat together, before they reached the club.'

'If Ott had already administered the poison condemning his one-time friend to death, is it likely they would have spent their last half-hour together in bitter argument? No, Miss Lane, I understand you do not care for Mr Ott, but he is not our killer. I have read about the effects of *Cerbera odollum,* and they do not include hallucinations or extreme emotional states. It is reckoned to be a bringer of a swift and peaceful death. Does that sound like Charles Manning at the end?'

I had to admit it did not. 'He looked terrified,' I agreed, as the memory of the man's face, pale and sweating and wide-eyed, came back to me.

'His pupils were dilated,' said Mr Jesperson. 'A common physiological response to opiates.'

'Well then, who do you think killed him – and how?' I demanded, a bit nettled by his rejection of my best suggestion.

'Manning ingested something, either intentionally or unknowingly. It caused the hallucinations, and the great stress on his heart, which manifested as fear and anxiety, until finally the strain was too much and his heart could take no more.'

'But if you do not think Mr Ott gave him this "something", who did?'

'Cunning Verrell.'

'What?' I stopped walking, then had to hurry to catch him up again. 'Why should Cunning Verrell kill Charles Manning?'

'Oh, not intentionally,' he replied calmly. 'And I may be completely wrong. It is certain that Verrell would not remain long in business – or indeed at liberty! – if his customers were dropping like flies. Spanish fly, the most famous aphrodisiac of all, known since ancient times, is also a deadly poison. The Medicis used it for both purposes. But that is an agonising death, causing internal damage which could not have been overlooked during the autopsy.'

He shook his head. 'Cunning Verrell will have his own recipe, and I would be willing to bet it includes something to make the heart race, as well as something to provoke wild dreams, and something else that looks like . . . er, the organ meant to be affected. As we found none of it on his person, Manning probably took a double or even a triple dose. And if he did suffer from some inherent weakness of the heart – which is possible, despite his brother's ignorance of it – his excitement may have turned to fear, and quickly overtaxed his system, leading to death.'

'How can we find out?'

He glanced down at me. 'I hope to have a telegram tomorrow with a complete list of ingredients.'

I gaped at him and he took pity on my slowness and explained: 'I left the mixture with a chemist in London who agreed to analyse it for me. I hope you did not think I purchased that concoction for my own use.' His eyes glittered in the moonlight and I suddenly felt unaccountably nervous, and looked away at the empty, tree-lined road ahead.

'It may be that we will find the answer there,' he said. 'Maybe even a bit of the old *Cerbera odollum* mashed up with powdered oyster shells and a bit of ginger root. You say the glasshouse is not locked; Verrell might have crept in one night and stolen anything that took his fancy. It would be a pity, though, if in his foolishness he has caused a man's death.'

A pity for the old cunning man, who would certainly have to be stopped from selling any more of his deadly medicines, but poetic justice if Charles Manning had brought about his own death by attempting to commit an outrage against an innocent young woman, I thought grimly.

One thing of which we did not speak, and which preyed upon my mind, was the question of Ann Bulstrode's involvement, and how much she or her sisters knew.

They had made it clear to me that visits to London were not usual for any of them, and it had been plainly stated that they had not been there for months. I could hardly blame them for not telling me about Ann's unhappy final encounter with Charles

Manning – a meeting I felt certain must have taken place, or why else would he have consumed the aphrodisiacs?

Any attempt I made to question Ann seemed likely to end with her in hysterics, so I thought my best hope was to try to find out what I could from Bella, and thus, the following morning, I followed her into her office, assuring her that I would leave as soon as 'a client appeared – or a patient – or whatever you call the people who come to you for help?'

She smiled. 'I call them by their names.'

'It is only women who come, is that right?'

'With their problems, yes.'

'Men, in similar situations, visit a cunning man instead, I understand. Are you acquainted with Cunning Verrell?'

'I know who he is.'

A coolness in her manner warned me to try a different approach. I said, 'Do women ever ask you for love potions?'

She gave me a curious look. 'Is that what you want?'

'I? No, certainly not! I was talking about other people,' I responded, flustered by this unexpectedly personal turn.

'Perhaps you would be surprised to learn how often someone may feel embarrassed by their own desires, unable to ask for what they want except "for a friend".'

'Bella, I assure you, I had no thought of asking you to make up anything for me, least of all a love potion!'

Repressing a smile, she dropped her gaze and moved away to add more coal to the fire.

'Love potions like the one in the story of *Tristan and Iseult* do not really exist,' she said, without looking at me. 'There is nothing anyone can buy to make someone fall in love. But there are ways of achieving the same end. A spell can be cast – but not by someone who is not involved. If a woman comes to me, desperate to win the heart of a man she loves, or to lure back a straying lover, I can instruct her in various ways and means. I might provide a recipe, it might be for a cake, or a warming drink, and if it is made of the right ingredients, and prepared with care and concentration and complete commitment on the part of the woman, then, when that cake or that drink is consumed by the object of her affections, there is a very good chance that it will cause a change in him, and the scales will fall from his eyes, and the next time he looks at her he will realise she is his own true love.'

'But men go to the cunning man, and he gives them something right away,' I said.

'Oh, but that is quite different.' She returned to her seat. 'He does not offer love potions, but aphrodisiacs.'

I knew the term 'aphrodisiac' came from my namesake goddess, Aphrodite, the goddess of love. 'Are they not the same thing?'

'Not at all.' She wrinkled her nose. 'What the cunning man sells has nothing to do with love, but only lust – and not even honest lust, but a simulation. They trick a man's body into performing – and much as they would like to believe otherwise, they only work on men, not women. Do you understand? Let me explain.'

And then, to my embarrassment, but even greater interest, she proceeded to give me a lecture on human sexuality, with the

273

aid of illustrations in a medical textbook. Although I thought I knew the basics of biology, it was quite an eye-opener.

'So now you see,' she concluded. 'When the male organ is engorged, and the man's heart races, he may believe himself to be excited – but it is a trick played upon his body. It can be a dangerous trick, and painful, but men who are foolish enough to think they can compel a woman's love, or buy it, are likely to treat their own bodies with similar brutality, as if they are stubborn creatures to be forced into performing . . . as if physical performance were the most important thing.'

She looked at me searchingly. 'No man who truly loved a woman should resort to such things as the cunning man supplies. If he has problems, there are better ways—'

A knock on the door startled us both; with an apologetic gesture to me, she called out, 'Yes? Come in.'

Nancy came in, holding out a folded piece of paper between finger and thumb with a look of distaste. 'For you, Miss. A strange man is at the door. He wants to look at some of your books.'

'Strange?'

'Very.'

Bella smiled and opened the note. Her eyebrows rose as she scanned it. 'Well, well! If *he* has sent you, perhaps I may forgive you dropping by without warning,' she murmured, and told the maid to show him in.

I got up to leave, but Bella detained me. 'Please, on no account leave me alone with this *strange man*.'

'Of course I will stay if you wish it. But – who is he?'

'A scholar, seemingly, and one with friends in high places. Usually I would expect to have a letter some weeks in advance, but sometimes – more often in the summer – someone who was formerly acquainted with my grandfather, or has simply heard about his collection, will call by in hope of seeing the library. Often there is a book they wish to purchase, or borrow – but in that case, they must be sent away disappointed.

'He may look at whatever he likes, but we will not leave him alone, to be sure he is not tempted to take anything away. I have discovered to my cost that even the most respectable address in Cambridge and even the most highly regarded scholars are not to be trusted if bibliophilia has them in its grip.'

She stopped speaking just before the door opened, and we waited in attentive silence as an odd-looking gentleman entered the room.

Now Nancy's reaction made sense, for I, too, found something very strange about this dirty, disreputable-looking character. Considering that he'd had his introduction from someone Bella respected, it seemed likely that his attire had more to do with the unworldliness of a dedicated scholar than outright poverty. He could not be blamed for the hunch-back which made him keep his head twisted to one side, and the green-glass spectacles he wore must be due to poor eyesight. I only wondered why, if he cared so little for appearances as his attire suggested, he spent money on perfumed grease to comb through his thick black hair. He smelled of attar of roses and stale clothes.

'Miss Bulstrode?' Noticing there were two women in the room, he moved his head slowly from one side to the other, reminding me of a tortoise. 'And, er, I beg your pardon.' His voice was rough and low, with a hint of Irish. 'I did not expect – your sister? Well, I am Seamus Rafferty, and sure I shall be eternally grateful for your kindness.'

'I am Miss Bulstrode, and this is Miss Lane. Let us not waste time; if you will tell me your area of interest, or which books you should like to consult . . . ?'

He nodded his head and bobbed a little as he rubbed his gloved hands together. 'Sure, sure. I am a philologist. You have, I believe, one or two Sanskrit texts? I should greatly love to see them.'

She looked surprised. 'Sanskrit. Yes . . . I could not tell you *what* they are, but I think I know *where* they are. Give me a moment.' She moved towards the bookcases and after a brief search returned with one large, bound volume, and two small ones.

He rubbed his hands again and made small squeaking sounds. I looked away, uncomfortable but also puzzled by something I could not quite put my finger on, as Bella showed him to a table with a reading lamp.

'I hope you will not let our presence disturb you,' she said. 'Miss Lane and I will speak quietly and try not to interrupt your reading.' She glanced at the clock on the mantelpiece and took a deep breath before saying firmly, 'You may have two hours. I hope that will be enough? If it is not, I will be happy to receive you another day.'

'Thank you,' he rasped, too entranced by the treasures now in his possession to look at anything else. He took no more notice of us as we retreated to the other side of the room, where Bella had her writing desk, upon the top of which Gabriel perched, as still as a statue.

Bella and I looked at each other. I could think of nothing to say, and although she may have been better than I at making polite conversation, she also appeared at a loss. Even if Mr Rafferty was effectively deaf in his absorption in Sanskrit texts, still, his presence limited our potential topics of conversation. We sat in silence for a few moments before she seized upon the usual recourse of the hostess and offered tea. I accepted with alacrity.

'Then – if you do not mind? I shall only be a few minutes in the kitchen.'

We both turned and cast our eyes in the direction of the oblivious scholar.

'I am happy to wait,' I said.

'Feel free to take any book down for yourself,' she offered.

'Thank you. There really is no need for you to hurry back. A cup of tea would be lovely.'

'Perhaps there will be cake as well,' she said, and gave me a grateful smile as she left. The heavy wooden door clicked quietly shut behind her, closing me in the library with Gabriel before me and the silent, studious Mr Rafferty behind me. I was still gazing at the beady-eyed crow when I heard Mr Jesperson's voice, clear and close at hand: 'Quick, where is it? The grimoire – which shelf?'

Startled, astonished, I jerked around and saw the bent figure of the Irish scholar standing up straight and miraculously tall, the bright-blue eyes of Mr Jesperson peering over the top of the green glass spectacles.

'Don't say I fooled you? You looked at me so suspiciously, I was afraid you'd give the game away! Now come, before Miss Bulstrode returns – where is the book?'

Thrown by this unexpected turn of events, for a moment I could not remember, but as I gazed up hopelessly at the row upon row of volumes, the memory returned and I pointed.

'There, see that fat green book? Next to that, between two books about birds, although you can hardly see it, it has a pinkish-brown spine.'

He went straight to the right place, and extracted the slender volume, which he opened at random. I hastened to his side, and we looked together at a few of the handwritten, illustrated pages. Then he closed it and stuffed it away inside his shirt.

My stomach gave an uneasy twist as I understood he meant to steal it. 'Why?'

'For a very good purpose.' He gave me a serious stare. 'I thought there might not be enough time to explain, so I've written you a letter.' From somewhere else amidst the layers of old clothes draped about him, he produced an envelope and handed it to me. 'Read it later. Now – I must resume my role – it would look suspicious if I left a moment before my two hours were up – we can speak again when we meet at four o'clock.' He adjusted the green glass spectacles so they once more obscured his eyes.

'Where?'

'You remember where we left the road for the path to the Poison Ring? I will meet you there, or on the road. It's all explained in the letter.' As he turned away, his posture changed, shoulder coming up on one side and his neck twisting to transform himself into the Sanskrit scholar once more.

I could hardly believe it, staring at the man in the chair, bent over an open book, his nose almost touching the page, lips moving slightly as he read. If not for the letter in my hand, I could have thought the last few minutes were nothing more than a waking dream.

The letter! I could think of no way to explain its sudden appearance to Bella, so I made haste to find a book of the right size in which to hide it. I was reading the book, and hoped I appeared engrossed in it, when Bella came back in with the tea tray.

'Scones in the oven for this afternoon, so we are to have nothing with our tea now,' she informed me. 'What have you found to read?'

I displayed the cover: '*Ghosts and Legends of Norfolk.*'

She smiled. 'I would wager there's nothing in there about the little people – at least, not in connection with the shrieking pits. Did you ask your friend where he came up with such an outlandish idea?'

Feeling uncomfortable because I knew he could hear us, I muttered an evasive reply. 'I suppose he found it in Mr Manning's notes. They were fragmentary and a bit of a jumble, but he made what sense of them he could.'

She poured out the tea, and I quickly changed the subject. 'You have your work here, but your sisters must find it rather quiet. Do they go out much? I suppose there must be some society in Cromer . . . or do they have friends they visit in Norwich?'

'Sugar?'

'Just one, thank you.'

'My sisters are rather homebodies, I suppose,' she said, handing me a cup and saucer. 'Although it is not quite so dull here from April through September, and they do often go to Cromer and even Norwich. You probably remember yesterday they spoke so yearningly of London, and how long it had been since we were there.'

'Yes, and Ann became so upset as she recalled that Mr Manning had promised to take her to the theatre. Was that something they had planned to do soon?' My heart beat a little faster as I put forward this leading question and I watched her intently for any signs of dissimulation.

But she answered calmly, 'I would not go so far as to call it a plan. They had spoken of it. He knew how much she loved the theatre, and naturally wished to please her. I think he offered it as a Christmas treat; Ann may have taken it as a more serious possibility than it really was. Of course, she could not have gone unchaperoned, and although he said we could all stay at the house in Gordon Square, I do not think his relations with his brother were friendly enough to make that likely – not in the immediate future, anyway.'

280

'Why did he go to London? Do you think he intended to lay the ground for reconciliation with his brother?'

'I have told you, I had no idea he intended to go to London. He said nothing about it.'

'He might have told Ann.'

Her manner cooled more rapidly than the tea. 'If he had, I am certain she would have mentioned it. Charles may have been Ann's suitor, but he was not a member of our family, and he did not live here; he did not even call every day. I would venture to say he was far more intimate with Felix Ott than with us – even if Ann was his intended bride.'

'I beg your pardon; I hope I have not offended—'

'Not at all. I understand your interest – naturally, his brother would be glad to know if Charles had been on his way to make up their differences before he died – but I cannot help you. There is no point in interrogating me *or* my sisters – and it is particularly upsetting to Ann, as you must realise.'

'I am very sorry—'

She stopped me with a gesture. 'Say no more about it.'

I drank the rest of my tea in silence. It was a relief when she mentioned a letter she had to write, and said she would not detain me any longer. One glance from her eloquent eyes was enough to tell me she felt there was no need for the continued 'protection' offered by my presence.

I was happy to get away to read my letter from Mr Jesperson. When I opened it, I found a page torn from his notebook, quickly scrawled without even a salutation:

Maria is gone. She said nothing to anyone, and no one heard her go, but she was nowhere to be found this morning. She may, like her baby, have been taken, but I believe she went of her own free will – taking her pathetically few belongings. Miss Flowerdew was probably the last person to see her. Whilst making herself a cup of cocoa before bedtime, Miss F gave Maria a dramatic account of the main points of my lecture. I expected this might happen, but did not anticipate how soon. Anyway, it is done; and there is no time to waste if we are to get her and her baby safely back. It may be helpful to have something to trade, so I have come for the so-called grimoire, which I believe was theirs before the cunning man dug it up. If bribery does not work we must resort to threats.

Meet me at 4 p.m. on the road beside the woods where the path to the Poison Ring/shrieking pit comes out. Dress warmly, bring a lantern & be prepared for a long, cold wait.

JJ

CHAPTER TWENTY-ONE

In the Woods

'It is almost sunset,' said Reverend Ringer with a grunt of dismay. 'And the mists are rising. In a few minutes we shall be able to see even less in these dark woods than we can now.' To express his disapproval, he lashed out with his sturdy walking stick and decapitated several spotted mushrooms, breaking the ring, and making me wince, although, as an act of destruction, it was very mild.

'I do not understand, Jasper,' he went on, his grumbles gaining force. 'If you suspected Maria had come here, why not tell me at once? At noon we might have had some chance – why in heaven's name leave it so late?'

'If we had arrived at noon we should have had a good deal longer to wait,' calmly responded Mr Jesperson, straightening up from a close inspection of the leaf mould that carpeted the forest floor. 'The wee folk do not come out in daylight. They rely on darkness and mist to hide them from our eyes. Our only chance of inducing one of them to come out and parley is after sunset.'

Reverend Ringer snorted. 'Do you really believe Maria has been taken by *fairies*?'

'Not taken. I think she *went* to them, hoping to save her child, and is now a prisoner underground, and we must negotiate for her release.' Jesperson shifted the lumpy weight of the canvas bag he carried over one shoulder. 'If so doubtful, why did you volunteer your help?'

I had been surprised but not displeased when I had arrived half an hour earlier to find Dr Ringer waiting by the side of the road along with Mr Jesperson. Dr Ringer was a strong and muscular man who would be a useful ally if physical strength were required, and if supernatural forces challenged us, the vicar's prayers might be of even greater help.

'You are a devilish convincing speaker, sir! Last night in the hall, and then today in my study, I found myself almost believing your fairy tales.'

'I shall not press you to stay. If you think this is a waste of time, go home. I shall manage well enough with the aid of my very capable partner, Miss Lane.'

'Now, now, don't go putting words in my mouth,' the vicar replied in a placatory tone. 'I promised you my help, and I stand by my word. No offence to Miss Lane, but if a bit of muscle is required, you may be glad of my stout stick and sturdy boots.' As he spoke, he stomped a few defenceless toadstools into the ground.

'Yet you think we are in the wrong place?'

The vicar shifted his stance and looked beyond the gloomy

284

clearing, towards the shrieking pit. Wisps of fog had started to appear between the trees, and darkness was falling fast. 'No . . . No . . . For as you pointed out, *someone* arranged Albert Cooke's body where it was found – may even have placed half a mushroom cap in his mouth. There is the temptation to think that was his murderer – but why should he have been murdered?'

'The police decided it was an accidental death,' Mr Jesperson interjected. 'But to accept their verdict we must believe that after he fell into the pit and struck his head, although the blow was fatal, he had enough strength left to clamber out and stagger over to the ring; to pluck a mushroom and bite into it as he arranged himself on the ground, as if for a nap, and then died.'

The vicar interrupted. 'Yes, yes, you needn't tell me! It's obvious someone else must have been involved, and any ordinary witness would be unlikely to have moved his body and then vanish without reporting the accident. If Mr Cooke died in the pit, and if the pit does in fact offer access to an underground dwelling . . . well, here we are, to try to prove it.

'But why not come in daylight, with tools, and dig until we uncover whatever hermit or troglodyte inhabits the lair beneath those stones?'

I had been wondering the same thing myself.

'We would risk frightening them into flight, and probably they would take Maria and her baby, too, and we would never be able to find them again.'

'How should they escape us?'

'The land around here is pocked with shrieking pits – at

least, it was formerly. And if each one gave access to an underground home, what could be more likely than that they are all connected to each other by a system of underground passages? At the bottom of the pit in the field across from the vicarage I found a hole beneath a stone. It was not a shallow hole, but seemed the mouth of a tunnel – I could not tell how far it stretched. I left it uncovered, but the next day, after Maria's baby went missing, I found the stone had been replaced. I also found a scrap of blue yarn that may have come from the shawl in which the baby was wrapped.' He stopped and nodded as he saw the vicar understood.

Dr Ringer said, 'So if they are attacked from one quarter, they will retreat to another.' He sighed. 'But why should they come out at all?'

'We must try to convince them it will be in their best interest. Come along, it is nearly dark now.' Setting down his bag, he rummaged within, extracting a lantern, which he lit. I was already equipped with my own, which Dr Ringer lit for me. Holding up our lights, we went in procession through the woods, to the edge of the shrieking pit.

'There, look, footprints.' Mr Jesperson stopped abruptly, and bent protectively over marks in the soft earth that might have been recent footprints, only a little smaller than my own.

I imagined Maria running to the pit and calling piteously for her baby. In my imagination, her hair was loose and dishevelled, and she resembled the figure of the shrieking woman on the poster that had advertised Mr Jesperson's lecture. What response had she received? How long had she waited? Where was she now?

Jesperson held out his lantern over the pit. There was no one in it, and little to be seen: bits of quartz glinted where they caught the light; otherwise it was a mass of stones and dirt, clumps of vegetation, a litter of dead leaves. 'Hold this,' he said, handing me his lantern, and then, as he had done before, he jumped down, reaching up to reclaim his light once he was standing within.

He made a closer inspection of the sides and floor of the pit, making no comment as he moved around from place to place, touching certain places, moving aside clumps of weeds, staring, and then moving on with nearly agonising slowness.

Clearly, he did not wish to be disturbed, and to keep Dr Ringer from erupting with more questions, I distracted his attention with a question about the strange noises that gave the pits their name: had he ever heard them?

'Only once, a few years ago, from the road. Perhaps it was only the wind. It was an altogether uncanny sound, I do confess, and I had never heard the like before. I should not myself have described it as being like a woman's wailing, but I could think of nothing else that it was like, either. Most unpleasant, to be sure, and no wonder that the common people might take it as a warning to stay well away from this spot at night!'

'You never heard the same sound issuing from the field across the road from the vicarage?'

'Never. Nor anywhere else.' He shifted and frowned, and

made a slight movement towards the pit where my friend was still at his incomprehensible detecting work.

I spoke quickly: 'Have you no idea what might cause such a sound? Is there really no explanation?'

'No one knows. However, I have my own theory,' he said, leaning towards me confidentially. 'I think it might be caused by certain atmospheric conditions, when the wind blows from the right quarter, and striking the stones that litter the bottom of the pit, perhaps whistling through them, there might be—'

'Aha! It has been moved!'

As one, we turned our attention downwards. 'What has?'

Mr Jesperson straightened and stepped back, holding out his lantern. 'There. See that stone slab? It appears immovable, and, indeed, I found it impossible to shift. My attention was drawn to it because of the pattern of vegetation around it . . . nothing sprouts from the side or below; but it is half-hidden from the casual eye by these draperies.' With his free hand, he gently lifted a mass of drooping grasses, revealing that all were embedded in the earth more than an inch above the top of this particular stone. 'Such a pattern might suggest that the rock is moved on occasion, possibly covering an access point very like the one I discovered in the other pit.'

'A theory your efforts would seem to disprove,' said Dr Ringer.

Jesperson took another step backwards. 'No; I have only proved that it is not easy to open from this side.'

'So what do you propose? Shall we dig it out? We should have brought shovels. I can go back – I'll bring the boy to help.'

Jesperson smiled slightly, holding up a cautionary hand. 'Not just yet.' He spoke, I thought, with unnecessary force and volume if he was aiming his words solely at us. 'First, I propose we try a little diplomacy. If *someone* – it may be Maria, or it may be whoever is keeping her prisoner – will come out and speak with us, we may be able to clear up our little problem without hard labour – no destructive digging. All we ask is the chance to speak with Maria, face to face.'

'I ask a bit more than that,' muttered Dr Ringer as Jesperson handed him up his lantern, and quickly hoisted himself out of the pit.

Dusting himself off, Jesperson leaned over the pit to call out his terms: 'Otherwise, we will bring men and shovels and dig until we find Maria and her baby. But if they come out now – we may come to mutually agreeable terms.'

We waited, but nothing happened; there was not a sound to be heard, and no movement except for the faint flickering of our lanterns as the darkness around us gradually deepened.

I looked at Mr Jesperson, wondering how long we were to wait, but his attention remained fixed on shadowed recess of the pit. After the passage of another minute he called out sternly, 'Send her out – send out the girl – and we will leave you in peace. Send her out – or prepare to be destroyed.'

Still nothing happened.

'Perhaps a prayer would be in order,' said Dr Ringer, taking a small book from his pocket. He began to leaf through it, until Mr Jesperson lifted his head, looking alert, and murmured, 'Did you hear that?'

I frowned, aware of some slight, distant sound – but surely it was only the wind?

The sound increased, becoming a high, eerie wailing. Although my skin prickled uneasily, I said, 'Could that be the baby?'

But as I spoke the noise grew louder and more intense, a howling shriek, impossible to mistake for a baby's cry. It was inhuman, like the sound of a gale force wind in a ship's rigging, or storms attacking the roof of a cottage on a lonely moor. And yet the night around us was utterly still, the bare limbs of the trees above us hung motionless. Only the wraithlike forms of the mist rising from the ground moved around us.

My skin crawled with goosebumps. It was easy to imagine a terrifying, ghostly figure of a wailing woman rushing through the landscape, and if I had not been in some measure prepared for this, I would have been tempted to run away. But we stood fast, and waited, and watched, whilst Dr Ringer recited 'Deliver me from mine enemies, O God; defend me from those that rise up against me.'

The shrieking died away, and through the words of the 59th Psalm we heard the faint crunch and slip of gravel instead. Then a pair of hands appeared over the top of the pit, and Jesperson hastened to lean down and help the small figure scramble out, as the vicar ceased his now inappropriate recitation.

I seized her hands. 'Maria, are you well?'

Remarkably cool and collected, she pulled her hands away and made it clear that she did not wish to be embraced by either me or the vicar. 'I am quite well, and I don't need no help from any of you, thank you very much. You shouldn't have come.'

'You had us worried,' her employer chided gently. 'Indeed, we feared for your life.'

'There was no need. Now you see me well and I may tell you I am very happy in my new position.'

Dr Ringer's eyes bulged slightly. 'New position? Whatever can you mean?'

Suspicious of her calm, I held my lantern to cast light on her face. She looked as cool as her words and showed no signs of fear or damage. Her clothes were dirty, yet on the whole, surprisingly clean for someone who had crawled out of the earth.

'You don't know nothing about it,' she said sharply in reply to the vicar, and then turned on Mr Jesperson. 'But *you* know better! How could you be so cruel, to speak of digging up and destroying our home?'

With what a feeling of disbelief did I register that single word.

'It was only a ruse,' he replied. 'After all, we did not know if you were free or held against your will; I could think of no better way to ensure you would be allowed to come out, so that we could see for ourselves. *Are* you free to go?'

She still stared at him distrustfully. 'You do not mean to harm them?'

'I promise you, we mean no harm. But under the circumstances, threats seemed more likely to work than pleading. If, instead of yourself, one of *them* had come out – then I would have offered them a trade.' He touched his breast. 'I have something I believe they want.'

Her brow wrinkled. 'What do you mean, "trade"? What could they give you? They have no treasure, whatever you may think.'

'They have you and your baby.'

Her lip curled. 'Are we chattel, to be bought and sold?'

I was baffled by Maria's response, and saw, too, that she had wrong-footed Mr Jesperson. But he was faster to seize upon the cause of her recalcitrance than I, dropping his voice to ask softly, 'Are you afraid for your baby?'

She raised her chin. 'Not any more. I was, when I came, of course. I couldn't think how I was to get her back; I only knew that somehow I must. But they let me see her right away. They were worried too. They tried their best, but they couldn't manage to feed her. Lucky I came in time.' She nodded, and her shoulders relaxed as a faint smile appeared on her face. 'My poor wee Annie! But now that I'm here, she's thriving again.'

'And for that, you would stay?'

'Why not?'

I broke in, shocked by her acceptance. 'Maria, you cannot. Have you forgotten – these people *stole* your child.'

She turned on me sharply. 'No. They rescued her – as they thought. Who would leave a *wanted* baby alone in a barn? They thought she had been abandoned. And as they had always longed for a child of their own – he took her back to his wife.'

She paused and moved closer to me to confide: 'They love

her, see? And because she needs me, I think they love me, too – or they will – for her sake.'

In that brave assertion, I felt all the sadness of her lonely, narrow little life.

Mr Jesperson spoke: 'So they will not try to stop you taking her away?'

'What? No!' She took a step back, and from the corner of my eye I saw Dr Ringer tense, and I was afraid he meant to lunge at her and grab her. 'No – they would not stop me, if I wished to, but I will not take her away.'

Jesperson dropped his voice. 'If you are fearful, forced against your will, give us a sign. We can help. I told you, I have something to trade—'

She drew herself up haughtily. 'I have told you what I think of your trading. Annie is my child. I have made my choice. This is the best place for both of us.'

Reverend Ringer gave a cry of protest. 'Maria! You cannot mean to stay *here*?'

'Oh, yes I can. And I will.'

'They are forcing you – using your natural maternal feelings to make you their prisoner. You do not know what you are doing.'

Seeing that the vicar's argument was having the opposite of its desired effect, Mr Jesperson intervened. 'Maria, truly, we want what is best for you. But how can we know if those . . . others . . . are your captors, holding the child hostage, or if they have your best interests at heart.'

'I have told you: they are my friends. I wish to stay.'

Looking at her small, dignified form, I believed her. If she had been speaking only for the sake of the unseen listeners, I was certain she could easily have indicated that she lied.

But the men were not so ready to believe she knew what she was talking about.

'Bring out your baby, Maria, so we may see for ourselves that she is well,' said the vicar coaxingly.

'And give you the chance to take her from me?' She gave a short, scornful laugh. 'She is better off where she is, with my friends.'

'Friends?' The word was like a bullet shot from the vicar's mouth. 'Have you forgotten those creatures stole your child – the anguish that they caused you?'

She squared her shoulders and turned on him. 'No, *master*, I have not forgotten – but I have forgiven – as you preach in your sermons. They never meant her any harm, and I understand why they thought she was unwanted. They did their best to care for her. It was not their fault they could not – now I am there, all is well.'

'Come home with me now,' he said. 'Take the baby – if they are your friends as you say, they will not stop you. Come back – your room is waiting, your same position – no one will reproach you; it will be as if you have never been away.'

She stared back him. 'Annie could stay in my room with me?'

He smiled. 'Of course.'

'And your good lady would not mind? With my own baby to tend, I could not be so quick about all my tasks.'

'I am sure she will understand. And it will only be for a little while.'

'How so? When she is older, she will need me still more – unless you think your wife would help, and then perhaps Miss Flowerdew will teach my Annie her letters, and she would be raised up as good as one of your own?'

He frowned. 'Come now, Maria. You know that it is impossible. You will wean her by three months, when we shall have found her a good home.'

'Her home is with me, and mine with her.'

'Be a good girl, Maria. Be sensible.'

'I am.'

He shook his head, grim-faced. 'Was it good or sensible of you to have a child without a father?'

'Nobody gave me a choice, did they?' She snapped back. More gently, she went on, 'But as soon as I saw her, I loved her. She was a gift. When I thought I'd lost her, I wanted to die. I've never felt like this about anyone. I'd rather live in a dark, smelly hole in the ground with my Annie than in the finest bedroom in your vicarage without her.'

Suddenly, almost shockingly, she broke into a huge grin, the likes of which I'd never seen on that wan little face. 'Only, it's *not* dark or cold or smelly. It's lovely – oh, you don't know how nice it is, really.'

The smile died away as she turned to gaze on Mr Jesperson, and implored, 'Please, don't hurt us! No more talk of digging. They are good people.'

'How many of them are there?' he asked.

'Two. They are the last in Norfolk – that's what they told me.'

He stared in fascination. 'Can you speak with them? You understand their language?'

'Oh!' She shook her head. 'No, but they can speak mine. Now – please, leave us be. I want your word that you will leave us in peace.'

'I should love to learn more about them,' he said wistfully.

She took a few steps back. 'Go away.'

'You are making a mistake, Maria,' said Reverend Ringer loudly. 'I shall pray on the matter, but I tell you now, these so-called friends of yours are not Christians. You put your soul, and the soul of your child, in danger by keeping company with them. For the last time, I implore you – come home.'

'This is my home now.' She turned her back on him, but Mr Jesperson touched her shoulder.

'Wait,' he said, 'Let me give you this – not in trade, as I had planned, but only as a gift, a token of my respect.' He fumbled inside his jacket until he found the old book and held it out to her. She gave him a wary look.

'Take it,' he urged. 'It is theirs – or it belonged to their fore-fathers once. Give it to them and say it is from Jasper Jesperson, with his respects, and he hopes we may meet as friends someday.'

'You will not hurt them?'

'Never. I swear it,' he said earnestly.

Seemingly mollified, she accepted the book and tucked it

away in an inner pocket of her skirt before she lowered herself down into the pit.

Hurrying after, holding out our lanterns, we saw how fearlessly she thrust her head into the hole that now gaped in the side of the pit, and watched her push and wriggle her way into the earth. Bit by bit she disappeared until, with a final kick of her feet, she vanished from view.

Once again we heard the high, shrill sound, as of a distant gale, and heard it grow in volume and intensity to an unholy shriek that raised the hairs on the back of my neck. This time, we saw the dark hole into which Maria had gone gradually shrink as the stone slab moved back into place and covered it again.

'Some sort of pulley system, I suppose,' Mr Jesperson muttered. 'I suppose the noise must be involved with that; it may be on a track, or . . . Hmm . . . I wonder . . .'

'We can find out soon enough, when we start digging,' said Dr Ringer.

'Dig – not when we have promised her,' I protested.

'I made no such promise,' he said sharply. 'And even if I had, I should not consider it binding – not when a Christian soul is at stake. I only wish we had brought shovels with us and could make a start now. But I suppose we will work better in daylight – and I will enlist the aid of five or six strong men from the village.'

'You must not,' I said anxiously. 'She does not want to be rescued, as she told you quite plainly.'

'She is a silly little girl,' he said, cutting me off and suggesting by his manner that he meant the same words to apply to me. 'I have a duty of care to her – and to her child – and I will not be dissuaded by any of her nonsense about *friends*.'

He gave a huffing breath and turned away from the pit. 'It will be better in daylight – too much chance of being misled in the dark – those creatures, whatever they are, might manage to evade us now, but not in the light of day.' He turned his challenging glare on Mr Jesperson. 'What about you – may I count on your help?'

'I gave her my word, and I mean to keep it. I wish you would reconsider – remember that she asked—'

'Asked to be thrown into the pits of hell? Would you collude in her damnation? And what of the babe – unbaptised? Would you have the destruction of those two young souls upon your conscience?'

'I do not think—'

'*You* do not think of what is right and good for her soul; that is *my* job. I shall dig into the side of that pit until I find the demons' hiding place – and I shall fetch out Maria and her babe – with or without your help. Then I shall exorcise the ground, sprinkle holy water and say all the requisite prayers and offices. The girls will be safe, and any abominations who dwelt in this place shall be destroyed and driven out forever.'

He turned and made his way back to the path, saying, 'They do not know what is coming!'

'Oh, I think they do,' said Mr Jesperson under his breath as we followed after.

When we reached the road, Mr Jesperson bid Dr Ringer good evening. The man looked affronted. 'What, you are so far lost to reason that you will not walk back with me?'

'I can hardly abandon Miss Lane to make her way alone along this dark highway. Surely you recall that she is no longer welcome at the vicarage, even if you remain my host,' he responded coldly.

The vicar shifted uncomfortably, stretching his neck and grimacing. 'Yes . . . yes, of course. Terribly sorry for that misunderstanding . . . but Mrs Ringer does have her little . . . Well, she has always been in charge of such matters, and I must not quarrel with my good wife, no matter how much I might disagree with some of her decisions. Well . . . goodnight and Godspeed, Miss Lane. Will you be back for dinner, Jasper?'

'No. Please tender my apologies to Mrs Ringer.'

Dr Ringer nodded. 'Very well. But take care not to stay out too late, or you must bed down in the stable. With all this unpleasant business lately, my good wife insists the doors are locked before we go to bed, and with Maria gone, there will be no one to let you in.'

'I understand. The prospect of a night in the open holds no fear for me, sir. But you may expect to see me for breakfast.'

Once the vicar was out of earshot, Mr Jesperson explained that we should probably both be spending most of the night in the woods, and that he had brought blankets to deal with that possibility.

I stared at him in bewilderment. 'But why?'

'Because I want to see them – don't you?' He grinned, and I saw that he was practically fizzing with excitement. 'Since Doctor Ringer has promised destruction to come in the morning, I do not expect they will linger for long. The fairies will be flitting tonight.'

How many people living today can say they have seen the fairies? And these were very likely the last two fairies in Norfolk.

Before we left the roadside to set up our hidden camp in the woods, Mr Jesperson revealed the contents of his mysteriously bulging bag included not only rugs and shawls to keep us warm, but also a loaf of bread, a slab of cheese, slices of beef, a fruit cake, and slabs of chocolate – all food we could quietly consume whilst waiting. He had also brought a flask of coffee, 'to stop us dozing off.'

'*Cold* coffee?' It sounded nasty, but when he told me that he had mixed it with milk and sugar, I put aside my preconceptions.

Earlier, although I had been quite unaware of it, Mr Jesperson had scouted out the best positions for observation, and now he led me slowly and cautiously through the dark woods to the chosen place, one well shielded by trees and bushes, but still offering a good view of the area around the shrieking pit.

We set up our rough camp, and made ourselves as comfortable as possible. Mr Jesperson sank easily into stillness, but I found it more difficult. How odd it was, to sit in the dark and cold – and how quickly one felt the cold when forced to keep still. I was particularly grateful for the food, which I consumed in small quantities, spacing it out, to have something to do. Eating in the dark was another unusual experience; I recognised each morsel by touch and smell, rather than sight, and with nothing else to distract me from it, the taste was somehow more intense, richer and more rewarding, whether it was a mouthful of bread, a sliver of cheese or a crumb of chocolate. It was good to have an occupation; chewing and tasting warmed me, if only for a moment, and helped the time to pass. Mr Jesperson was right about the cold coffee – although I should have preferred a hot drink, under the circumstances, it was actually very nice; I thought I might like to try it again sometime, but on a warm, sunny day.

Time passed slowly. Unable to speak to my friend as in ordinary circumstances, I could only reflect on matters as if I had been alone. I wondered again about the nature of Maria's new friends. Were they human? If not, were they animals, or spirits, or something else entirely? I wondered too at Jesperson's stillness. He was such a quick and lively person – restless, I should have said – but whereas I kept shifting my position, and could not hold back the occasional yawn, I never felt a fidget or sigh from the warm statue so close beside me in the dark.

I had to pinch myself to stay awake, and mentally recited poems and lists of kings and queens and other such material learnt in the schoolroom as I wondered if there was really any purpose to our vigil. What if they had already gone away through the underground tunnels Mr Jesperson had suggested must link all the remaining shrieking pits? At this moment, they might even be emerging unseen in the field opposite the vicarage, and we should be colder but no wiser when the morning came.

But at last – later we concluded the time must have been around midnight – we heard that same distant wailing that rose gradually to the unearthly, inhuman shriek that was responsible for the name and legend of the pits. Even though I had been wishing to hear it again, the sound made me shudder with an archaic and unreasoning fear, and I had a struggle to remain where I was and not run away. The noise stretched out, ghastly and unnatural, before it finally died. With the silence came a glimmer of light – so fleeting I thought I had imagined it. But, no, there it was again, and it issued from the pit.

Along with the light came other sounds, soft and muffled, and as the light grew, we glimpsed people clambering up out of the pit.

The first to emerge was a little man, no bigger than a three-year-old child, but looking like a vigorous, sturdy, well-proportioned man of advanced years, dressed in the manner of a Renaissance prince. He wore layers of sumptuous clothing, silks and velvets and furs, and there were rings on the fingers of his tiny hands, glittering golden in the eerie, apparently sourceless light.

Next out of the pit, helped up by the courteous gentleman, was a little lady, even smaller than he, and dressed in similarly rich antique style. Beneath a fur-lined velvet cloak her dark green dress was studded with pearls and winking gems, and her pale silver hair was piled atop her head and caught in a jewelled net.

Both these little people were encased in a glimmering glow,

as if they wore haloes of light. At the edge of the pit the man now bent down and took hold of two bags that were handed up to him by one who remained at the bottom; he stepped back with them to allow the woman to bend down to accept a smaller but more precious burden.

A moment later, Maria scrambled up beside them, pulling herself out of the pit as we had seen her do before. As she towered over her two little companions by at least a foot and a half, she looked a clumsy, malproportioned giant. She took the warmly wrapped bundle from the lady, kissed it several times and then cuddled it close to her breast.

The little man hoisted the bags, slinging one over each shoulder, and without any pause for discussion, he set off walking. His lady followed close behind, Maria in their wake.

Maria appeared wide-awake and self-possessed; it was clearly her considered decision to follow the little people rather than be forced to give up her baby; I only hoped she would not regret it. But it was not for us to say if she had made the right choice – unlike the vicar, we could not feel justified in 'rescuing' her against her will.

So we sat and watched the strange, glowing figures and Maria until they vanished in the darkness of the woods.

CHAPTER TWENTY-TWO

Explanation for a Death

I slept late the next morning, trapped by dreams in which I followed a ball of light through forests and across heath-land, into mines and through tunnels underground.

When at last I woke, I blinked groggily at the ceiling, still wondering what sort of life Maria would have now. Mr Jesperson thought the West Country was probably their destination. The ancient troglodytic race remembered as goblins, elves and fairies must have died out in most of Britain, but survivors may have found homes in the souterrains and tin-mines of Cornwall, or hidden away in caves on Dartmoor; the mountains of Wales were another strong possibility – beyond that, Scotland or Ireland.

Downstairs, I found Bella entertaining Mr Jesperson in the library.

'Your friend has been telling me what you witnessed,' she said as I entered. Her eyes and cheeks glowed with excitement. 'How marvellous! I never imagined there could be truth in those old stories . . . now I understand I have been too quick to dismiss some of Felix's ideas.'

'The folk we saw were more ancient even than the ancient Britons,' said Mr Jesperson. 'They were here, probably, before our earliest ancestors.'

'Are they immortal?'

'Is any living creature? I doubt it. They may be longer-lived than we are, but—'

'But their clothes! You said they were attired like members of court in the sixteenth century.'

'No, I said that was how they *appeared*. Their appearance, including the light that suffused them, and which would protect them from attack by any religiously inclined or superstitious who saw them, is an aspect of their glamour. You know that term, I think?'

She nodded, frowning slightly. 'Of course. A spell. You suggest they are able to perform magic?'

'If you include as "magic" all the arts of the conjurer.' He shrugged, smiling. 'Is it magic, or illusion? Just as some animals are able to blend into the background to escape their predators, our "good neighbours" must have their own protective coloration, the ability to disguise themselves. Folklore suggests that in reality they are naked, or clothed only in a few ragged scraps – another reason they avoid civilised society. The reason for their style of clothing may be tradition, or it may be a personal preference – how can we know?'

A shadow crossed his eyes and he looked wistful. 'I wish . . . I wish I could study them and their ways. How wonderful, to be in Maria's position – but she will not make use of it as I should.'

'How do you mean?' I asked.

'I mean she will simply accept them – she already has. She is part of their family now, and if she does come back to our world, she will say nothing of her sojourn in fairyland. She will protect them, and carry their secrets to the grave.'

'Felix may uncover their secrets,' said Bella. She spoke with a simple faith, and her eyes were bright at the thought of it. 'I think – do not you? – that these . . . people, and their ways, may be just what he has been searching for – something that belongs at the very heart of his School!'

'Perhaps, but now the last two fairies in Norfolk have made their escape, he has lost whatever small chance he might have had.' Mr Jesperson leaned back in his chair, tapping his long fingers on a padded armrest and looking obscurely dissatisfied, or perhaps impatient at needing to explain. 'They are gone, and their knowledge with them. When Doctor Ringer digs up their former home he will find no treasures, nothing of any value left behind.'

Bella seemed struck by this phrase and repeated it: 'Nothing of any value . . . Because they have so few *real* possessions? Because their things are illusory, products of the glamour?'

I felt suddenly apprehensive, and tried to think of something to say to turn the conversation, but it was too late; Bella had remembered.

'There was something! A book – my grandfather bought it from the cunning man.'

'Bought? The cunning man said stolen.'

She looked reproachful. 'My grandfather was always over-generous in his valuations and payments as a collector. If anyone stole that book, it was the cunning man himself. I have heard him brag about besting others; he was proud of himself for having tricked a dirty little man into letting him get his hands on a book neither of them could read. Once it was in his possession, he would not give it back. He brought it to my grandfather, thinking that as he had travelled in so many different lands, and knew so many of the world's languages, that he might be able to translate it. But it was like no language on Earth, my grandfather said; certainly it was none that he had ever seen before.'

She got to her feet and began to wander along the shelves, peering up at the array of spines. 'I remember, it was hand-written, with many drawings. I could recognise some of the plants, but not many. The pictures were more of roots than of leaves or flowers. And mushrooms; many mushrooms, and crystals . . . I wonder what has become of it?'

'Ott mentioned it to me,' said Mr Jesperson. 'He told me that it was in search of that book that he first came to Wayside Cross, and met you.'

Bella smoothed her hair – a quick, unconscious response that made the large orange stone in her ring flash. 'Yes, I was unable to find the book for him. Perhaps I did not try as hard as I might have done . . . but his eagerness made me suspicious. He made a ridiculous offer for it; an absurd valuation for a book he had never seen, one that features in no bibliographies or booksellers' catalogues. He called it a grimoire.'

'You think it is not?'

She shook her head. 'My grandfather was of the opinion that it was either a diary or a botanist's guide, written by someone well acquainted with our local area, in a private code or a made-up language. A curiosity; of no practical use to anyone.'

'Except to the person who wrote it.'

'Well, yes, but he was unlikely still to be alive.' Her eyes widened. 'Of course! You mean it was written by one of those . . . those . . . *others*. The "little man" Cunning Verrell got it from.'

'He told us he dug it up in a field,' I said.

She turned away, her eyes sweeping the room. 'It must be here somewhere. I recall it as a very small, slender volume, with no lettering or design on the spine . . . easily overlooked.' She began to pace and scan the shelves again. 'Probably it is tucked away on a high shelf.'

'Do you mean after all to sell it to Mr Ott?'

'Not *sell* it. But now that the little people have left, and I cannot restore it to them, Felix is the best person to have it. His School could be something very important to our country. He may do much good by preserving traditions and knowledge on the verge of being lost forever.'

A rusty scraping sound made me start, and I ducked my head at a rush of wings. The crow, until then invisible in a shadowy recess at the top of a bookcase, flapped across the room to land on the windowsill, where he let out another rasping caw.

'Another visitor?' said Bella. 'Who is it, Gabriel?'

The big black bird cocked his head at her and made another sound. One might almost have said he spoke – and from the smile that blossomed on the face of his mistress, she understood.

She went to the window and looked out. 'Yes, that is Mr Ott's carriage. What good timing – I'll tell Nancy to put the kettle on.' With a giddy laugh, she swept out of the room.

She was like a young girl with her first suitor – she was a woman in love. I exchanged a look with Mr Jesperson. 'Shall we make our excuses and leave?'

'No. I have some information to share – may as well tell everyone at once.'

'Something new?'

'Yes. I had a cable this morning – the very one I have been waiting for – and—' He stopped. 'There was no chance to tell you first – I hope you do not mind.'

I did, just a little, but as it was not his fault I had been so late in rising, I assured him it did not matter in the least.

A few moments later, Felix Ott followed a becomingly pink-cheeked Miss Bulstrode into the room.

Mr Jesperson was already on his feet, bowing, and so perhaps he did not see the annoyance that suffused Mr Ott's face upon his discovery that he was not Miss Bulstrode's first visitor of the day, but I took it all in.

'Jesperson, what the d—? I mean to say, I did not expect to find *you* here!'

Bella laid a gentle hand upon Mr Ott's arm. 'Felix, you know

that Miss Lane is our guest. Mr Jesperson came to call on *her*.'
How quickly, I thought, she accepted the role of his helpmeet,
and took it upon herself to soothe and explain, as if he were
a child.

'Yes, I came to tell Miss Lane we will return to London today,
now that we have resolved the question of the reason for Charles
Manning's untimely death,' Jesperson said coolly.

'You have?' cried Miss Bulstrode.

Ott stared. 'What do you mean?'

'I shall explain, as soon as we are all together. Miss Bulstrode,
would you be so kind as to ask your sisters to join us?'

I resumed my seat when Bella went out, but the two gentlemen remained standing, each taking the other's measure, as if
about to duel.

'You might have spoken to me about this first,' muttered
Mr Ott.

'Why?'

'Before intruding upon a young lady's grief with your dreadful stories . . .'

Mr Jesperson cocked his head. 'She has a right to know the
truth.'

'Perhaps, but what you bring is mere gossip – speculation – a
story you have cobbled together – you cannot possibly know
the whole truth.'

My friend smiled ironically. 'Are not there always gaps in
our understanding? I suspect that most of the details you wish
kept hidden from the young lady are already known to her.

Miss Lane's observations have suggested she is troubled more by feelings of *guilt* than grief.'

Mr Ott's eyes positively bulged, and he sucked in his breath. 'Sir! Surely you do not mean to suggest—'

The opening of the door cut him off, but he continued to direct a horrified stare at Mr Jesperson as the three sisters entered with much rustling of skirts, the younger two pale and nervous. Bella held Ann's hand, and all three crowded together on the small sofa.

Mr Jesperson remained standing to address us. 'First, a revelation, or you might call it a confession. As Mr Ott already knows, Miss Lane and I are partners in a detective agency. We kept this particular bit of information from you, but everything else we have told you is true. We did witness the death of Charles Manning as Miss Lane described, and were sent here by Mr Alexander Manning to discover, if we could, the circumstances that led up to his brother's death.

'Poison was suspected, but an autopsy revealed no trace of the usual culprits. The contents of his stomach included copious amounts of alcohol, and the substance of his last meal: oysters, rare beefsteak, and ginger cake.'

I saw Alys flinch at that, and Ann closed her eyes briefly.

'An odd meal,' Mr Jesperson went on in a musing voice. 'What did it signify? I had enquiries made at various oyster houses, but no one recalled serving him; I was unable to get any further in the matter of *where* he ate, or with whom, in the hours before his death, but the food itself was suggestive. Oysters are well known as an aphrodisiac; rare beef is likewise invigorating, and as for the ginger cake . . .' He shrugged. 'Ginger is said to warm the blood and inflame the passions; although it is generally prescribed raw, perhaps Charles did not know, or thought it would be better to have it in a cake than not at all. Was he very fond of cakes, Miss Ann?' He fired the final question suddenly.

Ann blinked rapidly, opened her mouth, but was unable to speak.

'It is a simple question,' said Mr Jesperson, gently now. 'Surely you know if your fiancé was fond of cakes and other sweet things?'

'Not particularly.' It was Alys rather than Ann who answered. 'Mr Charles did not have much of a sweet tooth – he drank tea without sugar. But he did like my ginger cake.'

'Did you take your ginger cake to him in London?'

Alys lifted her chin. 'It was for *Ann*. It was her cake. *He* helped himself, without a by-your-leave. That's the sort of man he was.'

'This was in London? Did he ask you to meet him there?'

'It was me!' Ann cried out. She wriggled until she had freed herself from the mild restraints of her sisters' arms. Her eyes were bright with unshed tears, and she trembled, but her colour was high and she looked in no danger of fainting. 'Charles said he loved me and he couldn't bear to wait – he wanted to elope, but I would not, I wanted to have a lovely wedding, and it takes time to do things properly. He could not afford to get married for at least a year, or two or three – that is what Bella said. We should need a house of our own, and it takes a lot of

money to rent and furnish and run even a very modest home.'
She took a deep breath.

'He pretended to agree with Bella, but afterwards he told
me that waiting was harder on a man than on a woman, it was
unfair; he said he would let me set the date, and he would work
with might and main to make enough money to support me as
I deserved, but I must do something for him. He asked me to
meet him in London.'

'She is such an innocent,' said Alys. 'I could not let her go
there alone.'

'I was not supposed to tell anyone,' said Ann sadly.

'You were quite right to tell me.'

'He bought me a first-class ticket and he gave me money to
take a cab from the terminus to the Midland Grand Hotel.'

I thought of the imposing building beside St Pancras Station,
only a short walk from our premises on Gower Street.

'Where he had reserved a room for "Miss Smith",' her sister
put in with a bitter twist to her mouth. 'He said he chose
the pseudonym to protect your privacy. They were a little bit
surprised when *two* "Miss Smiths" turned up, but I said it was
clearly a misunderstanding, because Mr Manning would never
have asked his fiancée to travel unaccompanied. No honest
gentleman would have expected you to conceal such a plan
from your sisters.'

Ann blinked and sniffed, and two bright lines of liquid ran
down her face as the welling tears at last spilt over. Bella, her
mouth set in a grim line, gave her a handkerchief and, flashing

313

her eyes at us, said in a low voice, 'Is this really necessary? Ann is very sorry; we are all very sorry to have been so mistaken in his character, but the man is dead now – may we not let him rest in peace?'

Mr Jesperson remained undisturbed, replying, 'Indeed, I hope we may, after we have learned the truth. Please continue, Miss Ann.'

After she had wiped away her tears the youngest sister took up the story again. 'Alys and I were shown into a set of rooms – a parlour and bedroom, very spacious and nicely furnished. After a little while a waiter came up with a bottle of champagne and oysters on ice – on instruction from Mr Manning, he said.' She wrinkled her nose. 'I hate oysters! I don't know how anyone can bear to eat the slimy things! Alys told him to take them away and bring us a pot of tea and sandwiches instead.'

Ann shook her head. 'I didn't want anything – I was too excited to eat, wondering when Charles would arrive. I was glad to have Alys with me.' She looked fondly at her sister and squeezed her hand. 'Even though Charles was so cross about it – he was as red as a cherry and puffing like a steam engine when he saw I was not alone!'

'When was this?'

'He arrived about the same time as the tea and sandwiches. That made him cross – he had ordered oysters and champagne, he shouted, not tea and cake!'

Mr Jesperson's gaze sharpened. 'There was cake?'

'I already told you,' said Alys reprovingly.

'It was our cake,' said Ann. 'And despite his bad temper, he did eat a piece of it and washed it down with tea whilst he waited for the waiter to bring back the champagne and oysters.'

'What else did he do?'

'He took out a sachet of powder, and when the champagne came, he mixed it into three glasses and ordered us to drink. He said it might warm our cold hearts. He drank one glass off himself, immediately, and when we did not follow his lead he became quite abusive. His language was vile – he was like a different person.'

'And did you drink?'

Ann shuddered and shook her head. 'After a while, he drank them both himself. And he tried to make Alys leave – he begged, he pleaded, and then he threatened. But dear Alys would not leave me alone with him in such a state! I began to realise that he did not love me at all – the things he said were so very dreadful.' Her pale cheeks had gradually darkened as the memories intensified, and now she pressed her fingers against them.

'I whispered to Alys to take me away, but he barred the door. He said if he could not have me alone, he would have us both.' The tears again rolled down her face, and at last she subsided into shuddering sobs, leaning against one sister and embraced by them both.

Mr Jesperson began to prowl about the room. 'Thank you,' he said. 'Please forgive me for putting you through such a strain, Miss Ann, but it was necessary for me to understand the situation.'

He stopped and faced us again. 'The powder that Manning drank in champagne was sold to him by Cunning Verrell. I managed to purchase what I believe to be the same "special mixture" and gave it to a chemist to analyse. I received his report today.'

Reaching into his vest pocket, he extracted a piece of paper, which he unfolded. 'The contents included *Atropa belladonna – Mandragora officinarum – Amanita muscaria – Cantharis vericatoria—*'

Bella leapt to her feet, crying, 'That compound is lethal – Verrell is a murderer!'

Felix Ott was quick to seize her by the arms, imploring her to be calm, and at his movement, Alys forgot all about her younger sister and jumped up in a fury to attack him, crying, 'Leave my Bella alone!'

The crow added to the general pandemonium, flapping about the room emitting raucous cries.

The upheaval quickly subsided as the ingrained decorum of the English lady and gentleman prevailed. Felix Ott fell back, apologising profusely for any misunderstanding; Bella assured him no harm had been done and told Alys to behave herself; and in a matter of moments, everyone had resumed their accustomed seats – except Gabriel, who now perched on Bella's left shoulder, and turned his glossy head this way and that, as if to warn all those his eye fell upon that they should feel the power of his beak and claws if they dared to disturb his beloved mistress.

Mr Jesperson cleared his throat. 'Ahem, yes, as Miss Bulstrode recognised, most of the ingredients I named are indeed poisonous – but as I am sure she also knows, the *amount* is a significant factor; minute doses of *Atropa belladonna,* for example, may actually have a beneficial effect, although too much is fatal. It causes dilated pupils – which we noticed in Mr Manning – hallucinations, ditto – aggressive behaviour – to which Miss Ann and Miss Alys have borne witness – and an increased heart-rate.

'*Mandragora* or mandrake also causes hallucinations and can affect the heart.

'*Cantharis vericatoria,* better known as Spanish Fly, is the most famous of all so-called aphrodisiacs – although its effects upon the body are painful and unpleasant – but although in larger doses it may be fatal, Mr Manning did not die from that.

'And I should say, in defence of Cunning Verrell, that a single dose of his mixture would not have caused the death of even a smaller, weaker man than Charles Manning. Verrell is specific about how much is to be taken at any one time, and even advises the man to halve the dose and share it with his lady in a glass of wine. My investigations suggest that the cunning man would be unlikely to sell a customer more than two or three of these mixtures at one time, but perhaps Manning managed to wheedle more out of him. Certainly, he ignored the warnings he was given and consumed the entire lot himself in a single evening. Is it fair to blame the cunning man for his customer's suicidal stupidity?'

Bella exhaled a long, soft sigh. 'Charles was the instrument of his own destruction.'

'I believe so,' said Mr Jesperson. 'From Ann's description, he was already under the influence before he arrived at the hotel, and then he took another dose. He was, I venture to say, in a state of self-loathing, having made the vicious decision to destroy a young woman's innocence and happiness through an act of brutality.'

'But why?' Bella stared at him. 'I do not understand. If he loved her . . .'

'He did not love me,' said Ann. 'I saw that, finally. If he had loved me, I would have done whatever he asked. But what I saw in that hotel room . . . He despised me.' She stared bleakly at nothing.

Alys groaned. 'You are romantic, Ann, but he was not. Love had nothing to do with it. You had something he wanted, and he meant to have it, by hook or by crook. If he ruined you, you would have to marry him. If he put you in the family way, even better.'

'But why did he want to marry me, if not for love?'

'It is not as if Ann has any serious expectations,' said Bella. 'She might eventually inherit this house from me, but surely Mr Manning was not so wicked as to have been planning to kill me and both my sisters for a small property in rural Norfolk?' She looked enquiringly at Mr Jesperson, who turned rather dramatically to gaze at Mr Ott.

The head of the School of British Wisdom shifted in his chair, gave an audible sigh, and said, rather haltingly, 'Perhaps I may shed some light on this distressing matter. I rather fear that *some* of Manning's actions – at least at first – may have been, er, performed in the misguided hope of pleasing *me*.'

Gaining in confidence as he made the decision to tell all, he continued:

'When I first arrived in the area, I had my sights fixed upon Wayside Cross, not only for the library, but because I had heard that the mistress of the house was a wise woman, called by some a witch – and thus, I felt certain, she was the inheritor of an ancient tradition. I was keen to enlist Miss Bulstrode in my School – I had visions of her as the head of the distaff side, as it were; the representative of traditions and knowledge traditionally reserved for females, and therefore on an equal footing with me.'

With a rueful smile, he said, 'Of course, my "plans" were made without reference to the real Miss Bulstrode – and when we did meet, I fear she was not very impressed with me.'

'Oh, Felix, that is not so!' cried the lady, and as their eyes met there was almost a chemical reaction; the very atmosphere of the room changed. Gabriel abruptly launched himself from Bella's shoulder and flapped noisily across the room to perch on the bookshelf.

The movement of the bird startled us all into moving or laughing; it was only a moment, yet it lightened the mood.

Mr Ott smiled as he continued, 'In any event, I fell deeply in love with Miss Bulstrode, and although I still wished – more fervently than ever – to win her support for my School, this was secondary to my personal desire to make her my wife. I hope you do not mind, Bella, if I say it so publically?'

'It is not so very public,' she replied, blushing slightly. 'My sisters already know, and perhaps our detectives may have deduced something of our feelings for each other.'

He gave a short nod. 'I proposed and was rejected. Miss Bulstrode said that although she appreciated my friendship, she had taken an oath of celibacy, being dedicated to her work of healing. Nor could she agree to take any official part in my School, feeling it, too, would be a distraction from her career. Well, I was deeply disappointed – I cannot pretend otherwise.'

His shoulders slumped and he looked down at the floor. 'My disappointment led me to behave very badly. I did not take my dismissal as a gentleman. Foolishly, I shared something of my feelings with Manning, who was, I fear, a very *worshipful* young man, when it came to myself. He admired me to an extreme . . . and it was balm to my soul, especially after the rejection. But I was less than honest with him, too, speaking of the loss to the School, rather than of my own personal heartbreak. If I had not . . .'

'You cannot mean that he thought he could make it up to you by marrying one of my sisters?' Bella spoke in tones of shocked disbelief.

Ott shrugged uncomfortably. 'Well . . . I think he felt that through him, the School should have a claim on your library.'

'That is absurd. He could use the library whenever he liked – indeed, he often did. And he needed no family connection for that – why, Miss Lane will confirm, we had a stranger here for several hours only the other day.'

Ott sighed. 'Really, I am only trying to make sense of his actions. I am not trying to justify them; they cannot be justified.

Somehow, he expected my gratitude and approval. He thought he was doing something great for the School. It may have had something to do with his mystical notions of bloodlines – he was thrilled to imagine he could forge a link between himself and a family that could trace its descent back to the old religion.'

'We are not Roman Catholics,' Alys exclaimed. 'Is *that* what he thought?'

'I believe Mr Ott refers to a much more ancient, pagan faith,' said Mr Jesperson.

'Of course – the idea that witches today are the descendants of a matriarchal, goddess-worshipping cult,' said Bella.

Felix Ott looked at her anxiously. 'You do not think it might be so?'

'Oh, it *might* be so,' she said. 'I do not worship, and am not qualified to pronounce on the matter. For I am not a witch – despite your best attempts to paint me as such in the eyes of the village.'

His eyes widened and he leaned forward. 'What?'

'You know what. Those dreadful remarks you made about witches – modern-day worshippers of Satan! Baby-murderers and cannibals! Did you think your libels would not get back to me?'

The colour drained from his face. 'Oh, my dear, my dear, can you forgive me? It was a moment of madness . . . I did not think . . . Can you ever forgive me?'

'I have forgiven you,' she replied, in a distant, regal manner. 'It took time, I admit, but I realised you spoke as a child lashes out in furious disappointment, not meaning it, and without thinking of consequences.'

'I should have given anything to be able to take those words back!' he exclaimed. 'Fortunately, the meeting was not well attended. And of course, I mentioned no names.'

'There was no need for *you* to name names when your unpleasant little acolyte, Miss Goodall, was more than happy to do it for you. How could you have imagined I would not hear of it, when she set out to turn the villagers against me?'

He groaned. 'I had words with her – I explained she had misunderstood – and threatened her with expulsion if she ever—'

Miss Bulstrode rose to her feet, and Mr Ott scrambled to his. 'Let it go,' she said briskly. 'It is all over now. You have apologised and I have forgiven you – and none of it is anything to do with the case Mr Jesperson and Miss Lane came here to solve.' She looked at us. 'You are satisfied that you have discovered the cause of Mr Manning's death?'

I looked at Mr Jesperson and was surprised to find him staring at the two younger sisters, rather than attending to Miss Bulstrode. 'Hmm?' He roused himself from his thoughts. 'Yes. Although it is not fair to blame him for the death, Cunning Verrell should be warned to dispense his powders only one at a time, no matter how much he is offered, and he might want to reassess his own skill at reading a man's physical health. Manning may have had a slight weakness of the heart; the combined stresses of his encounters that evening, his determination to go against his own nature, hallucinatory fears, and the combination of drugs was more than his heart could take. We need look no further than Manning himself to find the villain responsible.'

CHAPTER TWENTY-THREE

Second Thoughts

We returned to London that same day.

It should have been a triumphant return, for we had solved not only the mystery we had gone to Norfolk to investigate, but at least two others as well, but Mr Jesperson was unusually quiet on the journey.

I tried to discover what was preying on his mind. 'Are you thinking of what to tell his brother? Of course, the truth is not pleasant, and Charles may fall still lower in his esteem, but there must be some relief in learning his death was not the result of murder.'

'Oh, yes. This is the best result we could have hoped for. To have victim and villain one and the same, and not be required to bring the police into the matter,' he replied, without enthusiasm.

His mention of the police reminded me. 'You have not spoken with Sergeant Canright again, have you? Will you write to him?'

'No, why should I? If he is curious, he knows where to

reach me. But he never had anything to do with investigating Manning's death.'

'I was thinking not of Manning, but of Albert Cooke.'

The familiar sparkle returned to his eyes and he grinned at me. 'Ah! You think I should tell him that Cooke's lifeless body was removed from the shrieking pit where he struck his head, and laid out respectfully in the centre of the Poison Ring, possibly following the ancient funerary rituals of their race, by *fairies*?'

I bit my lip. 'When you put it like that . . .'

'*However* I put it, Canright would not be able to swallow it, and instead of seeing me as a bright and promising fellow detective, he should dismiss me as a lunatic. You may think it ridiculously vain of me to mind, but I should rather keep his good opinion. Let him solve the mystery in his own way – if he can.'

He had entirely recovered his usual good spirits by the time we reached Liverpool Street, and our evening meal prepared by his mother back in Gower Street was quite the celebration, marking the successful end of another curious affair.

We had been home for nearly a week when I received a letter from Bella Bulstrode.

Since she had already replied to my thank-you letter with her own brief note, this was unexpected, but although surprised, I was not displeased by the idea that we might develop an epistolary relationship, for I had found her to be an interesting and intelligent woman.

Mr Jesperson appeared utterly absorbed in his newspaper, and did not look up when I reached across the desk for the letter-opener. As soon as I read the first lines, I exclaimed aloud: 'What do you think of that? Miss Bulstrode has agreed to marry Felix Ott!'

There was a great crackling of newspapers as Mr Jesperson jumped to his feet. 'What? Who says so?' His blue eyes fairly blazed.

His intensity took me by surprise. 'Why, Bella herself – she has written to tell me.'

'Have they set a date?'

I was already scanning the brief missive for more information. 'She says as they are both of an age to know their own minds, there is no reason to put it off, or to make a big production of it. Probably before Christmas.'

'We must go.'

I laughed, puzzled by his reaction. 'Do you really think we shall be invited?'

'Not to the wedding. We must go now, today – before it is too late.'

'Too late for what?'

But he was too impatient to explain what seemed to him obvious, and headed for the door, tossing instructions at me as he went. 'Pack a few things – we shan't need to be away more than a night or two. And hurry. We might still get the last train to Cromer if we leave within the hour.'

Although it was maddening to be kept in the dark, and to

feel so slow-witted that I could not imagine any reason that our presence in Cromer – or Aylmerton – should suddenly be so urgently required, it seemed sensible to follow his lead, and I wasted no more time in questions or protests, but hurried upstairs to throw a few necessities into my bag.

Less than an hour later we were at Liverpool Street, and while I queued for tickets, Jesperson sent telegrams to Felix Ott and to the ladies at Wayside Cross announcing our impending arrival.

'But not to the Vicarage?' I noted.

He wrinkled his nose. 'I had rather not impose on the Ringers again. We will find it more comfortable to take lodgings in Cromer.'

'But you wish Mr Ott and Miss Bulstrode to expect us.'

'It may be that word that we are coming will be enough,' he said.

'Enough for what? Mr Jesperson, please – will you tell me why we are making this journey?'

He did not seem to hear me in his concentration on the barely comprehensible announcements of arrivals and departures. He seized my arm. 'Our train,' he muttered, and rushed me along to a distant platform.

When we were settled inside our compartment, I tried again to make him more forthcoming as to the reason for our urgent journey, but we were immediately interrupted by the arrival of a large and excessively sociable party of travellers, who put paid to any hope of private conversation.

Chameleon-like, Mr Jesperson quickly became one of the

crowd, complimenting the young ladies on their hats and discussing fly-fishing and cricket scores with the gentlemen – although I felt he was attending to it all with only a small part of his mind. As I had no desire to do the same, I took a copy of *Aurora Leigh* from my bag, and lost myself in Mrs Barrett Browning's verses.

In Norwich there was no time to waste; we raced to catch the last train to Cromer. It was packed with locals returning home after a day in the city, laden with parcels, and once again there was no opportunity to question Mr Jesperson as to his plans. But it no longer bothered me; soon enough, I knew, all would become clear.

My thoughts ran ahead to Alymerton and Wayside Cross. Remembering Bella's flushed cheeks and melting gaze, I was not really surprised by her announcement, for it was clear that she adored Felix Ott. Of his feelings for her, I was less certain. He struck me as selfish and self-absorbed, the sort of man who would love a woman not for herself, but for what she reflected back to him when he gazed at her. And perhaps, despite his denials, he wanted her for her property, and the good he imagined she would do for his School. *She* had forgiven him for his underhand attack that had libelled her as a witch, but I could not forget it, and wondered if she was right to trust him.

Ott had been our first suspect. Even before we had met him, we had heard him blamed for Charles Manning's death by Mr Alexander Manning and implicated by the Reverend Ringer. And Ott had lied to us, trying to keep his final meeting with Manning in London a secret. I wondered if Mr Jesperson had

had second thoughts; if he suspected Ott of having more of a hand in Charles' death – if Bella, having agreed to marry him, was now in danger.

Upon arriving in Cromer, Mr Jesperson did not head for the cab-stand as I had expected, but immediately strode out of the station and along the lamp-lit street towards the seafront.

'Where are we going?'

'To see Mr Ott.'

I asked no more questions, saving my breath to keep up with his rapid pace. But when we reached the fine stone house overlooking the sea, we found the windows all dark, and Mr Jesperson's fusillade of determined knocking elicited no response.

'Perhaps he has gone out to dine? It is the hour for it,' I reminded him. 'We might do the same, and try again later.' I was feeling hungry, and from past experience that should have meant my friend was positively famished, for we'd had no refreshments on our journey.

But Mr Jesperson did not take up my suggestion. 'We had better get to Wayside Cross, as quickly as possible.'

'May I be of service?' A woman's voice addressed us unexpectedly; as we turned, a woman in a long dark cloak stepped out of the shadows.

'Miss Goodall,' said Mr Jesperson, and now I recognised the woman I had seen in the first row at his lecture. 'I hope you may, indeed. Do you know where we may find Mr Ott?'

'I had hoped to find him here myself,' she said. 'But he has been spending much less time in his own quarters of late, and much more at the house I heard you mention. I must say I find his reasons hard to comprehend, although I understand the library there is meant to be a great attraction.'

As soon as she paused for breath Mr Jesperson said impatiently, 'Thank you for your thoughts on the matter, Miss Goodall, but now you must excuse us. We have urgent business with Mr Ott; I hope there may still be a cab for hire at the station.'

'There is no need for a cab – as you see, I have my own carriage,' she said, turning to indicate where it waited on the road below. 'It was not for nothing that I offered you my help. I am not on calling terms with Miss Bulstrode or her sisters, but, in company with you, perhaps I might dare drive out to Wayside Cross for once?'

'Thank you, that is most kind of you,' he said quickly. 'We will – forgive me; you are, I think, acquainted with my friend Miss Lane?'

She turned on me such a blank stare that I almost believed it was the first time she had registered my presence. 'How d'ye do, Miss Lane. Are you a member of the School?'

'No.'

'Never mind; if you are a friend of Mr Jesperson, 'tis good enough for me. Come along, let us not tarry, I hate this cold night air.'

She led the way down to her carriage, a one-horse cabriolet which she must have driven herself, despite her distaste for the cold; but as we drew near, she turned her sly smile on Mr

329

Jesperson and with much fluttering of eyelashes invited him to drive.

'It will be a treat for me to sit inside and keep warm, and Stormy will appreciate a man's surer hands upon the reins – you look like a good driver; I am not so bad, for a lady, but he can be a bit naughty with me, especially at night, when he's longing to get back home to his warm stall,' she gushed.

'My pleasure,' he murmured, opening the door for us.

She gestured for me to go inside first, pausing to instruct him: 'Go as fast as you like! We shall be quite comfortable and safe with you, I know.'

He took her at her word; scarcely had the door closed before we were moving off with a lurch that threw her against me. She didn't mind it, only laughed and advised me, 'Hang on tight! Pity you haven't got your fella to hold on to, eh?'

'I beg your pardon?'

'Oh, don't be an old maid! He may be young, but you make a handsome pair. Ain't he your fella?'

'He is not,' I said firmly. 'We are good friends.'

'Oh, yes? Felix and I, we are *good friends* too. I wish I could call Felix my fella, but with the business of organising the School and spreading the word and teaching, and research and study, and all of that, he has no time for courting. He as good as told me he could never even *think* of marriage until the School is well established. But when that day comes, he is sure to want a woman who understands and has been a part of it from the beginning to stand by his side and share his name.'

I felt a prickle of unease. 'Has he spoken of marriage?'

'No, I told you – he cannot think of it for years.'

'But you are friends.'

'Haven't I said so? How can you doubt it? I have been a supporter of the School since I first met Mr Ott. And it is not just words with me, like it is with some folk – I have given him a parcel of land – an outright gift – where I hope he will build a physical home for the School. He is very grateful for my support – he has told me so often enough.'

I looked at her and spoke tentatively: 'It must be hurtful, then, if he doesn't always keep his appointments with you.'

She looked puzzled, then took my meaning. 'Appointment? Oh, but there was no appointment – we had not arranged to meet this evening; not at all! It only chanced that I was driving past his house, and thought I would call in. Naturally, I saw at once that he was not at home, but I stopped, thinking he might come along at any minute, and thinking perhaps I might write a note to slip under his door. Then I saw you and Mr Jesperson approach and . . . You understand?'

I did. I also wondered how many times a week she 'chanced' to drive past his house – but of course I could not ask. I wondered how she would take the news of Mr Ott's intended marriage to Miss Bulstrode.

Peering out the window, I saw that we were already on the outskirts of Aylmerton.

'Have you never been to Wayside Cross?' I asked her.

She sniffed. 'Well, once – on a matter of business, as you

might say; you know of her business?' She gave me a sideways look and then nodded. 'Yes, it is true. She *is* a witch – although Mr Ott does not like us to use that word. But when I asked her to cast a spell for me, she would not. I know she has done such things for others, but she would not for me. She was not friendly at all – spoke to me as if – well, I fancy she looked down on me, the little country bumpkin, farmer's daughter – but of course, that was before I came into my inheritance.' She smoothed the fur collar of her cloak as if it were a darling pet. 'I am a landowner now, a woman of means, as well as a close personal friend of Mr Ott. I fancy she won't be so high and mighty with me now.'

'You mean to call on her this evening?' I asked, rather bemused.

'She'll have to have me, if she invites *you*. And if Felix is there, she would not dare insult him by refusing me. I am certain he would not allow it.'

The pace of the carriage slowed; looking out, I saw Wayside Cross, the house and walled gardens illuminated by moonlight.

There was a horse and carriage waiting at the gate, and as ours pulled up beside it, Miss Goodall recognised it as belonging to Mr Ott.

And there was the man himself: a coated, hatted figure leaving the house. As he walked down the path he dabbed at his mouth with a handkerchief which he then tucked away in a pocket.

I felt the carriage rock as Mr Jesperson leapt down from the driver's seat, calling out, 'I say, Ott. Might I have a word?'

Miss Goodall scrambled to exit and I made haste to follow.

'Felix!' She called eagerly. 'What a lovely surprise!'

The two men stopped and turned.

'Miss Goodall,' responded Mr Ott, with a curt nod of his head. 'Good evening. I fear I cannot stop.'

'But — we have only just arrived!' She fluttered her hands and gazed at him imploringly. 'Surely you will not go so soon?'

He glanced back at the house. 'It seems I must. I had better warn you, this is no time for a social call. One of the young ladies is indisposed, and Miss Bulstrode must attend to her needs.' His tone made it clear he took this as a personal affront. Had Miss Bulstrode not understood that in agreeing to marry him, she had accepted the role of handmaiden to her lord and master above all else? I hoped she would reconsider their engagement. If her work was as important to her as she had claimed, how could she give is up in order to attend to one selfish man? His demands would only increase once they were married; that was clear to me, even if her love had made her blind.

'You may call on me tomorrow, Jesperson.' Mr Ott took no further notice of Miss Goodall, and none at all of me. 'Whatever your business, it can wait until the morning.'

Jesperson kept his searching gaze fixed upon the other man as if trying to draw something more from him. 'If you say so.'

Ott shook his head impatiently. 'Goodnight,' he said, and in a few strides he had reached his carriage where he swiftly mounted to the driver's seat.

'We may as well also return to Cromer,' said Mr Jesperson. 'That is, if Miss Goodall will be so kind?'

I was startled, wondering why, when we had been in such haste to get here, we should turn away at the gate, but of course I said nothing. Miss Goodall gave a shrug and a sniff as she replied, '*I* have no wish to stay where Mr Ott has been turned out! You may drive me home.' Then she recollected our situation, and quickly added, 'Or, at least, as far as you wish to go. I regret I am unable to offer you rooms in my own house, but I live quite alone, in an old farmhouse some distance from the town, and it would not be suitable. There are some very nice hotels in Cromer . . .'

Mr Jesperson cut her off before she could go on to describe the possibilities, opening the carriage door and gesturing impatiently. We had scarcely a chance to get settled in our seats before he was back in the driver's seat and snapping the reins.

'What an impatient young man,' Miss Goodall murmured disapprovingly. 'There was no need to hurry us so. It makes no matter when we get back.'

Having been foiled of her desired visit with Mr Ott, her displeasure spread itself everywhere. But I found it more restful being snubbed by her than to be forced to listen to her self-absorbed chatter. While she sat glaring out the window, I let my mind leap ahead to the hotels of Cromer, and especially the prospect of a hot meal in one of the warm and pleasant public dining rooms.

Our return to Cromer was nothing like as swift as the journey out. Instead of attempting to overtake Mr Ott's sedately moving carriage, Mr Jesperson matched his pace, keeping close behind.

I felt certain that despite Mr Ott's dismissal, he meant to speak with him tonight, rather than wait until the morning.

We had just reached the outskirts of Cromer, the lights and buildings ahead offering an enticing, welcome prospect after the journey over heath and through forest, when, quite unexpectedly, Mr Jesperson pulled up the horse. The carriage stopped, and rocked slightly as he leapt down.

'What is the matter?' demanded Miss Goodall, peering out her window. 'Whatever is wrong with that man?'

I looked out my side and saw that Mr Jesperson was running after Mr Ott's carriage which was moving slowly and erratically on to the grassy road-verge.

I opened my own door and scrambled out, not bothering to make any reply.

Mr Jesperson caught up with Mr Ott's carriage and sprang up beside the driver, taking control. The carriage halted, and I ran up to find Mr Ott slumped down in his seat, and Mr Jesperson bending over him. In that instant, I knew Felix Ott was dead.

CHAPTER TWENTY-FOUR

Murderous Misses

The dead man's eyes were closed and his face in the moonlight was that of a peaceful dreamer, relaxed and without care. There could hardly have been a greater contrast with the dead visage of Charles Manning that had initiated our Norfolk adventure, and yet I had no doubt the two deaths were intimately connected.

Mr Jesperson straightened up from his investigation and looked at me. His entire aspect was drooping and melancholy. 'This is what I hoped to prevent. But we were too late, after all.'

'Have you any idea what—?'

'This.' He held out his hand to me, palm cupped upwards. 'This is what killed him.'

I stared at two small brown specks on his palm. 'That? What is it?'

'Crumbs caught in his moustache. No doubt there will be more in his pocket handkerchief, and even more in his stomach.'

I leaned closer, as he clearly wished me to do, and took a cautious sniff. 'Ginger cake?'

'Indeed. He must have consumed it at Wayside Cross. You remember, of course, that ginger cake was amongst the contents of Manning's stomach.'

My own empty stomach growled. At that moment, the sound of a carriage door, and then Miss Goodall's waspish voice carried to us on the still night air: 'Is it a private party, or may anyone join? What *are* you about?'

'Go,' said Mr Jesperson, his voice low and urgent. 'Keep her away. Delay her for an hour if you can, then bring her along to the police station. If she will not, then come yourself.'

I wasted no time asking questions, but scrambled down at once. As soon as my feet were on the ground, Jesperson clucked to the horse and slapped her neck with the reins, and they rattled off.

A loud squealing sound made me wince. Miss Goodall came pelting along the road, seized me by the arm, digging her fingernails in painfully hard, and gave me a petulant shake as she demanded, 'Why? Why'd you let them go without us? What is going on?'

'We are to meet them, never fear.'

'What . . . When? Where? Why?'

I clucked my tongue and gave her a reproving frown. 'Must Mr Ott explain his every plan to you in advance?'

'His *plan*? Oh! Where are we to meet, and when?' The annoyance was entirely gone from her expression, and she stopped squeezing my arm; now she looked like a child who has been promised a treat.

My stomach growled again. I hesitated, and then, reflecting that there would be nothing to eat at the police station, made a decision. 'We're to go to the Hotel de Paris,' I said. 'The restaurant there is open to non-residents, and it is supposed to be very good. Do you know it?'

'Why, of course!'

I marched her back to her carriage. 'You drive; I shall sit inside.' I did not wish to parry any more questions from her about Mr Ott's imaginary plan. I could use the rest from her company whilst thinking about the meaning of this latest death.

The restaurant at the Hotel de Paris was as good – and as expensive – as the guidebooks suggested. Still uncertain how long I could, or should, delay revealing the true state of affairs to Miss Goodall, I decided that a bowl of soup followed by an omelette would be enough of a meal for me. She, very much puzzled by my insistence that we would dine *before* the gentlemen arrived, objected also on the grounds that she rarely ate anything so late. Just to keep me company, she agreed to a bowl of soup, and when I'd finished my omelette (*aux fines herbes* – perfectly light and delicious) she ventured to suggest that something sweet would not go amiss, so we both had the *tarte tatin* with heavy cream.

'Where are our friends?' she asked, surreptitiously licking the tines of her fork. 'It is not very gentlemanly to keep ladies waiting so long.'

Something like stage fright clutched at my stomach and dried my mouth. 'Oh, dear. I am afraid . . .'

She dropped her fork. 'What?'

I took a deep breath. 'Mr Jesperson told me that . . . there was a possibility . . . and if they had not turned up by the time we finished our meal, we weren't to wait any longer, but to go directly to the police station.'

Her eyes widened. She opened her mouth – for a moment, I thought she would scream, but social graces intervened. Her eyes darting about the room in search of spies or villains, she whispered across the table, 'Police! Why, what has happened – what did he think might happen?'

'Do you know where the police station is?'

'Certainly.' She scorched me with her look. 'I had to go there when my father died.'

'I am sorry to stir up unhappy memories. If you do not wish to come with me . . .'

She nearly overturned the chair in her eagerness. 'He asked for me – of course I must go.'

The old man on the desk made haste to show us through to Sergeant Canright's office, where we were expected. As he opened the door to the inner office, I heard a man's deep voice say, 'Predicting what he ate is no evidence he was poisoned.'

'Excuse me, sir, sirs,' said the old man. 'The ladies are here.'

Miss Goodall's eager, hopeful expression faded as quickly as her eyes went from the tall, slender form of Mr Jesperson to the stockier figure of the police officer and found no one else in the room.

'Where is he? Where is Mr Ott?'

'Please sit down, Miss Goodall. And Miss Lane.'

'Why are we here? What has happened to Mr Ott – you drove his carriage,' she said, turning her accusing gaze upon Mr Jesperson. 'I saw you take the reins and drive away with him.'

'Miss Goodall.' The policeman had the voice and delivery used to commanding obedience. 'Please sit down, and I will explain.' This time, she did as he asked.

'You were well acquainted with Mr Ott, I believe – a member of his School?'

She lifted her head. 'I am. Why do you say it like that?'

He grimaced. 'It is never easy. I have sad news, I fear—'

She held up her hands in horror. 'No!'

'Felix Ott expired suddenly, earlier this evening.'

'Who did it? Who killed him?'

Frowning, the policeman glanced at Jesperson, who raised his eyebrows. Sergeant Canright sighed and replied to Miss Goodall, 'Why should you imagine him *killed* when I tell you he died?'

'I heard you mention poison as we came in.'

'Ah!' He wagged a finger at her, half-smiling. 'The dangers of hearing a word out of context. You heard me tell Mr Jesperson that there was no evidence of poison. All the signs point to death by natural causes – a sudden, overwhelming heart attack. They happen more frequently to older men, but sometimes they strike someone in the prime of life, like Mr Ott.' He shook his head. 'Just one of Mother Nature's nasty little tricks.'

340

Miss Goodall bit her lip. 'Do you mean to arrest Mother Nature?'

'I beg your pardon?'

She glared at him furiously and snapped, 'Why are we in a police station? If my . . . If dear Mr Ott died of natural causes, what have the police to do with it?'

He grunted. 'Nothing, so far as I am concerned. If you must have someone to blame, do not look at me. Jesperson and his partner came to Norfolk to investigate the death of Charles Manning. As you probably know, he was one of Mr Ott's closest associates, and he died of a sudden heart attack. Jesperson considers it highly suspicious that Ott should go the same way – but the two deaths are not so similar after all.

'Manning died because he took too much quack medicine. It got his heart to racing, it made him half-crazed, he was seeing demons and witches all around, and it was too much for his heart. Our surgeon didn't find anything like that in poor Mr Ott's belly – and our doctor here is as good as any in London; he knows the workings of various poisons on the body, and would not have failed to spot anything in the system that could have stopped his heart. Also unlike Manning, who dined and drank heartily in the hours before his death, Mr Ott was quite abstemious. He had eaten nothing at all in the last six hours or more except a piece of ginger cake.'

'You say he was not killed by poison,' said she. Her eyes glittered, but I thought the tears she held back were of anger rather than sorrow. 'But that was no natural death, nor a coincidence.

341

I say he was killed by a spell, and I know who cast it – a witch! It was that evil Miss Bulstrode – he knew she was a witch, and that was why she killed him.'

'You have good reason to know about the casting of spells, do you not?'

I was surprised to see Mr Jesperson move around the policeman's desk to confront Miss Goodall with this unexpected question.

She blinked at him. 'How do you mean?'

'I mean that you tried to hire Miss Bulstrode to cast a deathly spell. She refused. Although she agreed that such spells *could* be cast – as you knew from your own studies – she was not an assassin for hire.'

As he spoke, I remembered the story Miss Goodall had told me, about the spell Miss Bulstrode had refused to cast.

'She may also have told you – or perhaps it was Mr Ott? I know you had several intense discussions with him on the subject – that if any witch did cast such a spell, it would work if the victim deserved to die. If he did not, the spell would rebound on the ill-wisher – not the witch herself, as she would have many potent guards in place, but on the one who had commissioned the spell.'

He cocked his head thoughtfully. 'A pretty idea, but it hardly accords with the world we live in. We want to believe in natural justice and just desserts, but all around us we see the evil profiting by their actions and bad things happening to good people. But it was a notion Mr Ott was keen to promote, to give his School the gloss of morality, and to counteract the old slander equating witchcraft with devil worship.

'However, it hardly matters if it was true; it worried you enough to cause you to abandon the idea of causing your parents to die by magical means. You used poison instead.'

Sergeant Canright breathed an oath.

Miss Goodall, who had been attending to Mr Jesperson's lecture with something of the hypnotic fascination of a snake to a snake-charmer, abruptly crumpled. Burying her face in her hands, she shook and sobbed.

'See here, Jesperson,' Canright exclaimed. 'That's an awfully serious charge.'

Mr Jesperson kept his attention focused on the weeping woman. 'It is true, is it not, Miss Goodall? You hated and feared your father, a rough and often violent fellow who was a handy man with the stick. He used to beat your mother – and you, too – on the slightest excuse. I do not think anyone who knew him was terribly surprised when he turned up dead by poisoning – you told me so yourself, Canright. You said the local gossips surmised that his wife had finally had enough, and gave him a fatal dose in his tea. But you had no evidence, and she seemed genuinely distraught over his death: he was a brute, but she loved him.

'Then, when Mrs G was found dead, killed by the same batch of poison, you probably felt natural justice had been served. The murderess could not live with her husband, but neither could she go on living without him, so she killed herself. This was the general presumption, but it was wrong.' He leaned in closer to Miss Goodall, and now his voice changed, becoming gentle and concerned: 'Why did you do it, Miss Goodall? Why did you kill that good soul who never did you any harm?'

She raised her head and looked at him from red and swollen eyes. Her face was streaked with tears, but there was no remorse in her look or her tone as she answered, only a selfish indignation. 'She would not give me my inheritance. She refused to give me anything; she would not even agree to sell off the smallest bit of land, not even a few acres for the School.'

'I see. You did it for him – for Mr Ott's School of British Wisdom. You wanted nothing for yourself, but only to help the man you loved?'

'Yes. It's true. All I ever wanted was to help him.' A sob welled up in her throat and she almost wailed the next words. 'And it was all for nothing! Oh, Felix – I did everything for you – and for what? Now you are gone, nothing matters.' She collapsed again into hopeless tears.

Jesperson turned away from her. 'I leave her to you, Canright. I think we may borrow Ott's carriage, since we're about his business.' He took his coat from the stand by the door.

'Where are you going?' Canright asked.

'Wayside Cross.'

The policeman snorted. 'You think he died by witchcraft?'

'Not at all. As I told you before, Ott was poisoned. It happened in that house. The poison is one hardly known in this country, so there is no shame to your surgeon that he did not find it. But I will prove it – make sure he keeps the contents of the stomach. If we can find the rest of the ginger cake, he can test its toxicity and we'll have our proof. Oh, and you may wish to come along to Wayside Cross yourself in . . . shall we say, an hour? Yes, that should give us enough time to find out the villain, so you can make the arrest.'

Grinning, Canright shook his head. 'You are a regular card, Jesperson. You expect me to believe—'

'Believe it or not, as you please – just come. We shall have something for you by then.'

'And if you do not?'

'Then I shall treat you to a meal. Is that good enough?'

'Make it a bottle of whisky.'

'Done. Come along, Miss Lane, the clock is ticking.'

Despite the cold, I chose to sit beside Mr Jesperson as he drove, for I felt he still had a great deal of explaining to do.

'When we left Norfolk last week you were certain that Mr Manning had killed himself by an accidental overdose,' I said as we started off. 'But now you seem to say that he was murdered, and that whoever killed him went on to kill Mr Ott.'

'No.'

I stared at him. 'Where am I wrong?'

'I never believed the cunning man's mixture was the cause of Manning's death,' he replied. 'It was a possibility, however, and once I had learnt the extent of Manning's viciousness – how he had meant to treat Miss Ann – I thought it better that his death be considered self-administered than that either or both of the young ladies he tried to wrong should be dragged into the mire of a murder case. I thought that what she had done was justified as self-defence; he had brought it upon himself, and got his just deserts, and she . . .' He groaned, and slapped the reins against the horse's neck, urging it to go faster.

'But I was wrong! I should never have set myself up as judge and jury! I am a detective. My job is to find out the facts and put them together until they make a true picture – and let others be the judge of what to do about that picture. I should *never* have kept it all to myself.'

I chewed my lip thoughtfully. 'You might have told me, at least.'

'Certainly I should have. Can you forgive me?'

'You are forgiven,' I said, a trifle uncomfortably. 'Anyway, I blame myself for not questioning you more closely – for simply accepting—'

'Yes, I thought you would be more suspicious, considering that it was you who discovered the murder weapon – the fruit of the suicide tree – the *Cerbera odollam*,' he said more cheerfully.

'So Alys is the killer. She is the one who made the cake.'

'But she said she made it for Ann,' he reminded me.

'Oh, Ann.' I dismissed the idea of that timid, weeping girl having the nerve to kill anyone. 'That baby.'

'Is she a baby who has not yet learnt morality? If babies had enough strength, their passions would be deadly,' he said.

'But why should Ann want to kill the man she was looking forward to marrying? I admit, once she knew what he meant to do to her, she might have been inspired to strike back – but the cake had already been baked and brought to London. Such premeditation does not sit with the idea of self-defence.'

'Whereas Alys may have planned to kill Manning for the same reason she has now killed Ott. Out of jealousy and fear – or you might say, out of love; a possessive love for her sisters that will not brook anything that might break their unity.'

'That was why you were so desperate to return, when you learnt that Bella was betrothed to Felix Ott?'

He agreed. 'The picture rose in my mind of the three sisters – a self-contained unit, a coven – menaced by a male outsider expecting to be admitted into their sacred female space. But it is even more complicated by the fact that Miss Bulstrode is like a mother to Ann and Alys – and they are like spoilt, demanding children who will not allow their mother any other love interest, or any life of her own. Marriage for her – the intrusion of a stepfather – is an idea they could not bear.

'And having once got away with murder, believing herself unsuspected, what could there be to stop her from killing again?'

CHAPTER TWENTY-FIVE

The Final Interview

We left the carriage by the front gate, but Mr Jesperson suggested that rather than go to the front door, we should take the opportunity to look in the glasshouse first.

'I should like to see this suicide tree.'

I led him around the house to the back where, as expected, the glasshouse was unlocked and easily accessed. But finding the plant was not quite so easy, in the deeply shadowed aisles, with nothing but the uncertain yellow light from Mr Jesperson's lamp. I recalled that it had been in an out-of-the-way corner, but stared in perplexity at several different potted bushes with little to distinguish them.

'I should have said it was that one – the leaves look right. But where are the fruits? I must be wrong.' I searched in vain for anything resembling the large, green nuts that had first attracted my attention.

'How many fruits did you say it was bearing?'

'Three. In appearance, rather like limes. But they depended

from thick, scaly stems, and it appeared that there should have been a fourth, which had either dropped off or been picked.'

'I should say they have all been picked now,' he said. 'Whether harvested for future use, or destroyed as evidence against one of her sisters, I will not try to guess. Let us waste no more time – there is nothing for us here. On to the house.'

The back door was only a few steps from the glasshouse, and that was the route taken by Mr Jesperson. He did not bother to knock, and the door was not locked. My heart beat faster with apprehensive fear, but I followed him inside without a murmur.

We were alone in the neat, tidy kitchen. Mr Jesperson prowled about, his gaze raking the room from ceiling to floor. 'Surely she will have hidden it; she would not leave it where someone, a maid or her sister, could be tempted and fall victim to its poison.'

'It would be safest hidden in her own room,' I said, remembering the cake box I had seen underneath Ann's bed. I felt a useless wave of annoyance, wishing I had thought to look inside it. But what would it have meant to me then? I would probably have smiled at the cake, imagining it as a symbol of childish greed, thinking she had hidden it away for a private, midnight feast. I shivered, and told Mr Jesperson: 'I think it was in a box under Ann's bed.'

'Well, she took it out – or someone else did – and gave a piece to Mr Ott. If she has not hidden it away again, it must be—'

The door swung open and there was Bella, staring at us in surprise. 'I thought I heard someone . . . But who let you in?'

Mr Jesperson bowed to her and, with his most charming smile, replied, 'I blush to admit it, but we let ourselves in.'

His charm had no effect upon Miss Bulstrode. Her eyes flashed. 'Indeed? Then I hope you will show yourselves out again, and without delay.' She stepped back, opening the door wide, indicating she wished us not to retreat through the back door, but to go past her and down the hall to the front.

As we hesitated, she said, 'I notice Mr Ott's carriage is at the gate. Did he bring you here?'

'No. But I borrowed his carriage, as we have come on his business.'

'Indeed?' She looked surprised, puzzled, and no longer quite so unfriendly. 'What business is that?'

'We should like the chance to discuss it with you.'

'Go ahead.' When Mr Jesperson did not respond immediately she looked surprised. 'What are you waiting for?'

'It is not a simple matter – and it is something your sisters must hear as well.'

'I will not bother Alys now; she has gone to bed with a sick headache – I have given her a powder – she is not to be disturbed.'

'I must insist.'

His manner was steely and determined, but so was hers.

'Tell me whatever it is; I will inform my sisters in the morning.'

He simply shook his head, and stared at her. She stared back. I had the unwelcome thought that their silent battle might last for hours, if not days.

'Please, Bella,' I said. 'It is very important. Will you not agree, for Mr Ott's sake?'

I saw her waver. 'I will get Ann.'

'Get them both,' I said. 'And what about Elsie and Nancy?'

'What of them? Elsie has a bad cold; we have not seen her today. And it was so clear that Nancy was sickening for something, too, that I sent her home early.'

'So neither of the maids were here when Felix Ott arrived?'

'No – but what does that matter? He did not mind – I would have made dinner, and he would have stayed for a simple family meal with us – but then Alys began to feel poorly, so it was better not.'

'So you sent him away without his supper,' said Mr Jesperson. 'He was evidently not happy about that. Luncheon was a very long time ago. Did he have anything to eat before he left?'

'Anything . . . ?' She stared. 'Mr Jesperson, I do not understand what business any of this is of yours. Why all these questions? Is Felix ill?'

'Please fetch your sisters, Miss Bulstrode.'

Her mouth a tight line, she stared at him, eyes blazing, but it must have been clear to her by now that there would be no speedy end to any staring match with him, and concern for Mr Ott tipped the balance. Turning away, she spoke to me without catching my eye, her manner that of mistress speaking to an inept servant: 'Take him through to my library, and wait there.'

As soon as she had gone, Mr Jesperson made a dive for the pantry door. Inside, on a high shelf, were stacked several lidded tins, but apart from the smallest, half-full of table water biscuits, they were clean and empty. He looked into the bread-bin and inside the oven and even checked the ash-can without finding any sign of the ginger cake.

'Perhaps Mr Ott ate the last of it,' I said, but he shook his head. I persisted: 'There may not have been much left, if it was the same cake the girls took to London—'

'Certainly it was the same. No ginger cake was baked here today,' he said, tapping the side of his nose. 'Now, we had better go – or Miss Bulstrode may be forced to come searching for us again.'

But when we reached the library, it was empty except for the baleful presence of the crow Gabriel, who was perched upon the marble mantelpiece. Undaunted by the bird's glare, Mr Jesperson approached the fireplace and crouched down to work at reviving the fitful, smouldering fire. I kept my eye on the bird as I took my seat, noting how it turned its head from one side to the other and peered down at the top of my friend's head. I wondered if Gabriel was tempted to try to snatch one of those gleaming red-gold curls.

The door opened and the draught made the fire flare up for a moment. Something else in the room caught the light and flashed silver. That silver flash caught my attention, and I recognised the gilt coffer I had first glimpsed beneath Ann's bed, now on a table beside a bottle, a glass, a crumpled linen napkin and a bowl of fruit.

'Here we all are, at your command,' said Bella Bulstrode. 'Oh, don't worry yourself about the fire, Mr Jesperson. It doesn't matter if it dies down – we'll only be with you a few minutes.'

She bustled around Alys, making sure she was well wrapped in her shawl before she looked at Mr Jesperson. 'What are you waiting for?'

'Only for your attention,' he said quietly. 'Let me put again my question – this time to all three of you. Did Mr Ott have anything to eat during his visit here this evening?'

Alys shook her head, and winced as if the movement had caused a stab of pain.

Bella said, 'I already told you. When Felix called by unexpectedly, I invited him to stay for dinner. But Alys had meant to cook and she suddenly felt unwell, so I said we must make it another time.'

'How did he respond to you rescinding your invitation?'

She made a gesture of impatience. 'It was nothing so formal, and naturally he understood. No servants, Alys indisposed . . . Why not ask Felix, if it bothers you?'

'I should like to hear your story.'

She frowned, displeased by his choice of words. 'It is not a *story.*'

'Was he angry?'

'What was there to be angry about? It had been a casual suggestion, and the situation had changed. He understood that.'

'And then?'

She sighed. 'He did offer to take me to Cromer for a meal. But I did not like to leave Alys alone, and it was hardly fair on

Ann, to leave her here to a bit of bread and cheese on her own whilst I dined in a restaurant, so I said we must make it another time. He tried to argue, but I suppose I am as stubborn as he is.'

Then Ann spoke up from her corner. 'And *he* said he hoped – no, he said you *had better* think more of him when you were his wedded wife – then you would have to put him before your half-sisters.'

'Ann!' Bella stared. 'He never did! How can you—?'

'He did not say it to you,' Ann said with a smug smile. 'He said it to himself, after you had left – and I heard him. He meant to be your lord and master. He was only pretending to be otherwise, to trick you – and when you were married, it would have been too late.'

Bella went to her and sank down by her side, perching on the edge of the sofa. 'Darling,' she said gently, caressing her hands. 'It is not true. All men are not the same. Mr Ott is not like Mr Manning.'

'Yes he is.' Ann smiled to herself. 'He is now. Now they are exactly the same.' She let out a brief, shrill giggle. Alys moaned and clutched at her head. Bella looked baffled and frantic as she turned from one to the other.

Mr Jesperson looked at me. With my eyes, I indicated the box on the table. His own eyes widened fractionally and then he said conversationally, 'I say, Miss Ann – did you give him a piece of cake?'

'It was my cake. We were supposed to share it. But he grabbed it – he grabbed me too, and slobbered on me, the beast! – and after he stuffed it into his mouth like that, I did not want to – and Alys told me I should not.'

Alys moaned even more loudly and Jesperson pitched his voice to be heard over her noise: 'You are speaking of Charles Manning?'

'Yes, him! The beast. I thought he loved me and I loved him. It would have been so beautiful to die together, and never be parted. Like Romeo and Juliet. I think I had a dream about it, but I was awake, and then it never happened,' she said with wistful incoherence.

'You were both going to eat the cake,' Jesperson prodded when her voice trailed away.

Ann nodded. 'But Alys would not let me. And I am not sorry – I would not want to be dead with Mr Manning. He was horrible. He called us witches, and worse.'

Bella groaned. 'Stop it, Ann! You don't know what you're saying!' She got to her feet and turned on Mr Jesperson. 'Leave her alone. The child is half mad with grief and fear. We know what caused Mr Manning's death – it was his own fault. Why rake it up now?'

'We did not come here tonight to speak of Charles Manning, but of Felix Ott,' he replied. 'It is Ann who has made the connection.'

Bella caught her breath. 'Felix,' she murmured. 'You said you were here on his business.'

'Yes. I am sorry – very sorry – to have to tell you that Felix Ott is dead.'

As she swayed on her feet, Mr Jesperson caught hold of her and eased her into a chair. 'It was very sudden,' he said gently. 'He died as he was driving back to Cromer. From the look on his face, it was a quick and a peaceful passing.'

Bella stared blankly ahead and said nothing.

After a pause, Mr Jesperson continued, 'The police surgeon was of the opinion that Ott must have suffered from an unsuspected weakness of the heart – which, you will recall, was the same diagnosis offered in explanation of Manning's death. I believe both men were poisoned – and if you think about it, I am sure you must agree. The only question is *what* poison, and how did they come to ingest it? The autopsy revealed that Ott had eaten nothing for hours except a piece of ginger cake.'

'And a glass of Madeira wine,' Ann piped up suddenly. 'There is nothing nicer with a glass of Madeira than a piece of cake. Fruit cake is best, but a slice of ginger cake would do very nicely, thank you.'

I felt the skin crawling on the back of my neck at the sound of her strangely innocent, mad young voice. She was certainly guilty, but was she sane?

'It is not true,' cried Bella. 'Ann has dreams . . . fantasies . . . pay her no heed. Poor Felix . . . It was a natural death; his heart was weak.'

Jesperson's eyes narrowed. 'You knew him to have a weak heart?'

'He never spoke of it; perhaps he did not know himself; but it is the only explanation.'

'No, Miss Bulstrode, it is not the only explanation. The police in Norfolk may not be familiar with *Cerbera odollam,* called the *pong-pong* by the people in one of the countries where it grows, and better known as the suicide tree, but *you* are – and your sisters, too. Your specimen of this deadly plant had three nuts hanging from it when Miss Lane saw it last week – they are gone now. The meat of one nut is enough to stop the heart within an hour.'

Bella shot a reproachful look in my direction. 'Anyone may enter my glasshouse, if they wish to take the trouble – as you know for yourself, Mr Jesperson! Perhaps I should have it fitted with a sturdy lock. But no one took those seeds for any evil purpose – I destroyed them myself.'

'The police might call that destroying the evidence,' he drawled.

'How dare you!' Her fists clenched; the look she gave him was quite murderous. 'I invited Miss Lane into my house and treated her as a friend, and this is my reward – to have *her* friend accuse me of causing the death of the man I loved.'

'We do not accuse *you,* Bella,' I said. 'But *someone* killed Mr Ott – and before that, Mr Manning – you cannot deny it.'

'I can deny it – I do deny it,' she replied coldly. 'Do the police call it murder? I think not. This is the fantasy of a man who wishes to show off his cleverness.'

I looked across at the sofa where Ann had Alys in an embrace, saw her pulling her head into her lap so she could gently stroke her brow. 'Bella, I understand your desire to protect your sisters, but look what has happened. Getting away with murder once has emboldened her to do it again. And why should she stop at two? If she ever feels threatened, if she imagines anyone threatens your happy little family – she will kill again.'

Bella glared. 'You are worse than absurd. The two of you fancy yourselves as detectives – so you want a crime to solve. There has been no crime committed here. Only a' – her voice wavered – 'personal tragedy, the unexpected, sudden death of a dear friend, a man who might have achieved greatness if he had not been cut off in his prime. Felix Ott died too soon – but it was not any malicious act or person who killed him. You are cruel, knowing how hard this bereavement must strike me, to add to my pain by pretending he could have been murdered by one of my own sisters!'

'We shall have to let the court decide,' said Mr Jesperson.

'Fantasist! There is no evidence, and no case to answer, except in your imagination.'

'No evidence?' He smiled slightly and looked past her, at her sisters. 'Miss Ann, I wonder if there is any of your ginger cake left?'

She smiled coyly and shook her head. 'Not for you.'

'Please? I have not had any supper – and I do like ginger cake.'

She shut her eyes. 'Stop it. There's none left. Go away.'

'Forgive me if I do not believe you,' he said, and in two long strides he was beside the table and the silver box was in his hands. He opened it; I caught a whiff of the moist rich cake, sugar and ginger and other spices at the same moment that Bella came up out of her chair, whirling towards him.

'Give me that!' She seized hold of the silver box and gave it a yank. The contents were jarred; the cake bounced, and then as she pulled at the box again it came flying out, to land on the carpet.

'Oh, look what you have done,' she cried, and stooped for it.

Mr Jesperson was as quick as she to try to snatch the piece of cake, but both of them were slower than the bird. Swift and silent, the great black bird soared down from its high perch, dipped and grabbed up a large gobbet of the sweet brown cake and flew away with it.

Bella immediately forgot about the cake that remained on the floor in her anxiety about her pet. 'Gabriel, no!' she cried, straightening. 'Drop it! Oh, drop it, Gabriel, my sweet! Nasty! Drop it!'

The bird landed on the top shelf he so often favoured and cocked his head, peering down with one bright, beady eye at his mistress. The bit of cake, bigger than a grape, was still gripped in his beak. So often before, I had noticed how intelligent the bird seemed, or at least how great an understanding there was between it and the woman he served. Surely, I thought, he would do what she told him now.

Mr Jesperson stood up, wrapping the remains of the ginger cake in his handkerchief and carefully stowing it away in a pocket while Bella's attention was fixed on the bird.

'Gabriel,' she called clearly. 'Drop it; drop it now.'

The bird stretched its neck out, putting its head back until the beak was pointed up at the ceiling. Then it opened its beak, and swallowed the morsel.

Bella gave a despairing cry and dropped her face into her hands.

For a moment the room was silent except for the faint crackling of the flames in the hearth, and the faint snoring of Alys, asleep in her sister's lap.

Then Ann spoke. 'Mr Jesperson, I have changed my mind,' she said. 'You may have a piece of my ginger cake, after all. It is mine, you know. Alys said she made it for me, and so she did, but I added something to it, a special ingredient, when she was not looking. That is why I had to tell her *she* was not allowed to eat any of it; no one was to touch it, unless I said so. And now I say that you may eat it.'

'Thank you, Miss Ann,' he said with a little bow.

'Will you have something to drink with it? There is that bottle of Madeira wine. Forgive me for not serving you, but I do not wish to disturb my sister.'

'Do not trouble yourself. Miss Lane and I are leaving now.'

Her eyes widened and she gave a little gasp. 'Not before you have eaten your cake?'

'I shall take it away with me, for later.'

'No – you must not – you must eat it now.' She scowled. 'Do you hear me? Eat it now; otherwise, I shall think you very rude, and not at all a gentleman.'

Bella raised her face, which looked as pale and lifeless as a mask. 'Throw it on the fire,' she whispered. 'Please.'

'I am sorry,' he said, and turned toward the door.

I took one last look at the three sisters in that room with the dying fire, and looked up at the bird, as still as a statue in the shadows near the ceiling, and then I followed my friend.

Outside the house, we met the police arriving.